Mummy Fearest
From Italian *Topolino* #1109 (1977)
Writer and Artist: Romano Scarpa
Inker: Sandro Zemolin
Colorists: Disney Italia and Digikore Studios
Translation and Dialogue: Joe Torcivia

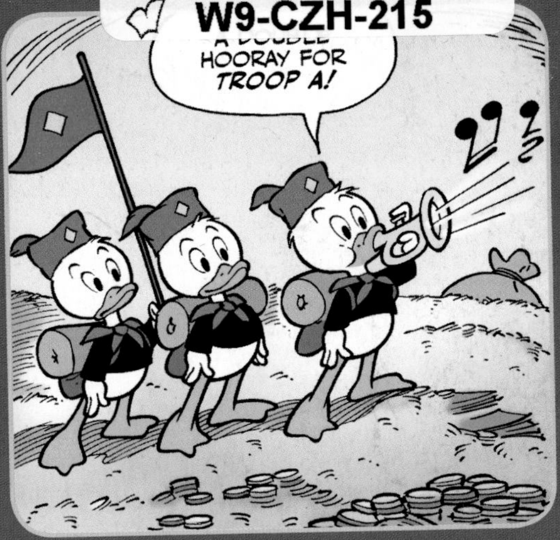
HOORAY FOR TROOP A!

Of Mice and Magic
From Dutch *Donald Duck* #5/1980
Artist: Mark De Jonge
Colorists: Disney Italia and Digikore Studios
Translation and Dialogue: Thad Komorowski

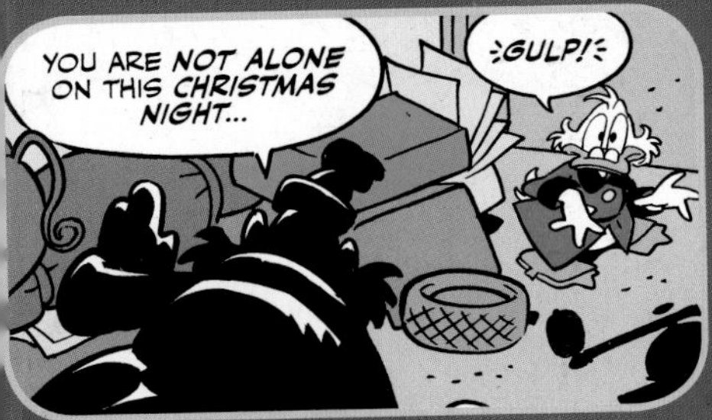
YOU ARE NOT ALONE ON THIS CHRISTMAS NIGHT...
GULP!

Another Christmas on Bear Mountain
From Italian *Topolino* #2717 (2007)
Writer: Tito Faraci
Artist: Giorgio Cavazzano
Inker: Sandro Zemolin
Colorists: Disney Italia with Travis and Nicole Seitler
Translation and Dialogue: Gary Leach

Blizzard Blues
From Dutch *Donald Duck* #50/1995
Writer: Evert Geradts
Artist: Jaap Stavenuiter
Colorists: Sanoma with Travis and Nicole Seitler
Translation and Dialogue: Maura McManus

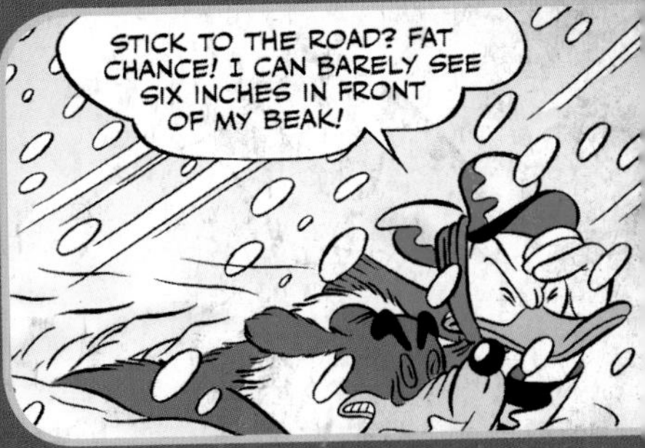
STICK TO THE ROAD? FAT CHANCE! I CAN BARELY SEE SIX INCHES IN FRONT OF MY BEAK!

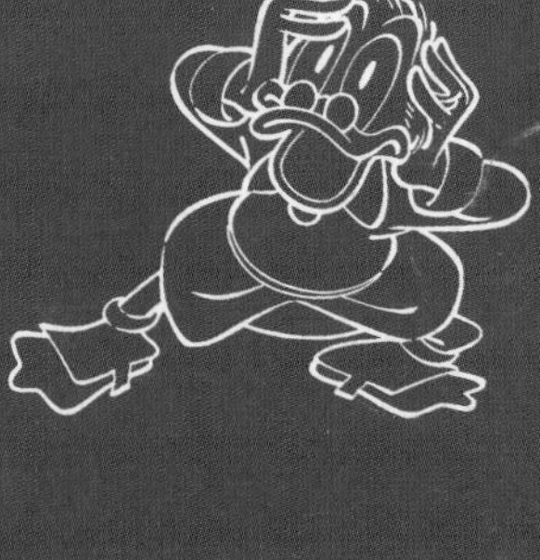

Letterers: Travis and Nicole Seitler
Series Editor: Sarah Gaydos
Archival Editor: David Gerstein

Cover Artist: Michel Nadorp
Cover Colorist: Sanoma with Travis and Nicole Seitler
Collection Editors: Justin Eisinger and Alonzo Simon
Publisher: Ted Adams
Collection Designer: Clyde Grapa

Disney COMICS

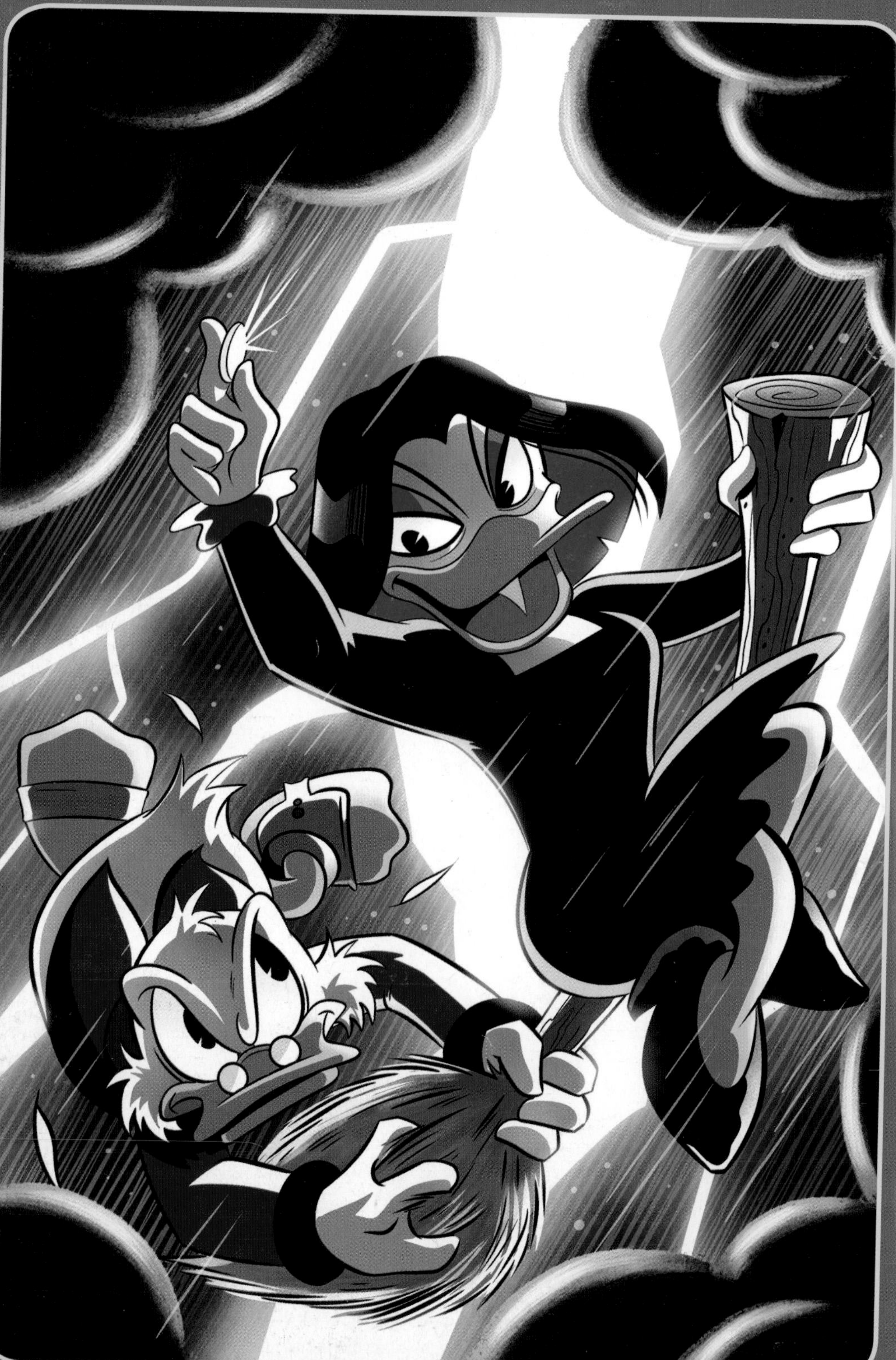

Art by Derek Charm

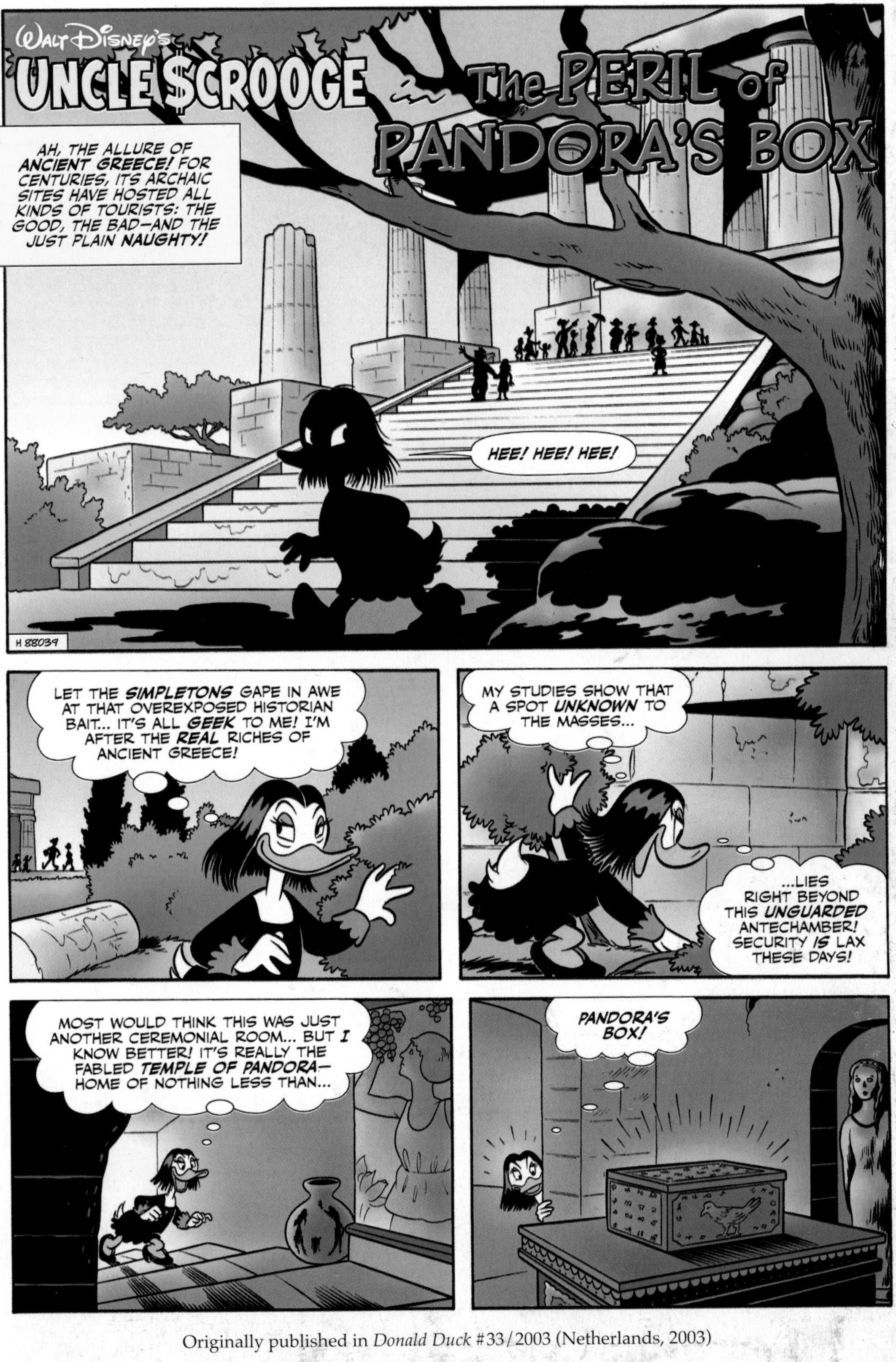
WALT DISNEY'S
UNCLE $CROOGE
The PERIL of PANDORA'S BOX
AH, THE ALLURE OF ANCIENT GREECE! FOR CENTURIES, ITS ARCHAIC SITES HAVE HOSTED ALL KINDS OF TOURISTS: THE GOOD, THE BAD—AND THE JUST PLAIN NAUGHTY!
HEE! HEE! HEE!
H 88039
LET THE SIMPLETONS GAPE IN AWE AT THAT OVEREXPOSED HISTORIAN BAIT... IT'S ALL GEEK TO ME! I'M AFTER THE REAL RICHES OF ANCIENT GREECE!
MY STUDIES SHOW THAT A SPOT UNKNOWN TO THE MASSES...
...LIES RIGHT BEYOND THIS UNGUARDED ANTECHAMBER! SECURITY IS LAX THESE DAYS!
MOST WOULD THINK THIS WAS JUST ANOTHER CEREMONIAL ROOM... BUT I KNOW BETTER! IT'S REALLY THE FABLED TEMPLE OF PANDORA—HOME OF NOTHING LESS THAN...
PANDORA'S BOX!

Originally published in *Donald Duck* #33/2003 (Netherlands, 2003)

I HAVE LONG SOUGHT THE MIDAS TOUCH—BUT *HERE* LIES MY MEANS OF GAINING *MORE POWER* STILL!

GREEK MYTHOLOGY SAYS THE WORLD OWES *ALL* ITS *EVIL* TO THIS LITTLE BOX!

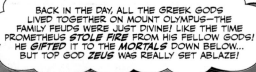

BACK IN THE DAY, ALL THE GREEK GODS LIVED TOGETHER ON MOUNT OLYMPUS—THE FAMILY FEUDS WERE JUST DIVINE! LIKE THE TIME PROMETHEUS *STOLE FIRE* FROM HIS FELLOW GODS! HE *GIFTED* IT TO THE *MORTALS* DOWN BELOW... BUT TOP GOD *ZEUS* WAS REALLY SET ABLAZE!

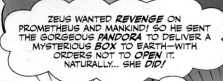

ZEUS WANTED *REVENGE* ON PROMETHEUS AND MANKIND! SO HE SENT THE GORGEOUS *PANDORA* TO DELIVER A MYSTERIOUS *BOX* TO EARTH—WITH ORDERS NOT TO *OPEN* IT. NATURALLY... SHE *DID!*

EVIL ESCAPED FROM INSIDE—AND GAVE EARTH THE *WORKS!*

ACCORDING TO LEGEND, THERE'S A TEENY BIT *MORE* MISFORTUNE LEFT IN THE BOX... YES, I CAN SEE IT!

AND WHO BETTER TO INFLICT *ANCIENT EVIL* UPON THAN A CERTAIN *ANCIENT TIGHTWAD* WITH A CERTAIN *ANCIENT DIME?* I HEAR HE'S IN THIS VERY VICINITY!

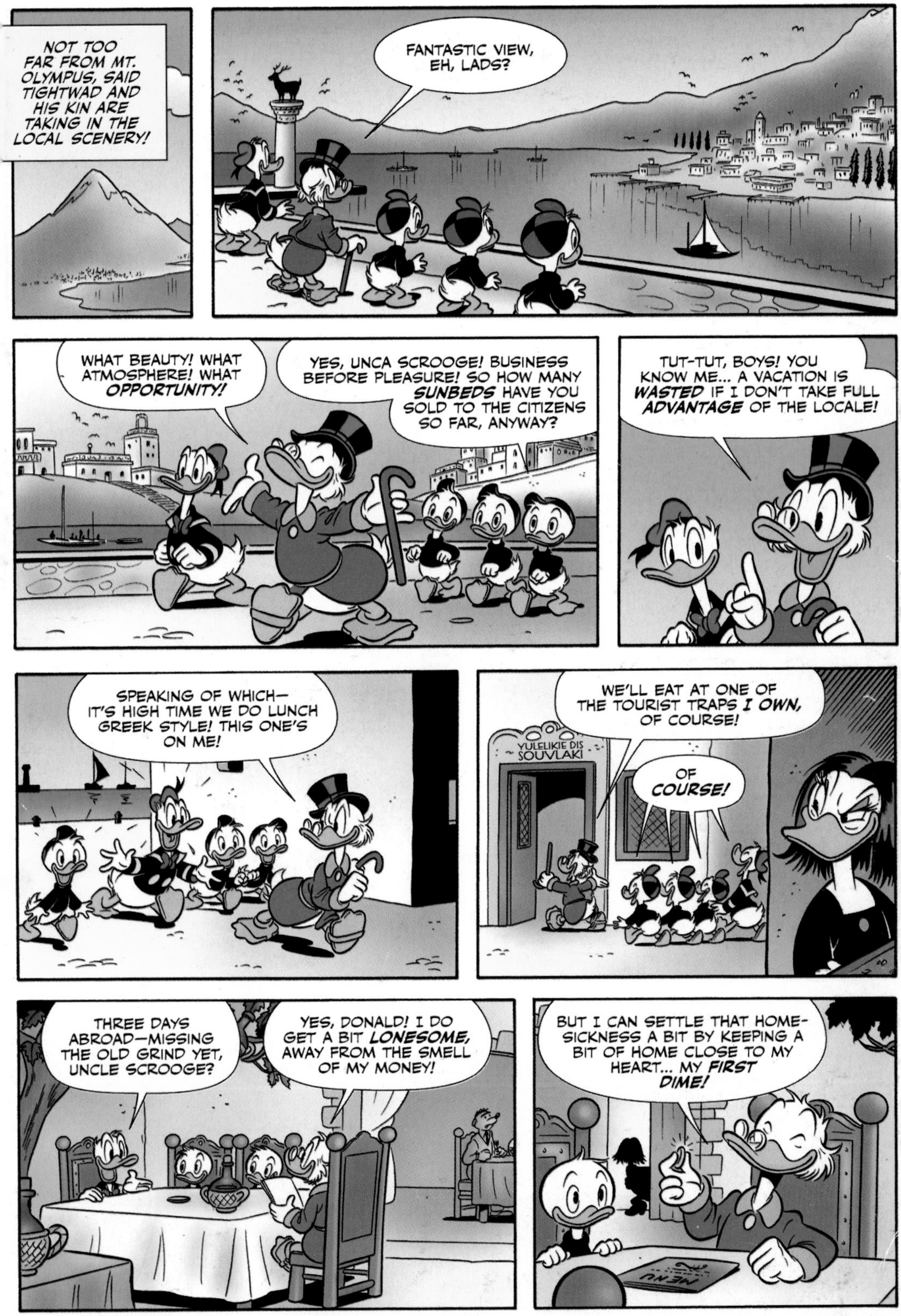

NOT TOO FAR FROM MT. OLYMPUS, SAID TIGHTWAD AND HIS KIN ARE TAKING IN THE LOCAL SCENERY!
FANTASTIC VIEW, EH, LADS?
WHAT BEAUTY! WHAT ATMOSPHERE! WHAT OPPORTUNITY!
YES, UNCA SCROOGE! BUSINESS BEFORE PLEASURE! SO HOW MANY SUNBEDS HAVE YOU SOLD TO THE CITIZENS SO FAR, ANYWAY?
TUT-TUT, BOYS! YOU KNOW ME... A VACATION IS WASTED IF I DON'T TAKE FULL ADVANTAGE OF THE LOCALE!
SPEAKING OF WHICH— IT'S HIGH TIME WE DO LUNCH GREEK STYLE! THIS ONE'S ON ME!
WE'LL EAT AT ONE OF THE TOURIST TRAPS I OWN, OF COURSE!
YULELIKIE DIS SOUVLAKI
OF COURSE!
THREE DAYS ABROAD—MISSING THE OLD GRIND YET, UNCLE SCROOGE?
YES, DONALD! I DO GET A BIT LONESOME, AWAY FROM THE SMELL OF MY MONEY!
BUT I CAN SETTLE THAT HOME-SICKNESS A BIT BY KEEPING A BIT OF HOME CLOSE TO MY HEART... MY FIRST DIME!
MENU

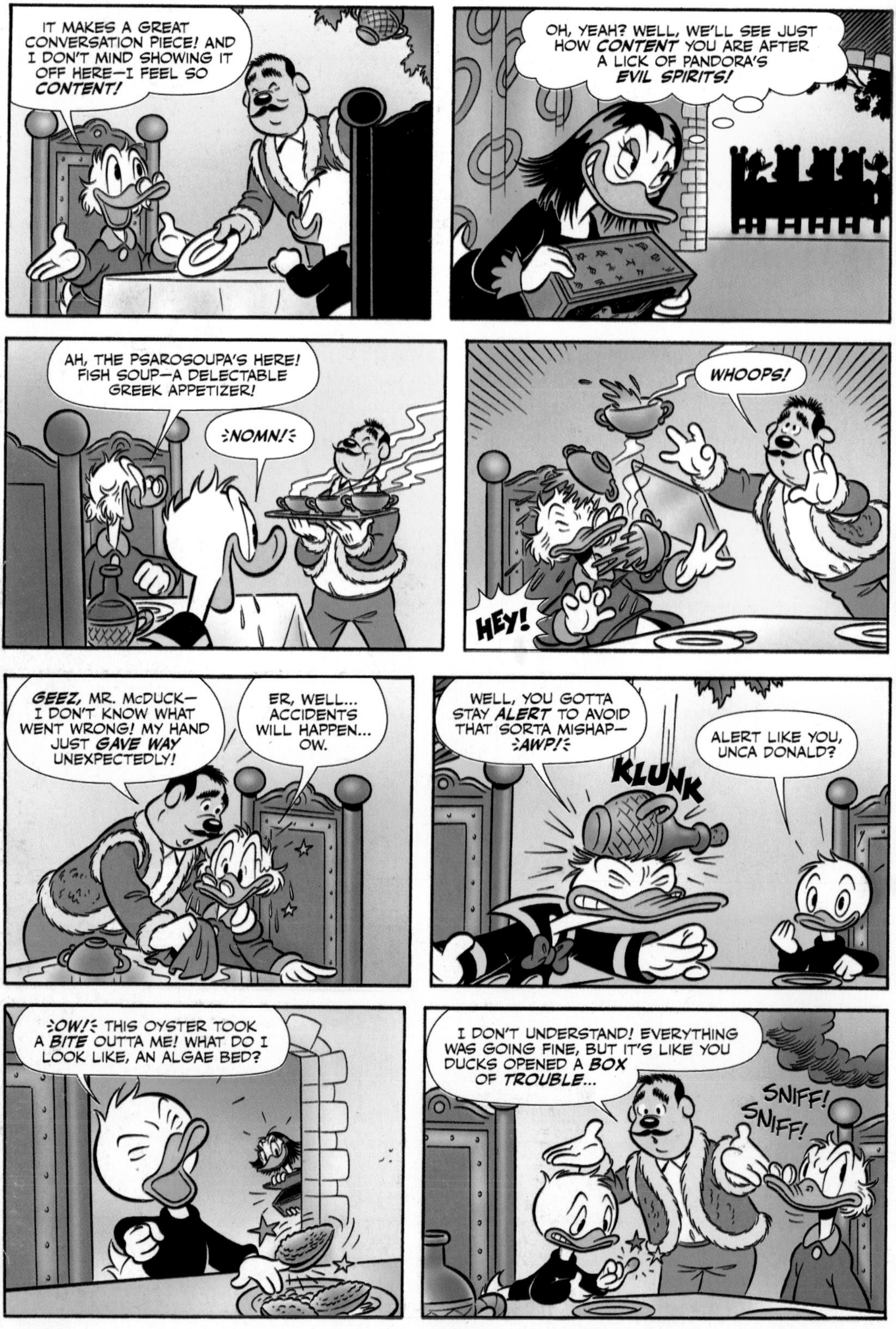
IT MAKES A GREAT CONVERSATION PIECE! AND I DON'T MIND SHOWING IT OFF HERE—I FEEL SO CONTENT!
OH, YEAH? WELL, WE'LL SEE JUST HOW CONTENT YOU ARE AFTER A LICK OF PANDORA'S EVIL SPIRITS!
AH, THE PSAROSOUPA'S HERE! FISH SOUP—A DELECTABLE GREEK APPETIZER!
NOMN!
WHOOPS!
HEY!
GEEZ, MR. McDUCK—I DON'T KNOW WHAT WENT WRONG! MY HAND JUST GAVE WAY UNEXPECTEDLY!
ER, WELL... ACCIDENTS WILL HAPPEN... OW.
WELL, YOU GOTTA STAY ALERT TO AVOID THAT SORTA MISHAP—AWP!
KLUNK
ALERT LIKE YOU, UNCA DONALD?
OW! THIS OYSTER TOOK A BITE OUTTA ME! WHAT DO I LOOK LIKE, AN ALGAE BED?
I DON'T UNDERSTAND! EVERYTHING WAS GOING FINE, BUT IT'S LIKE YOU DUCKS OPENED A BOX OF TROUBLE...
SNIFF! SNIFF!

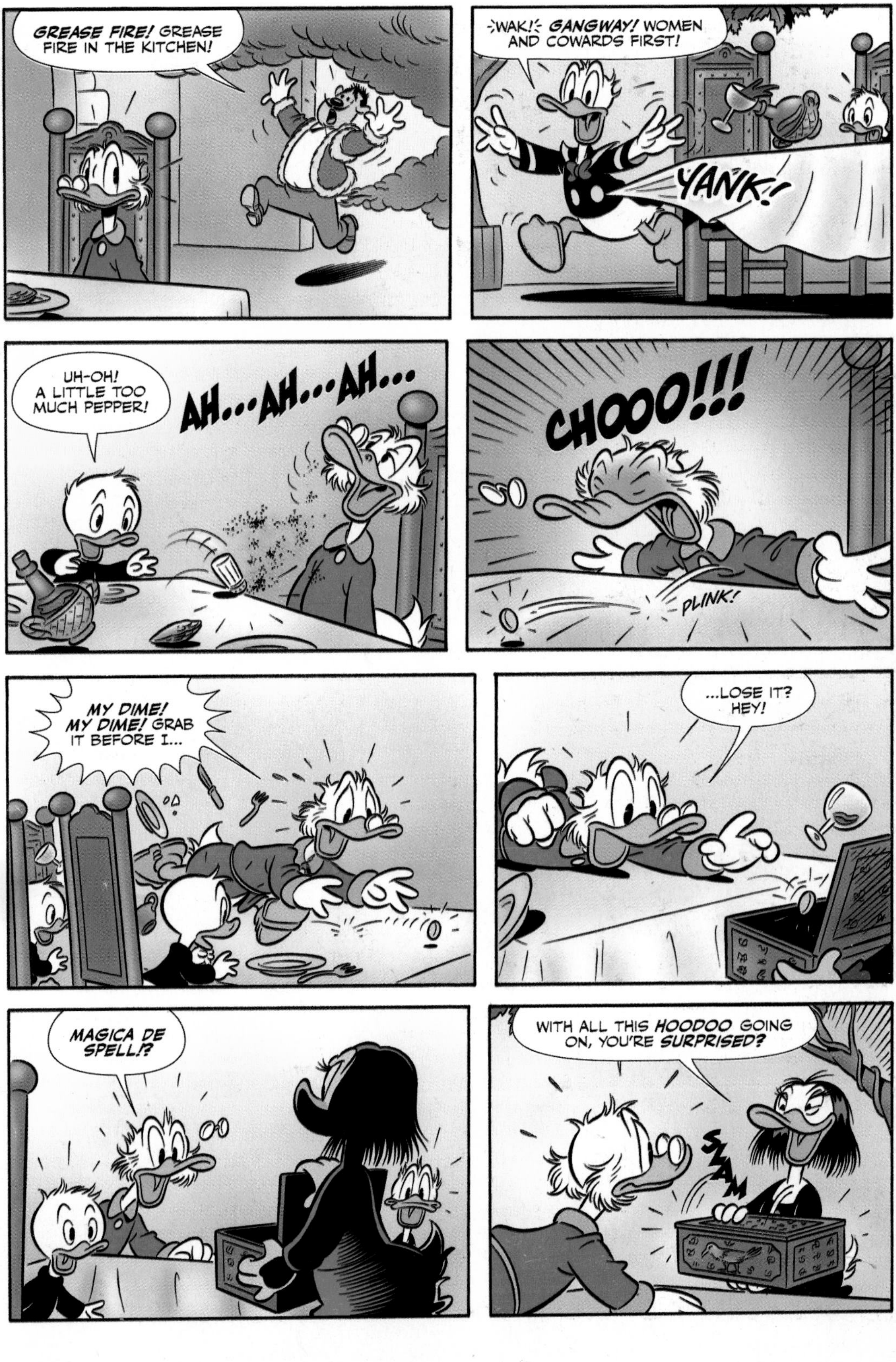
GREASE FIRE! GREASE FIRE IN THE KITCHEN!
WAK! GANGWAY! WOMEN AND COWARDS FIRST!
YANK!
UH-OH! A LITTLE TOO MUCH PEPPER!
AH...AH...AH...
CHOOO!!!
PLINK!
MY DIME! MY DIME! GRAB IT BEFORE I...
...LOSE IT? HEY!
MAGICA DE SPELL!?
WITH ALL THIS HOODOO GOING ON, YOU'RE SURPRISED?
SLAM

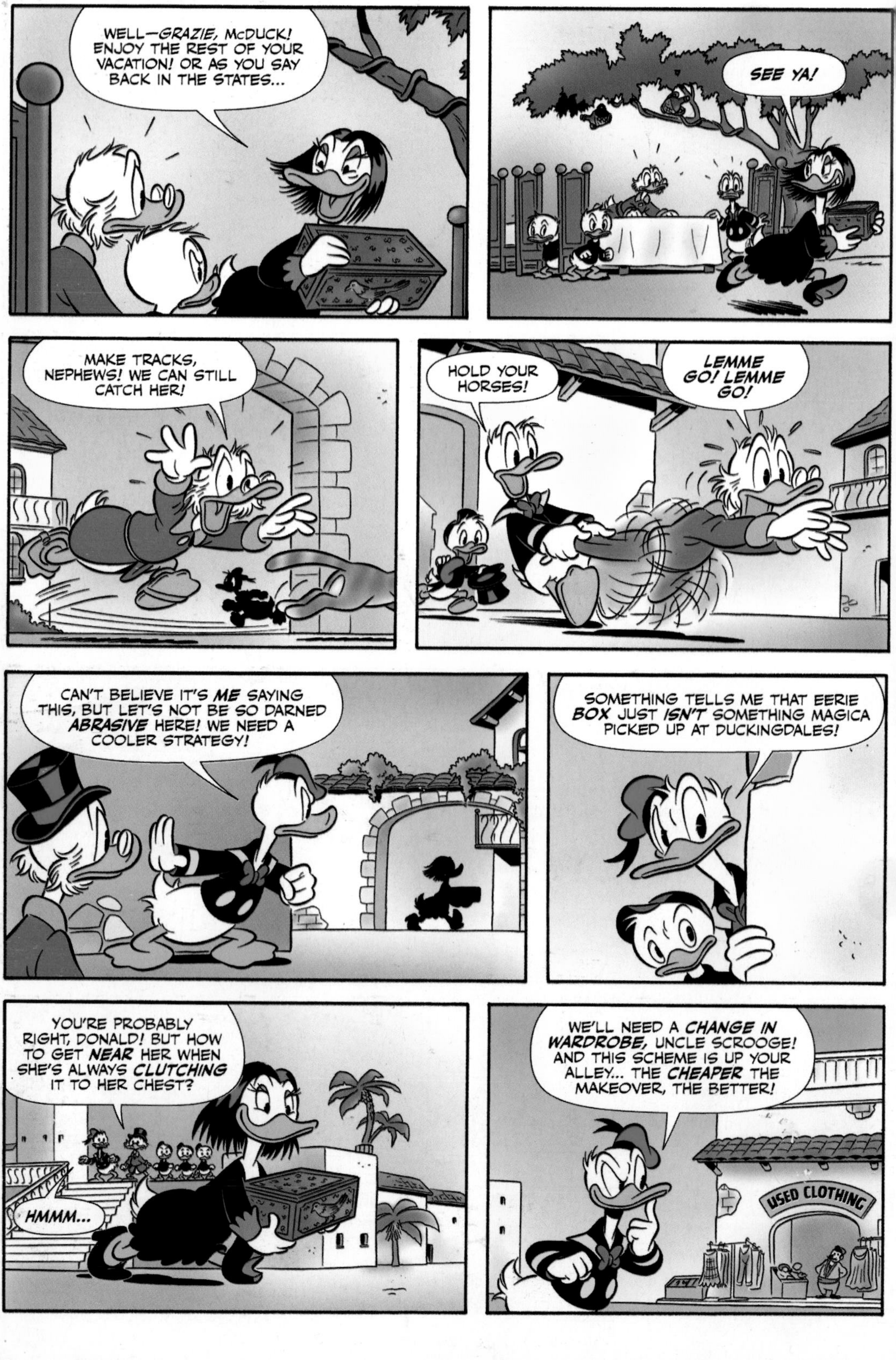
WELL—GRAZIE, McDUCK! ENJOY THE REST OF YOUR VACATION! OR AS YOU SAY BACK IN THE STATES...
SEE YA!
MAKE TRACKS, NEPHEWS! WE CAN STILL CATCH HER!
HOLD YOUR HORSES!
LEMME GO! LEMME GO!
CAN'T BELIEVE IT'S ME SAYING THIS, BUT LET'S NOT BE SO DARNED ABRASIVE HERE! WE NEED A COOLER STRATEGY!
SOMETHING TELLS ME THAT EERIE BOX JUST ISN'T SOMETHING MAGICA PICKED UP AT DUCKINGDALES!
YOU'RE PROBABLY RIGHT, DONALD! BUT HOW TO GET NEAR HER WHEN SHE'S ALWAYS CLUTCHING IT TO HER CHEST?
HMMM...
WE'LL NEED A CHANGE IN WARDROBE, UNCLE SCROOGE! AND THIS SCHEME IS UP YOUR ALLEY... THE CHEAPER THE MAKEOVER, THE BETTER!
USED CLOTHING

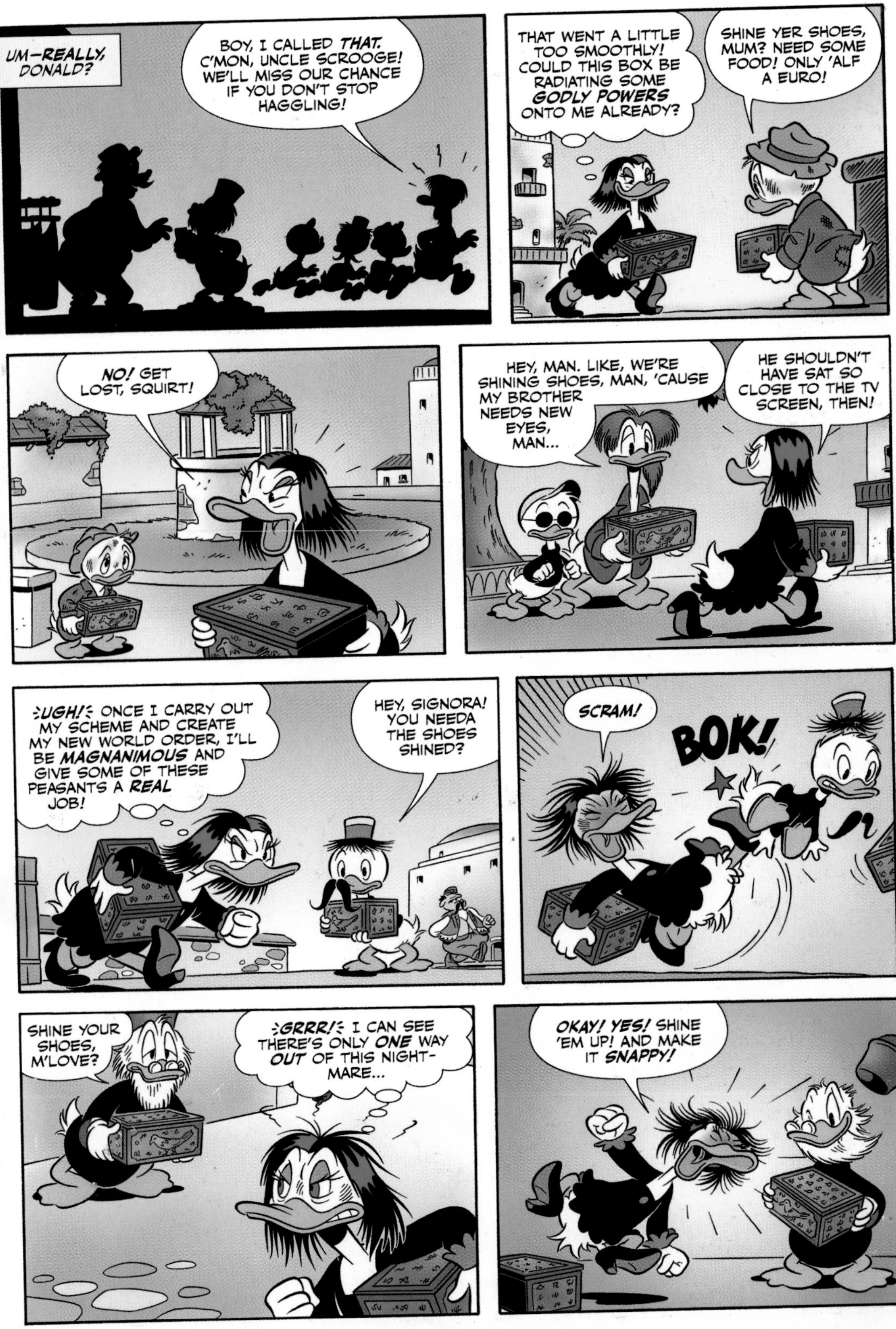
UM—REALLY, DONALD?
BOY, I CALLED THAT. C'MON, UNCLE SCROOGE! WE'LL MISS OUR CHANCE IF YOU DON'T STOP HAGGLING!
THAT WENT A LITTLE TOO SMOOTHLY! COULD THIS BOX BE RADIATING SOME GODLY POWERS ONTO ME ALREADY?
SHINE YER SHOES, MUM? NEED SOME FOOD! ONLY 'ALF A EURO!
NO! GET LOST, SQUIRT!
HEY, MAN. LIKE, WE'RE SHINING SHOES, MAN, 'CAUSE MY BROTHER NEEDS NEW EYES, MAN...
HE SHOULDN'T HAVE SAT SO CLOSE TO THE TV SCREEN, THEN!
UGH! ONCE I CARRY OUT MY SCHEME AND CREATE MY NEW WORLD ORDER, I'LL BE MAGNANIMOUS AND GIVE SOME OF THESE PEASANTS A REAL JOB!
HEY, SIGNORA! YOU NEEDA THE SHOES SHINED?
SCRAM!
BOK!
SHINE YOUR SHOES, M'LOVE?
GRRR! I CAN SEE THERE'S ONLY ONE WAY OUT OF THIS NIGHT-MARE...
OKAY! YES! SHINE 'EM UP! AND MAKE IT SNAPPY!

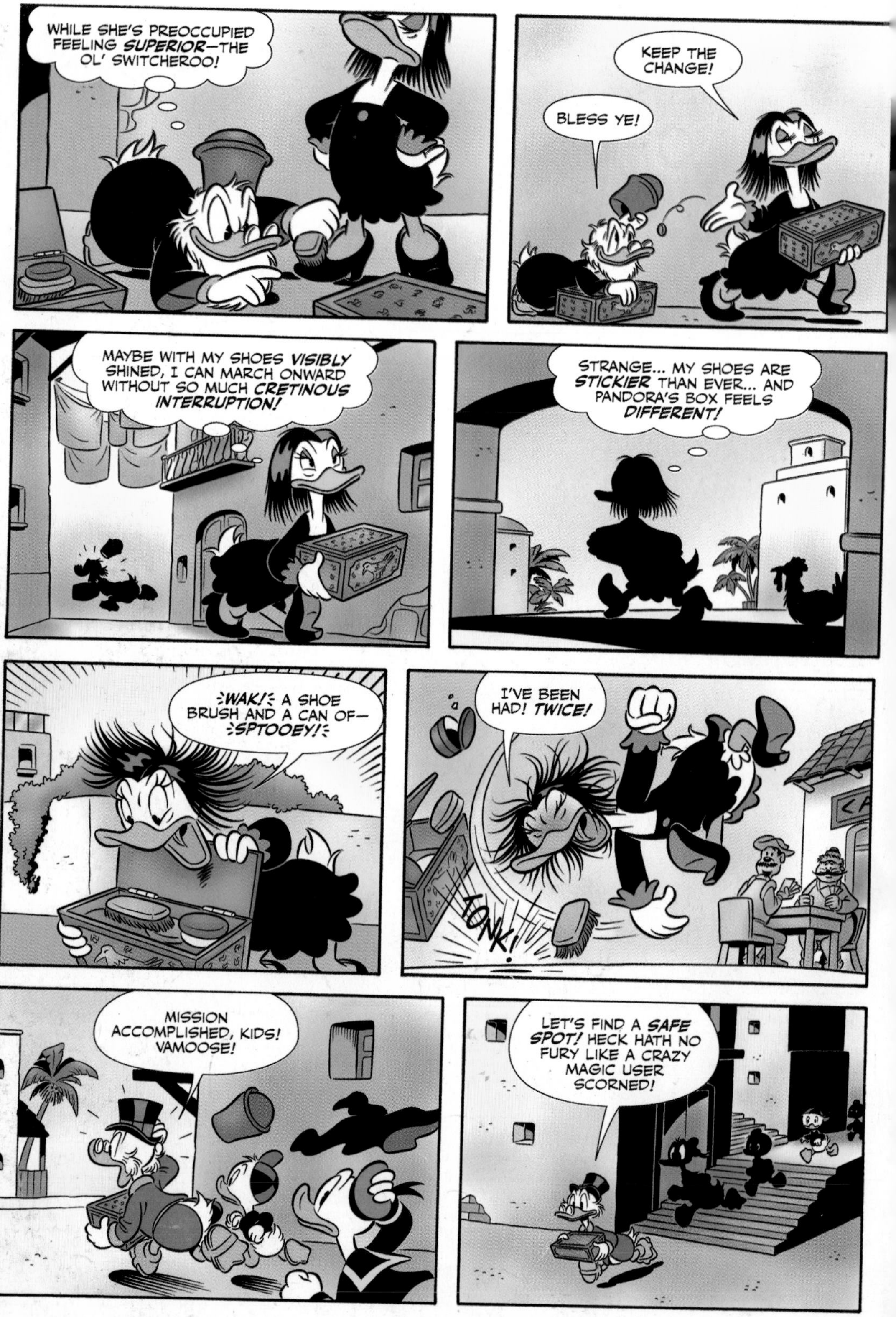
WHILE SHE'S PREOCCUPIED FEELING SUPERIOR—THE OL' SWITCHEROO!
KEEP THE CHANGE!
BLESS YE!
MAYBE WITH MY SHOES VISIBLY SHINED, I CAN MARCH ONWARD WITHOUT SO MUCH CRETINOUS INTERRUPTION!
STRANGE... MY SHOES ARE STICKIER THAN EVER... AND PANDORA'S BOX FEELS DIFFERENT!
WAK! A SHOE BRUSH AND A CAN OF—SPTOOEY!
I'VE BEEN HAD! TWICE!
TONK!
MISSION ACCOMPLISHED, KIDS! VAMOOSE!
LET'S FIND A SAFE SPOT! HECK HATH NO FURY LIKE A CRAZY MAGIC USER SCORNED!

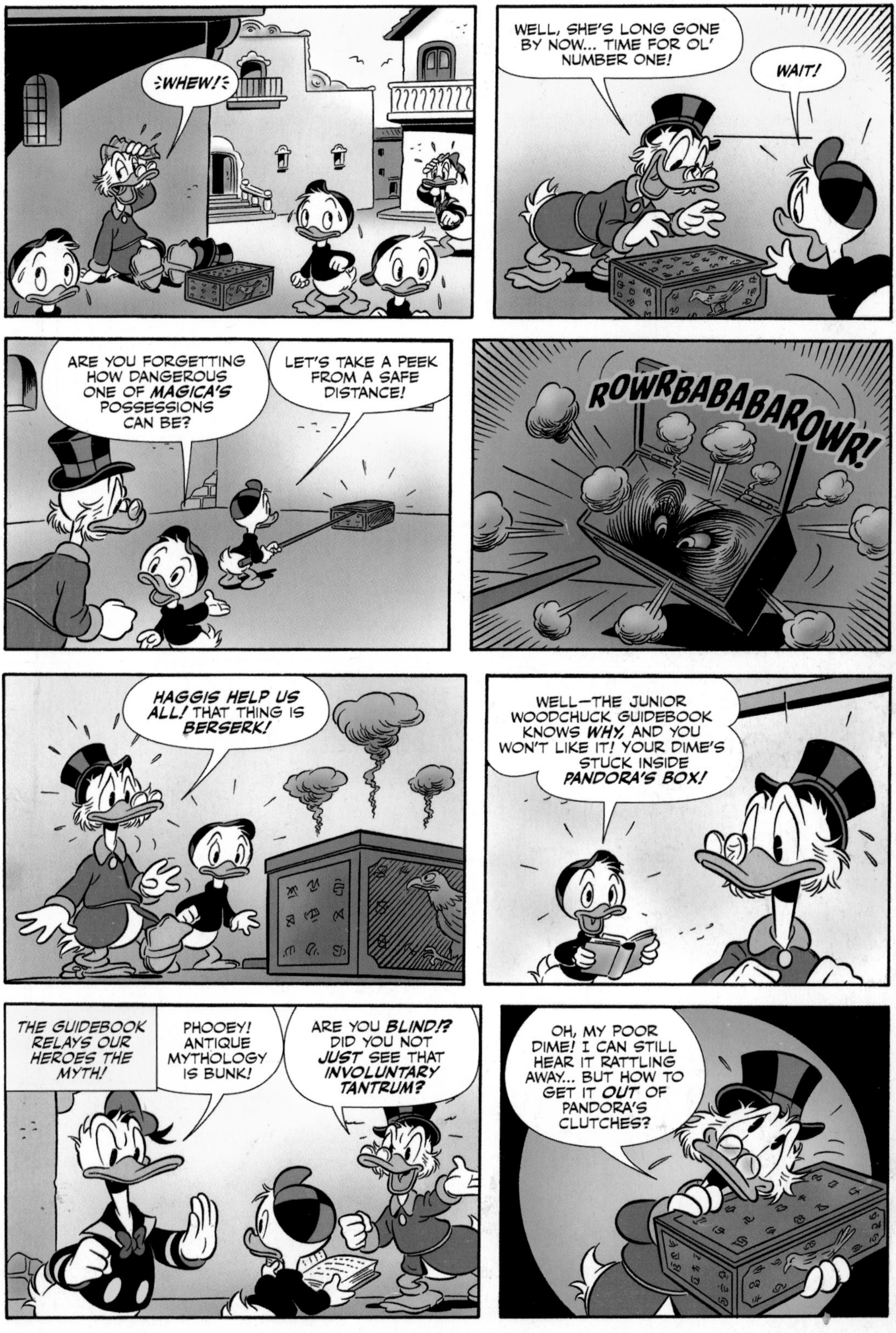
WHEW!
WELL, SHE'S LONG GONE BY NOW... TIME FOR OL' NUMBER ONE!
WAIT!
ARE YOU FORGETTING HOW DANGEROUS ONE OF MAGICA'S POSSESSIONS CAN BE?
LET'S TAKE A PEEK FROM A SAFE DISTANCE!
ROWRBABABAROWR!
HAGGIS HELP US ALL! THAT THING IS BERSERK!
WELL—THE JUNIOR WOODCHUCK GUIDEBOOK KNOWS WHY, AND YOU WON'T LIKE IT! YOUR DIME'S STUCK INSIDE PANDORA'S BOX!
THE GUIDEBOOK RELAYS OUR HEROES THE MYTH!
PHOOEY! ANTIQUE MYTHOLOGY IS BUNK!
ARE YOU BLIND!? DID YOU NOT JUST SEE THAT INVOLUNTARY TANTRUM?
OH, MY POOR DIME! I CAN STILL HEAR IT RATTLING AWAY... BUT HOW TO GET IT OUT OF PANDORA'S CLUTCHES?

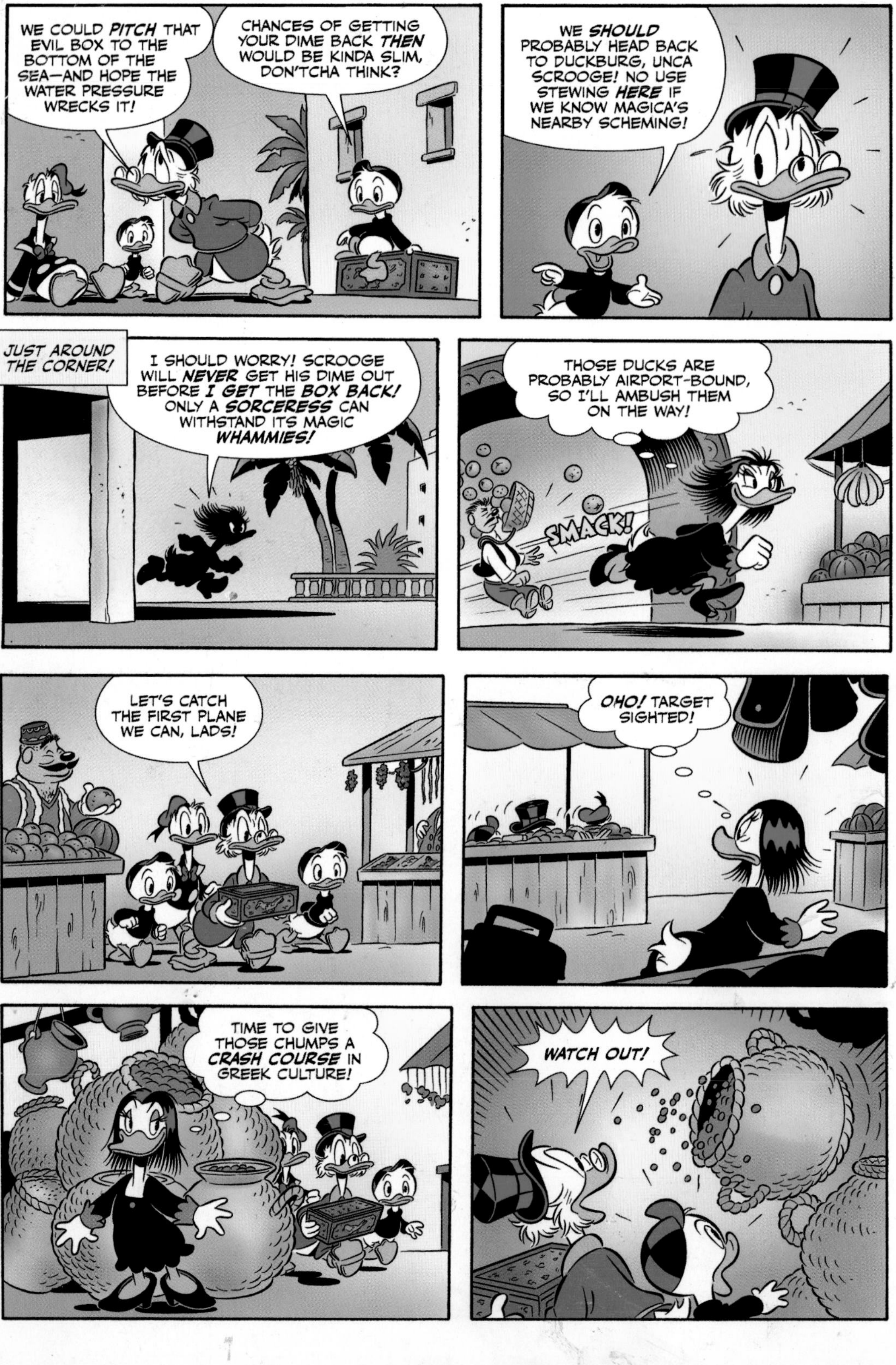
WE COULD PITCH THAT EVIL BOX TO THE BOTTOM OF THE SEA—AND HOPE THE WATER PRESSURE WRECKS IT!
CHANCES OF GETTING YOUR DIME BACK THEN WOULD BE KINDA SLIM, DON'TCHA THINK?
WE SHOULD PROBABLY HEAD BACK TO DUCKBURG, UNCA SCROOGE! NO USE STEWING HERE IF WE KNOW MAGICA'S NEARBY SCHEMING!
JUST AROUND THE CORNER!
I SHOULD WORRY! SCROOGE WILL NEVER GET HIS DIME OUT BEFORE I GET THE BOX BACK! ONLY A SORCERESS CAN WITHSTAND ITS MAGIC WHAMMIES!
THOSE DUCKS ARE PROBABLY AIRPORT-BOUND, SO I'LL AMBUSH THEM ON THE WAY!
SMACK!
LET'S CATCH THE FIRST PLANE WE CAN, LADS!
OHO! TARGET SIGHTED!
TIME TO GIVE THOSE CHUMPS A CRASH COURSE IN GREEK CULTURE!
WATCH OUT!

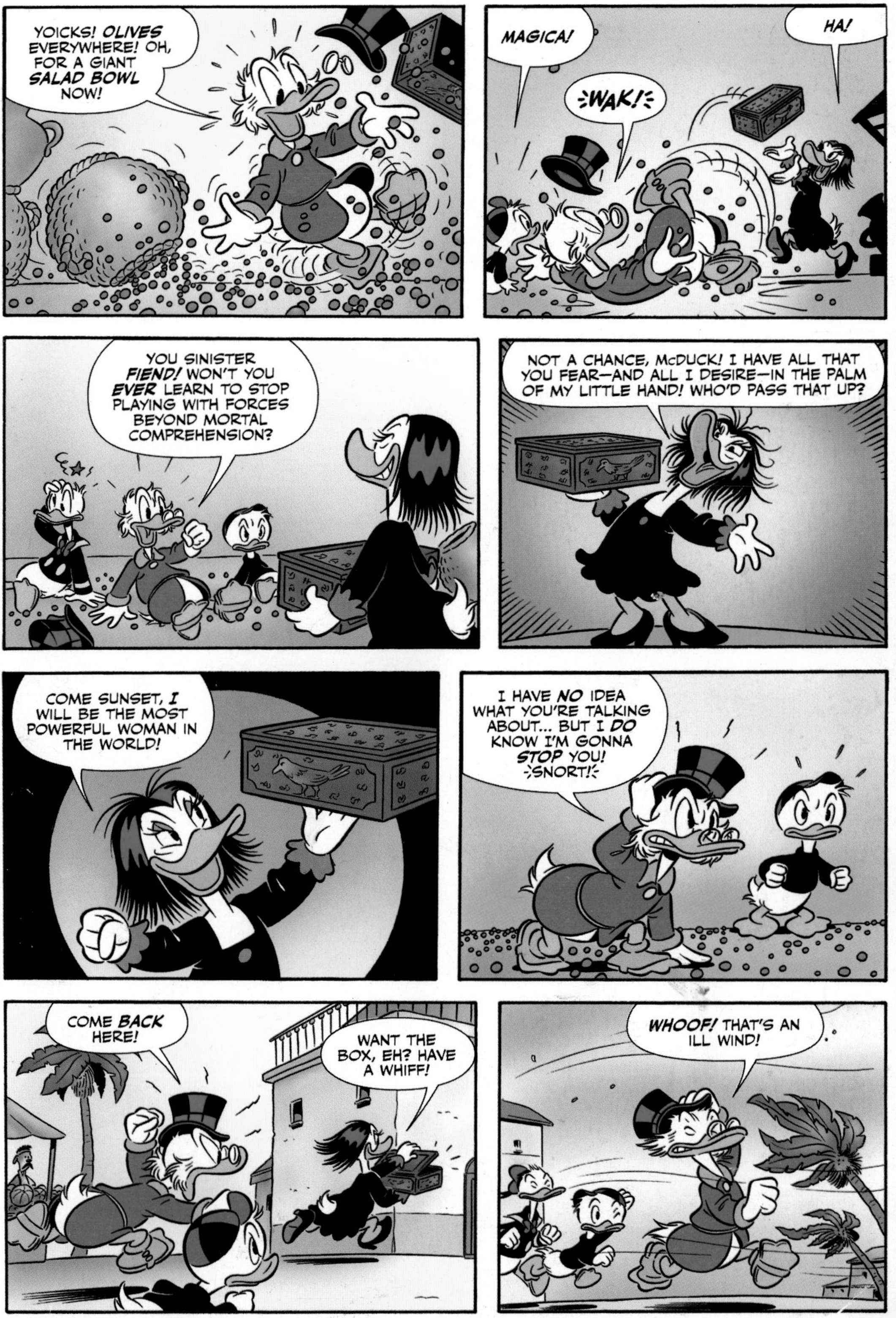
YOICKS! OLIVES EVERYWHERE! OH, FOR A GIANT SALAD BOWL NOW!
MAGICA!
-WAK!-
HA!
YOU SINISTER FIEND! WON'T YOU EVER LEARN TO STOP PLAYING WITH FORCES BEYOND MORTAL COMPREHENSION?
NOT A CHANCE, McDUCK! I HAVE ALL THAT YOU FEAR—AND ALL I DESIRE—IN THE PALM OF MY LITTLE HAND! WHO'D PASS THAT UP?
COME SUNSET, I WILL BE THE MOST POWERFUL WOMAN IN THE WORLD!
I HAVE NO IDEA WHAT YOU'RE TALKING ABOUT... BUT I DO KNOW I'M GONNA STOP YOU! -SNORT!-
COME BACK HERE!
WANT THE BOX, EH? HAVE A WHIFF!
WHOOF! THAT'S AN ILL WIND!

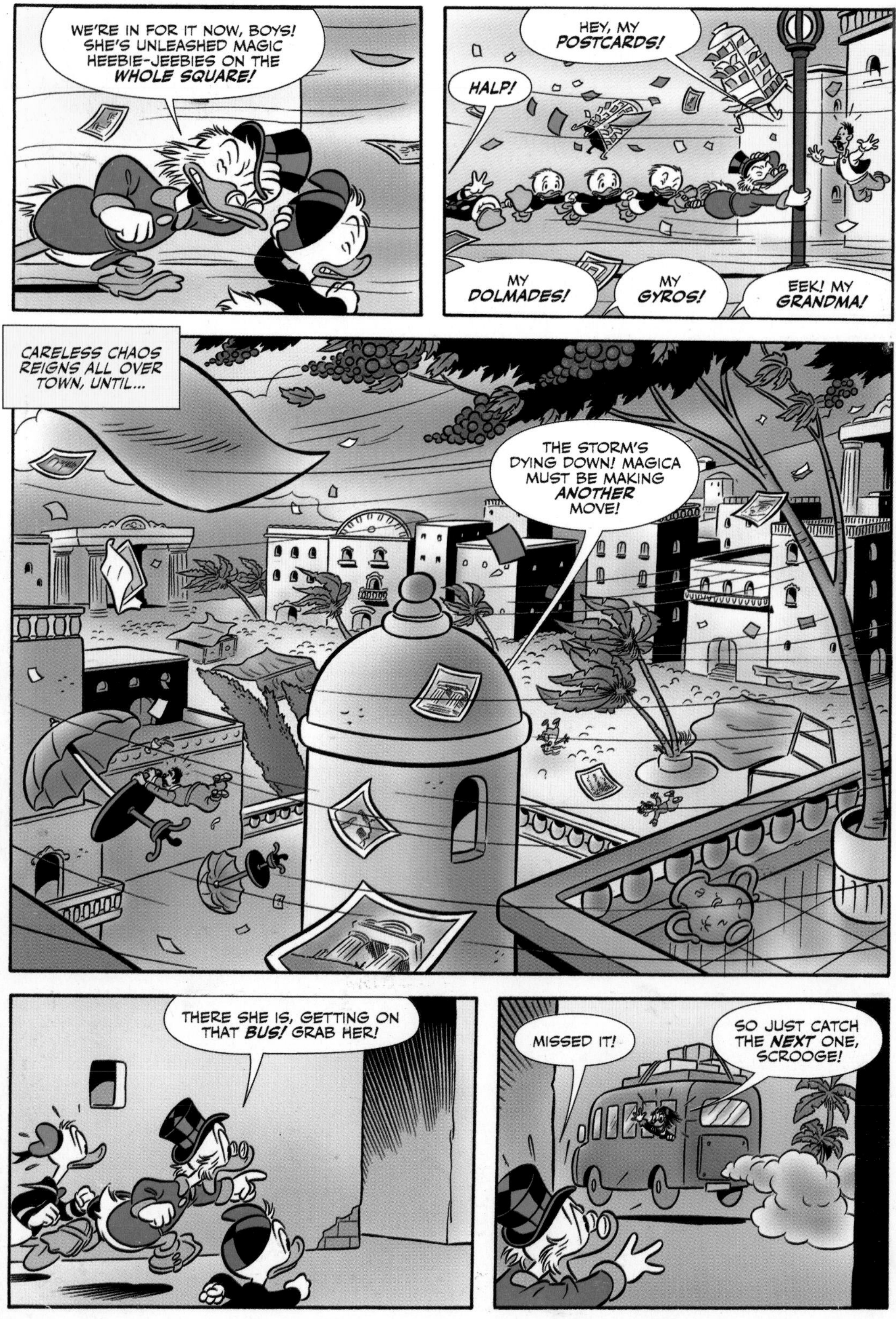
WE'RE IN FOR IT NOW, BOYS! SHE'S UNLEASHED MAGIC HEEBIE-JEEBIES ON THE **WHOLE SQUARE!**
HEY, MY **POSTCARDS!**
HALP!
MY **DOLMADES!**
MY **GYROS!**
EEK! MY **GRANDMA!**
CARELESS CHAOS REIGNS ALL OVER TOWN, UNTIL...
THE STORM'S DYING DOWN! MAGICA MUST BE MAKING **ANOTHER** MOVE!
THERE SHE IS, GETTING ON THAT **BUS!** GRAB HER!
MISSED IT!
SO JUST CATCH THE **NEXT** ONE, SCROOGE!

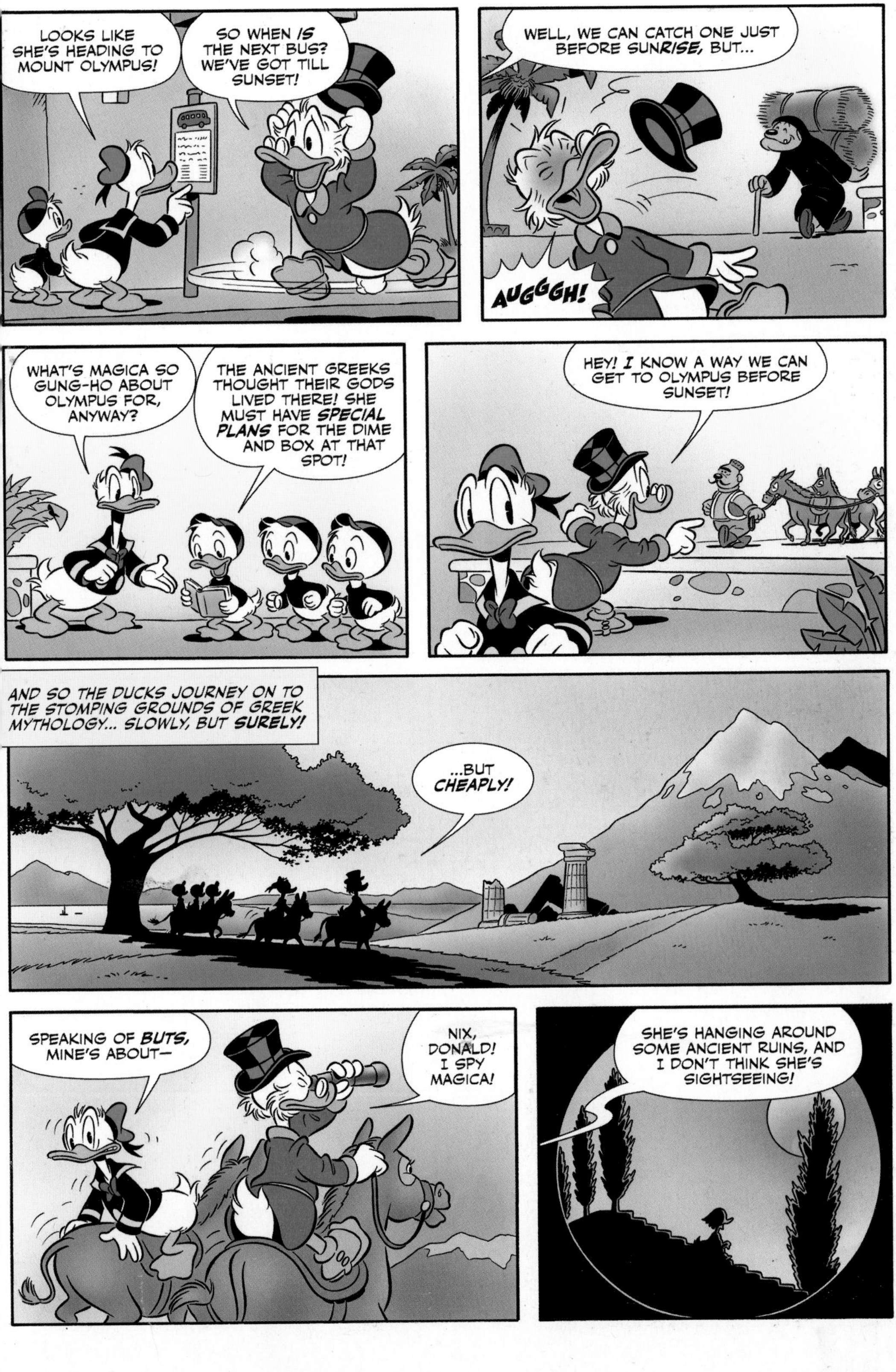
LOOKS LIKE SHE'S HEADING TO MOUNT OLYMPUS!
SO WHEN IS THE NEXT BUS? WE'VE GOT TILL SUNSET!
WELL, WE CAN CATCH ONE JUST BEFORE SUNRISE, BUT...
AUGGGH!
WHAT'S MAGICA SO GUNG-HO ABOUT OLYMPUS FOR, ANYWAY?
THE ANCIENT GREEKS THOUGHT THEIR GODS LIVED THERE! SHE MUST HAVE SPECIAL PLANS FOR THE DIME AND BOX AT THAT SPOT!
HEY! I KNOW A WAY WE CAN GET TO OLYMPUS BEFORE SUNSET!
AND SO THE DUCKS JOURNEY ON TO THE STOMPING GROUNDS OF GREEK MYTHOLOGY... SLOWLY, BUT SURELY!
...BUT CHEAPLY!
SPEAKING OF BUTS, MINE'S ABOUT—
NIX, DONALD! I SPY MAGICA!
SHE'S HANGING AROUND SOME ANCIENT RUINS, AND I DON'T THINK SHE'S SIGHTSEEING!

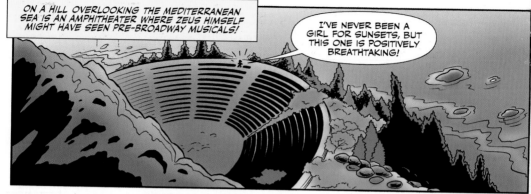

ON A HILL OVERLOOKING THE MEDITERRANEAN SEA IS AN AMPHITHEATER WHERE ZEUS HIMSELF MIGHT HAVE SEEN PRE-BROADWAY MUSICALS!

I'VE NEVER BEEN A GIRL FOR SUNSETS, BUT THIS ONE IS POSITIVELY BREATHTAKING!

HIGH ABOVE THE MIGHTY SEA, I HATCH AN ANCIENT SPELL TO GRANT DIVINITY UNTO—ME!

THE SECOND MR. SUN SINKS SLOWLY IN THE WEST, SO TOO WILL THE DIME—AND PANDORA'S CHEST!

TAKE THE SOURCE OF ALL THE WORLD'S UNHAPPINESS... ADD SCROOGE'S DIME, A SOURCE OF INFINITE HAPPINESS—SINK BOTH TO THE SEA BOTTOM... AND UP COMES A TIDAL WAVE OF UNSPEAKABLE MAGIC POWERS FOR THE TAKING!... FAR BETTER THAN THE MIDAS TOUCH!

OH-OH-OH!

≷PSST!≷ UNCA SCROOGE! YOU'LL NEVER BELIEVE THIS ONE!

IT LOOKS LIKE IT'S SINK OR SWIM FOR SCROOGE!

HER PLAN COULD BE MISGUIDED—BUT THEN I'M STILL OUT MY DIME! AND ON THE OTHER HAND, IF SHE'S RIGHT... OHHHHH, BROTHER!

WAIT! I THINK I'VE GOT A WAY TO STOP THAT MYTHOLOGY-OBSESSED LOON!

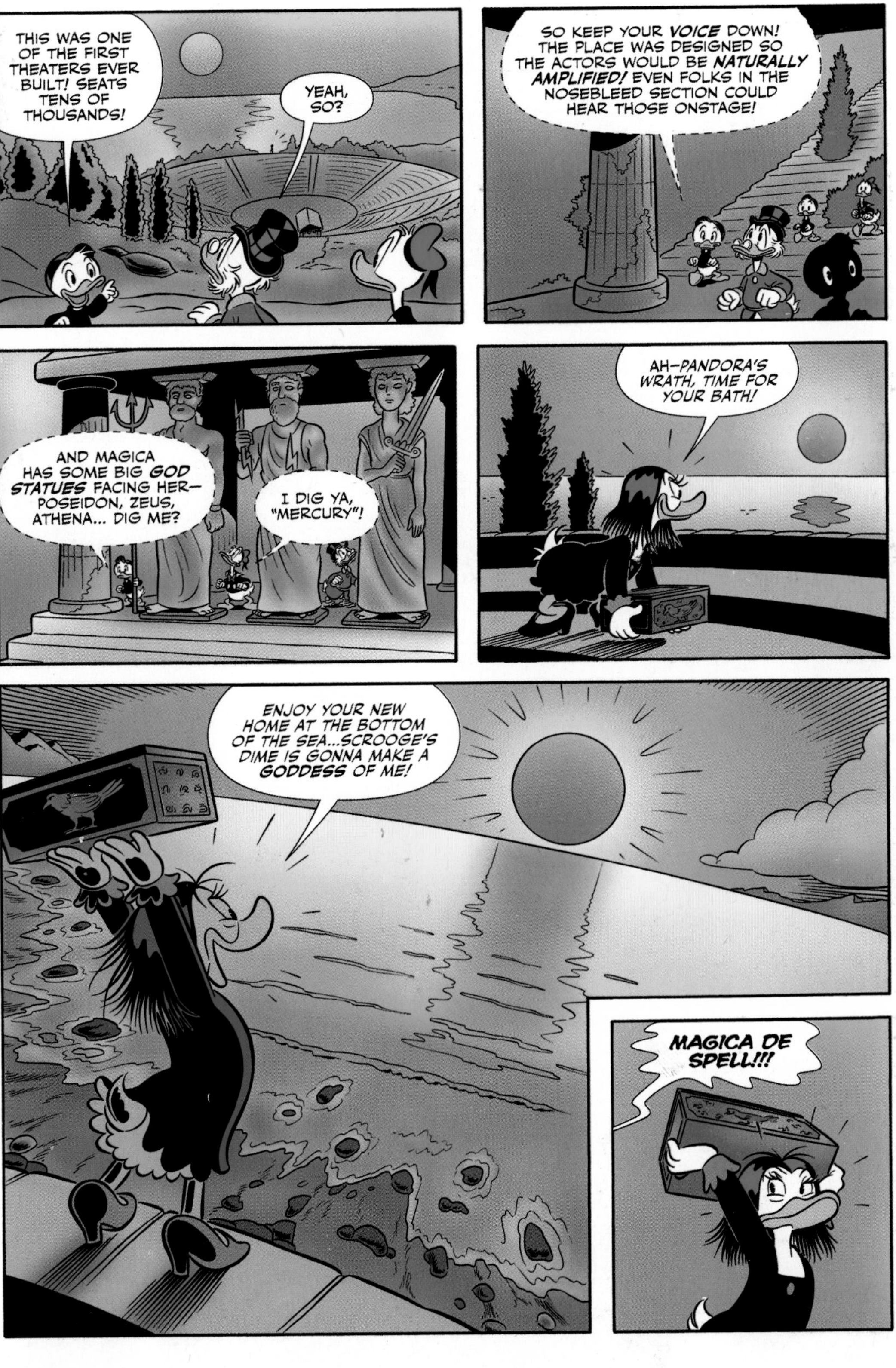

THIS WAS ONE OF THE FIRST THEATERS EVER BUILT! SEATS TENS OF THOUSANDS!
YEAH, SO?
SO KEEP YOUR VOICE DOWN! THE PLACE WAS DESIGNED SO THE ACTORS WOULD BE NATURALLY AMPLIFIED! EVEN FOLKS IN THE NOSEBLEED SECTION COULD HEAR THOSE ONSTAGE!
AND MAGICA HAS SOME BIG GOD STATUES FACING HER— POSEIDON, ZEUS, ATHENA... DIG ME?
I DIG YA, "MERCURY"!
AH—PANDORA'S WRATH, TIME FOR YOUR BATH!
ENJOY YOUR NEW HOME AT THE BOTTOM OF THE SEA...SCROOGE'S DIME IS GONNA MAKE A GODDESS OF ME!
MAGICA DE SPELL!!!

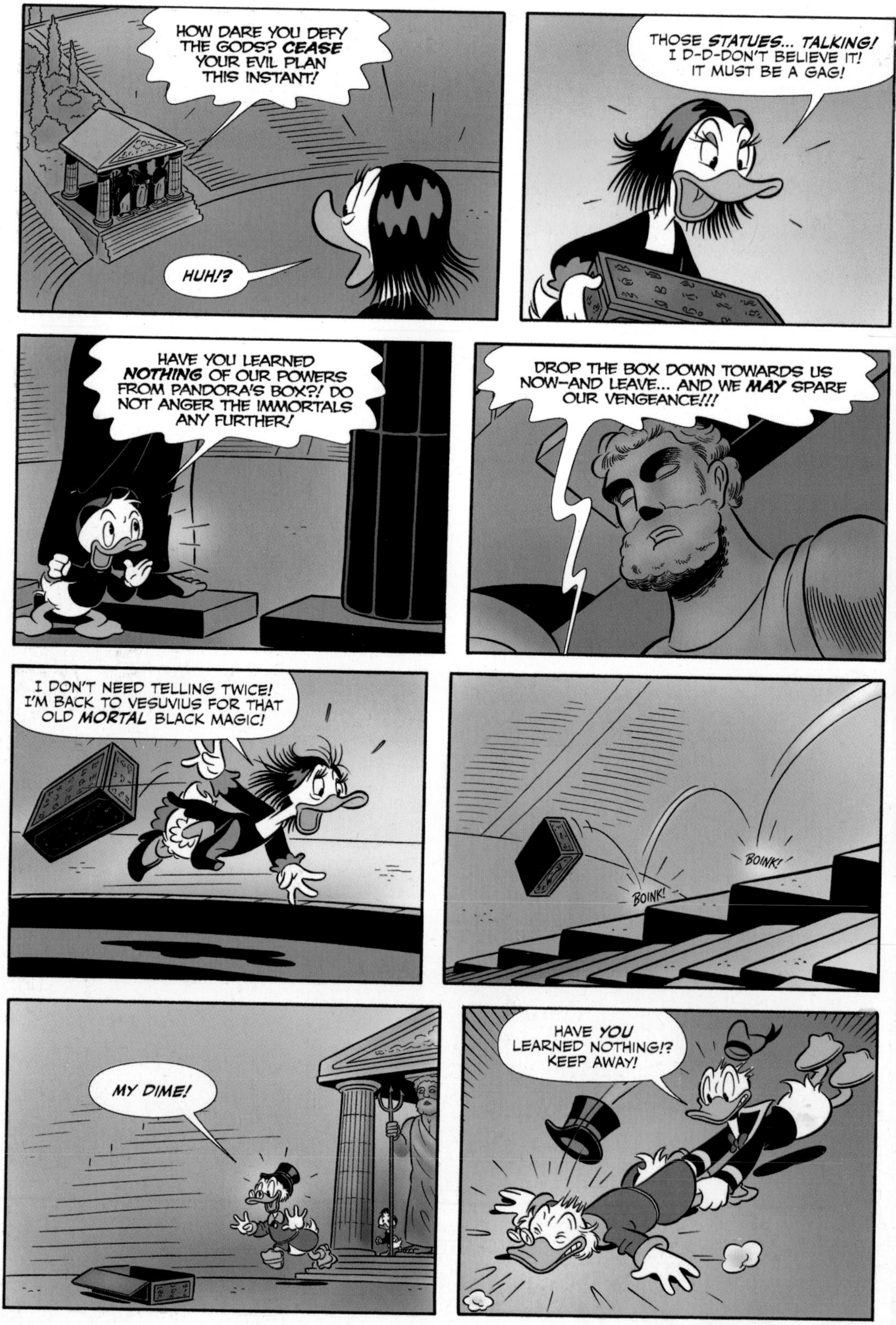
HOW DARE YOU DEFY THE GODS? CEASE YOUR EVIL PLAN THIS INSTANT!
HUH!?
THOSE STATUES... TALKING! I D-D-DON'T BELIEVE IT! IT MUST BE A GAG!
HAVE YOU LEARNED NOTHING OF OUR POWERS FROM PANDORA'S BOX?! DO NOT ANGER THE IMMORTALS ANY FURTHER!
DROP THE BOX DOWN TOWARDS US NOW—AND LEAVE... AND WE MAY SPARE OUR VENGEANCE!!!
I DON'T NEED TELLING TWICE! I'M BACK TO VESUVIUS FOR THAT OLD MORTAL BLACK MAGIC!
BOINK!
BOINK!
MY DIME!
HAVE YOU LEARNED NOTHING!? KEEP AWAY!

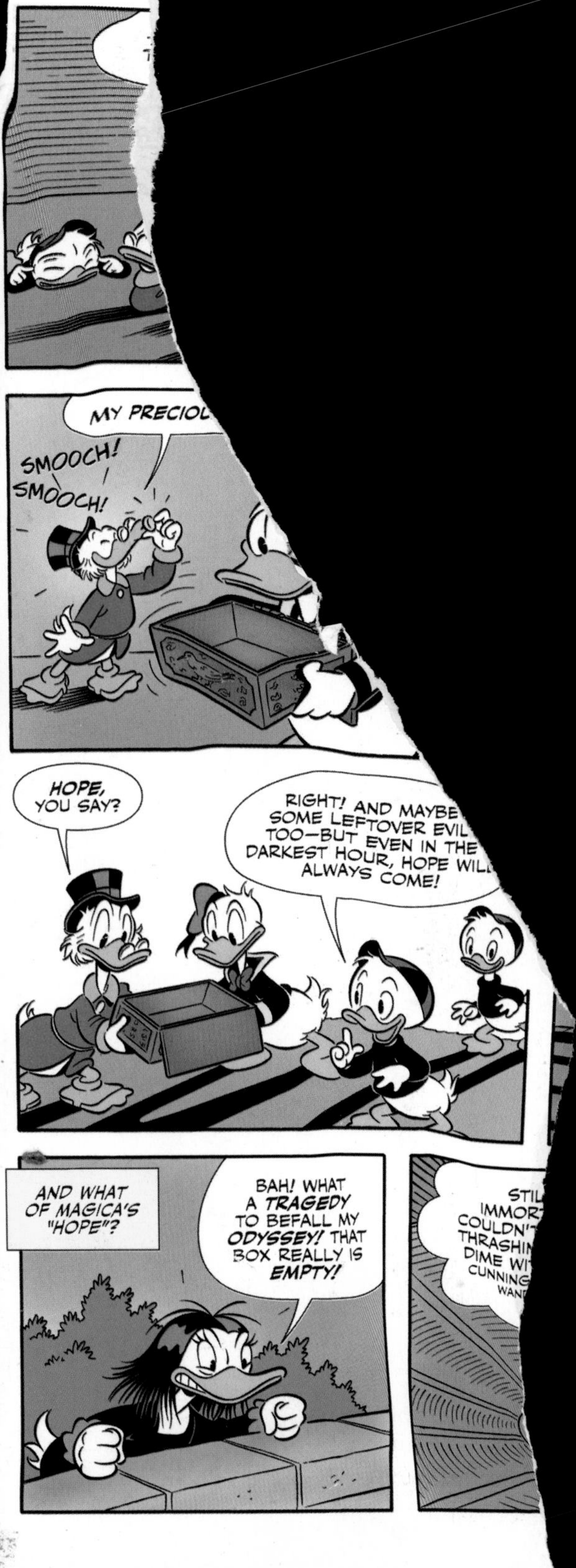
MY PRECIOU
SMOOCH! SMOOCH!
HOPE, YOU SAY?
RIGHT! AND MAYBE SOME LEFTOVER EVIL TOO—BUT EVEN IN THE DARKEST HOUR, HOPE WILL ALWAYS COME!
AND WHAT OF MAGICA'S "HOPE"?
BAH! WHAT A TRAGEDY TO BEFALL MY ODYSSEY! THAT BOX REALLY IS EMPTY!
STIL IMMORT COULDN'T THRASHIN DIME WIT CUNNING WAND

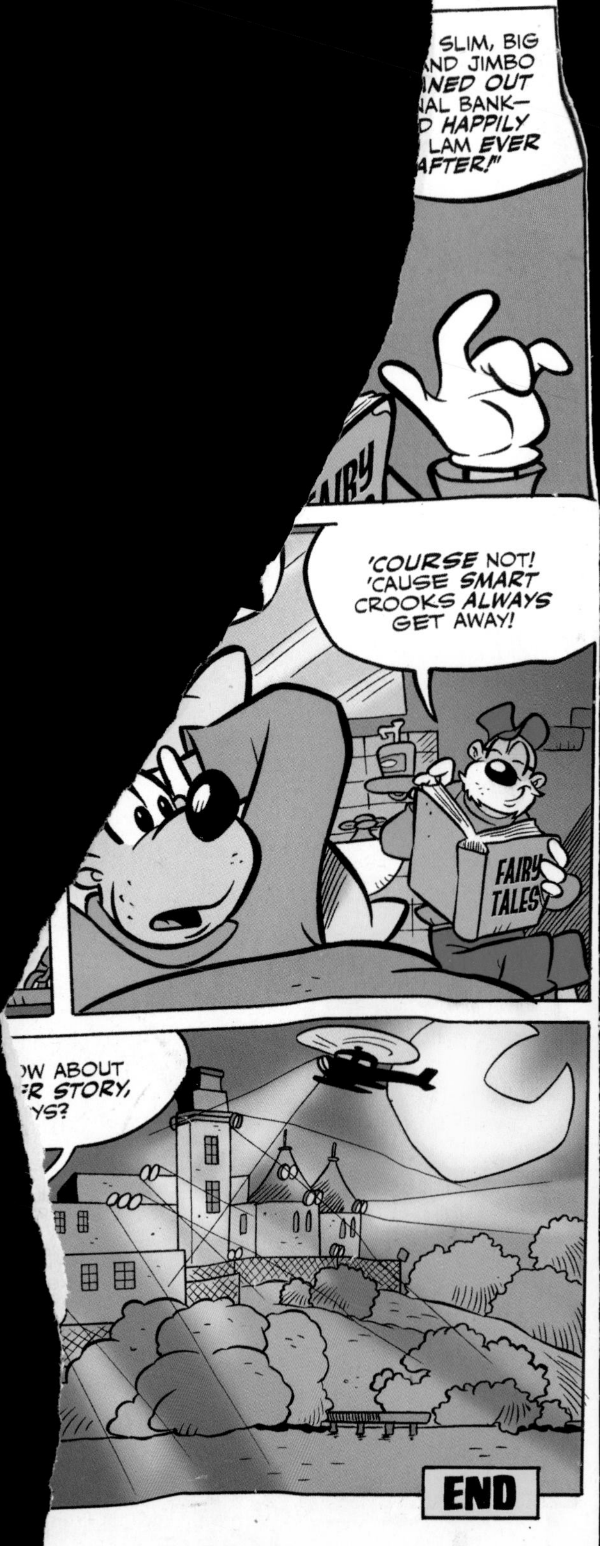
SLIM, BIG
AND JIMBO
NED OUT
NAL BANK—
D HAPPILY
LAM EVER
AFTER!"
FAIRY
'COURSE NOT! 'CAUSE SMART CROOKS ALWAYS GET AWAY!
FAIRY TALES
OW ABOUT
R STORY,
YS?
END

in *Topolino* #2922 (Italy, 2011)

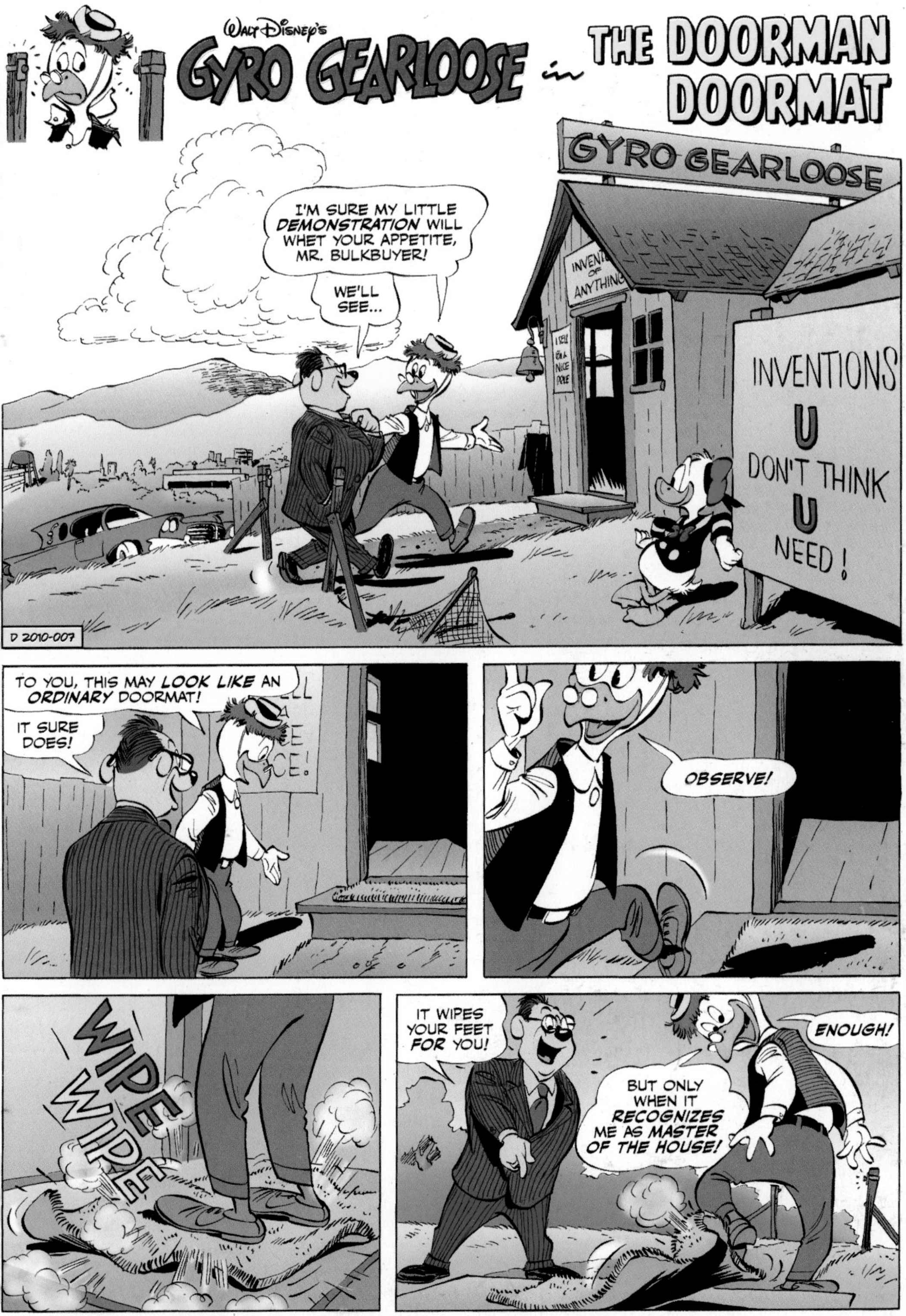
Walt Disney's
GYRO GEARLOOSE in
THE DOORMAN DOORMAT
GYRO GEARLOOSE
INVENTIONS U DON'T THINK U NEED!
I'M SURE MY LITTLE *DEMONSTRATION* WILL WHET YOUR APPETITE, MR. BULKBUYER!
WE'LL SEE...
D 2010-007
TO YOU, THIS MAY *LOOK LIKE* AN *ORDINARY* DOORMAT!
IT SURE DOES!
OBSERVE!
WIPE WIPE WIPE
IT WIPES YOUR FEET *FOR* YOU!
BUT ONLY WHEN IT *RECOGNIZES* ME AS *MASTER OF THE HOUSE!*
ENOUGH!

Originally published in *Kalle Anka & Co.* #15-16/2011 (Sweden, 2011)

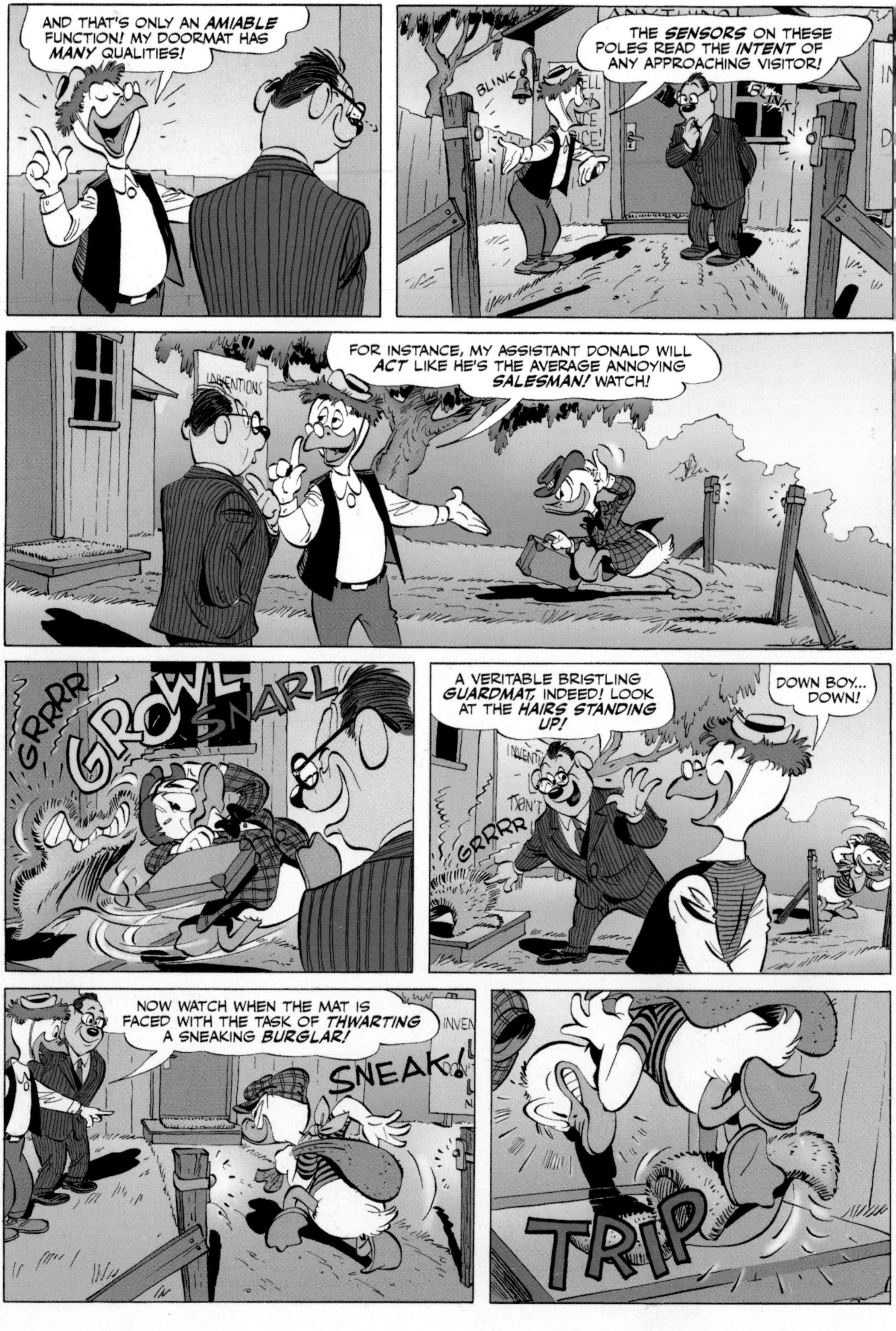
AND THAT'S ONLY AN AMIABLE FUNCTION! MY DOORMAT HAS MANY QUALITIES!
THE SENSORS ON THESE POLES READ THE INTENT OF ANY APPROACHING VISITOR!
BLINK
BLINK
FOR INSTANCE, MY ASSISTANT DONALD WILL ACT LIKE HE'S THE AVERAGE ANNOYING SALESMAN! WATCH!
INVENTIONS
GRRRR
GROWL
SNARL
A VERITABLE BRISTLING GUARDMAT, INDEED! LOOK AT THE HAIRS STANDING UP!
DOWN BOY... DOWN!
GRRRR
NOW WATCH WHEN THE MAT IS FACED WITH THE TASK OF THWARTING A SNEAKING BURGLAR!
SNEAK!
TRIP

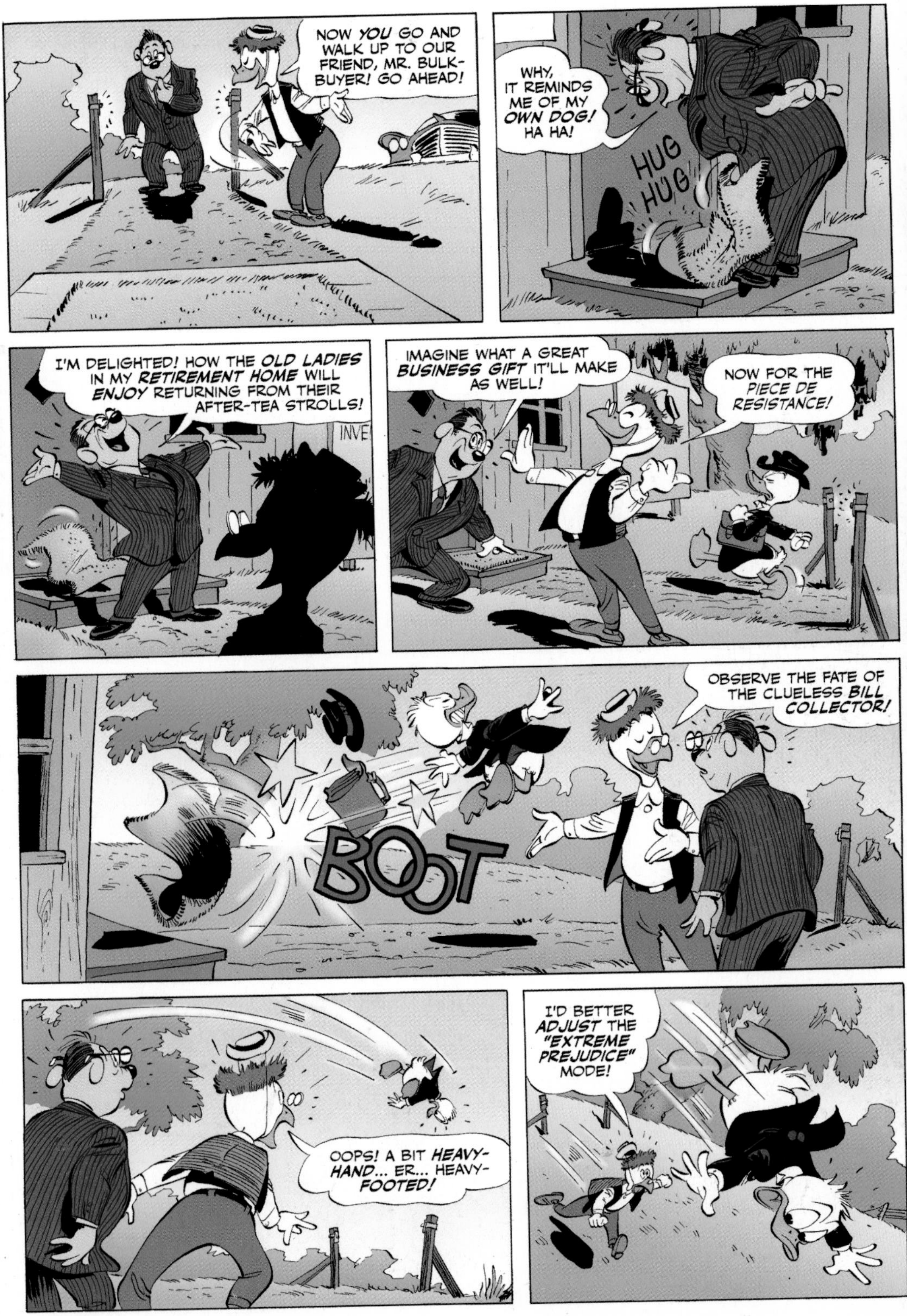
NOW YOU GO AND WALK UP TO OUR FRIEND, MR. BULK-BUYER! GO AHEAD!
WHY, IT REMINDS ME OF MY OWN DOG! HA HA!
HUG HUG
I'M DELIGHTED! HOW THE OLD LADIES IN MY RETIREMENT HOME WILL ENJOY RETURNING FROM THEIR AFTER-TEA STROLLS!
INVE
IMAGINE WHAT A GREAT BUSINESS GIFT IT'LL MAKE AS WELL!
NOW FOR THE PIECE DE RESISTANCE!
OBSERVE THE FATE OF THE CLUELESS BILL COLLECTOR!
BOOT
OOPS! A BIT HEAVY-HAND... ER... HEAVY-FOOTED!
I'D BETTER ADJUST THE "EXTREME PREJUDICE" MODE!

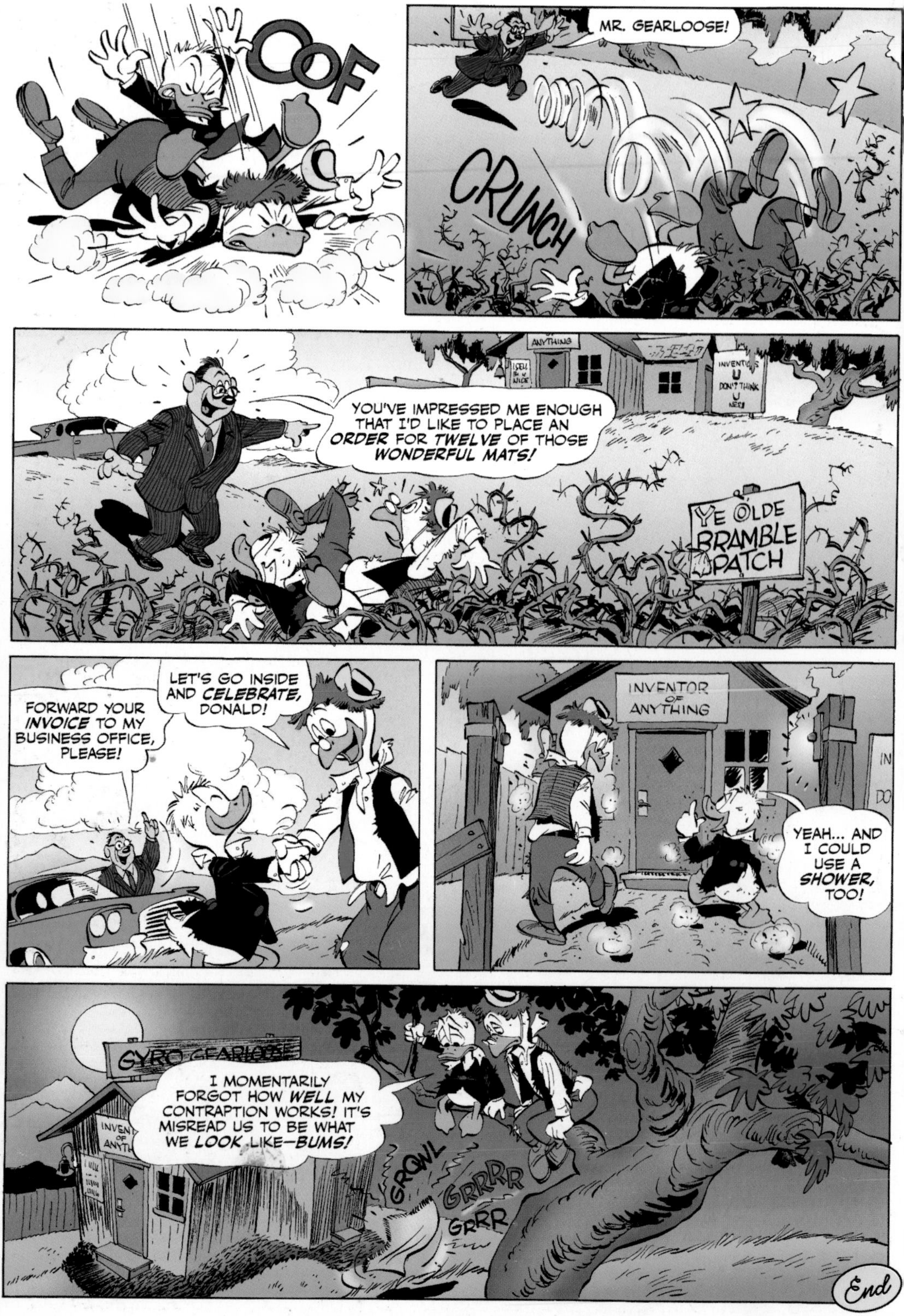
OOF
MR. GEARLOOSE!
CRUNCH
ANYTHING
YOU'VE IMPRESSED ME ENOUGH THAT I'D LIKE TO PLACE AN ORDER FOR TWELVE OF THOSE WONDERFUL MATS!
YE OLDE BRAMBLE PATCH
FORWARD YOUR INVOICE TO MY BUSINESS OFFICE, PLEASE!
LET'S GO INSIDE AND CELEBRATE, DONALD!
INVENTOR OF ANYTHING
YEAH... AND I COULD USE A SHOWER, TOO!
I MOMENTARILY FORGOT HOW WELL MY CONTRAPTION WORKS! IT'S MISREAD US TO BE WHAT WE LOOK LIKE—BUMS!
GROWL
GRRRR
GRRR
End

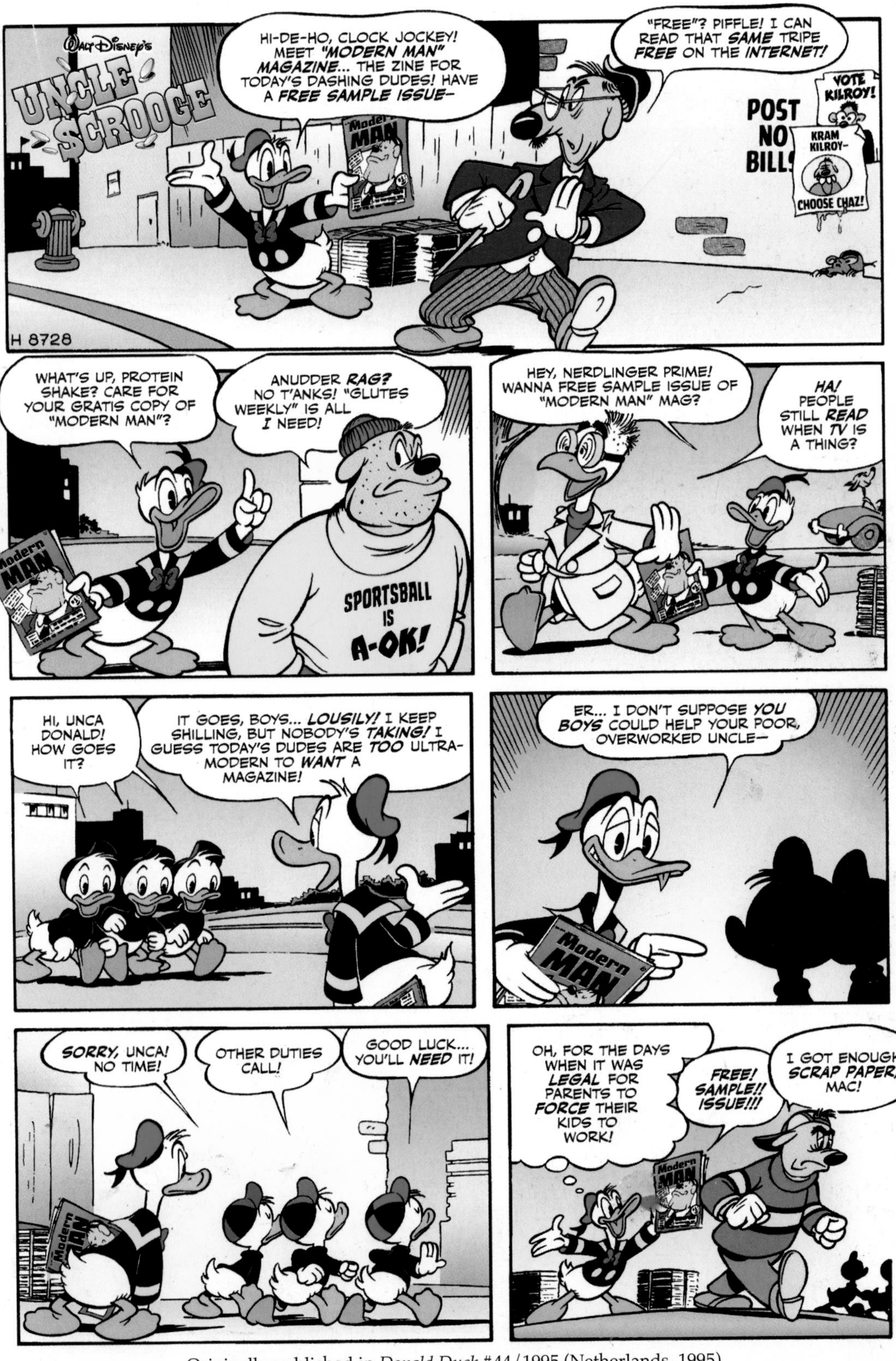
WALT DISNEY'S
UNCLE $CROOGE
HI-DE-HO, CLOCK JOCKEY! MEET "MODERN MAN" MAGAZINE... THE ZINE FOR TODAY'S DASHING DUDES! HAVE A FREE SAMPLE ISSUE—
"FREE"? PIFFLE! I CAN READ THAT SAME TRIPE FREE ON THE INTERNET!
POST NO BILLS
VOTE KILROY!
KRAM KILROY—
CHOOSE CHAZ!
H 8728
WHAT'S UP, PROTEIN SHAKE? CARE FOR YOUR GRATIS COPY OF "MODERN MAN"?
ANUDDER RAG? NO T'ANKS! "GLUTES WEEKLY" IS ALL I NEED!
SPORTSBALL IS A-OK!
HEY, NERDLINGER PRIME! WANNA FREE SAMPLE ISSUE OF "MODERN MAN" MAG?
HA! PEOPLE STILL READ WHEN TV IS A THING?
HI, UNCA DONALD! HOW GOES IT?
IT GOES, BOYS... LOUSILY! I KEEP SHILLING, BUT NOBODY'S TAKING! I GUESS TODAY'S DUDES ARE TOO ULTRA-MODERN TO WANT A MAGAZINE!
ER... I DON'T SUPPOSE YOU BOYS COULD HELP YOUR POOR, OVERWORKED UNCLE—
Modern MAN
SORRY, UNCA! NO TIME!
OTHER DUTIES CALL!
GOOD LUCK... YOU'LL NEED IT!
OH, FOR THE DAYS WHEN IT WAS LEGAL FOR PARENTS TO FORCE THEIR KIDS TO WORK!
FREE! SAMPLE!! ISSUE!!!
I GOT ENOUGH SCRAP PAPER, MAC!

Originally published in *Donald Duck* #44/1995 (Netherlands, 1995)

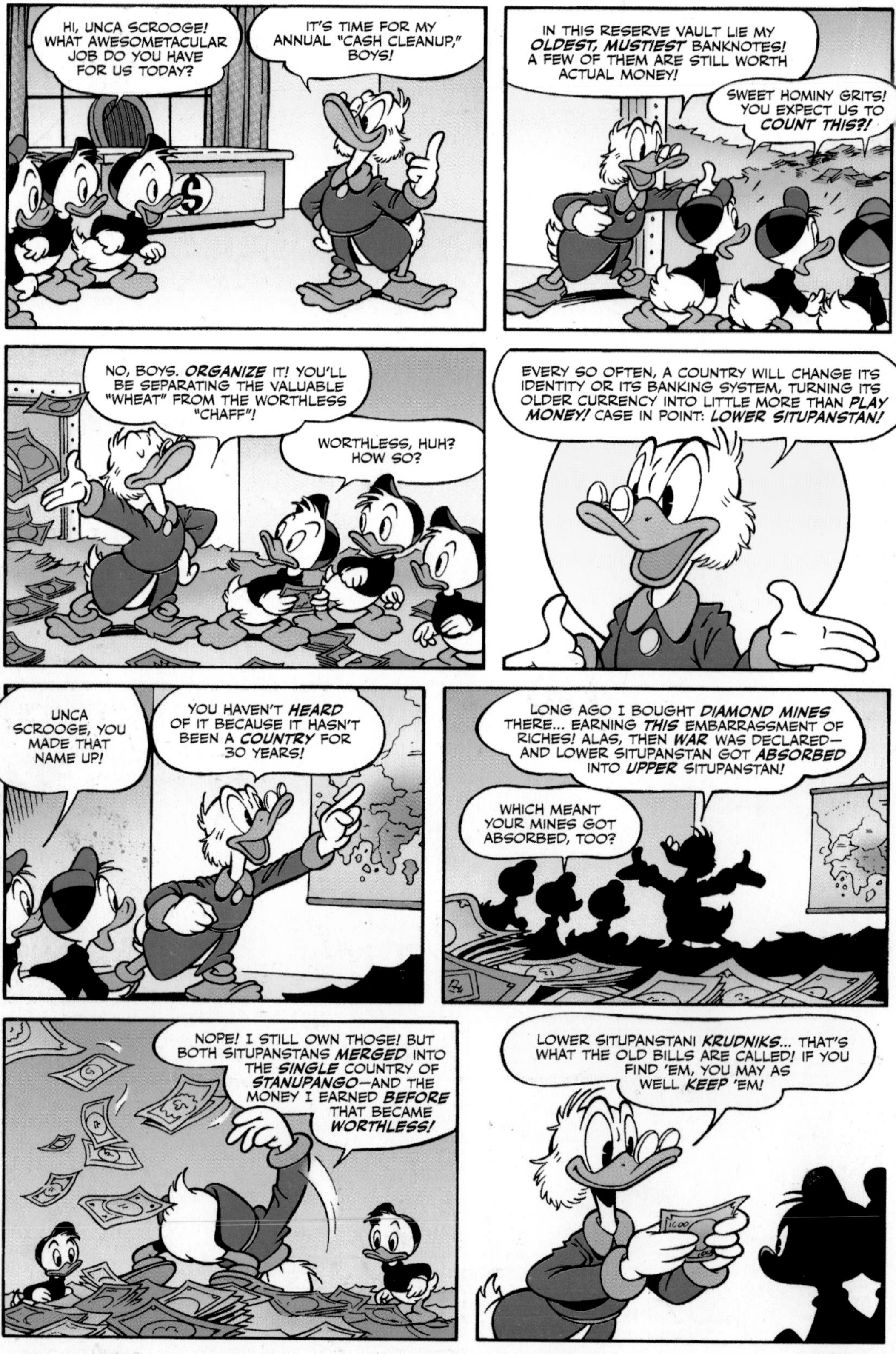
HI, UNCA SCROOGE! WHAT AWESOMETACULAR JOB DO YOU HAVE FOR US TODAY?
IT'S TIME FOR MY ANNUAL "CASH CLEANUP," BOYS!
IN THIS RESERVE VAULT LIE MY OLDEST, MUSTIEST BANKNOTES! A FEW OF THEM ARE STILL WORTH ACTUAL MONEY!
SWEET HOMINY GRITS! YOU EXPECT US TO COUNT THIS?!
NO, BOYS. ORGANIZE IT! YOU'LL BE SEPARATING THE VALUABLE "WHEAT" FROM THE WORTHLESS "CHAFF"!
WORTHLESS, HUH? HOW SO?
EVERY SO OFTEN, A COUNTRY WILL CHANGE ITS IDENTITY OR ITS BANKING SYSTEM, TURNING ITS OLDER CURRENCY INTO LITTLE MORE THAN PLAY MONEY! CASE IN POINT: LOWER SITUPANSTAN!
UNCA SCROOGE, YOU MADE THAT NAME UP!
YOU HAVEN'T HEARD OF IT BECAUSE IT HASN'T BEEN A COUNTRY FOR 30 YEARS!
LONG AGO I BOUGHT DIAMOND MINES THERE... EARNING THIS EMBARRASSMENT OF RICHES! ALAS, THEN WAR WAS DECLARED— AND LOWER SITUPANSTAN GOT ABSORBED INTO UPPER SITUPANSTAN!
WHICH MEANT YOUR MINES GOT ABSORBED, TOO?
NOPE! I STILL OWN THOSE! BUT BOTH SITUPANSTANS MERGED INTO THE SINGLE COUNTRY OF STANUPANGO—AND THE MONEY I EARNED BEFORE THAT BECAME WORTHLESS!
LOWER SITUPANSTANI KRUDNIKS... THAT'S WHAT THE OLD BILLS ARE CALLED! IF YOU FIND 'EM, YOU MAY AS WELL KEEP 'EM!

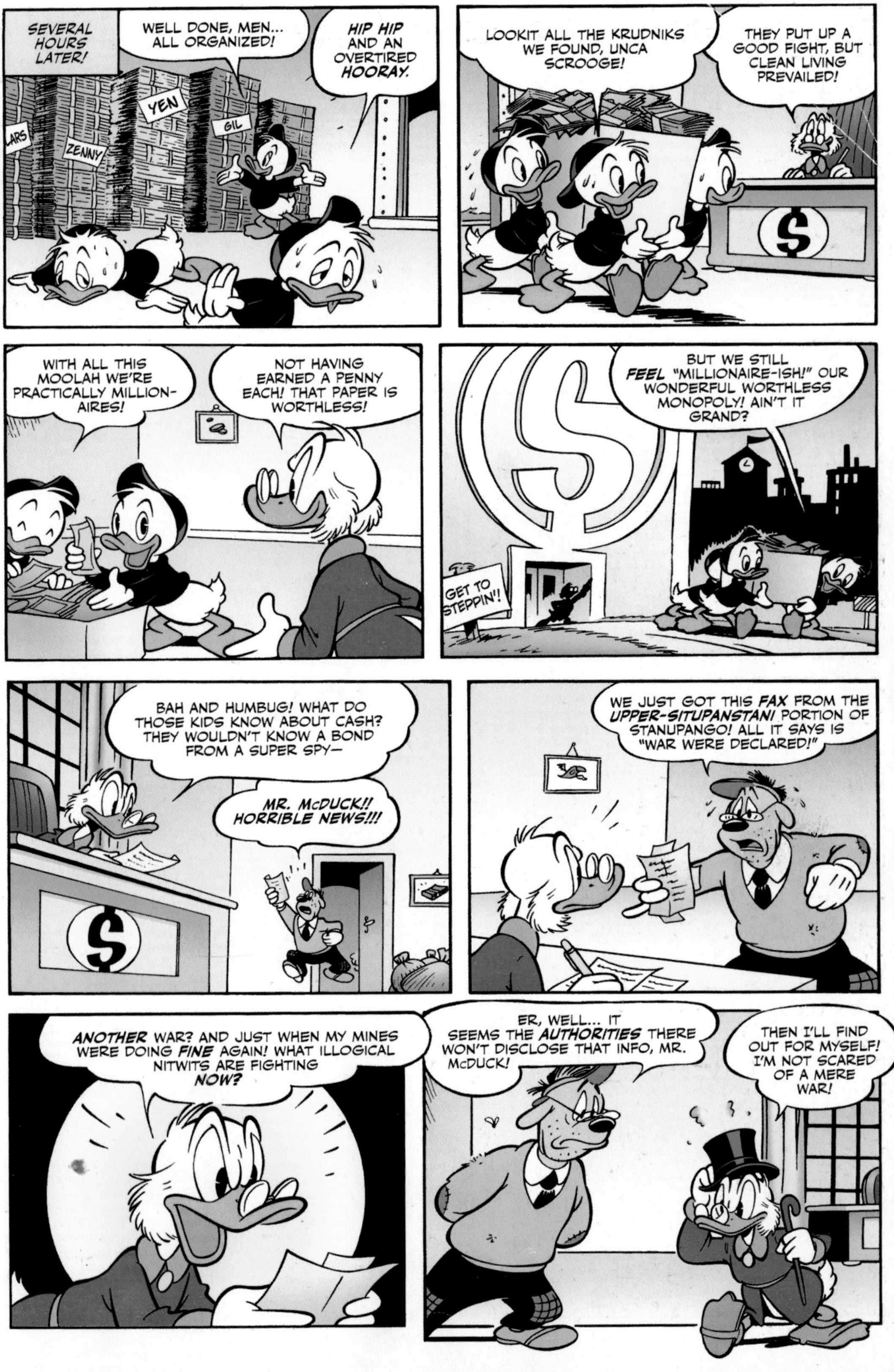

SEVERAL HOURS LATER!
WELL DONE, MEN... ALL ORGANIZED!
HIP HIP AND AN OVERTIRED HOORAY.
YEN
GIL
ZENNY
LOOKIT ALL THE KRUDNIKS WE FOUND, UNCA SCROOGE!
THEY PUT UP A GOOD FIGHT, BUT CLEAN LIVING PREVAILED!
WITH ALL THIS MOOLAH WE'RE PRACTICALLY MILLION-AIRES!
NOT HAVING EARNED A PENNY EACH! THAT PAPER IS WORTHLESS!
BUT WE STILL FEEL "MILLIONAIRE-ISH!" OUR WONDERFUL WORTHLESS MONOPOLY! AIN'T IT GRAND?
GET TO STEPPIN'!
BAH AND HUMBUG! WHAT DO THOSE KIDS KNOW ABOUT CASH? THEY WOULDN'T KNOW A BOND FROM A SUPER SPY—
MR. McDUCK!! HORRIBLE NEWS!!!
WE JUST GOT THIS FAX FROM THE UPPER-SITUPANSTANI PORTION OF STANUPANGO! ALL IT SAYS IS "WAR WERE DECLARED!"
ANOTHER WAR? AND JUST WHEN MY MINES WERE DOING FINE AGAIN! WHAT ILLOGICAL NITWITS ARE FIGHTING NOW?
ER, WELL... IT SEEMS THE AUTHORITIES THERE WON'T DISCLOSE THAT INFO, MR. McDUCK!
THEN I'LL FIND OUT FOR MYSELF! I'M NOT SCARED OF A MERE WAR!

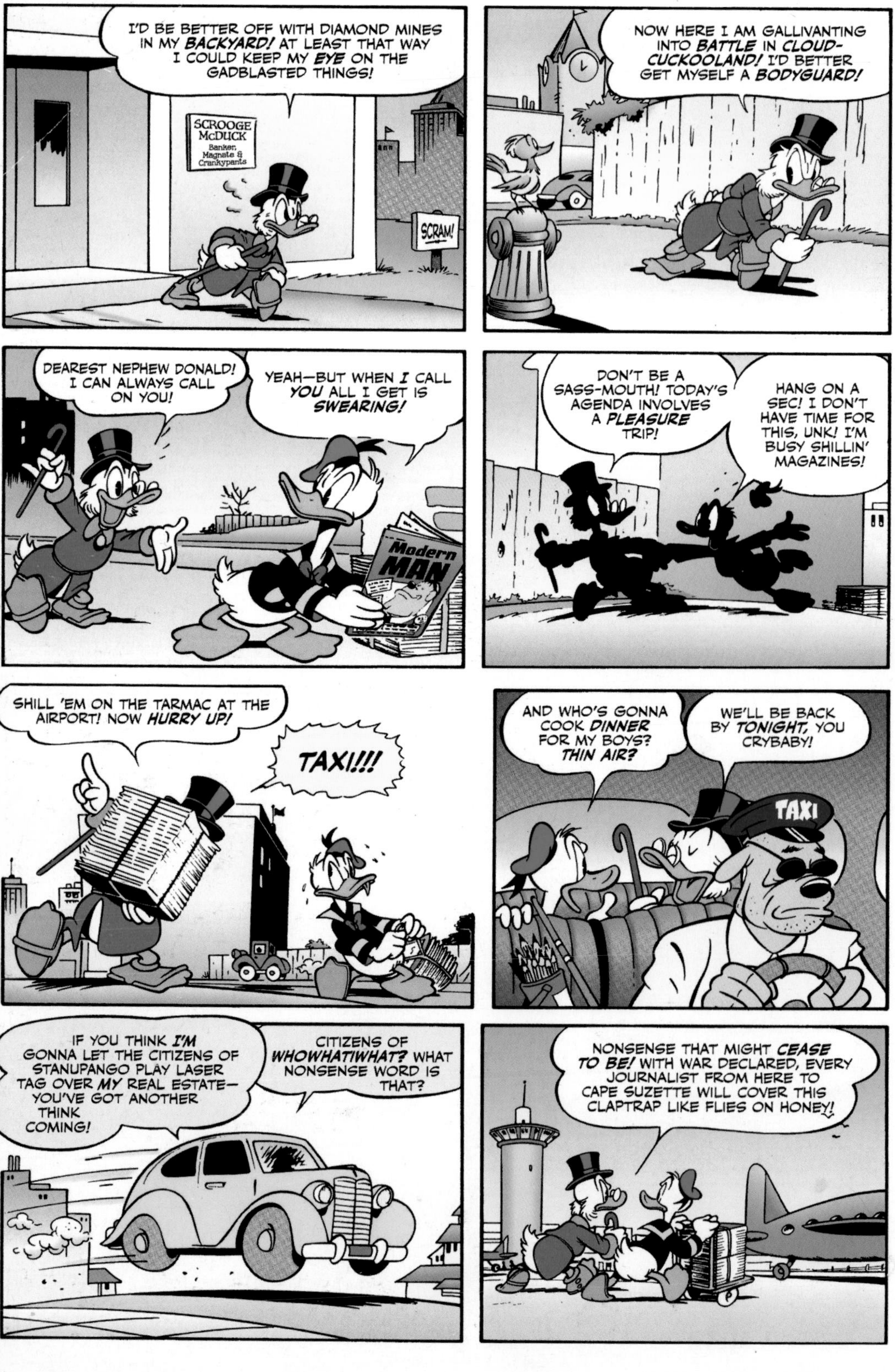
I'D BE BETTER OFF WITH DIAMOND MINES IN MY BACKYARD! AT LEAST THAT WAY I COULD KEEP MY EYE ON THE GADBLASTED THINGS!
SCROOGE McDUCK Banker, Magnate & Crankypants
SCRAM!
NOW HERE I AM GALLIVANTING INTO BATTLE IN CLOUD-CUCKOOLAND! I'D BETTER GET MYSELF A BODYGUARD!
DEAREST NEPHEW DONALD! I CAN ALWAYS CALL ON YOU!
YEAH—BUT WHEN I CALL YOU ALL I GET IS SWEARING!
Modern MAN
DON'T BE A SASS-MOUTH! TODAY'S AGENDA INVOLVES A PLEASURE TRIP!
HANG ON A SEC! I DON'T HAVE TIME FOR THIS, UNK! I'M BUSY SHILLIN' MAGAZINES!
SHILL 'EM ON THE TARMAC AT THE AIRPORT! NOW HURRY UP!
TAXI!!!
AND WHO'S GONNA COOK DINNER FOR MY BOYS? THIN AIR?
WE'LL BE BACK BY TONIGHT, YOU CRYBABY!
TAXI
IF YOU THINK I'M GONNA LET THE CITIZENS OF STANUPANGO PLAY LASER TAG OVER MY REAL ESTATE— YOU'VE GOT ANOTHER THINK COMING!
CITIZENS OF WHOWHATIWHAT? WHAT NONSENSE WORD IS THAT?
NONSENSE THAT MIGHT CEASE TO BE! WITH WAR DECLARED, EVERY JOURNALIST FROM HERE TO CAPE SUZETTE WILL COVER THIS CLAPTRAP LIKE FLIES ON HONEY!

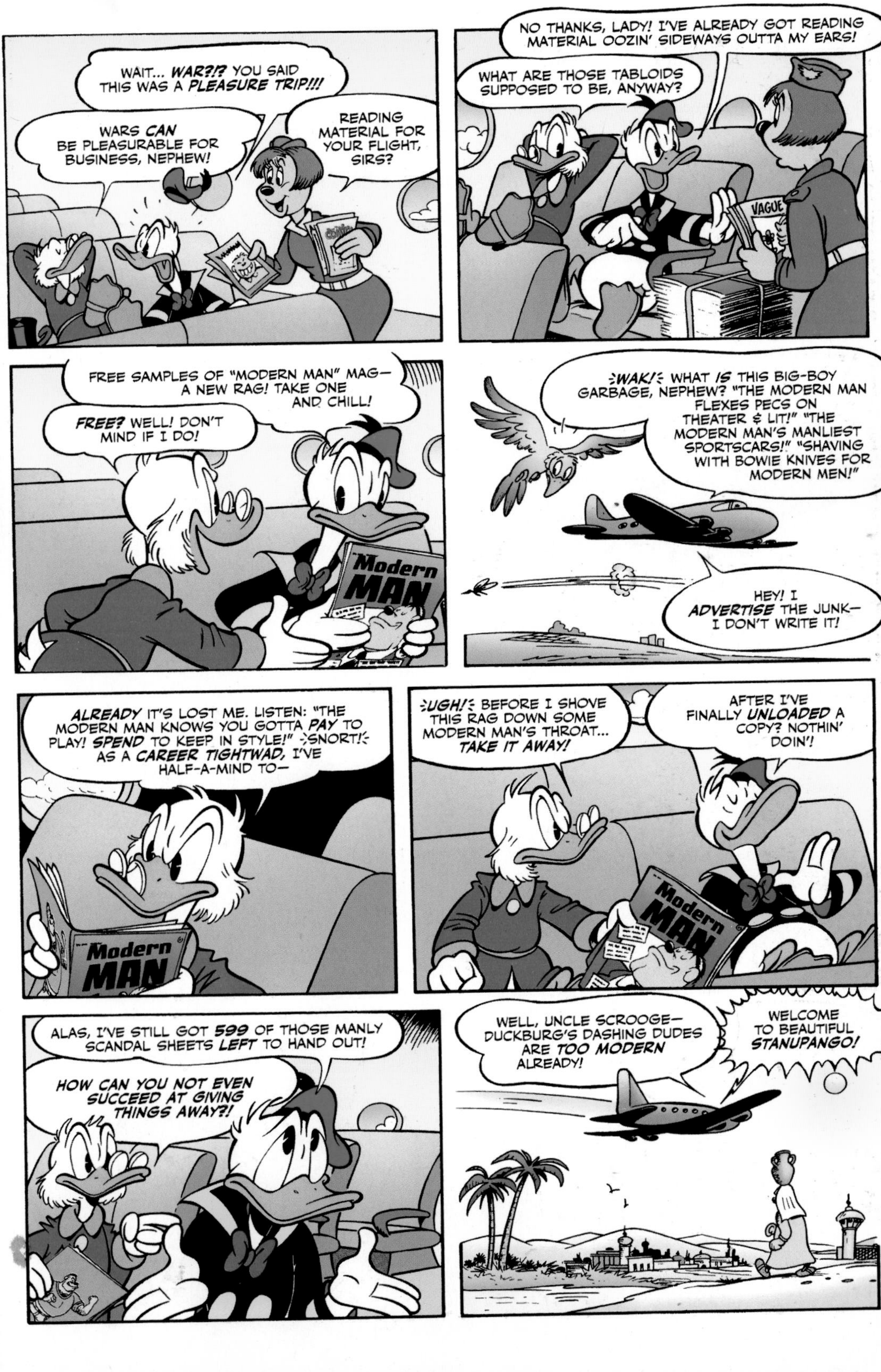
WAIT... WAR?!? YOU SAID THIS WAS A PLEASURE TRIP!!!
WARS CAN BE PLEASURABLE FOR BUSINESS, NEPHEW!
READING MATERIAL FOR YOUR FLIGHT, SIRS?
NO THANKS, LADY! I'VE ALREADY GOT READING MATERIAL OOZIN' SIDEWAYS OUTTA MY EARS!
WHAT ARE THOSE TABLOIDS SUPPOSED TO BE, ANYWAY?
VAGUE
FREE SAMPLES OF "MODERN MAN" MAG— A NEW RAG! TAKE ONE AND CHILL!
FREE? WELL! DON'T MIND IF I DO!
Modern MAN
WAK! WHAT IS THIS BIG-BOY GARBAGE, NEPHEW? "THE MODERN MAN FLEXES PECS ON THEATER & LIT!" "THE MODERN MAN'S MANLIEST SPORTSCARS!" "SHAVING WITH BOWIE KNIVES FOR MODERN MEN!"
HEY! I ADVERTISE THE JUNK— I DON'T WRITE IT!
ALREADY IT'S LOST ME. LISTEN: "THE MODERN MAN KNOWS YOU GOTTA PAY TO PLAY! SPEND TO KEEP IN STYLE!" SNORT! AS A CAREER TIGHTWAD, I'VE HALF-A-MIND TO—
Modern MAN
UGH! BEFORE I SHOVE THIS RAG DOWN SOME MODERN MAN'S THROAT... TAKE IT AWAY!
AFTER I'VE FINALLY UNLOADED A COPY? NOTHIN' DOIN'!
Modern MAN
ALAS, I'VE STILL GOT 599 OF THOSE MANLY SCANDAL SHEETS LEFT TO HAND OUT!
HOW CAN YOU NOT EVEN SUCCEED AT GIVING THINGS AWAY?!
WELL, UNCLE SCROOGE— DUCKBURG'S DASHING DUDES ARE TOO MODERN ALREADY!
WELCOME TO BEAUTIFUL STANUPANGO!

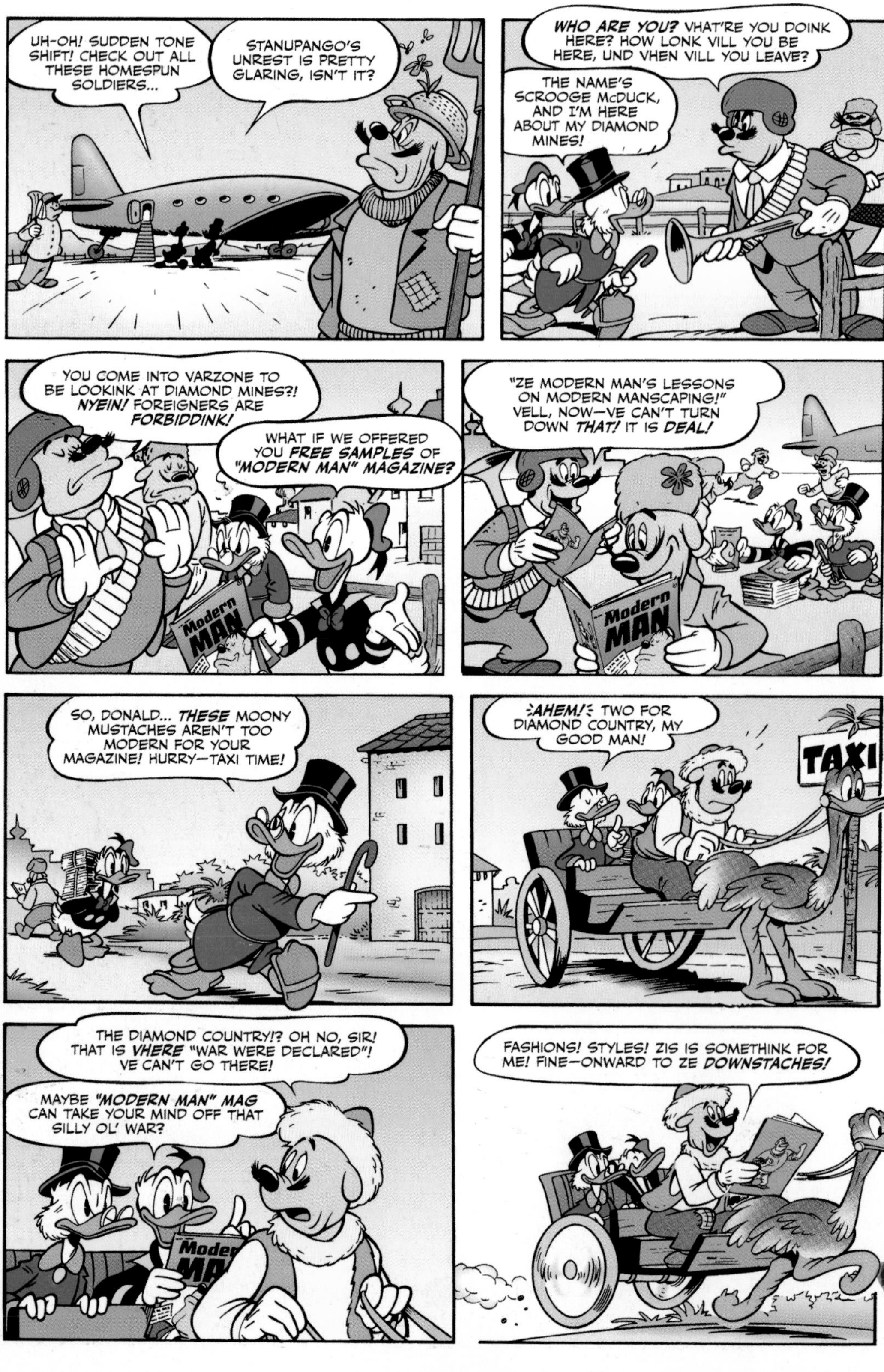
UH-OH! SUDDEN TONE SHIFT! CHECK OUT ALL THESE HOMESPUN SOLDIERS...
STANUPANGO'S UNREST IS PRETTY GLARING, ISN'T IT?
WHO ARE YOU? VHAT'RE YOU DOINK HERE? HOW LONK VILL YOU BE HERE, UND VHEN VILL YOU LEAVE?
THE NAME'S SCROOGE McDUCK, AND I'M HERE ABOUT MY DIAMOND MINES!
YOU COME INTO VARZONE TO BE LOOKINK AT DIAMOND MINES?! NYEIN! FOREIGNERS ARE FORBIDDINK!
WHAT IF WE OFFERED YOU FREE SAMPLES OF "MODERN MAN" MAGAZINE?
Modern MAN
"ZE MODERN MAN'S LESSONS ON MODERN MANSCAPING!" VELL, NOW—VE CAN'T TURN DOWN THAT! IT IS DEAL!
Modern MAN
SO, DONALD... THESE MOONY MUSTACHES AREN'T TOO MODERN FOR YOUR MAGAZINE! HURRY—TAXI TIME!
AHEM! TWO FOR DIAMOND COUNTRY, MY GOOD MAN!
TAXI
THE DIAMOND COUNTRY!? OH NO, SIR! THAT IS VHERE "WAR WERE DECLARED"! VE CAN'T GO THERE!
MAYBE "MODERN MAN" MAG CAN TAKE YOUR MIND OFF THAT SILLY OL' WAR?
FASHIONS! STYLES! ZIS IS SOMETHINK FOR ME! FINE—ONWARD TO ZE DOWNSTACHES!

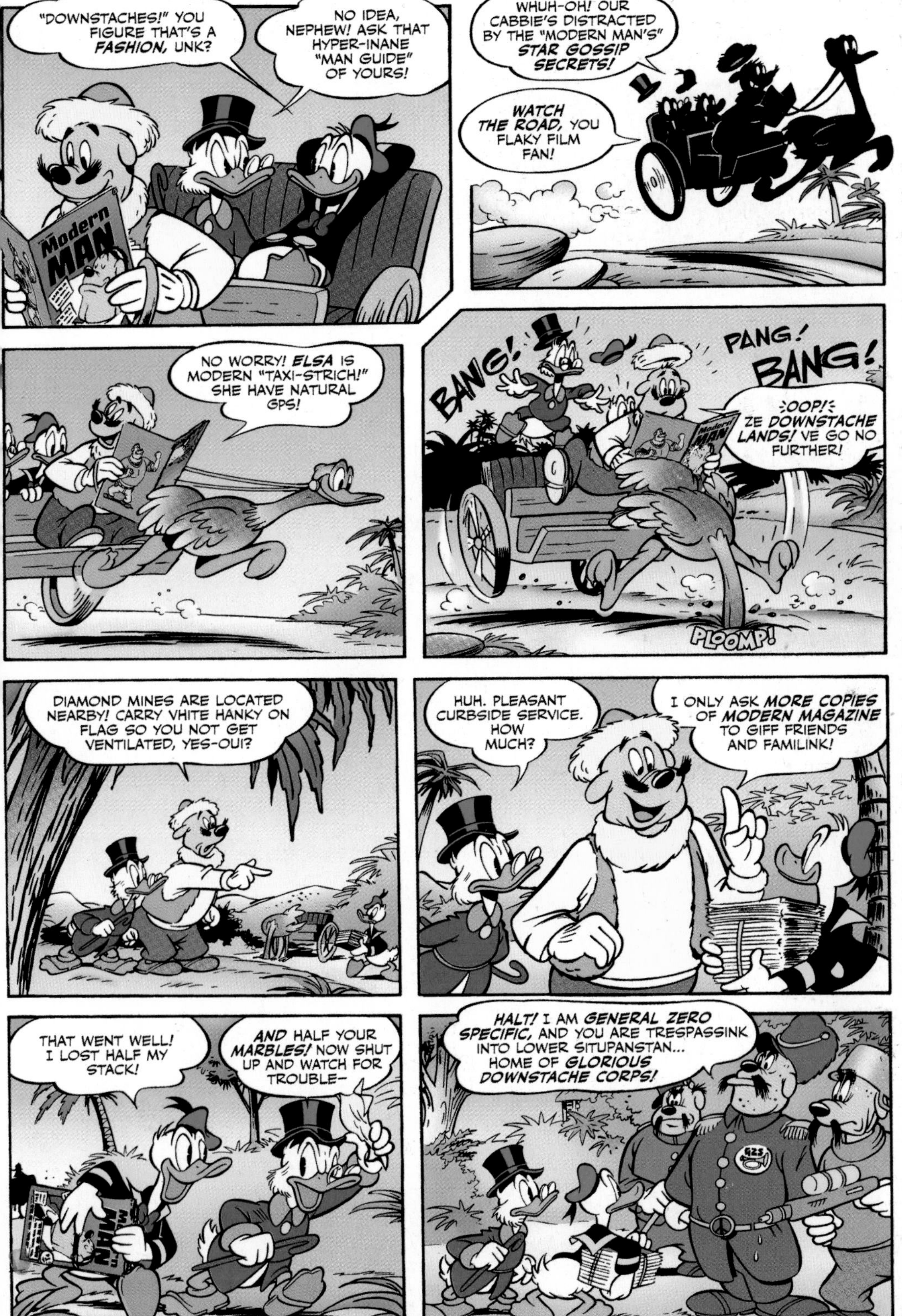
"DOWNSTACHES!" YOU FIGURE THAT'S A FASHION, UNK?
NO IDEA, NEPHEW! ASK THAT HYPER-INANE "MAN GUIDE" OF YOURS!
Modern MAN
WHUH-OH! OUR CABBIE'S DISTRACTED BY THE "MODERN MAN'S" STAR GOSSIP SECRETS!
WATCH THE ROAD, YOU FLAKY FILM FAN!
NO WORRY! ELSA IS MODERN "TAXI-STRICH!" SHE HAVE NATURAL GPS!
BANG!
PANG!
BANG!
OOP! ZE DOWNSTACHE LANDS! VE GO NO FURTHER!
PLOOMP!
DIAMOND MINES ARE LOCATED NEARBY! CARRY VHITE HANKY ON FLAG SO YOU NOT GET VENTILATED, YES-OUI?
HUH. PLEASANT CURBSIDE SERVICE. HOW MUCH?
I ONLY ASK MORE COPIES OF MODERN MAGAZINE TO GIFF FRIENDS AND FAMILINK!
THAT WENT WELL! I LOST HALF MY STACK!
AND HALF YOUR MARBLES! NOW SHUT UP AND WATCH FOR TROUBLE–
HALT! I AM GENERAL ZERO SPECIFIC, AND YOU ARE TRESPASSINK INTO LOWER SITUPANSTAN... HOME OF GLORIOUS DOWNSTACHE CORPS!

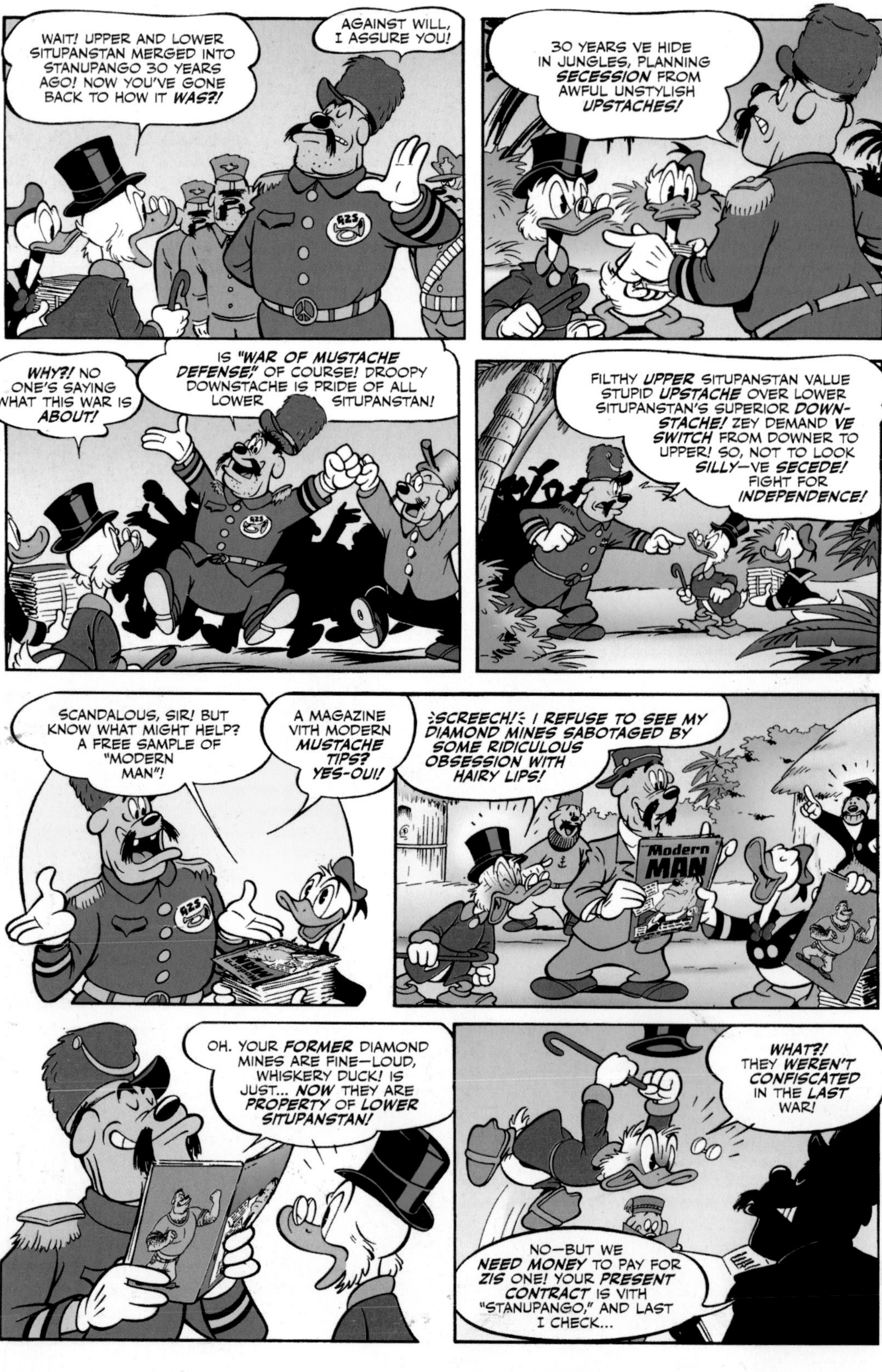
WAIT! UPPER AND LOWER SITUPANSTAN MERGED INTO STANUPANGO 30 YEARS AGO! NOW YOU'VE GONE BACK TO HOW IT WAS?!
AGAINST WILL, I ASSURE YOU!
30 YEARS VE HIDE IN JUNGLES, PLANNING SECESSION FROM AWFUL UNSTYLISH UPSTACHES!
WHY?! NO ONE'S SAYING WHAT THIS WAR IS ABOUT!
IS "WAR OF MUSTACHE DEFENSE," OF COURSE! DROOPY DOWNSTACHE IS PRIDE OF ALL LOWER SITUPANSTAN!
FILTHY UPPER SITUPANSTAN VALUE STUPID UPSTACHE OVER LOWER SITUPANSTAN'S SUPERIOR DOWN-STACHE! ZEY DEMAND VE SWITCH FROM DOWNER TO UPPER! SO, NOT TO LOOK SILLY—VE SECEDE! FIGHT FOR INDEPENDENCE!
SCANDALOUS, SIR! BUT KNOW WHAT MIGHT HELP? A FREE SAMPLE OF "MODERN MAN"!
A MAGAZINE VITH MODERN MUSTACHE TIPS? YES-OUI!
SCREECH! I REFUSE TO SEE MY DIAMOND MINES SABOTAGED BY SOME RIDICULOUS OBSESSION WITH HAIRY LIPS!
Modern MAN
OH. YOUR FORMER DIAMOND MINES ARE FINE—LOUD, WHISKERY DUCK! IS JUST... NOW THEY ARE PROPERTY OF LOWER SITUPANSTAN!
WHAT?! THEY WEREN'T CONFISCATED IN THE LAST WAR!
NO—BUT WE NEED MONEY TO PAY FOR ZIS ONE! YOUR PRESENT CONTRACT IS VITH "STANUPANGO," AND LAST I CHECK...

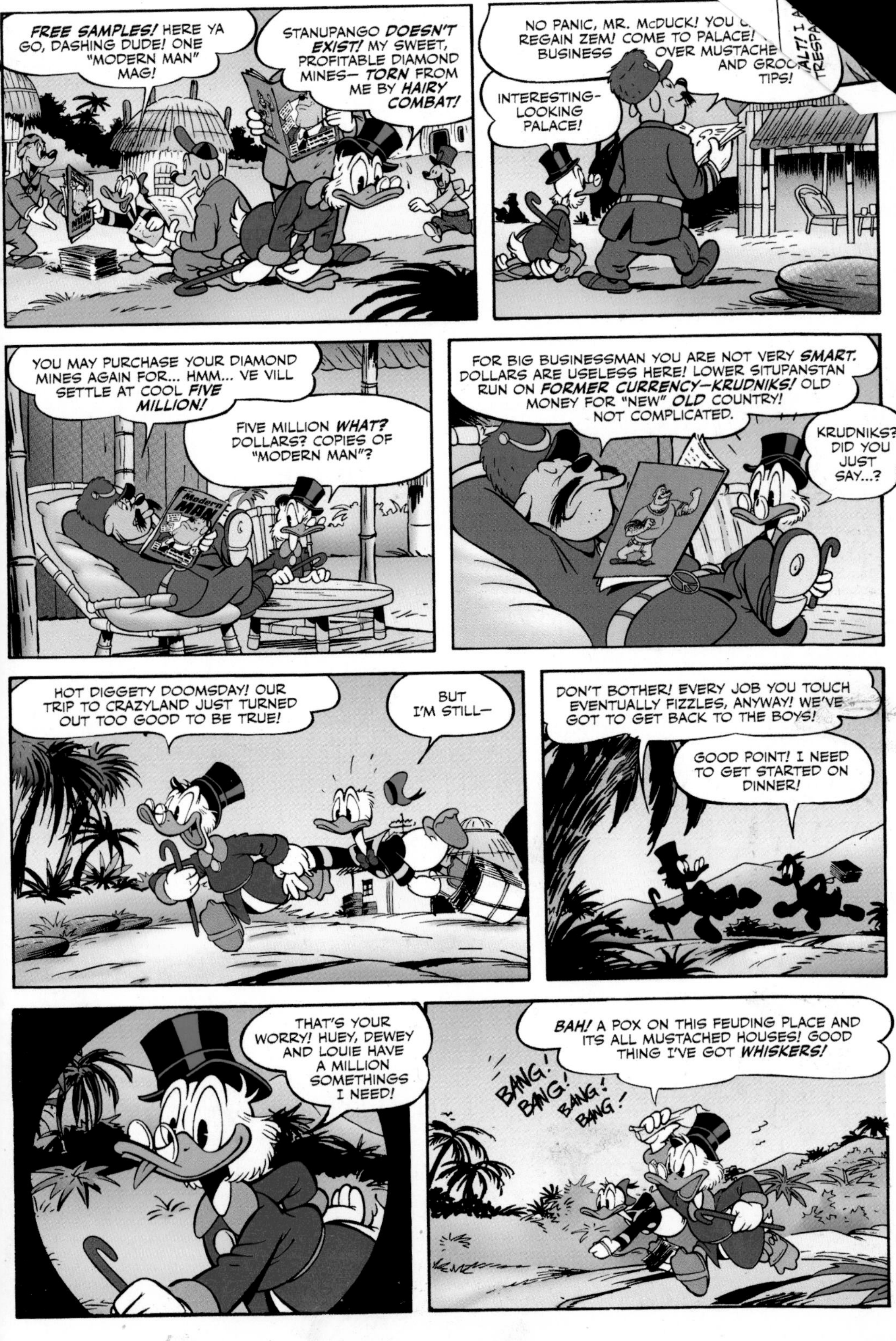
FREE SAMPLES! HERE YA GO, DASHING DUDE! ONE "MODERN MAN" MAG!
STANUPANGO DOESN'T EXIST! MY SWEET, PROFITABLE DIAMOND MINES— TORN FROM ME BY HAIRY COMBAT!
NO PANIC, MR. McDUCK! YOU C REGAIN ZEM! COME TO PALACE! BUSINESS OVER MUSTACHE AND GROO TIPS!
INTERESTING-LOOKING PALACE!
ALT! I A TRESPA
YOU MAY PURCHASE YOUR DIAMOND MINES AGAIN FOR... HMM... VE VILL SETTLE AT COOL FIVE MILLION!
FIVE MILLION WHAT? DOLLARS? COPIES OF "MODERN MAN"?
Modern MAN
FOR BIG BUSINESSMAN YOU ARE NOT VERY SMART. DOLLARS ARE USELESS HERE! LOWER SITUPANSTAN RUN ON FORMER CURRENCY—KRUDNIKS! OLD MONEY FOR "NEW" OLD COUNTRY! NOT COMPLICATED.
KRUDNIKS? DID YOU JUST SAY...?
HOT DIGGETY DOOMSDAY! OUR TRIP TO CRAZYLAND JUST TURNED OUT TOO GOOD TO BE TRUE!
BUT I'M STILL—
DON'T BOTHER! EVERY JOB YOU TOUCH EVENTUALLY FIZZLES, ANYWAY! WE'VE GOT TO GET BACK TO THE BOYS!
GOOD POINT! I NEED TO GET STARTED ON DINNER!
THAT'S YOUR WORRY! HUEY, DEWEY AND LOUIE HAVE A MILLION SOMETHINGS I NEED!
BAH! A POX ON THIS FEUDING PLACE AND ITS ALL MUSTACHED HOUSES! GOOD THING I'VE GOT WHISKERS!
BANG! BANG! BANG! BANG!

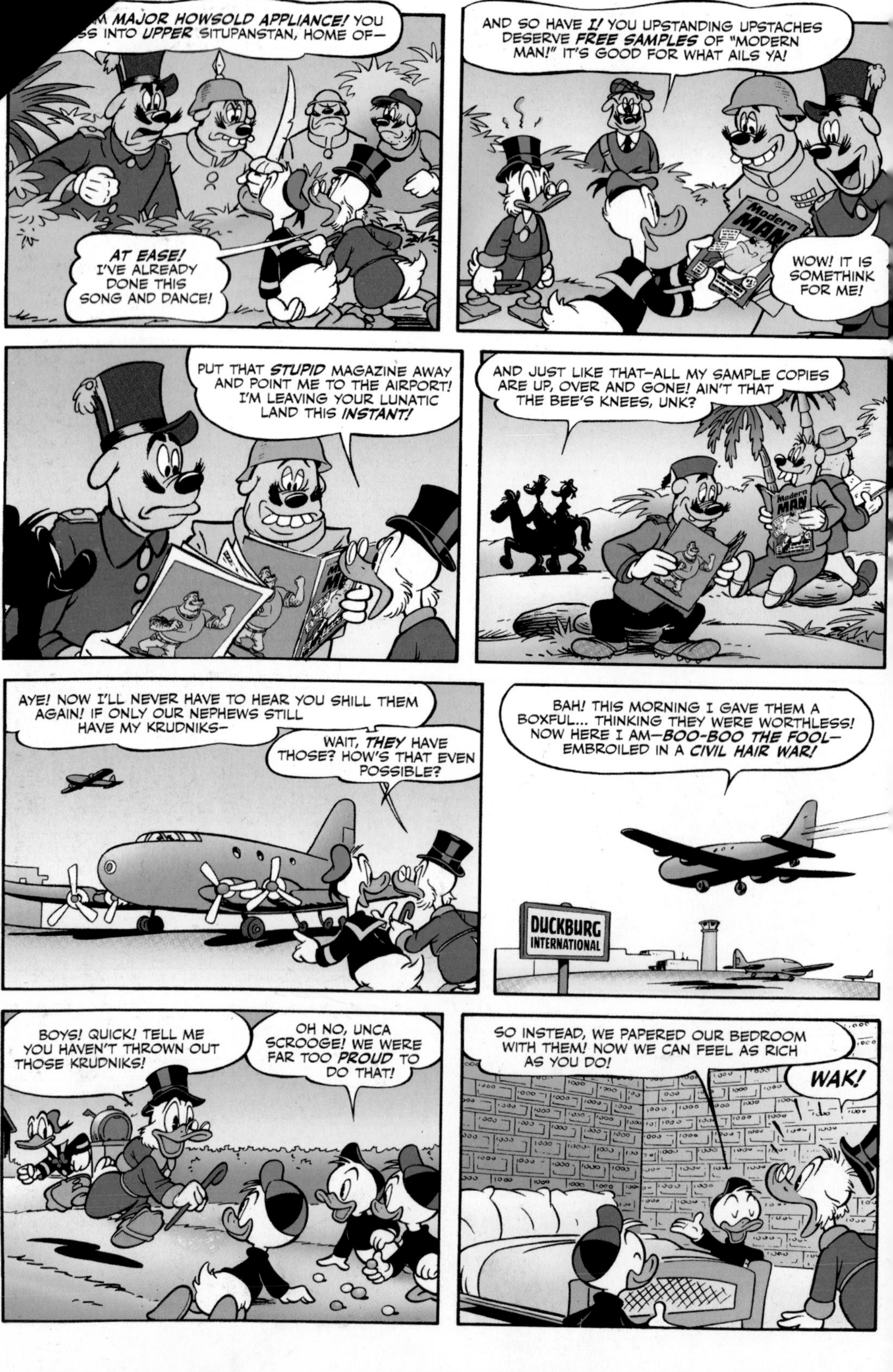

M MAJOR HOWSOLD APPLIANCE! YOU SS INTO UPPER SITUPANSTAN, HOME OF—
AT EASE! I'VE ALREADY DONE THIS SONG AND DANCE!
AND SO HAVE I! YOU UPSTANDING UPSTACHES DESERVE FREE SAMPLES OF "MODERN MAN!" IT'S GOOD FOR WHAT AILS YA!
Modern MAN
WOW! IT IS SOMETHINK FOR ME!
PUT THAT STUPID MAGAZINE AWAY AND POINT ME TO THE AIRPORT! I'M LEAVING YOUR LUNATIC LAND THIS INSTANT!
AND JUST LIKE THAT—ALL MY SAMPLE COPIES ARE UP, OVER AND GONE! AIN'T THAT THE BEE'S KNEES, UNK?
Modern MAN
AYE! NOW I'LL NEVER HAVE TO HEAR YOU SHILL THEM AGAIN! IF ONLY OUR NEPHEWS STILL HAVE MY KRUDNIKS—
WAIT, THEY HAVE THOSE? HOW'S THAT EVEN POSSIBLE?
BAH! THIS MORNING I GAVE THEM A BOXFUL... THINKING THEY WERE WORTHLESS! NOW HERE I AM—BOO-BOO THE FOOL—EMBROILED IN A CIVIL HAIR WAR!
DUCKBURG INTERNATIONAL
BOYS! QUICK! TELL ME YOU HAVEN'T THROWN OUT THOSE KRUDNIKS!
OH NO, UNCA SCROOGE! WE WERE FAR TOO PROUD TO DO THAT!
SO INSTEAD, WE PAPERED OUR BEDROOM WITH THEM! NOW WE CAN FEEL AS RICH AS YOU DO!
WAK!

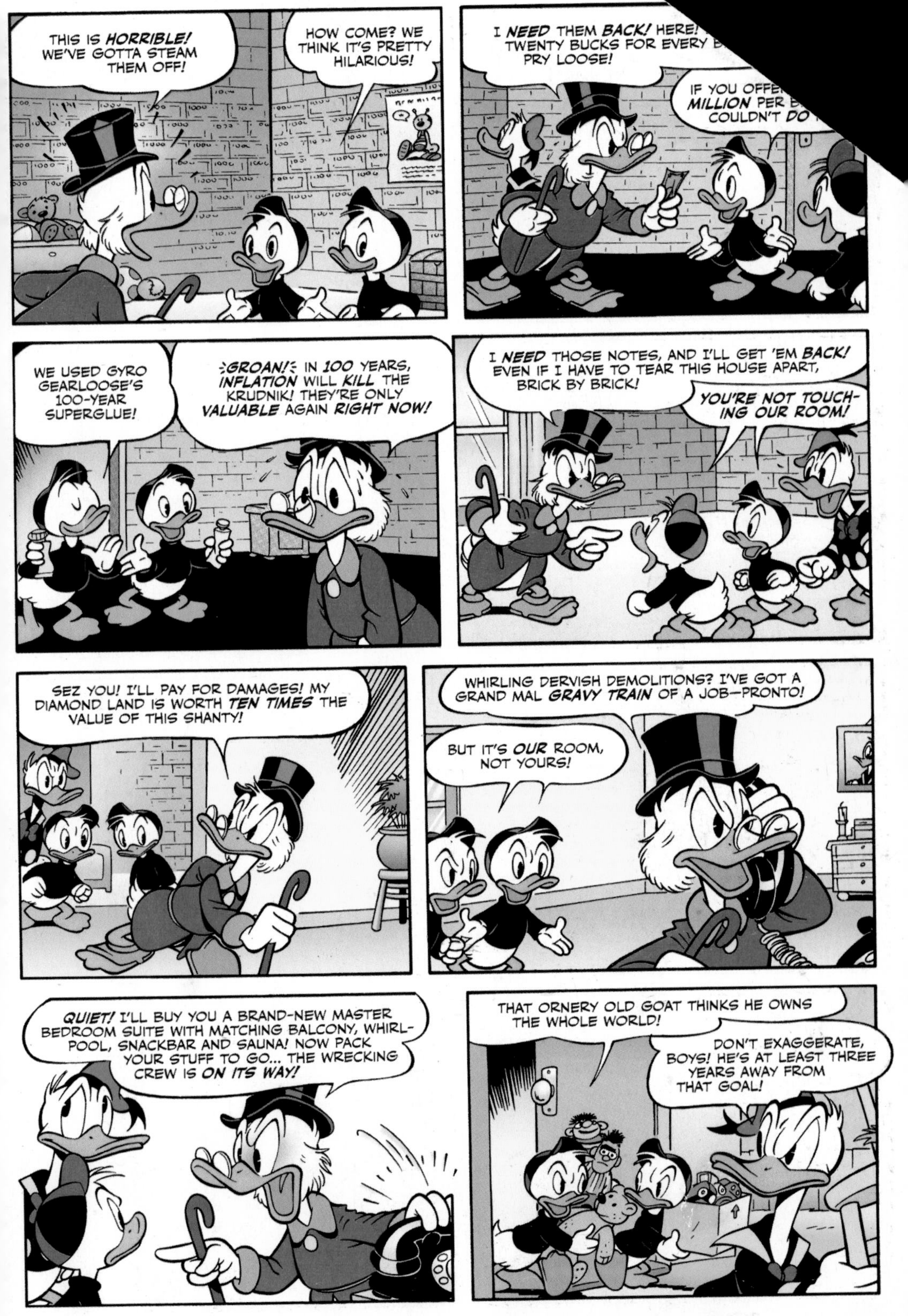
THIS IS HORRIBLE! WE'VE GOTTA STEAM THEM OFF!
HOW COME? WE THINK IT'S PRETTY HILARIOUS!
I NEED THEM BACK! HERE! TWENTY BUCKS FOR EVERY B PRY LOOSE!
IF YOU OFFE MILLION PER B COULDN'T DO
WE USED GYRO GEARLOOSE'S 100-YEAR SUPERGLUE!
GROAN! IN 100 YEARS, INFLATION WILL KILL THE KRUDNIK! THEY'RE ONLY VALUABLE AGAIN RIGHT NOW!
I NEED THOSE NOTES, AND I'LL GET 'EM BACK! EVEN IF I HAVE TO TEAR THIS HOUSE APART, BRICK BY BRICK!
YOU'RE NOT TOUCHING OUR ROOM!
SEZ YOU! I'LL PAY FOR DAMAGES! MY DIAMOND LAND IS WORTH TEN TIMES THE VALUE OF THIS SHANTY!
WHIRLING DERVISH DEMOLITIONS? I'VE GOT A GRAND MAL GRAVY TRAIN OF A JOB—PRONTO!
BUT IT'S OUR ROOM, NOT YOURS!
QUIET! I'LL BUY YOU A BRAND-NEW MASTER BEDROOM SUITE WITH MATCHING BALCONY, WHIRLPOOL, SNACKBAR AND SAUNA! NOW PACK YOUR STUFF TO GO... THE WRECKING CREW IS ON ITS WAY!
THAT ORNERY OLD GOAT THINKS HE OWNS THE WHOLE WORLD!
DON'T EXAGGERATE, BOYS! HE'S AT LEAST THREE YEARS AWAY FROM THAT GOAL!

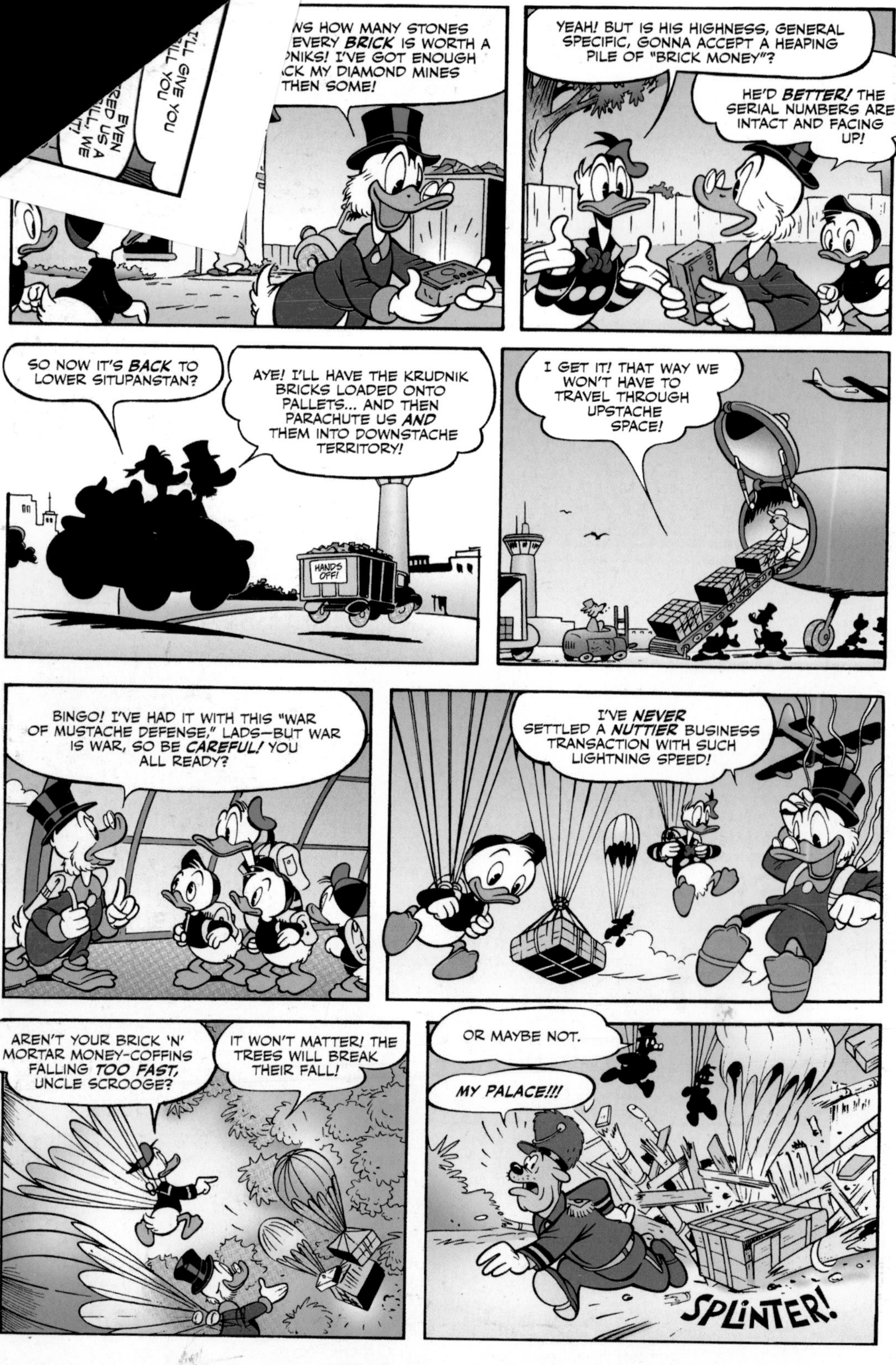
WS HOW MANY STONES
EVERY BRICK IS WORTH A
NIKS! I'VE GOT ENOUGH
ACK MY DIAMOND MINES
THEN SOME!
YEAH! BUT IS HIS HIGHNESS, GENERAL SPECIFIC, GONNA ACCEPT A HEAPING PILE OF "BRICK MONEY"?
HE'D BETTER! THE SERIAL NUMBERS ARE INTACT AND FACING UP!
SO NOW IT'S BACK TO LOWER SITUPANSTAN?
AYE! I'LL HAVE THE KRUDNIK BRICKS LOADED ONTO PALLETS... AND THEN PARACHUTE US AND THEM INTO DOWNSTACHE TERRITORY!
HANDS OFF!
I GET IT! THAT WAY WE WON'T HAVE TO TRAVEL THROUGH UPSTACHE SPACE!
BINGO! I'VE HAD IT WITH THIS "WAR OF MUSTACHE DEFENSE," LADS—BUT WAR IS WAR, SO BE CAREFUL! YOU ALL READY?
I'VE NEVER SETTLED A NUTTIER BUSINESS TRANSACTION WITH SUCH LIGHTNING SPEED!
AREN'T YOUR BRICK 'N' MORTAR MONEY-COFFINS FALLING TOO FAST, UNCLE SCROOGE?
IT WON'T MATTER! THE TREES WILL BREAK THEIR FALL!
OR MAYBE NOT.
MY PALACE!!!
SPLINTER!

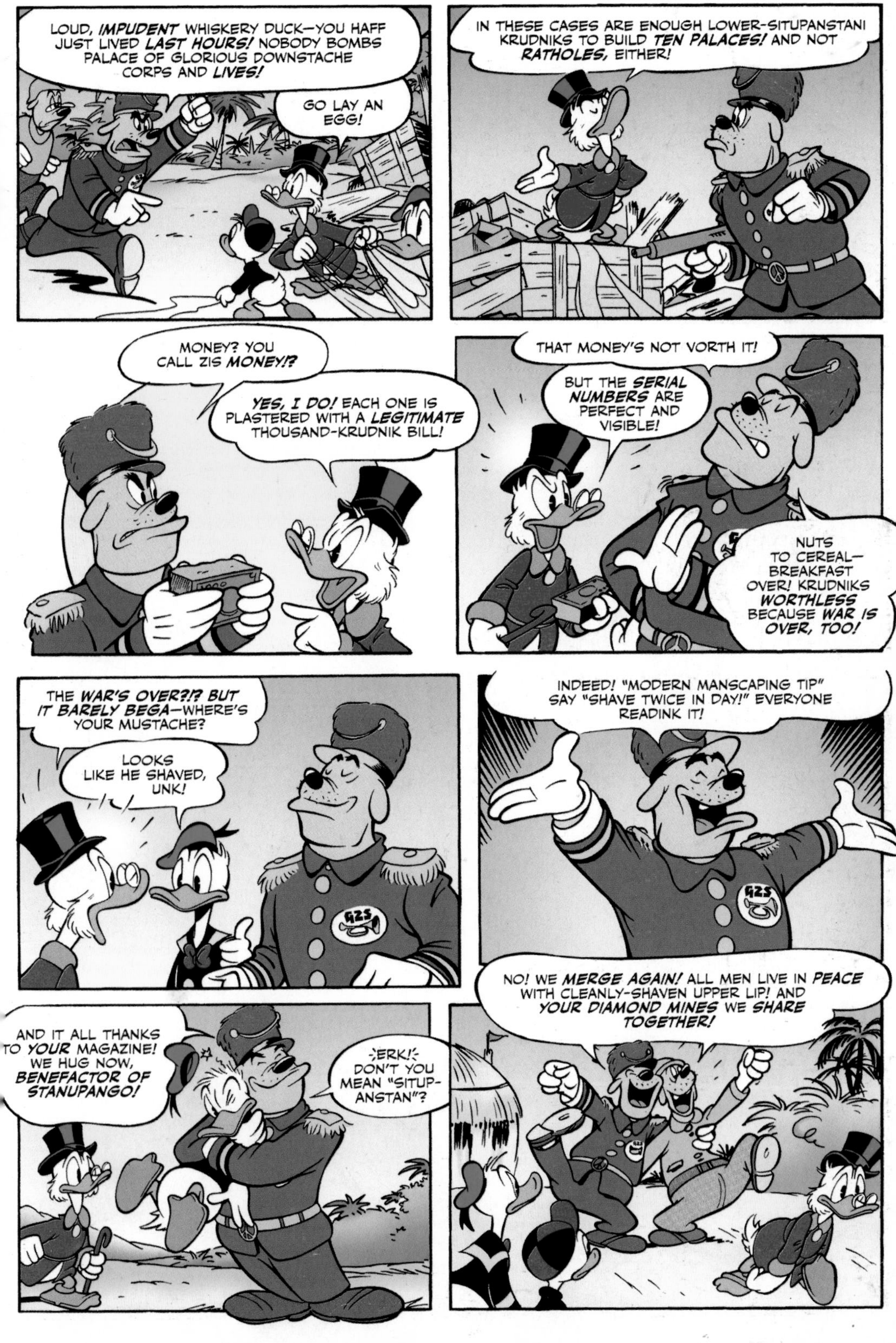
LOUD, IMPUDENT WHISKERY DUCK—YOU HAFF JUST LIVED LAST HOURS! NOBODY BOMBS PALACE OF GLORIOUS DOWNSTACHE CORPS AND LIVES!
GO LAY AN EGG!
IN THESE CASES ARE ENOUGH LOWER-SITUPANSTANI KRUDNIKS TO BUILD TEN PALACES! AND NOT RATHOLES, EITHER!
MONEY? YOU CALL ZIS MONEY!?
YES, I DO! EACH ONE IS PLASTERED WITH A LEGITIMATE THOUSAND-KRUDNIK BILL!
THAT MONEY'S NOT VORTH IT!
BUT THE SERIAL NUMBERS ARE PERFECT AND VISIBLE!
NUTS TO CEREAL—BREAKFAST OVER! KRUDNIKS WORTHLESS BECAUSE WAR IS OVER, TOO!
THE WAR'S OVER?!? BUT IT BARELY BEGA—WHERE'S YOUR MUSTACHE?
LOOKS LIKE HE SHAVED, UNK!
INDEED! "MODERN MANSCAPING TIP" SAY "SHAVE TWICE IN DAY!" EVERYONE READINK IT!
AND IT ALL THANKS TO YOUR MAGAZINE! WE HUG NOW, BENEFACTOR OF STANUPANGO!
ERK! DON'T YOU MEAN "SITUP-ANSTAN"?
NO! WE MERGE AGAIN! ALL MEN LIVE IN PEACE WITH CLEANLY-SHAVEN UPPER LIP! AND YOUR DIAMOND MINES WE SHARE TOGETHER!

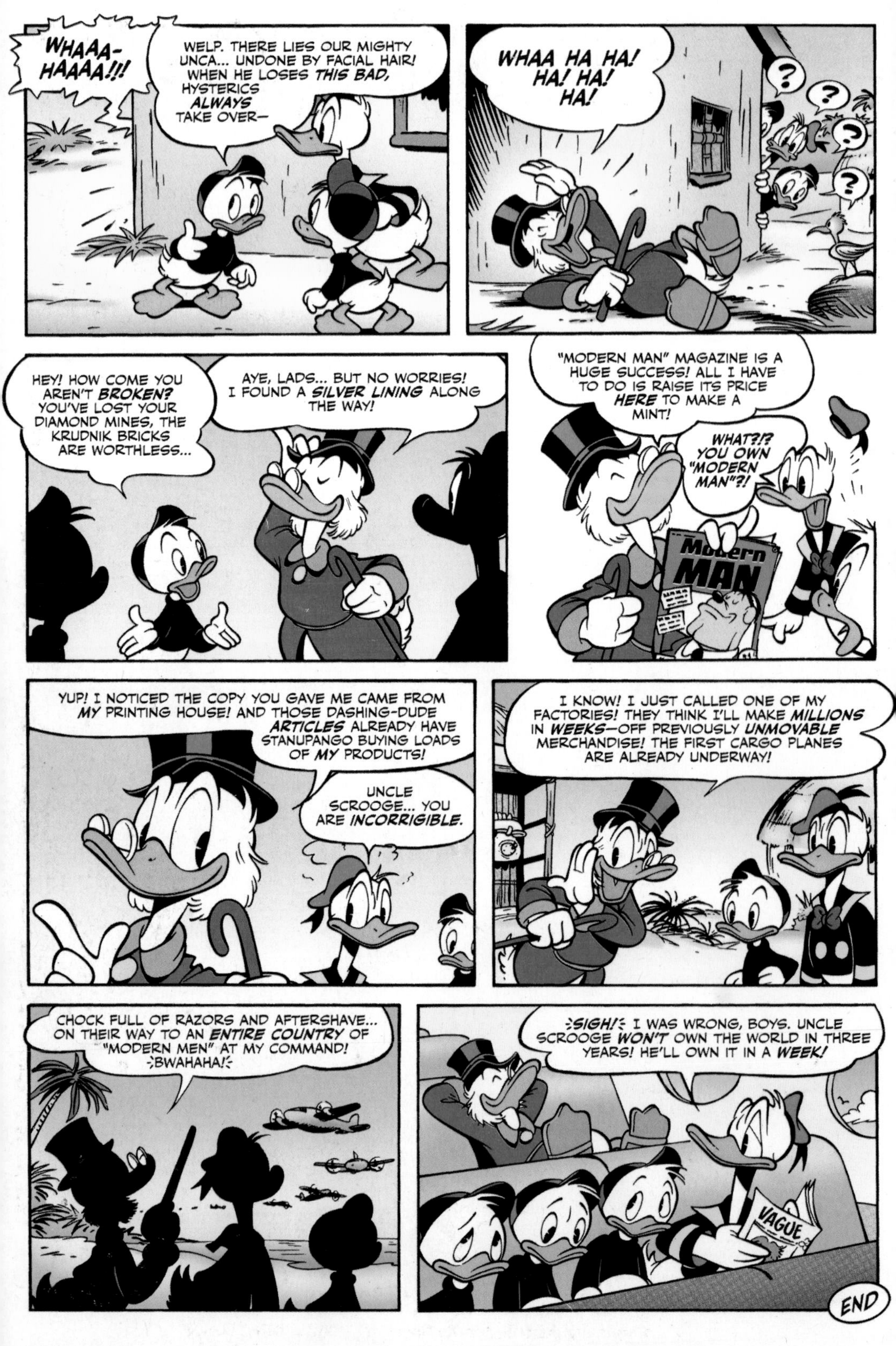
WHAAA-HAAAA!!!
WELP. THERE LIES OUR MIGHTY UNCA... UNDONE BY FACIAL HAIR! WHEN HE LOSES THIS BAD, HYSTERICS ALWAYS TAKE OVER—
WHAA HA HA! HA! HA! HA!
?
?
?
?
HEY! HOW COME YOU AREN'T BROKEN? YOU'VE LOST YOUR DIAMOND MINES, THE KRUDNIK BRICKS ARE WORTHLESS...
AYE, LADS... BUT NO WORRIES! I FOUND A SILVER LINING ALONG THE WAY!
"MODERN MAN" MAGAZINE IS A HUGE SUCCESS! ALL I HAVE TO DO IS RAISE ITS PRICE HERE TO MAKE A MINT!
WHAT?!? YOU OWN "MODERN MAN"?!
Modern MAN
YUP! I NOTICED THE COPY YOU GAVE ME CAME FROM MY PRINTING HOUSE! AND THOSE DASHING-DUDE ARTICLES ALREADY HAVE STANUPANGO BUYING LOADS OF MY PRODUCTS!
UNCLE SCROOGE... YOU ARE INCORRIGIBLE.
I KNOW! I JUST CALLED ONE OF MY FACTORIES! THEY THINK I'LL MAKE MILLIONS IN WEEKS—OFF PREVIOUSLY UNMOVABLE MERCHANDISE! THE FIRST CARGO PLANES ARE ALREADY UNDERWAY!
CHOCK FULL OF RAZORS AND AFTERSHAVE... ON THEIR WAY TO AN ENTIRE COUNTRY OF "MODERN MEN" AT MY COMMAND! BWAHAHA!
SIGH! I WAS WRONG, BOYS. UNCLE SCROOGE WON'T OWN THE WORLD IN THREE YEARS! HE'LL OWN IT IN A WEEK!
VAGUE
END

Walt Disney's Uncle $crooge in Mummy Fearest

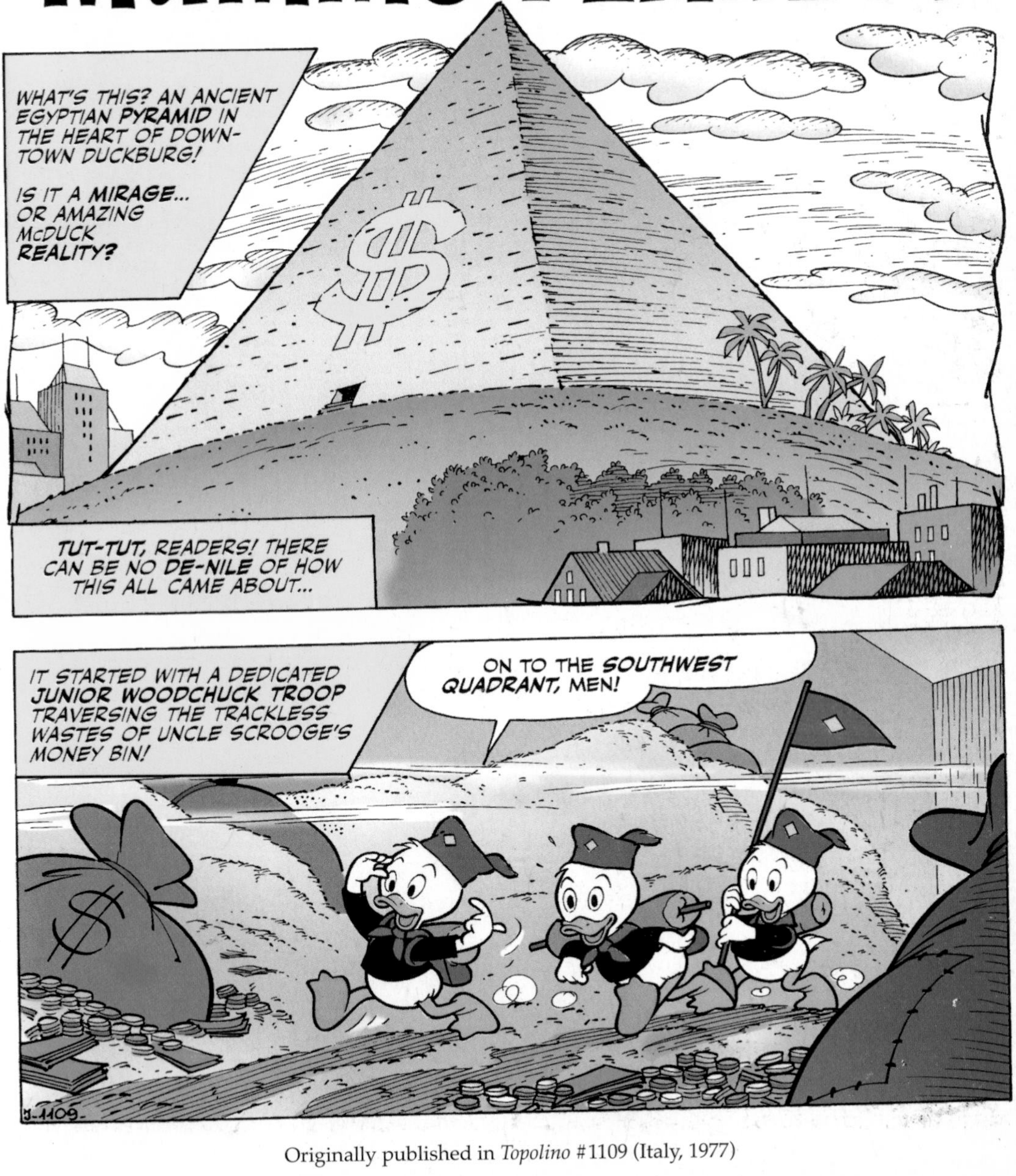
WHAT'S THIS? AN ANCIENT EGYPTIAN PYRAMID IN THE HEART OF DOWN-TOWN DUCKBURG!
IS IT A MIRAGE... OR AMAZING McDUCK REALITY?
TUT-TUT, READERS! THERE CAN BE NO DE-NILE OF HOW THIS ALL CAME ABOUT...
IT STARTED WITH A DEDICATED JUNIOR WOODCHUCK TROOP TRAVERSING THE TRACKLESS WASTES OF UNCLE SCROOGE'S MONEY BIN!
ON TO THE SOUTHWEST QUADRANT, MEN!
I-1109-

Originally published in *Topolino* #1109 (Italy, 1977)

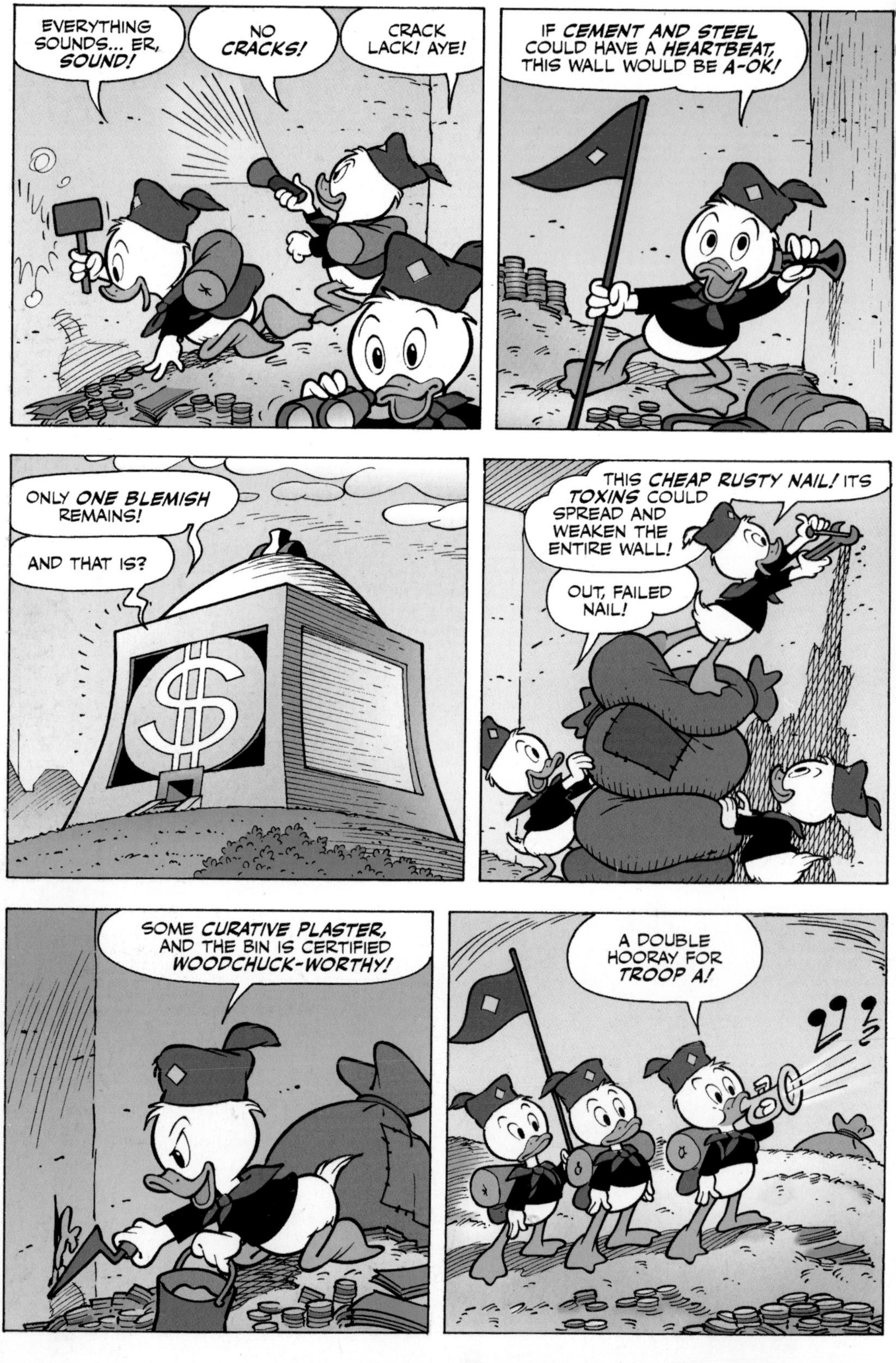
EVERYTHING SOUNDS... ER, SOUND!
NO CRACKS!
CRACK LACK! AYE!
IF CEMENT AND STEEL COULD HAVE A HEARTBEAT, THIS WALL WOULD BE A-OK!
ONLY ONE BLEMISH REMAINS!
AND THAT IS?
THIS CHEAP RUSTY NAIL! ITS TOXINS COULD SPREAD AND WEAKEN THE ENTIRE WALL!
OUT, FAILED NAIL!
SOME CURATIVE PLASTER, AND THE BIN IS CERTIFIED WOODCHUCK-WORTHY!
A DOUBLE HOORAY FOR TROOP A!

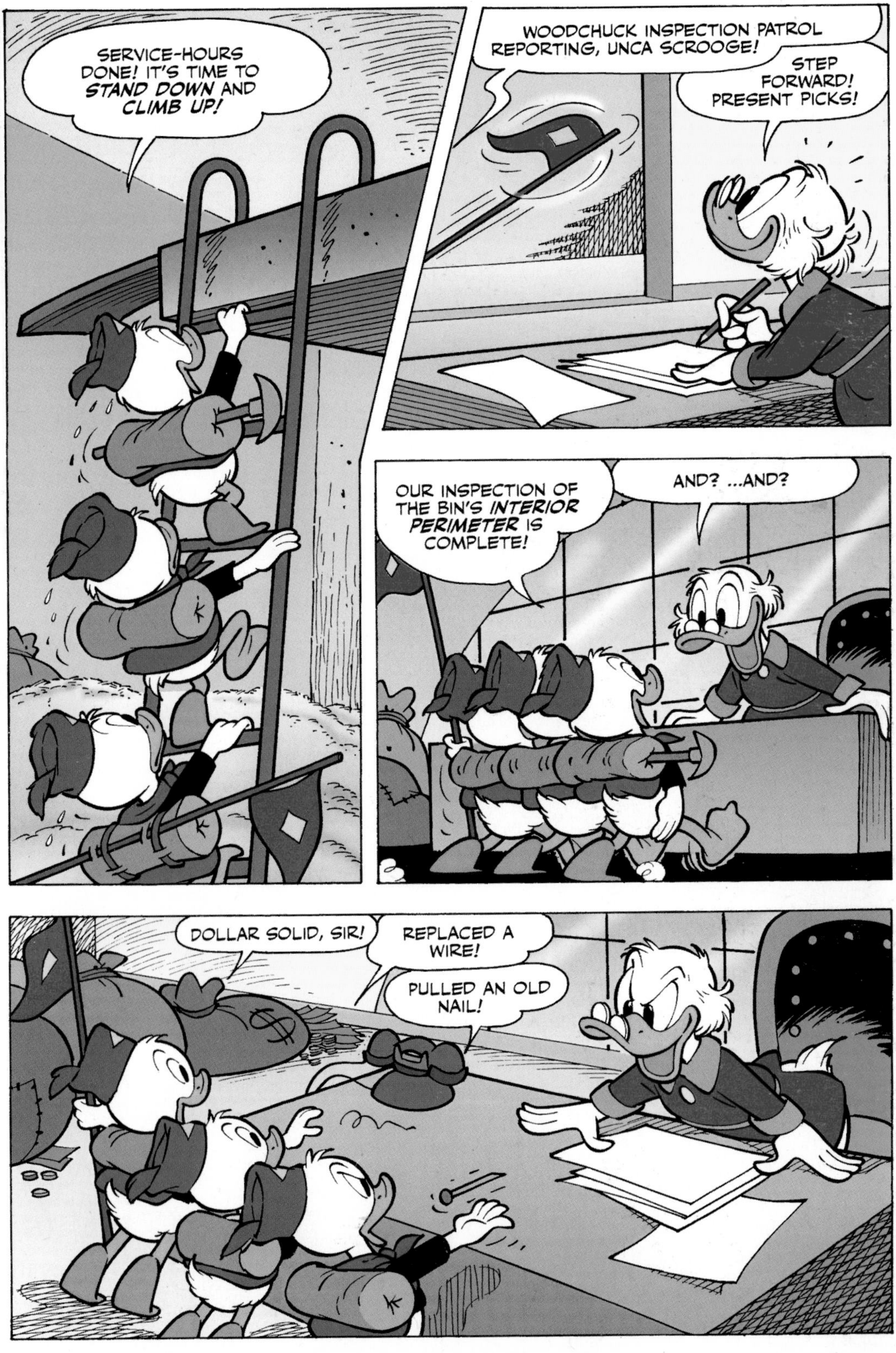
SERVICE-HOURS DONE! IT'S TIME TO *STAND DOWN* AND *CLIMB UP!*
WOODCHUCK INSPECTION PATROL REPORTING, UNCA SCROOGE!
STEP FORWARD! PRESENT PICKS!
OUR INSPECTION OF THE BIN'S *INTERIOR PERIMETER* IS COMPLETE!
AND? ...AND?
DOLLAR SOLID, SIR!
REPLACED A WIRE!
PULLED AN OLD NAIL!

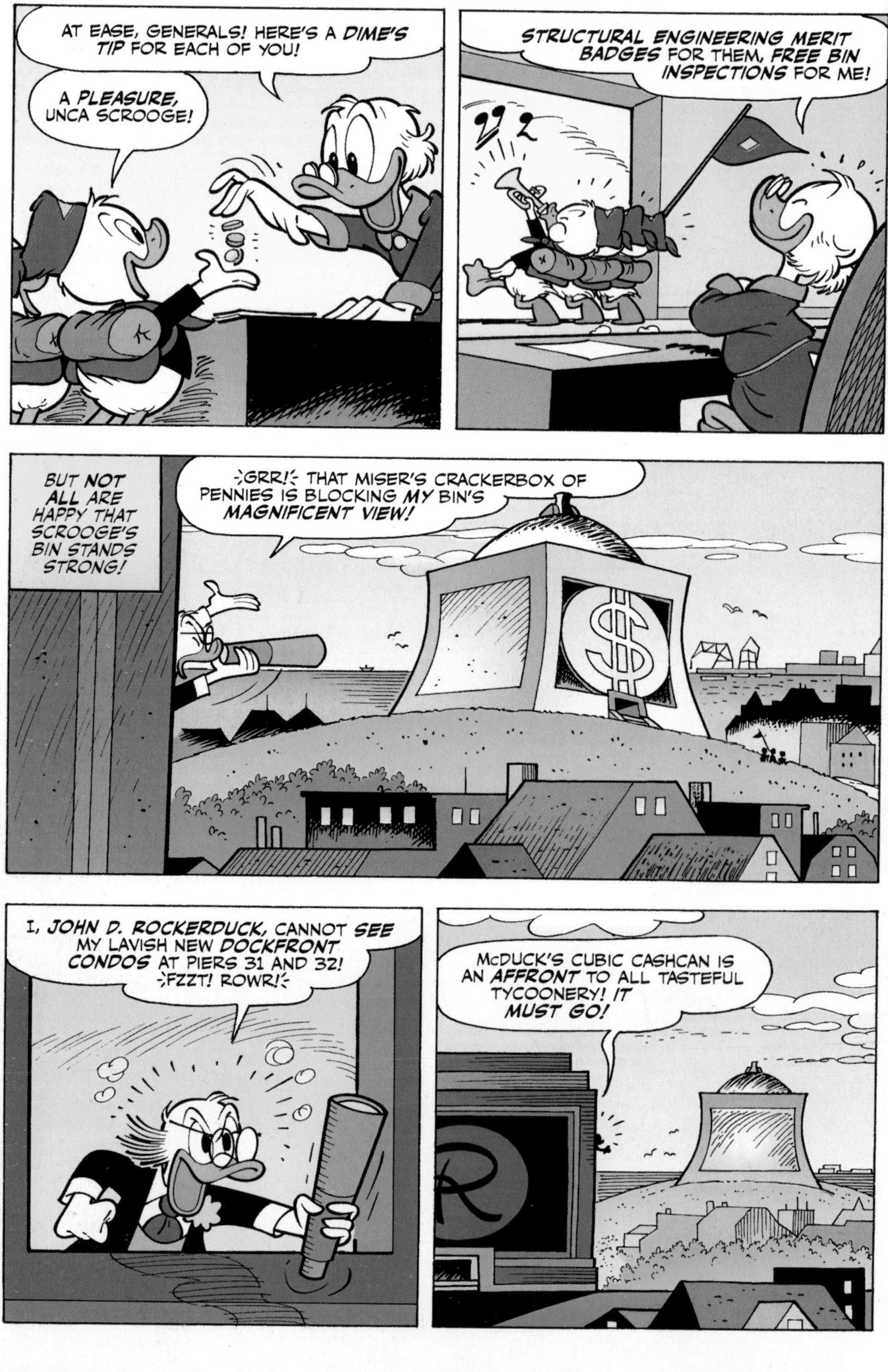
AT EASE, GENERALS! HERE'S A DIME'S TIP FOR EACH OF YOU!
A PLEASURE, UNCA SCROOGE!
STRUCTURAL ENGINEERING MERIT BADGES FOR THEM, FREE BIN INSPECTIONS FOR ME!
BUT NOT ALL ARE HAPPY THAT SCROOGE'S BIN STANDS STRONG!
GRR! THAT MISER'S CRACKERBOX OF PENNIES IS BLOCKING MY BIN'S MAGNIFICENT VIEW!
I, JOHN D. ROCKERDUCK, CANNOT SEE MY LAVISH NEW DOCKFRONT CONDOS AT PIERS 31 AND 32! FZZT! ROWR!
McDUCK'S CUBIC CASHCAN IS AN AFFRONT TO ALL TASTEFUL TYCOONERY! IT MUST GO!

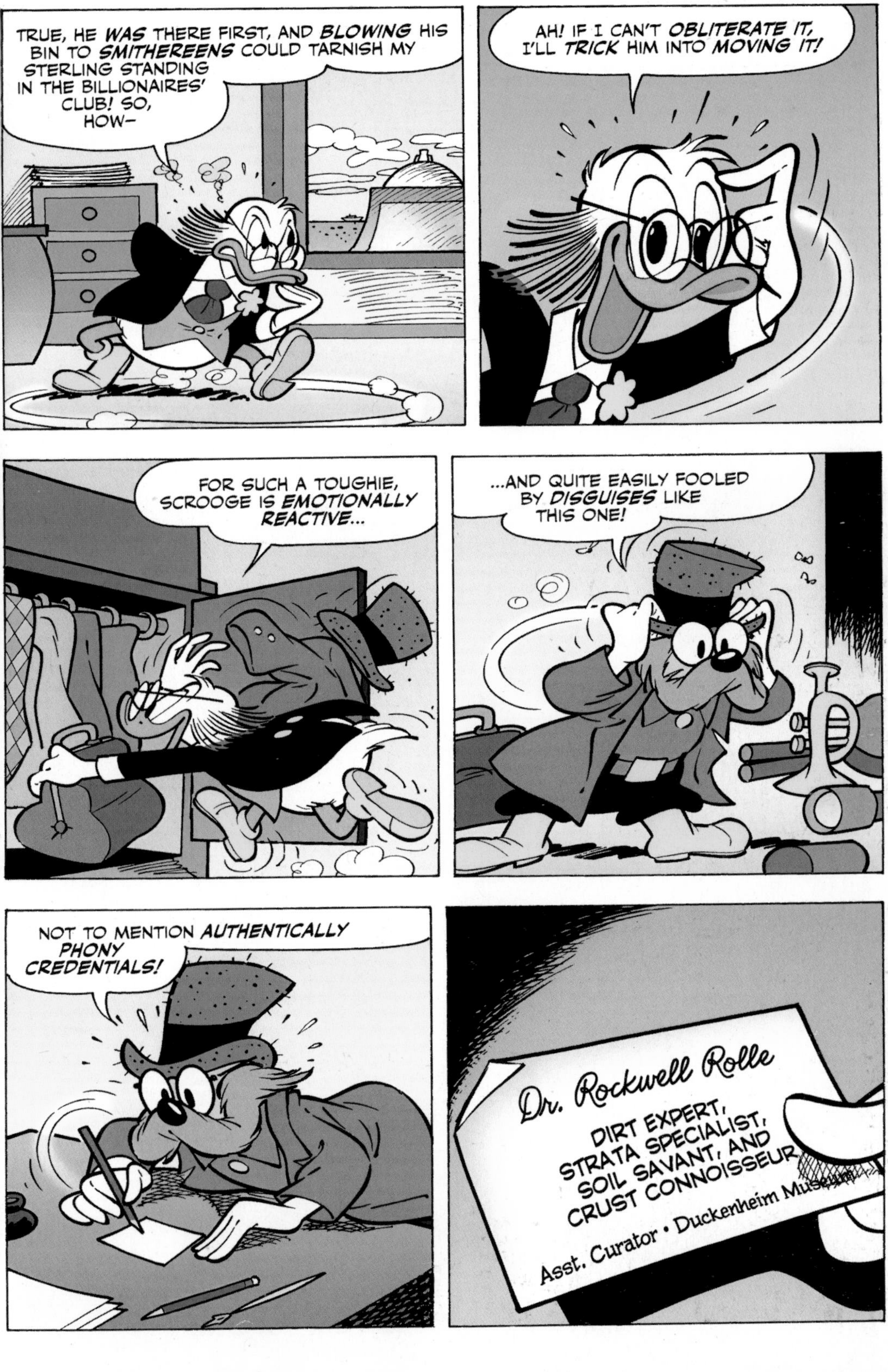
TRUE, HE WAS THERE FIRST, AND BLOWING HIS BIN TO SMITHEREENS COULD TARNISH MY STERLING STANDING IN THE BILLIONAIRES' CLUB! SO, HOW–
AH! IF I CAN'T OBLITERATE IT, I'LL TRICK HIM INTO MOVING IT!
FOR SUCH A TOUGHIE, SCROOGE IS EMOTIONALLY REACTIVE...
...AND QUITE EASILY FOOLED BY DISGUISES LIKE THIS ONE!
NOT TO MENTION AUTHENTICALLY PHONY CREDENTIALS!
Dr. Rockwell Rolle
DIRT EXPERT, STRATA SPECIALIST, SOIL SAVANT, AND CRUST CONNOISSEUR
Asst. Curator • Duckenheim Museum

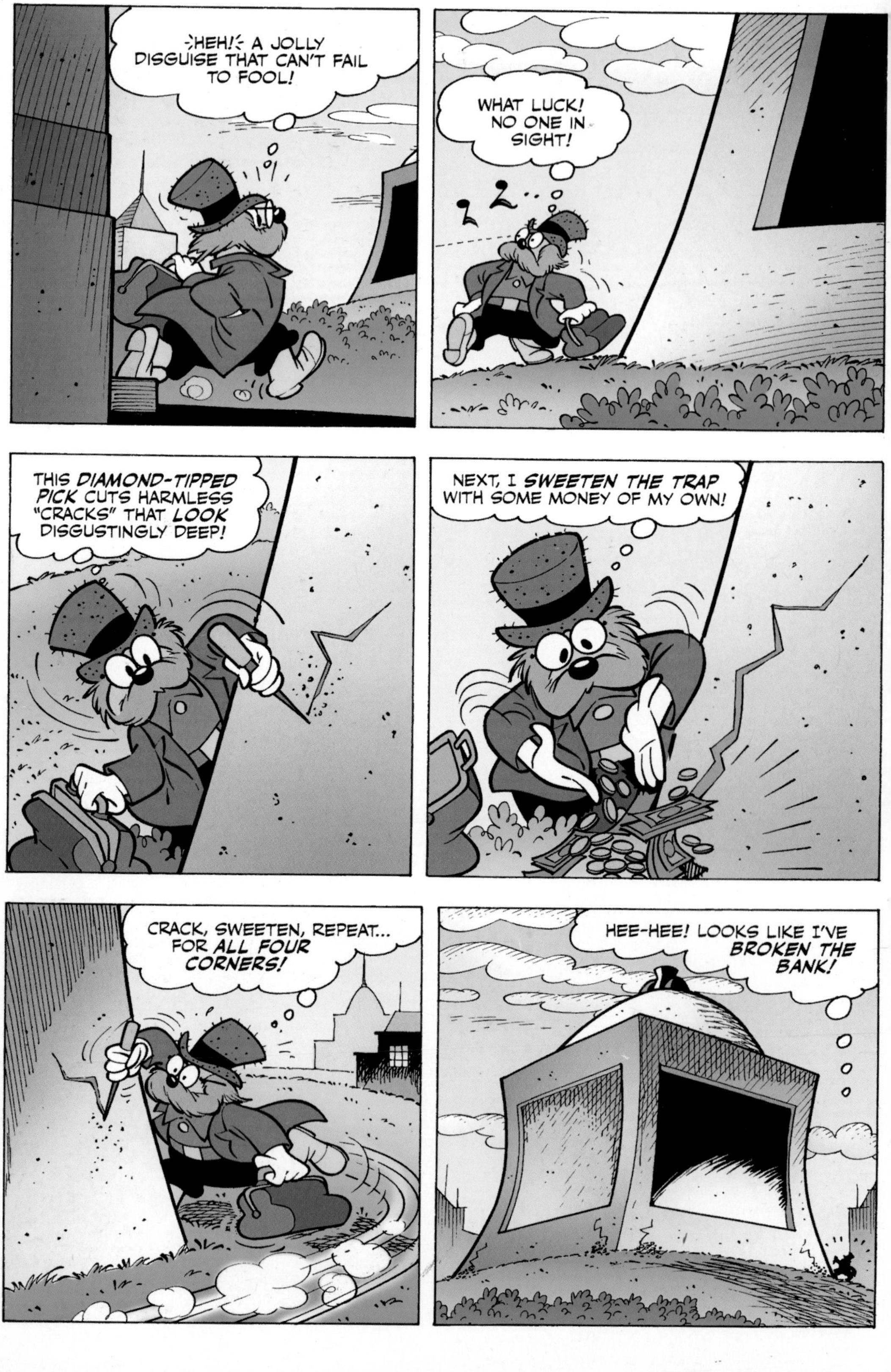

-HEH!- A JOLLY DISGUISE THAT CAN'T FAIL TO FOOL!
WHAT LUCK! NO ONE IN SIGHT!
THIS *DIAMOND-TIPPED PICK* CUTS HARMLESS "CRACKS" THAT *LOOK* DISGUSTINGLY DEEP!
NEXT, I *SWEETEN THE TRAP* WITH SOME MONEY OF MY OWN!
CRACK, SWEETEN, REPEAT... FOR *ALL FOUR CORNERS!*
HEE-HEE! LOOKS LIKE I'VE *BROKEN THE BANK!*

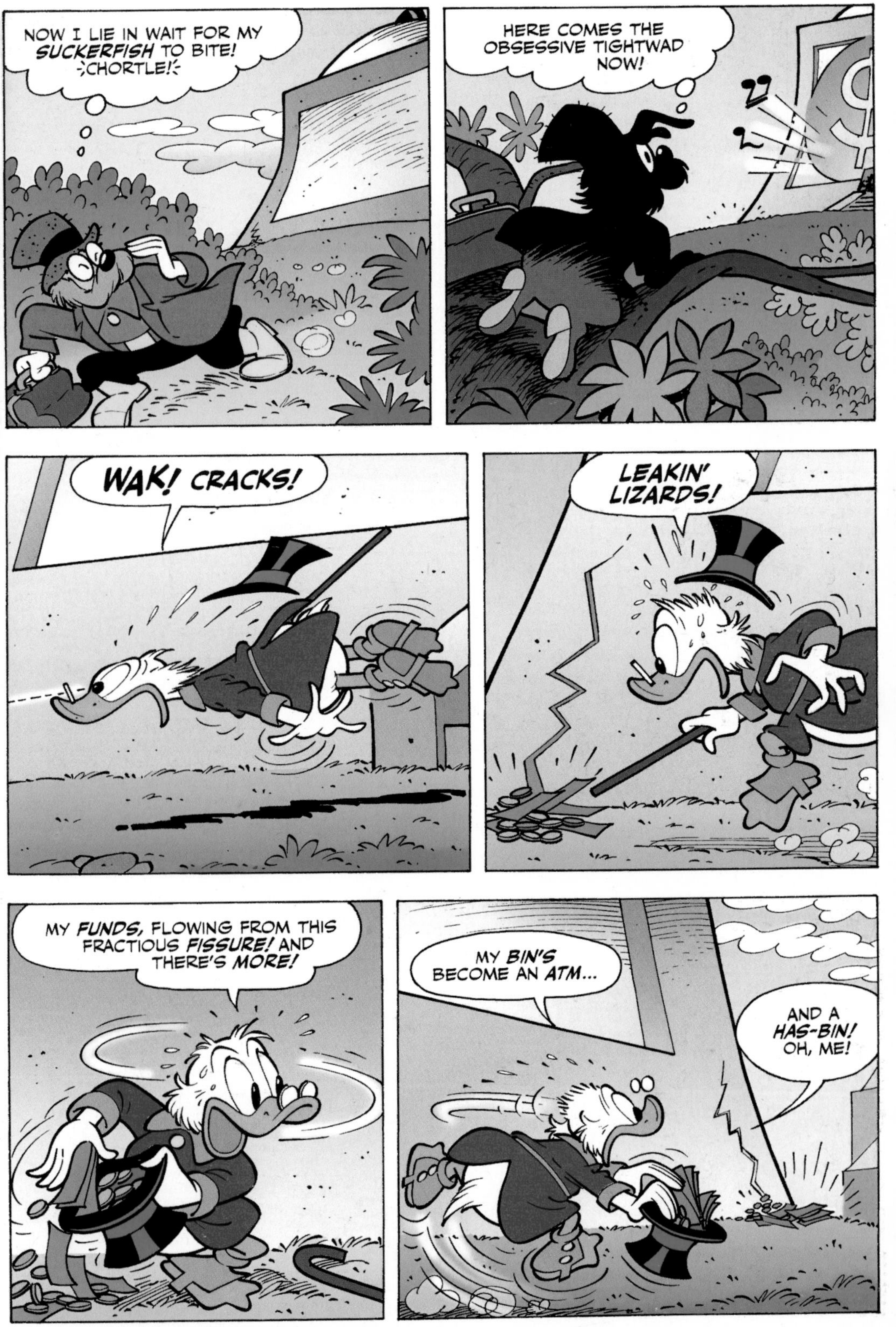
NOW I LIE IN WAIT FOR MY SUCKERFISH TO BITE! CHORTLE!
HERE COMES THE OBSESSIVE TIGHTWAD NOW!
WAK! CRACKS!
LEAKIN' LIZARDS!
MY FUNDS, FLOWING FROM THIS FRACTIOUS FISSURE! AND THERE'S MORE!
MY BIN'S BECOME AN ATM...
AND A HAS-BIN! OH, ME!

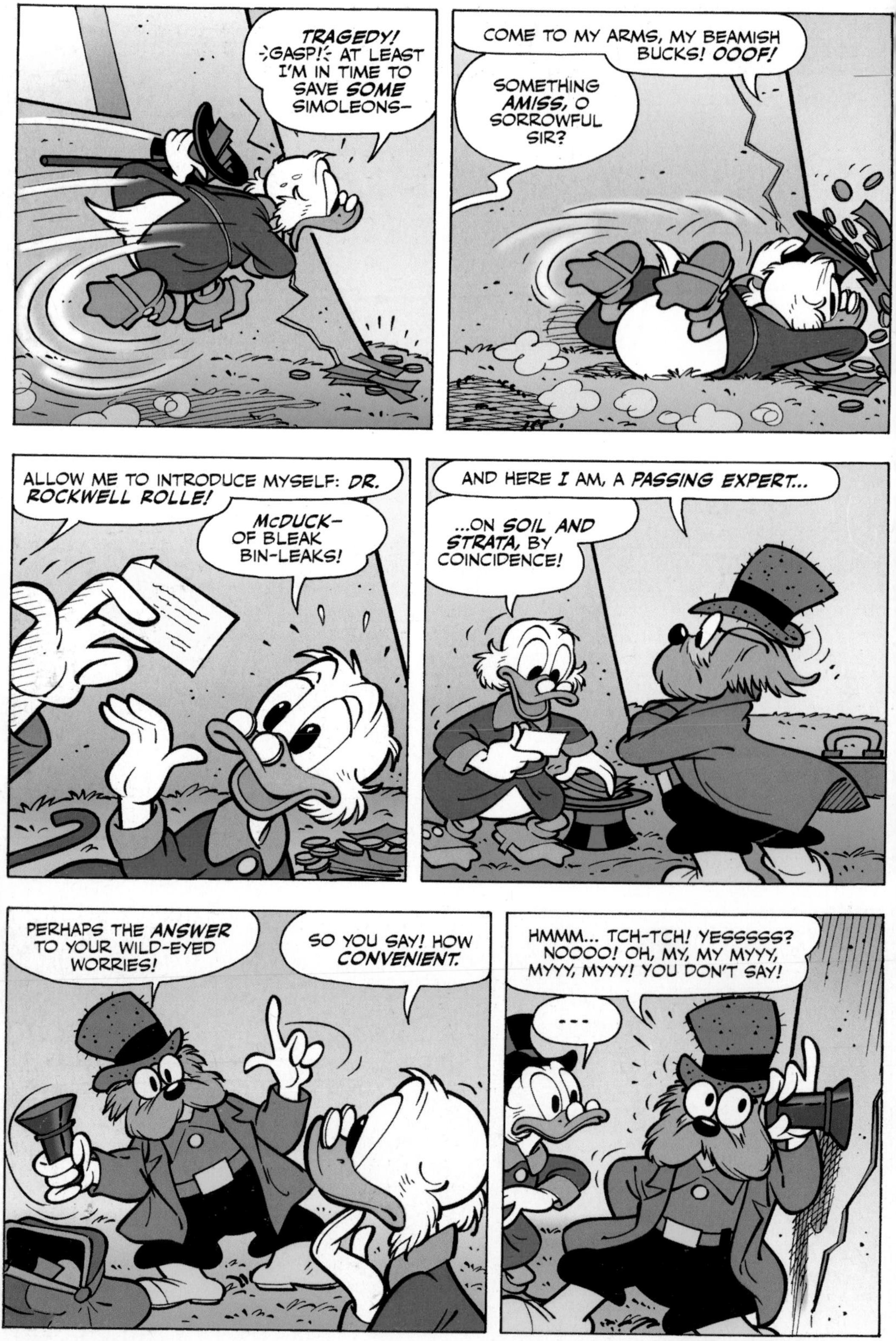
TRAGEDY! -GASP!- AT LEAST I'M IN TIME TO SAVE SOME SIMOLEONS–
COME TO MY ARMS, MY BEAMISH BUCKS! OOOF!
SOMETHING AMISS, O SORROWFUL SIR?
ALLOW ME TO INTRODUCE MYSELF: DR. ROCKWELL ROLLE!
McDUCK– OF BLEAK BIN-LEAKS!
AND HERE I AM, A PASSING EXPERT...
...ON SOIL AND STRATA, BY COINCIDENCE!
PERHAPS THE ANSWER TO YOUR WILD-EYED WORRIES!
SO YOU SAY! HOW CONVENIENT.
HMMM... TCH-TCH! YESSSSS? NOOOO! OH, MY, MY MYYY, MYYY, MYYY! YOU DON'T SAY!

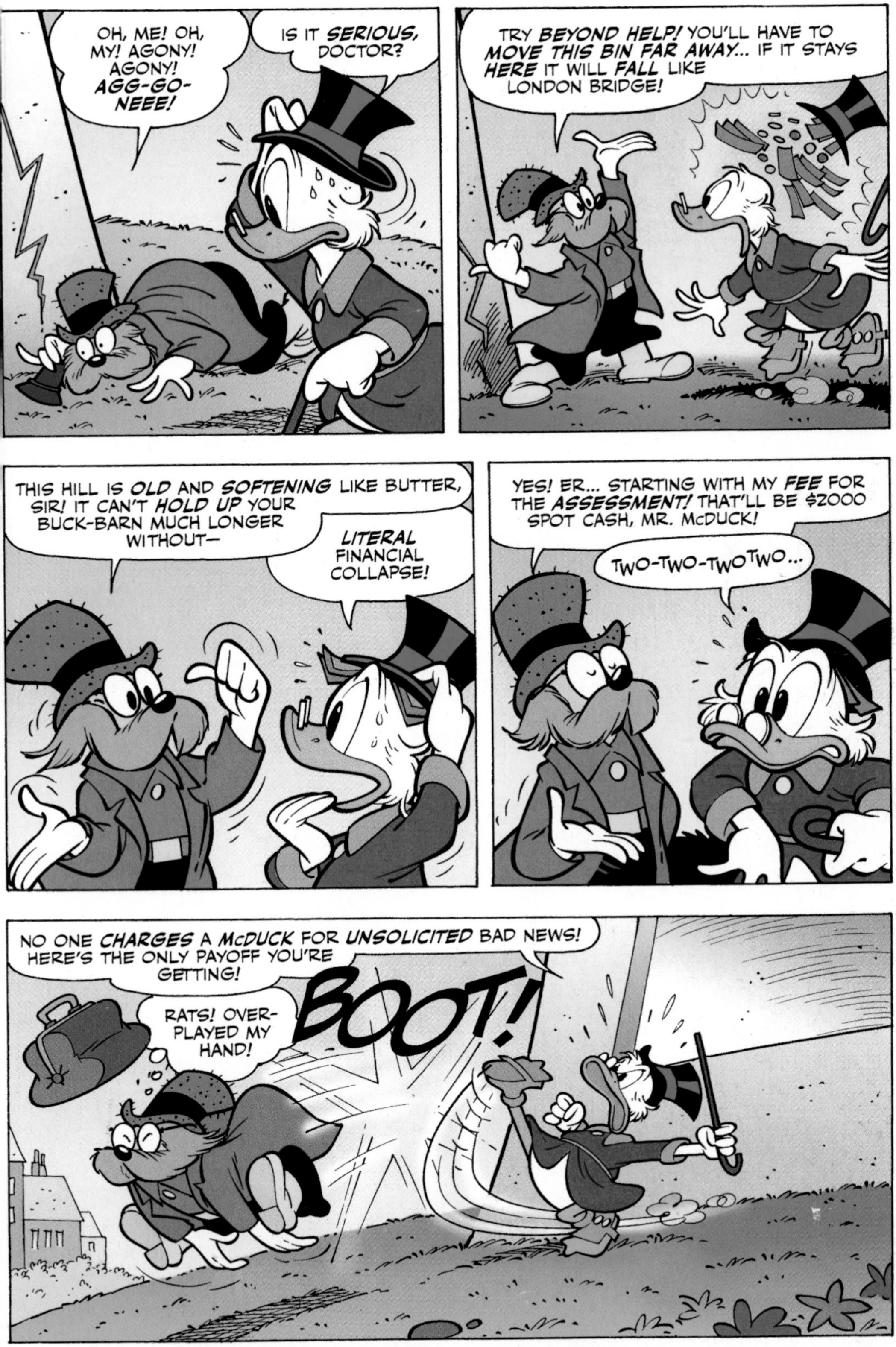
OH, ME! OH, MY! AGONY! AGONY! AGG-GO-NEEE!
IS IT SERIOUS, DOCTOR?
TRY BEYOND HELP! YOU'LL HAVE TO MOVE THIS BIN FAR AWAY... IF IT STAYS HERE IT WILL FALL LIKE LONDON BRIDGE!
THIS HILL IS OLD AND SOFTENING LIKE BUTTER, SIR! IT CAN'T HOLD UP YOUR BUCK-BARN MUCH LONGER WITHOUT—
LITERAL FINANCIAL COLLAPSE!
YES! ER... STARTING WITH MY FEE FOR THE ASSESSMENT! THAT'LL BE $2000 SPOT CASH, MR. McDUCK!
TWO-TWO-TWOTWO...
NO ONE CHARGES A McDUCK FOR UNSOLICITED BAD NEWS! HERE'S THE ONLY PAYOFF YOU'RE GETTING!
RATS! OVER-PLAYED MY HAND!
BOOT!

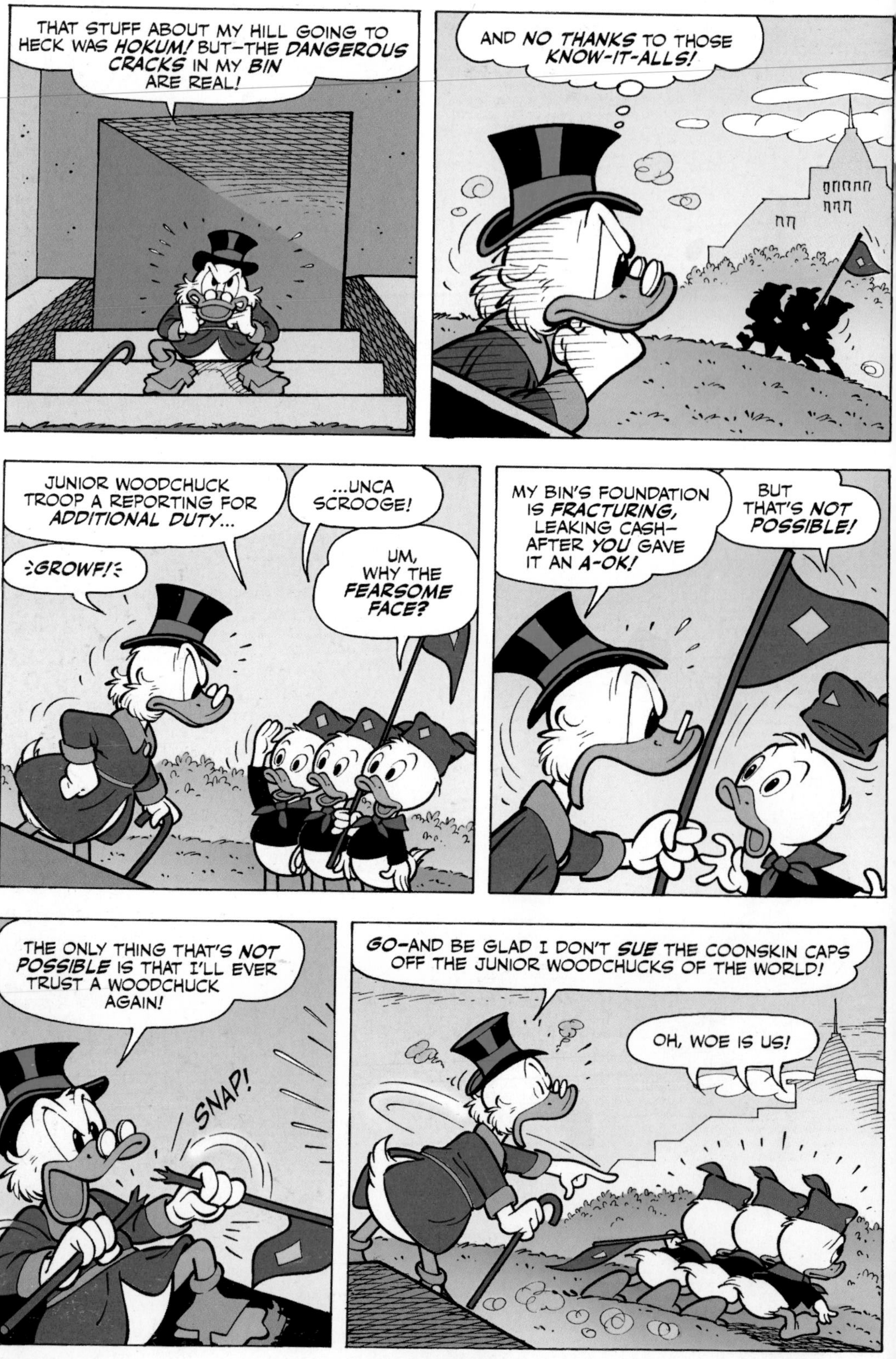
THAT STUFF ABOUT MY HILL GOING TO HECK WAS HOKUM! BUT—THE DANGEROUS CRACKS IN MY BIN ARE REAL!
AND NO THANKS TO THOSE KNOW-IT-ALLS!
JUNIOR WOODCHUCK TROOP A REPORTING FOR ADDITIONAL DUTY...
...UNCA SCROOGE!
GROWF!
UM, WHY THE FEARSOME FACE?
MY BIN'S FOUNDATION IS FRACTURING, LEAKING CASH—AFTER YOU GAVE IT AN A-OK!
BUT THAT'S NOT POSSIBLE!
THE ONLY THING THAT'S NOT POSSIBLE IS THAT I'LL EVER TRUST A WOODCHUCK AGAIN!
SNAP!
GO—AND BE GLAD I DON'T SUE THE COONSKIN CAPS OFF THE JUNIOR WOODCHUCKS OF THE WORLD!
OH, WOE IS US!

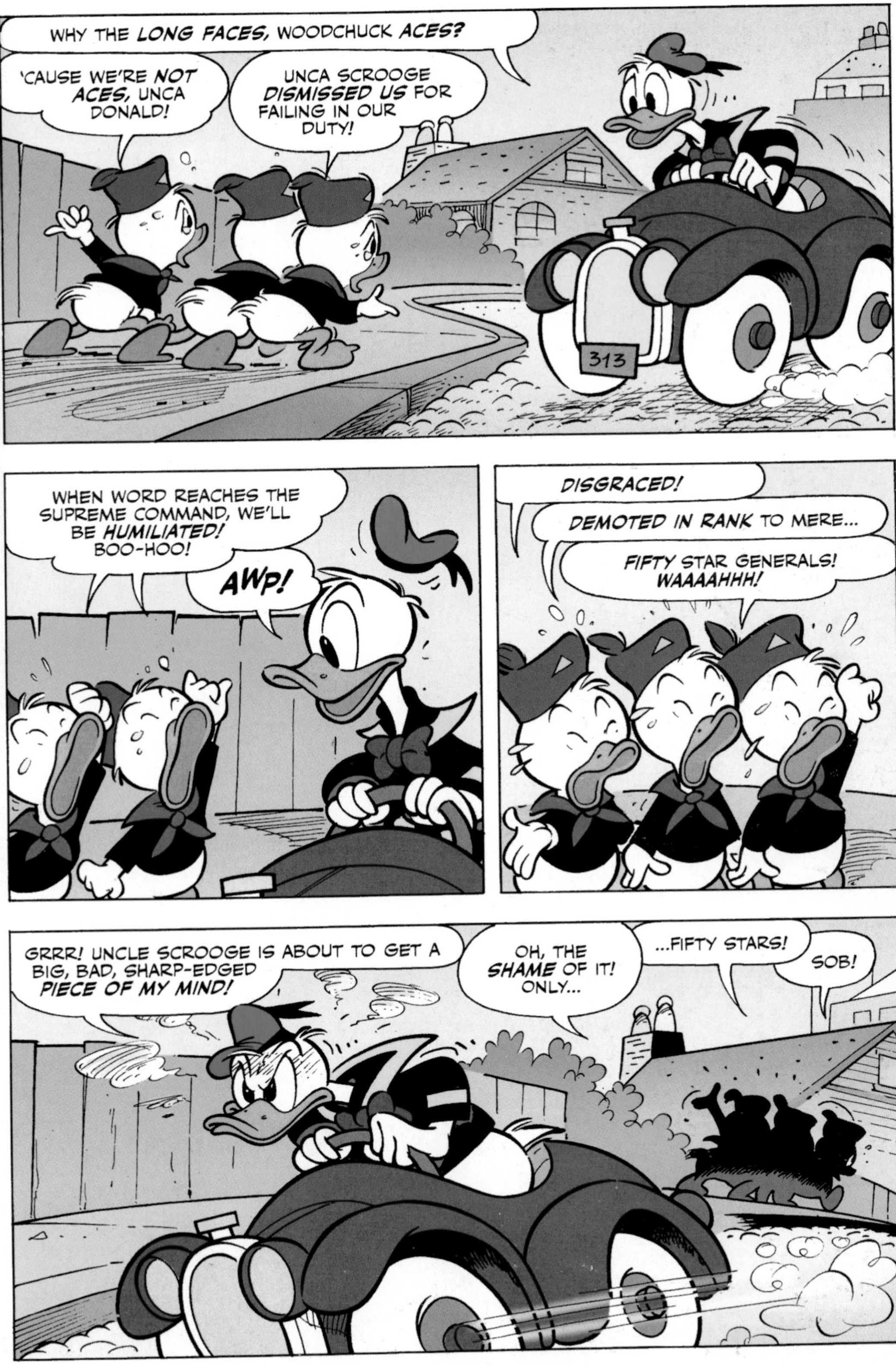
WHY THE LONG FACES, WOODCHUCK ACES?
'CAUSE WE'RE NOT ACES, UNCA DONALD!
UNCA SCROOGE DISMISSED US FOR FAILING IN OUR DUTY!
313
WHEN WORD REACHES THE SUPREME COMMAND, WE'LL BE HUMILIATED! BOO-HOO!
AWP!
DISGRACED!
DEMOTED IN RANK TO MERE...
FIFTY STAR GENERALS! WAAAAHHH!
GRRR! UNCLE SCROOGE IS ABOUT TO GET A BIG, BAD, SHARP-EDGED PIECE OF MY MIND!
OH, THE SHAME OF IT! ONLY...
...FIFTY STARS!
SOB!

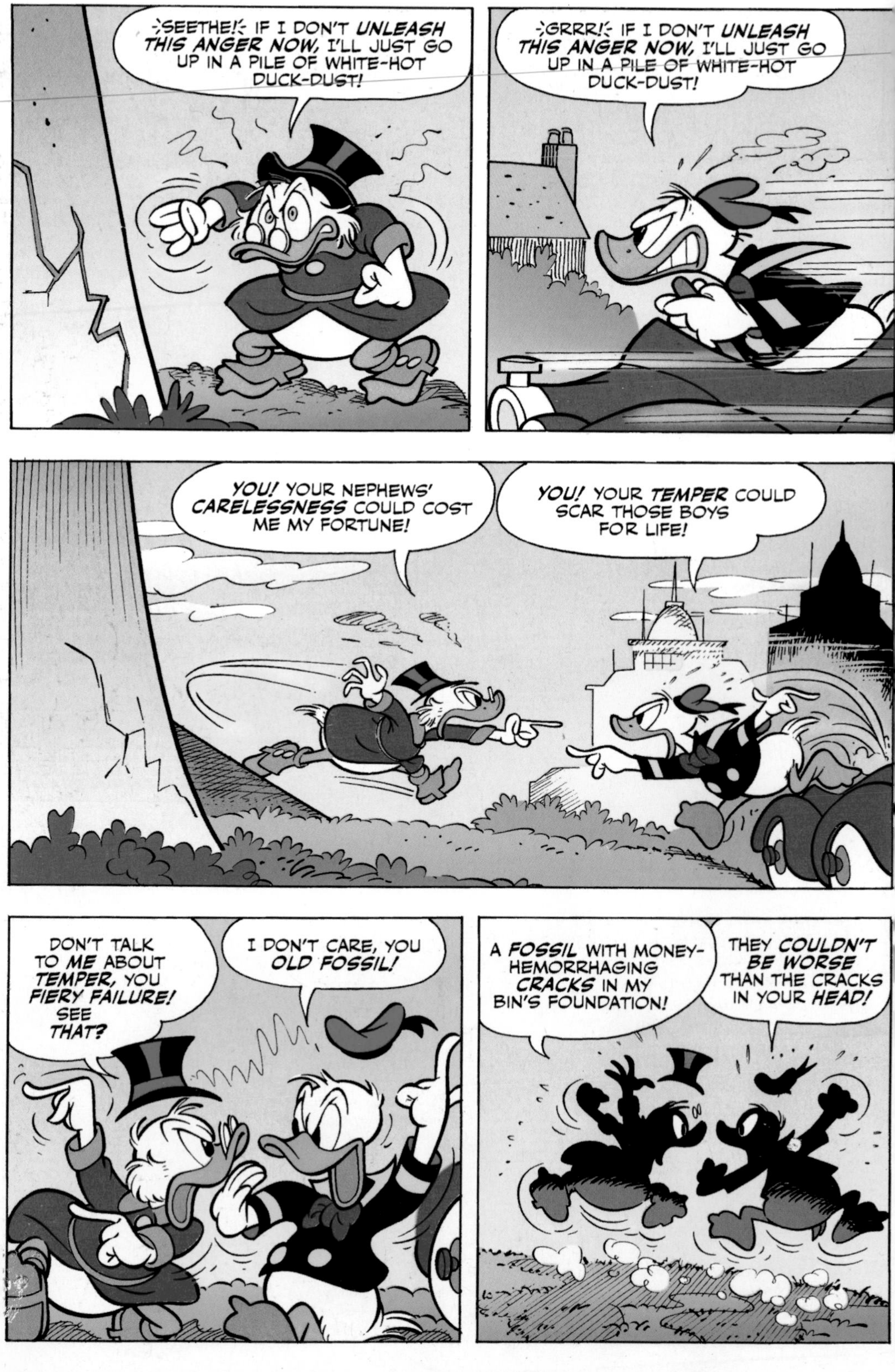
-SEETHE!- IF I DON'T UNLEASH THIS ANGER NOW, I'LL JUST GO UP IN A PILE OF WHITE-HOT DUCK-DUST!
-GRRR!- IF I DON'T UNLEASH THIS ANGER NOW, I'LL JUST GO UP IN A PILE OF WHITE-HOT DUCK-DUST!
YOU! YOUR NEPHEWS' CARELESSNESS COULD COST ME MY FORTUNE!
YOU! YOUR TEMPER COULD SCAR THOSE BOYS FOR LIFE!
DON'T TALK TO ME ABOUT TEMPER, YOU FIERY FAILURE! SEE THAT?
I DON'T CARE, YOU OLD FOSSIL!
A FOSSIL WITH MONEY-HEMORRHAGING CRACKS IN MY BIN'S FOUNDATION!
THEY COULDN'T BE WORSE THAN THE CRACKS IN YOUR HEAD!

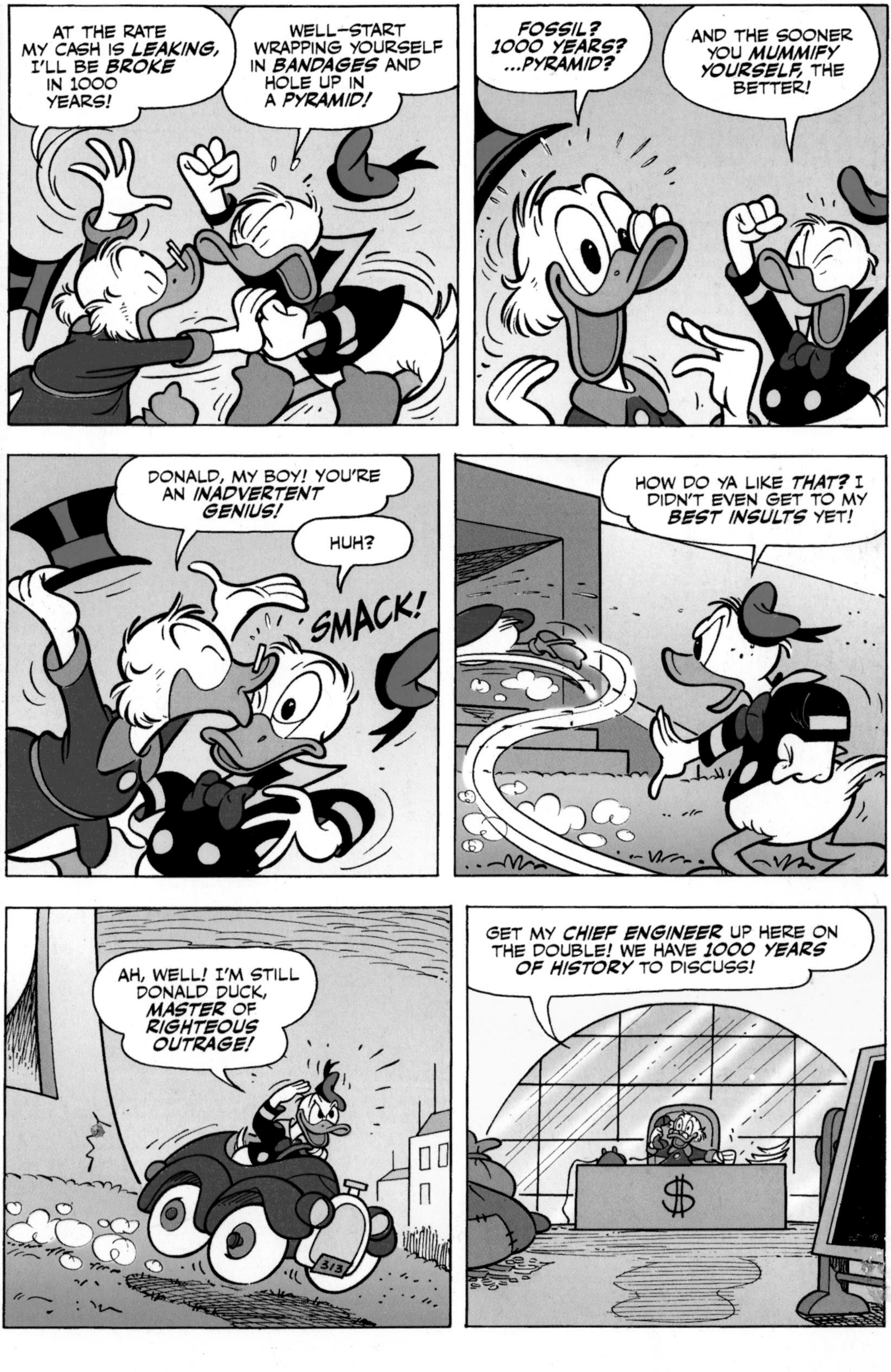
AT THE RATE MY CASH IS *LEAKING,* I'LL BE *BROKE* IN 1000 YEARS!
WELL—START WRAPPING YOURSELF IN *BANDAGES* AND HOLE UP IN A *PYRAMID!*
FOSSIL? 1000 YEARS? ...PYRAMID?
AND THE SOONER YOU *MUMMIFY YOURSELF,* THE BETTER!
DONALD, MY BOY! YOU'RE AN *INADVERTENT GENIUS!*
HUH?
SMACK!
HOW DO YA LIKE *THAT?* I DIDN'T EVEN GET TO MY *BEST INSULTS* YET!
AH, WELL! I'M STILL DONALD DUCK, *MASTER* OF *RIGHTEOUS OUTRAGE!*
313
GET MY *CHIEF ENGINEER* UP HERE ON THE DOUBLE! WE HAVE *1000 YEARS OF HISTORY* TO DISCUSS!
$

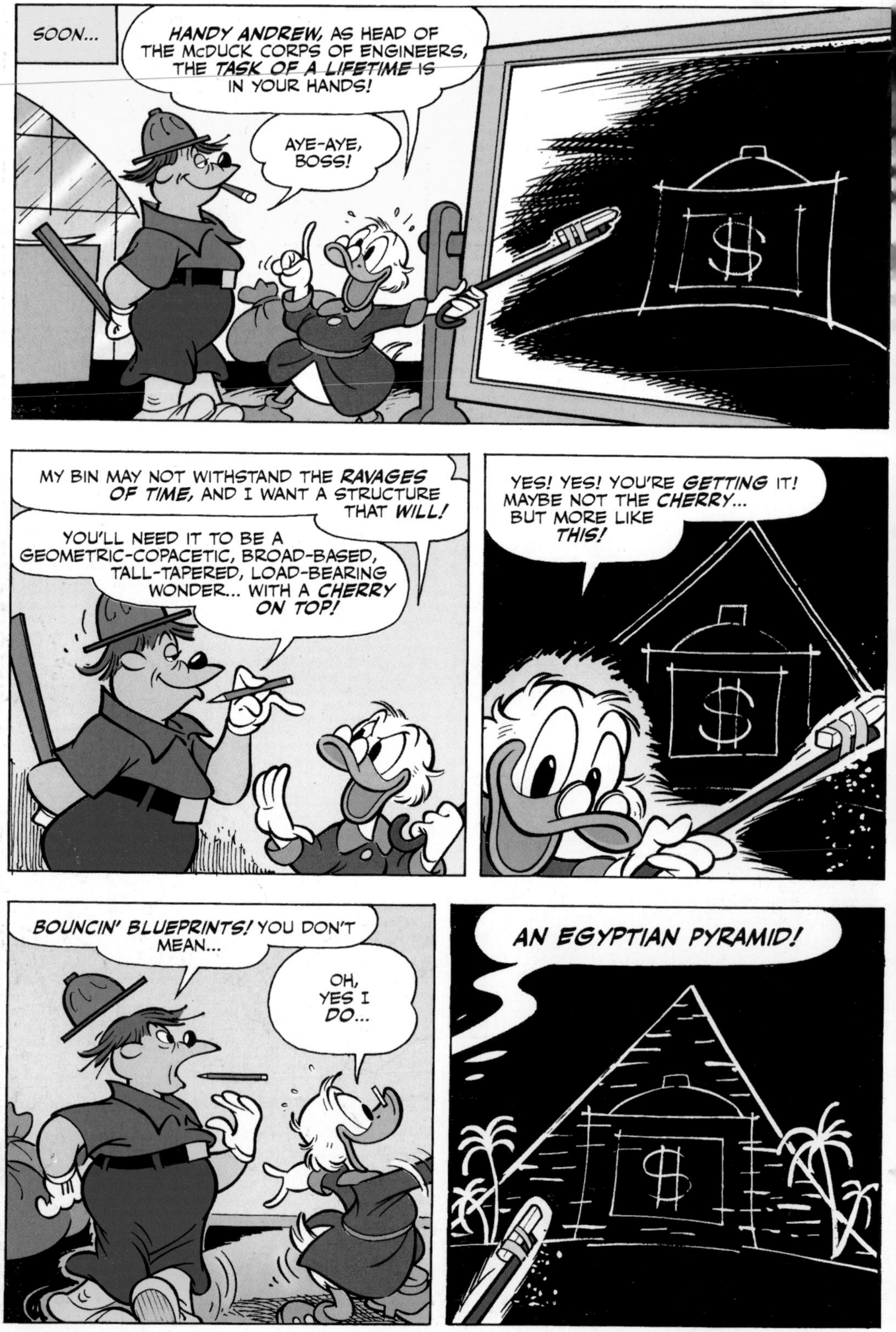
SOON...
HANDY ANDREW, AS HEAD OF THE McDUCK CORPS OF ENGINEERS, THE TASK OF A LIFETIME IS IN YOUR HANDS!
AYE-AYE, BOSS!
MY BIN MAY NOT WITHSTAND THE RAVAGES OF TIME, AND I WANT A STRUCTURE THAT WILL!
YOU'LL NEED IT TO BE A GEOMETRIC-COPACETIC, BROAD-BASED, TALL-TAPERED, LOAD-BEARING WONDER... WITH A CHERRY ON TOP!
YES! YES! YOU'RE GETTING IT! MAYBE NOT THE CHERRY... BUT MORE LIKE THIS!
BOUNCIN' BLUEPRINTS! YOU DON'T MEAN...
OH, YES I DO...
AN EGYPTIAN PYRAMID!

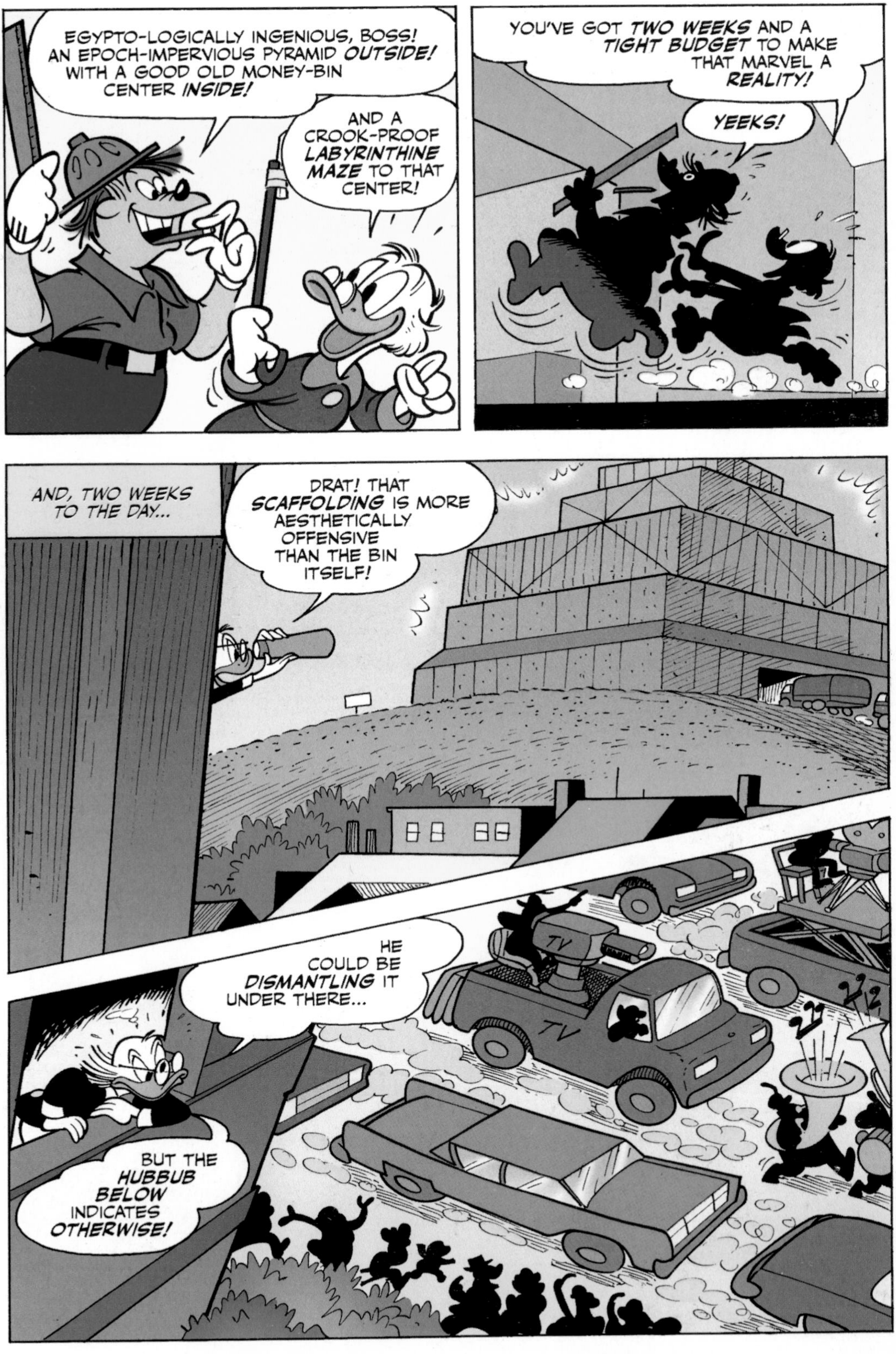
EGYPTO-LOGICALLY INGENIOUS, BOSS! AN EPOCH-IMPERVIOUS PYRAMID OUTSIDE! WITH A GOOD OLD MONEY-BIN CENTER INSIDE!
AND A CROOK-PROOF LABYRINTHINE MAZE TO THAT CENTER!
YOU'VE GOT TWO WEEKS AND A TIGHT BUDGET TO MAKE THAT MARVEL A REALITY!
YEEKS!
AND, TWO WEEKS TO THE DAY...
DRAT! THAT SCAFFOLDING IS MORE AESTHETICALLY OFFENSIVE THAN THE BIN ITSELF!
HE COULD BE DISMANTLING IT UNDER THERE...
BUT THE HUBBUB BELOW INDICATES OTHERWISE!
TV
TV

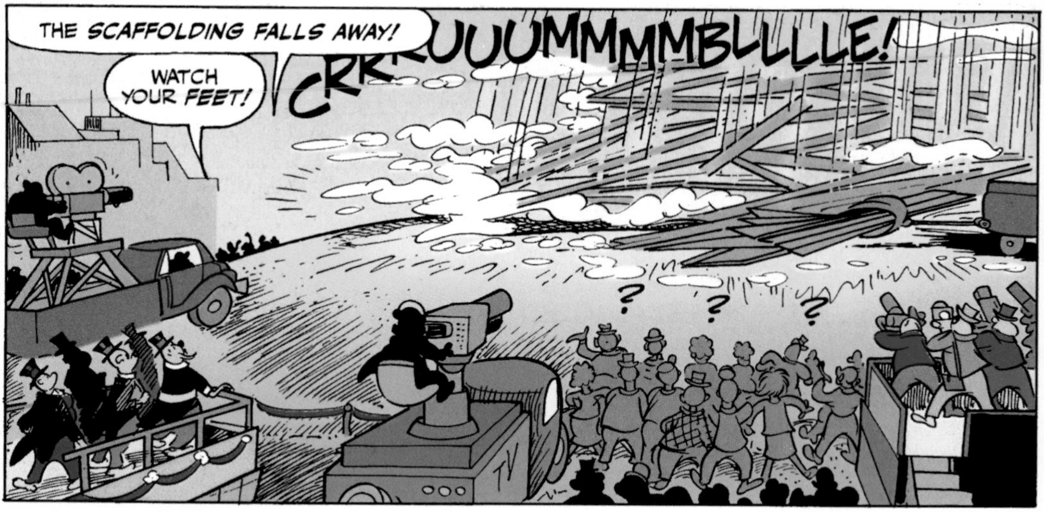
THE SCAFFOLDING FALLS AWAY!
WATCH YOUR FEET!
CRRRUUUMMMMBLLLLE!
TV

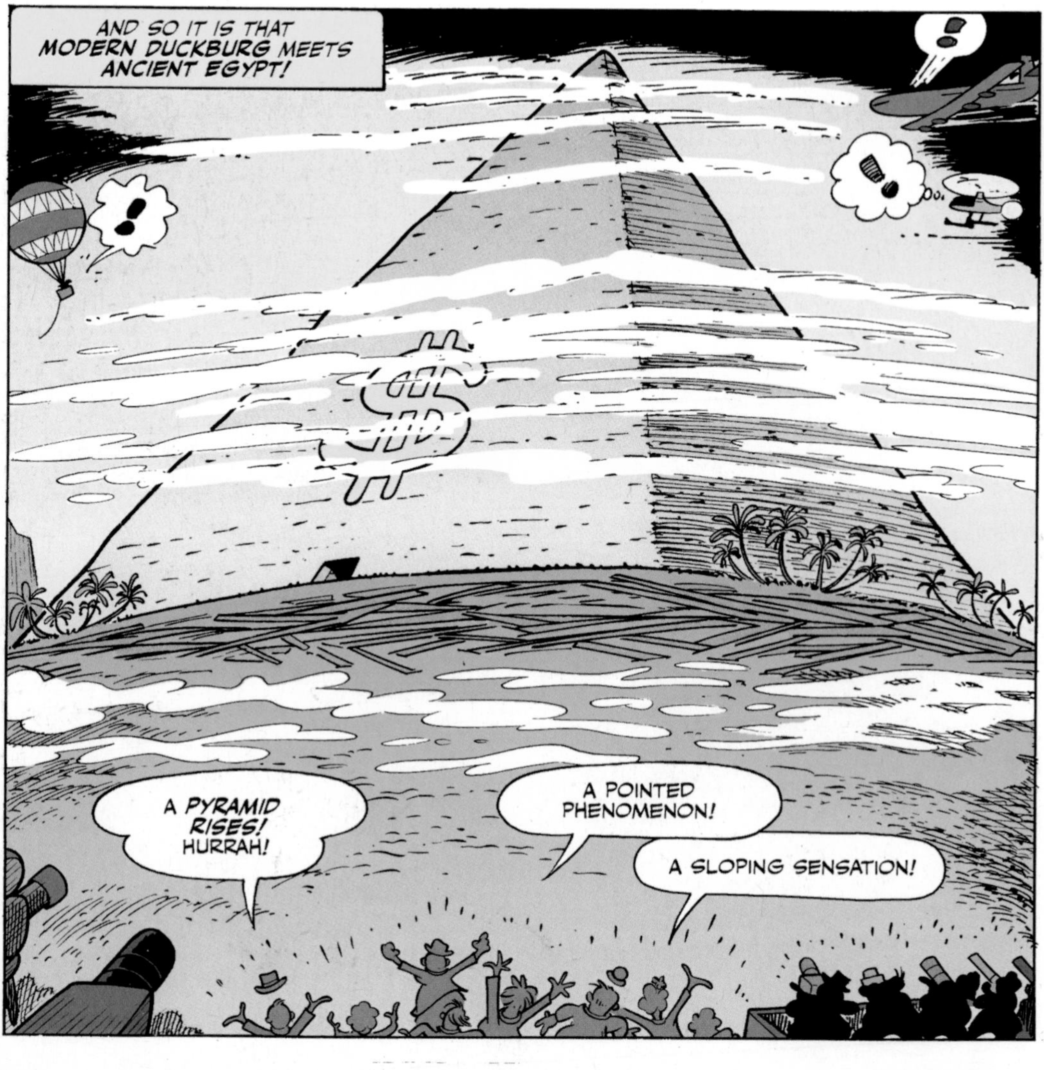
AND SO IT IS THAT MODERN DUCKBURG MEETS ANCIENT EGYPT!
A PYRAMID RISES! HURRAH!
A POINTED PHENOMENON!
A SLOPING SENSATION!

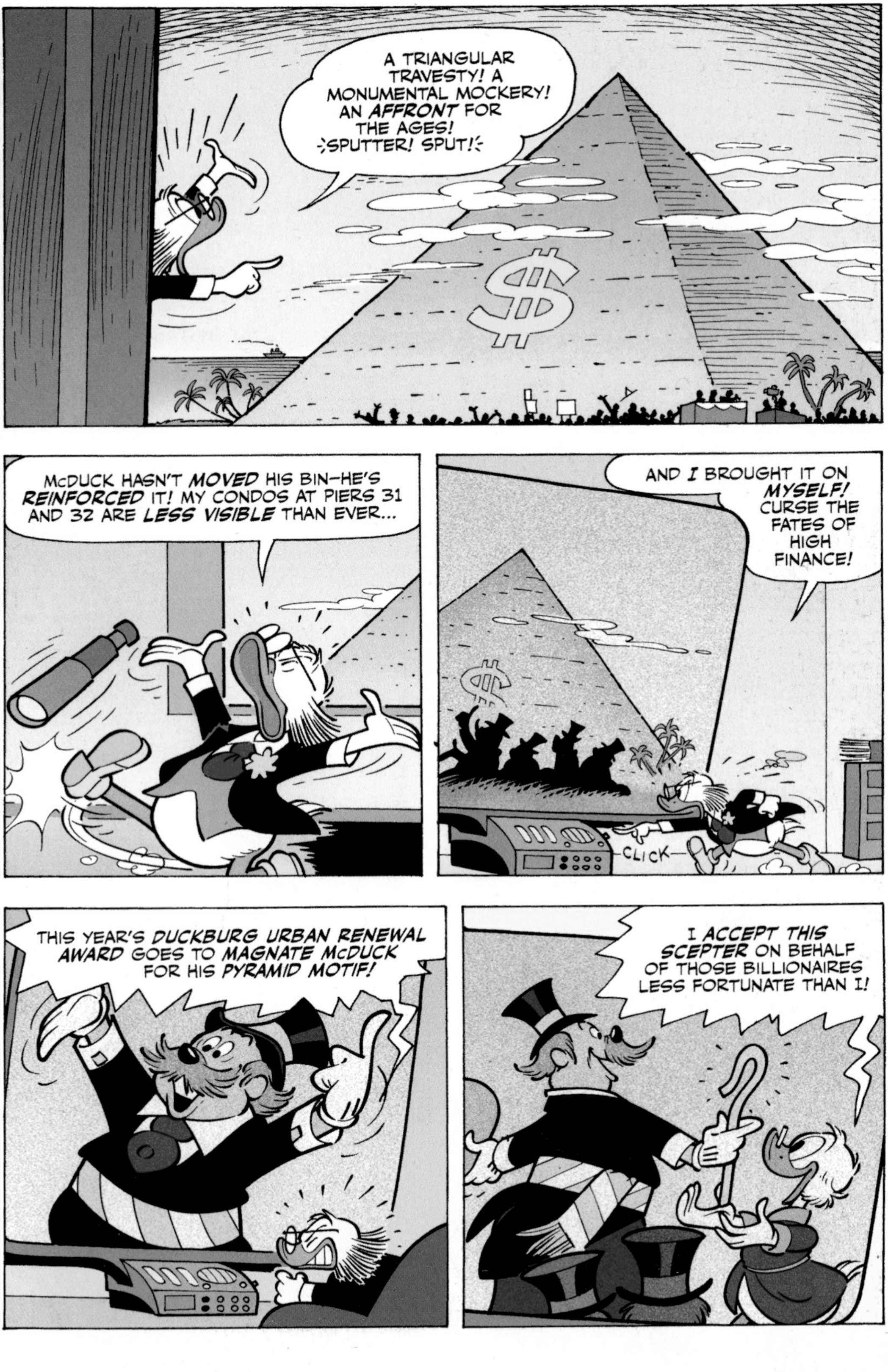
A TRIANGULAR TRAVESTY! A MONUMENTAL MOCKERY! AN AFFRONT FOR THE AGES! -SPUTTER! SPUT!-
McDUCK HASN'T MOVED HIS BIN—HE'S REINFORCED IT! MY CONDOS AT PIERS 31 AND 32 ARE LESS VISIBLE THAN EVER...
AND I BROUGHT IT ON MYSELF! CURSE THE FATES OF HIGH FINANCE!
CLICK
THIS YEAR'S DUCKBURG URBAN RENEWAL AWARD GOES TO MAGNATE McDUCK FOR HIS PYRAMID MOTIF!
I ACCEPT THIS SCEPTER ON BEHALF OF THOSE BILLIONAIRES LESS FORTUNATE THAN I!

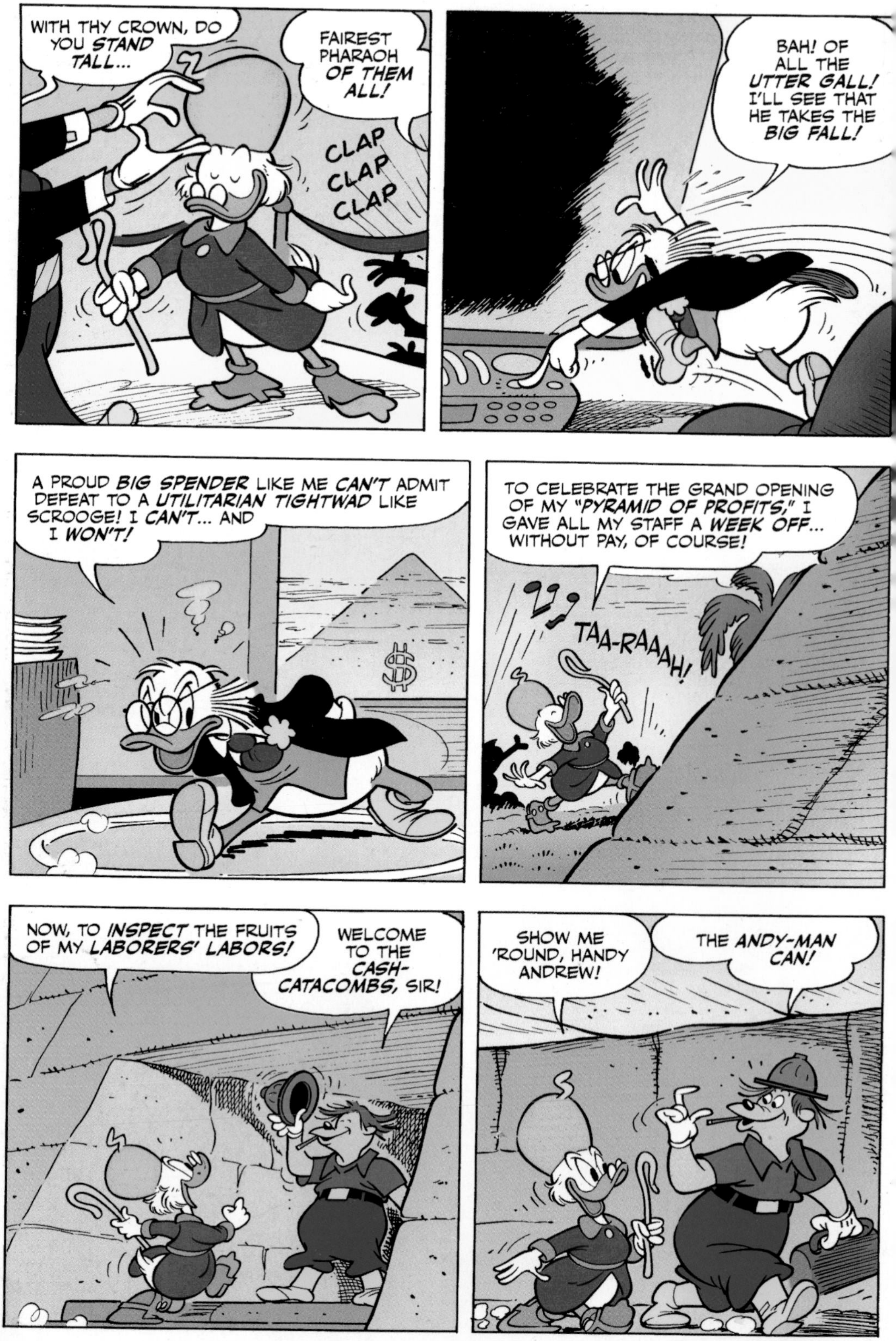
WITH THY CROWN, DO YOU STAND TALL...
FAIREST PHARAOH OF THEM ALL!
CLAP CLAP CLAP
BAH! OF ALL THE UTTER GALL! I'LL SEE THAT HE TAKES THE BIG FALL!
A PROUD BIG SPENDER LIKE ME CAN'T ADMIT DEFEAT TO A UTILITARIAN TIGHTWAD LIKE SCROOGE! I CAN'T... AND I WON'T!
TO CELEBRATE THE GRAND OPENING OF MY "PYRAMID OF PROFITS," I GAVE ALL MY STAFF A WEEK OFF... WITHOUT PAY, OF COURSE!
TAA-RAAAH!
NOW, TO INSPECT THE FRUITS OF MY LABORERS' LABORS!
WELCOME TO THE CASH-CATACOMBS, SIR!
SHOW ME 'ROUND, HANDY ANDREW!
THE ANDY-MAN CAN!

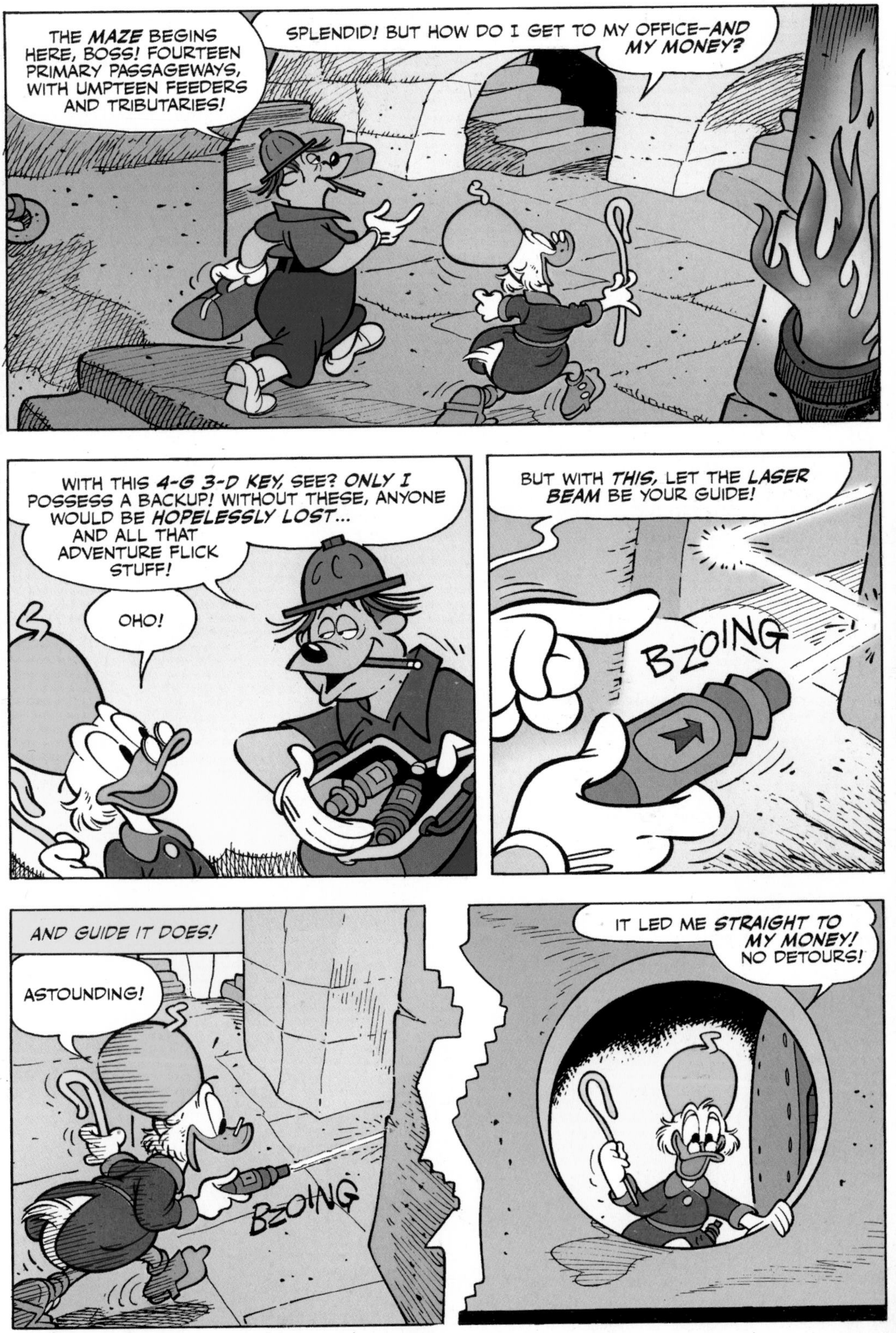
THE MAZE BEGINS HERE, BOSS! FOURTEEN PRIMARY PASSAGEWAYS, WITH UMPTEEN FEEDERS AND TRIBUTARIES!
SPLENDID! BUT HOW DO I GET TO MY OFFICE—AND MY MONEY?
WITH THIS 4-G 3-D KEY, SEE? ONLY I POSSESS A BACKUP! WITHOUT THESE, ANYONE WOULD BE HOPELESSLY LOST... AND ALL THAT ADVENTURE FLICK STUFF!
OHO!
BUT WITH THIS, LET THE LASER BEAM BE YOUR GUIDE!
BZOING
AND GUIDE IT DOES!
ASTOUNDING!
BZOING
IT LED ME STRAIGHT TO MY MONEY! NO DETOURS!

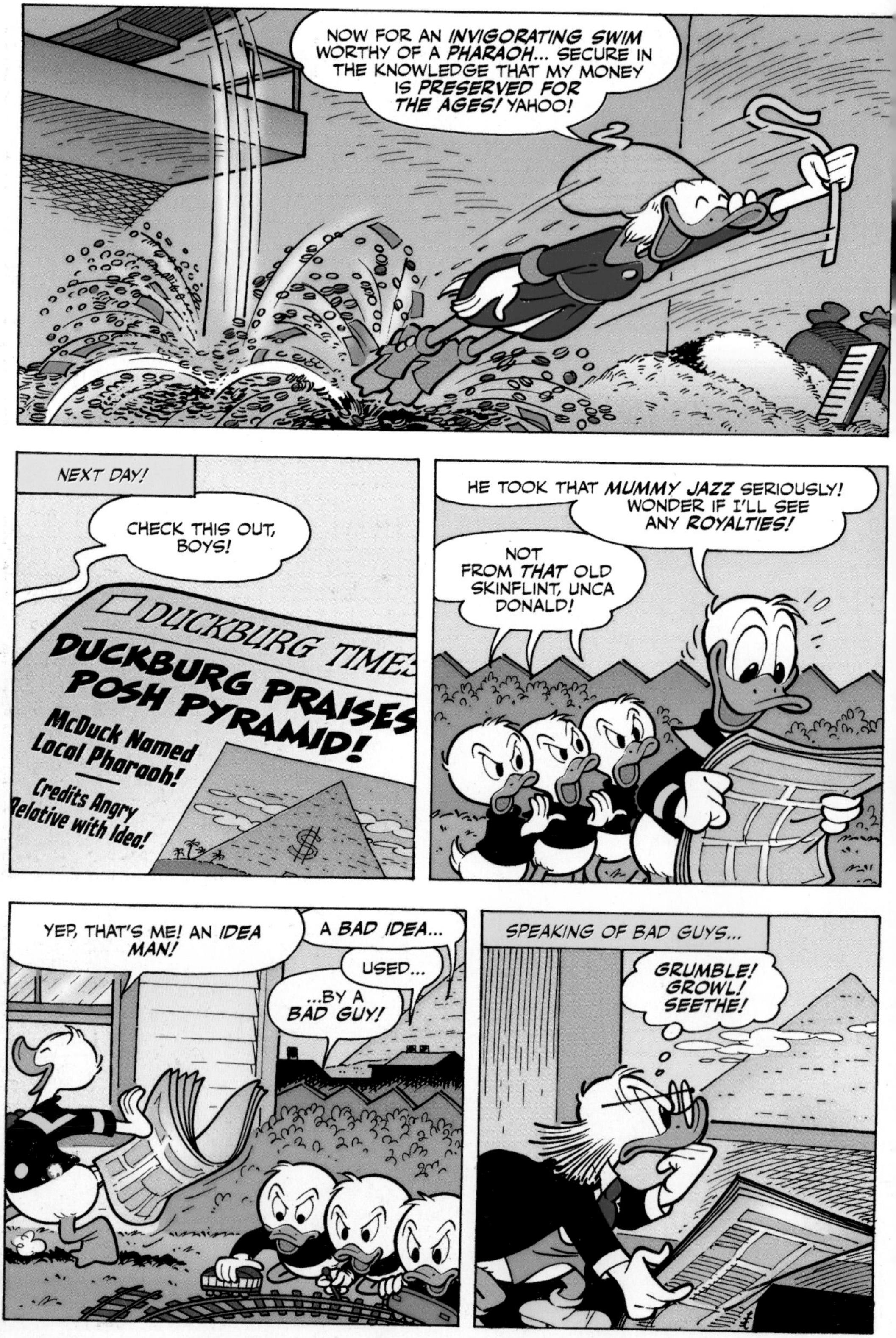

NOW FOR AN INVIGORATING SWIM WORTHY OF A PHARAOH... SECURE IN THE KNOWLEDGE THAT MY MONEY IS PRESERVED FOR THE AGES! YAHOO!
NEXT DAY!
CHECK THIS OUT, BOYS!
DUCKBURG TIMES
DUCKBURG PRAISES POSH PYRAMID!
McDuck Named Local Pharaoh!
Credits Angry Relative with Idea!
HE TOOK THAT MUMMY JAZZ SERIOUSLY! WONDER IF I'LL SEE ANY ROYALTIES!
NOT FROM THAT OLD SKINFLINT, UNCA DONALD!
YEP, THAT'S ME! AN IDEA MAN!
A BAD IDEA...
USED...
...BY A BAD GUY!
SPEAKING OF BAD GUYS...
GRUMBLE! GROWL! SEETHE!

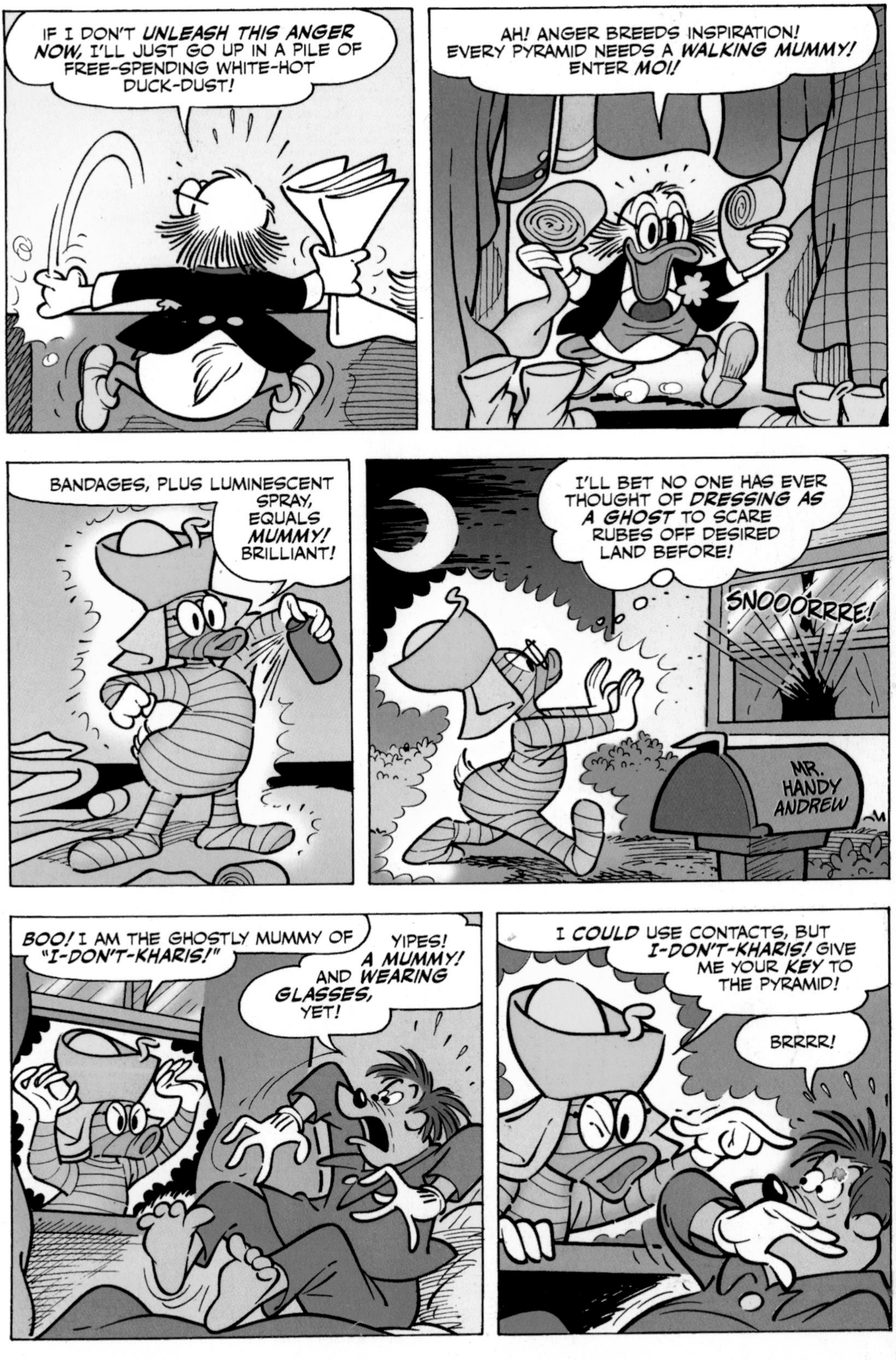
IF I DON'T *UNLEASH THIS ANGER NOW,* I'LL JUST GO UP IN A PILE OF FREE-SPENDING WHITE-HOT DUCK-DUST!
AH! ANGER BREEDS INSPIRATION! EVERY PYRAMID NEEDS A *WALKING MUMMY!* ENTER *MOI!*
BANDAGES, PLUS LUMINESCENT SPRAY, EQUALS *MUMMY!* BRILLIANT!
I'LL BET NO ONE HAS EVER THOUGHT OF *DRESSING AS A GHOST* TO SCARE RUBES OFF DESIRED LAND BEFORE!
SNOOORRRE!
MR. HANDY ANDREW
BOO! I AM THE GHOSTLY MUMMY OF *"I-DON'T-KHARIS!"*
YIPES! *A MUMMY!* AND *WEARING GLASSES,* YET!
I *COULD* USE CONTACTS, BUT *I-DON'T-KHARIS!* GIVE ME YOUR *KEY* TO THE PYRAMID!
BRRRR!

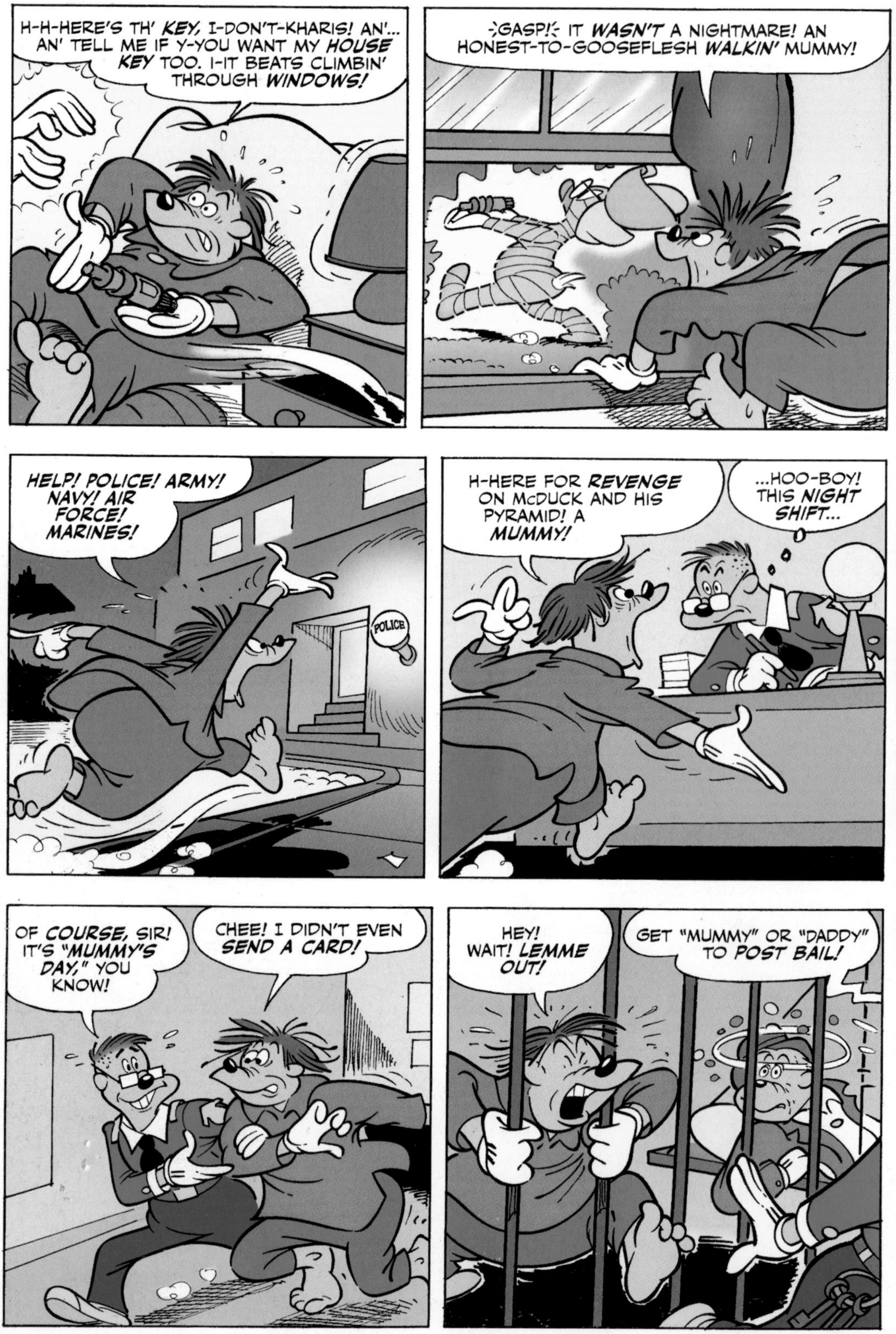
H-H-HERE'S TH' KEY, I-DON'T-KHARIS! AN'... AN' TELL ME IF Y-YOU WANT MY HOUSE KEY TOO. I-IT BEATS CLIMBIN' THROUGH WINDOWS!
GASP! IT WASN'T A NIGHTMARE! AN HONEST-TO-GOOSEFLESH WALKIN' MUMMY!
HELP! POLICE! ARMY! NAVY! AIR FORCE! MARINES!
POLICE
H-HERE FOR REVENGE ON McDUCK AND HIS PYRAMID! A MUMMY!
...HOO-BOY! THIS NIGHT SHIFT...
OF COURSE, SIR! IT'S "MUMMY'S DAY," YOU KNOW!
CHEE! I DIDN'T EVEN SEND A CARD!
HEY! WAIT! LEMME OUT!
GET "MUMMY" OR "DADDY" TO POST BAIL!

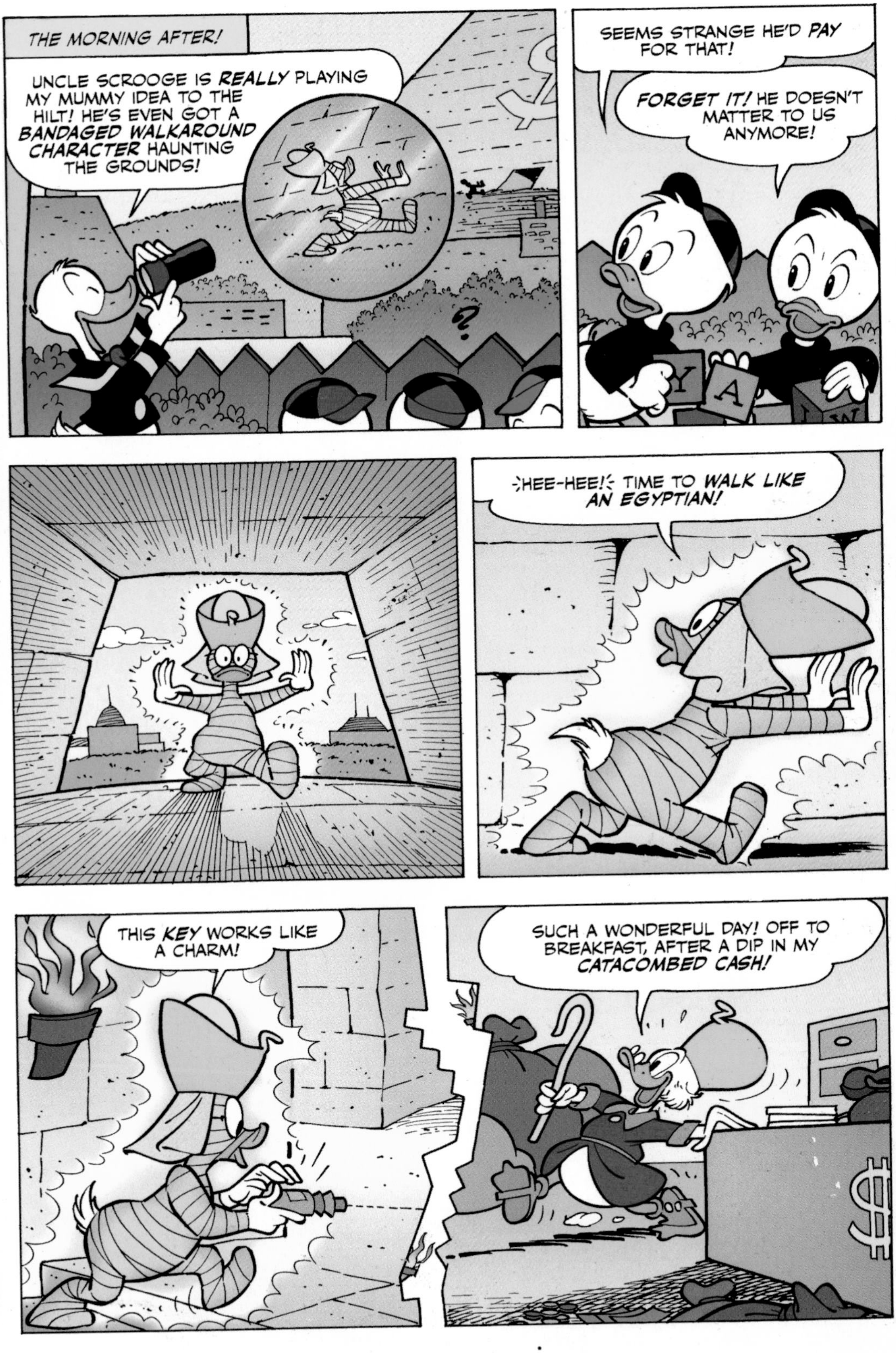
THE MORNING AFTER!
UNCLE SCROOGE IS REALLY PLAYING MY MUMMY IDEA TO THE HILT! HE'S EVEN GOT A BANDAGED WALKAROUND CHARACTER HAUNTING THE GROUNDS!
SEEMS STRANGE HE'D PAY FOR THAT!
FORGET IT! HE DOESN'T MATTER TO US ANYMORE!
HEE-HEE! TIME TO WALK LIKE AN EGYPTIAN!
THIS KEY WORKS LIKE A CHARM!
SUCH A WONDERFUL DAY! OFF TO BREAKFAST, AFTER A DIP IN MY CATACOMBED CASH!

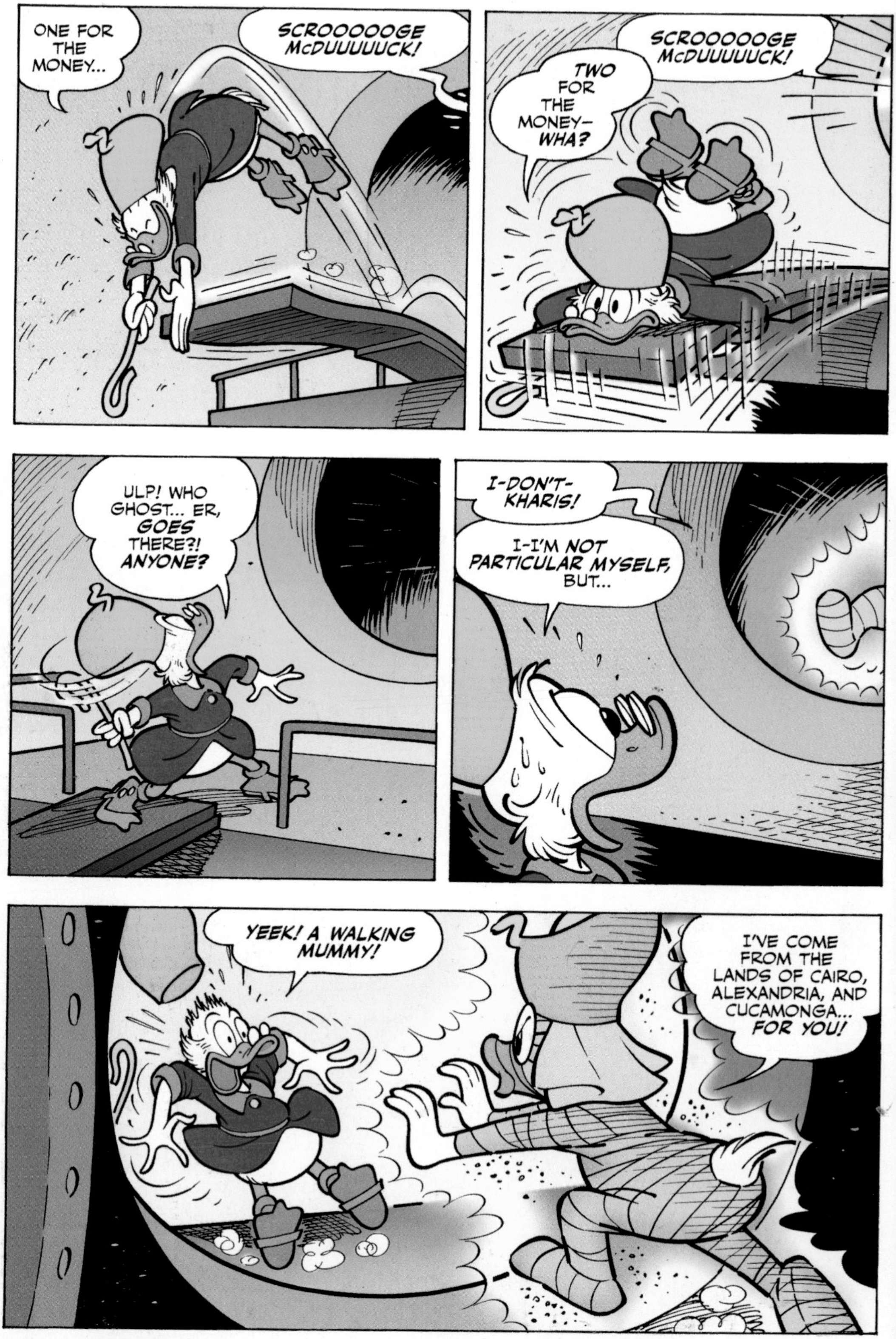
ONE FOR THE MONEY...
SCROOOOOGE McDUUUUUCK!
SCROOOOOGE McDUUUUUCK!
TWO FOR THE MONEY— WHA?
ULP! WHO GHOST... ER, GOES THERE?! ANYONE?
I-DON'T-KHARIS!
I-I'M NOT PARTICULAR MYSELF, BUT...
YEEK! A WALKING MUMMY!
I'VE COME FROM THE LANDS OF CAIRO, ALEXANDRIA, AND CUCAMONGA... FOR YOU!

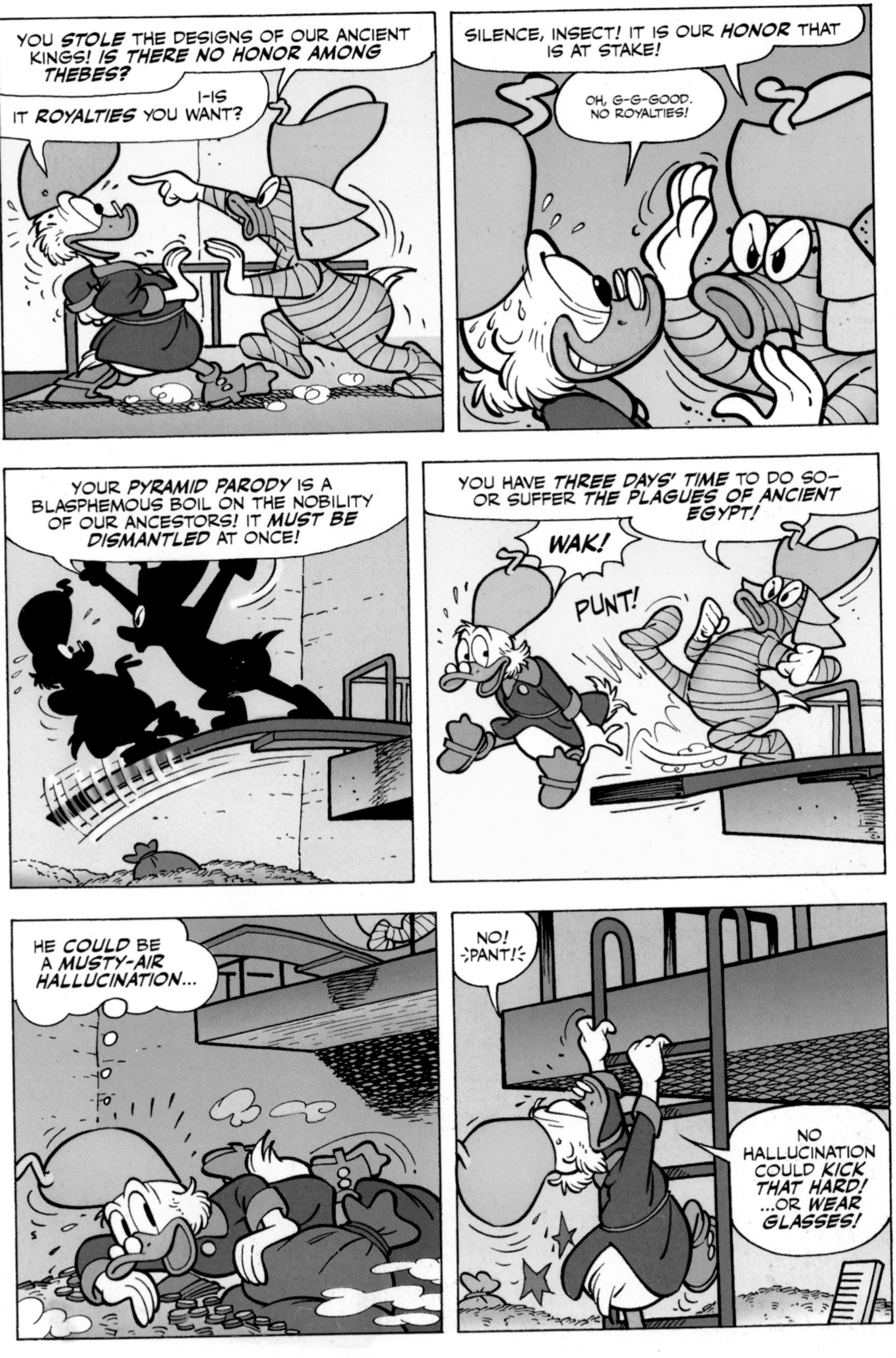
YOU STOLE THE DESIGNS OF OUR ANCIENT KINGS! IS THERE NO HONOR AMONG THEBES?
I-IS IT ROYALTIES YOU WANT?
SILENCE, INSECT! IT IS OUR HONOR THAT IS AT STAKE!
OH, G-G-GOOD. NO ROYALTIES!
YOUR PYRAMID PARODY IS A BLASPHEMOUS BOIL ON THE NOBILITY OF OUR ANCESTORS! IT MUST BE DISMANTLED AT ONCE!
YOU HAVE THREE DAYS' TIME TO DO SO— OR SUFFER THE PLAGUES OF ANCIENT EGYPT!
WAK!
PUNT!
HE COULD BE A MUSTY-AIR HALLUCINATION...
NO! PANT!
NO HALLUCINATION COULD KICK THAT HARD! ...OR WEAR GLASSES!

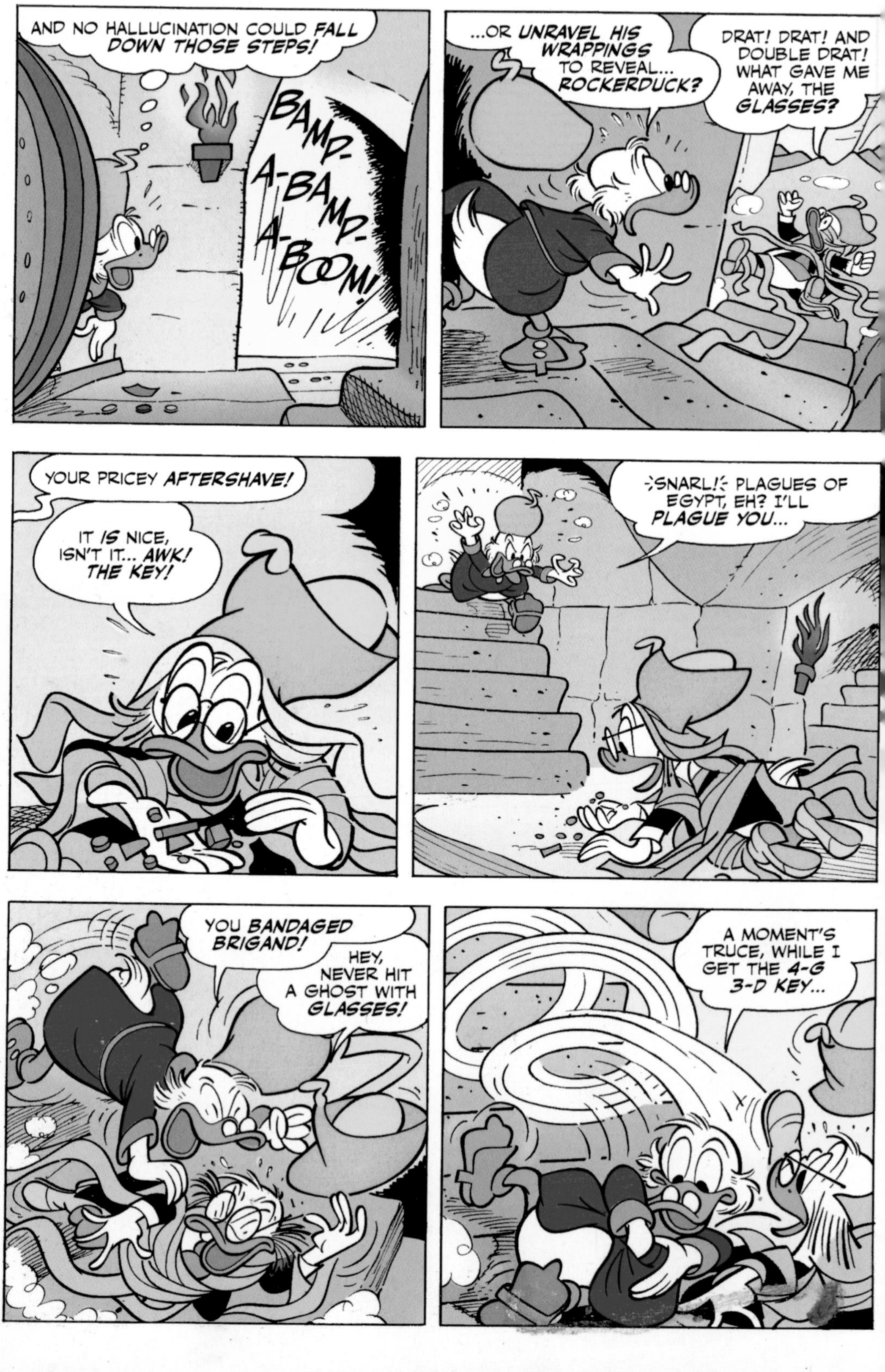
AND NO HALLUCINATION COULD FALL DOWN THOSE STEPS!
BAMP-A-BAMP-A-BOOM!
...OR UNRAVEL HIS WRAPPINGS TO REVEAL... ROCKERDUCK?
DRAT! DRAT! AND DOUBLE DRAT! WHAT GAVE ME AWAY, THE GLASSES?
YOUR PRICEY AFTERSHAVE!
IT IS NICE, ISN'T IT... AWK! THE KEY!
SNARL! PLAGUES OF EGYPT, EH? I'LL PLAGUE YOU...
YOU BANDAGED BRIGAND!
HEY, NEVER HIT A GHOST WITH GLASSES!
A MOMENT'S TRUCE, WHILE I GET THE 4-G 3-D KEY...

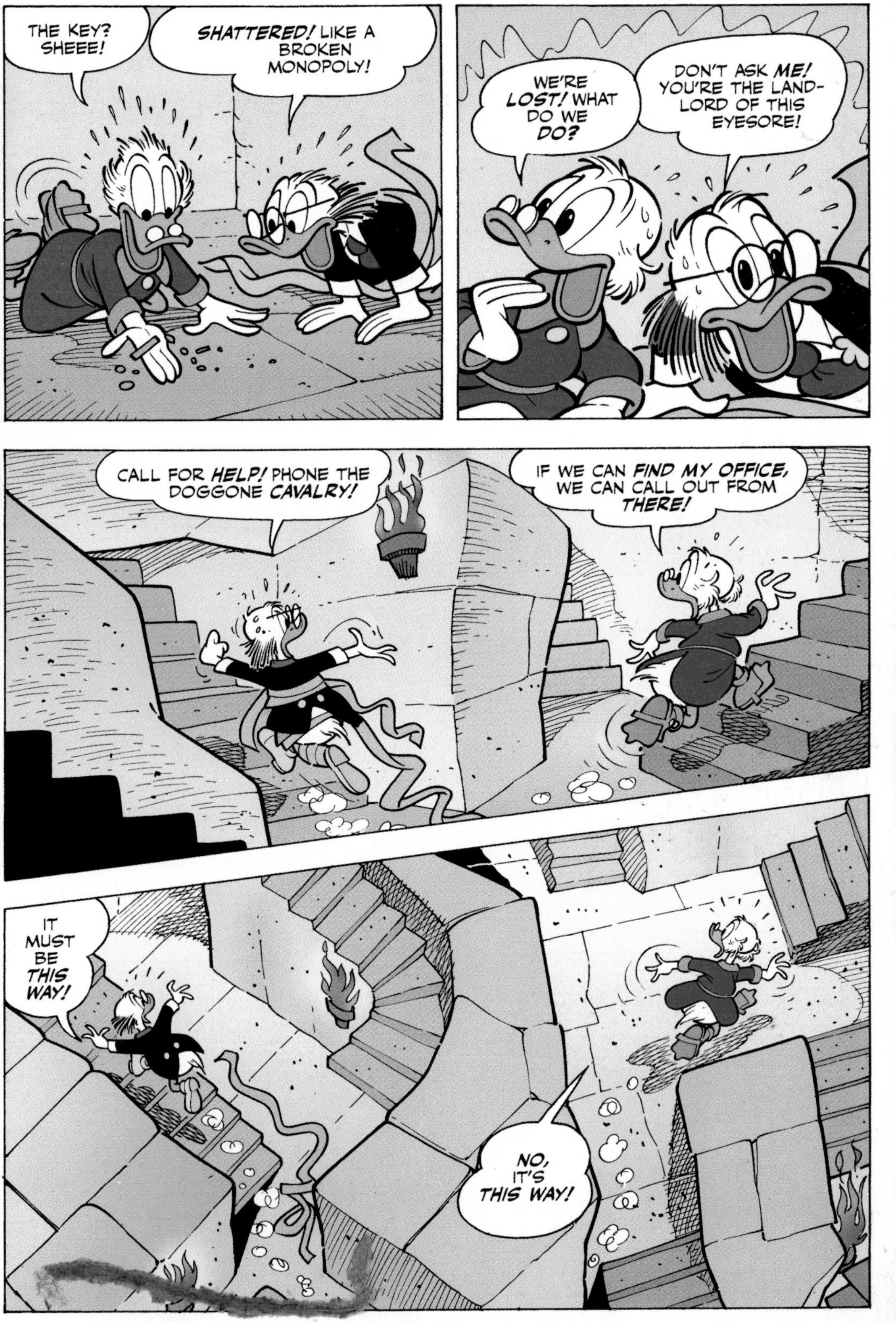
THE KEY? SHEEE!
SHATTERED! LIKE A BROKEN MONOPOLY!
WE'RE LOST! WHAT DO WE DO?
DON'T ASK ME! YOU'RE THE LAND-LORD OF THIS EYESORE!
CALL FOR HELP! PHONE THE DOGGONE CAVALRY!
IF WE CAN FIND MY OFFICE, WE CAN CALL OUT FROM THERE!
IT MUST BE THIS WAY!
NO, IT'S THIS WAY!

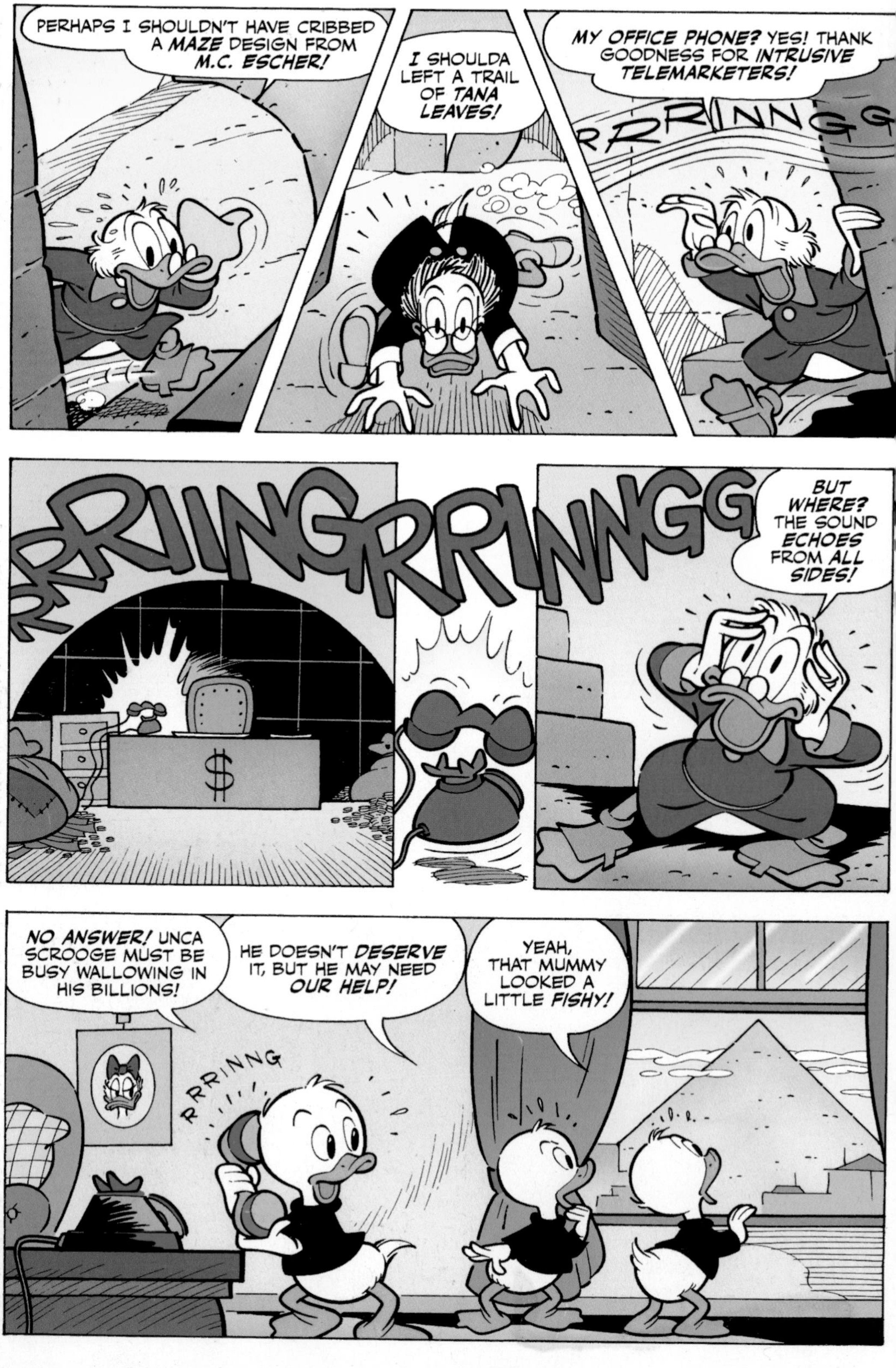
PERHAPS I SHOULDN'T HAVE CRIBBED A MAZE DESIGN FROM M.C. ESCHER!
I SHOULDA LEFT A TRAIL OF TANA LEAVES!
MY OFFICE PHONE? YES! THANK GOODNESS FOR INTRUSIVE TELEMARKETERS!
RRRINNGG
RRRIINGRRRINNGG
BUT WHERE? THE SOUND ECHOES FROM ALL SIDES!
NO ANSWER! UNCA SCROOGE MUST BE BUSY WALLOWING IN HIS BILLIONS!
HE DOESN'T DESERVE IT, BUT HE MAY NEED OUR HELP!
YEAH, THAT MUMMY LOOKED A LITTLE FISHY!
RRRINNG

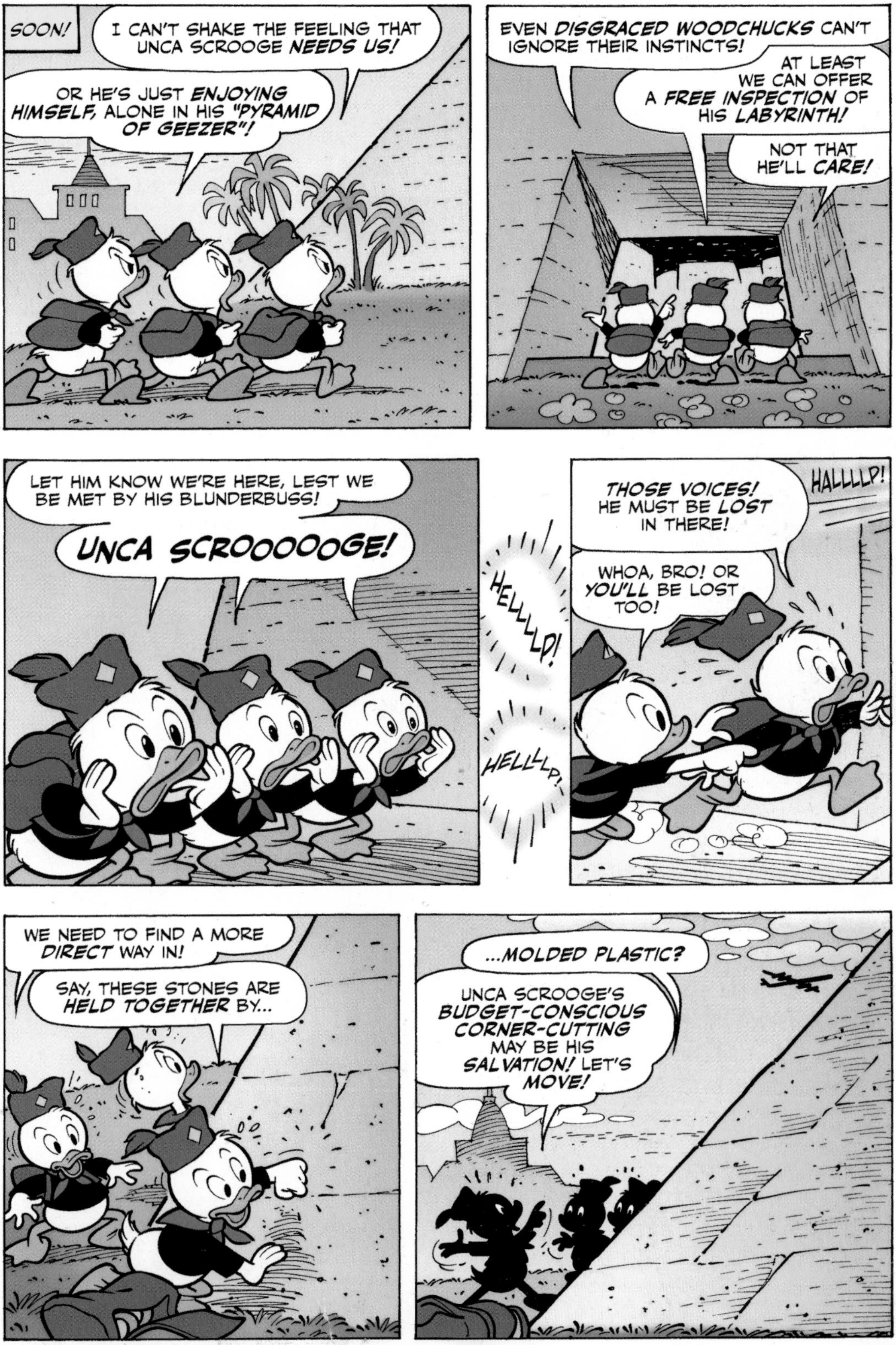
SOON!
I CAN'T SHAKE THE FEELING THAT UNCA SCROOGE NEEDS US!
OR HE'S JUST ENJOYING HIMSELF, ALONE IN HIS "PYRAMID OF GEEZER"!
EVEN DISGRACED WOODCHUCKS CAN'T IGNORE THEIR INSTINCTS!
AT LEAST WE CAN OFFER A FREE INSPECTION OF HIS LABYRINTH!
NOT THAT HE'LL CARE!
LET HIM KNOW WE'RE HERE, LEST WE BE MET BY HIS BLUNDERBUSS!
UNCA SCROOOOOGE!
HELLLLLP!
HELLLLP!
HALLLLP!
THOSE VOICES! HE MUST BE LOST IN THERE!
WHOA, BRO! OR YOU'LL BE LOST TOO!
WE NEED TO FIND A MORE DIRECT WAY IN!
SAY, THESE STONES ARE HELD TOGETHER BY...
...MOLDED PLASTIC?
UNCA SCROOGE'S BUDGET-CONSCIOUS CORNER-CUTTING MAY BE HIS SALVATION! LET'S MOVE!

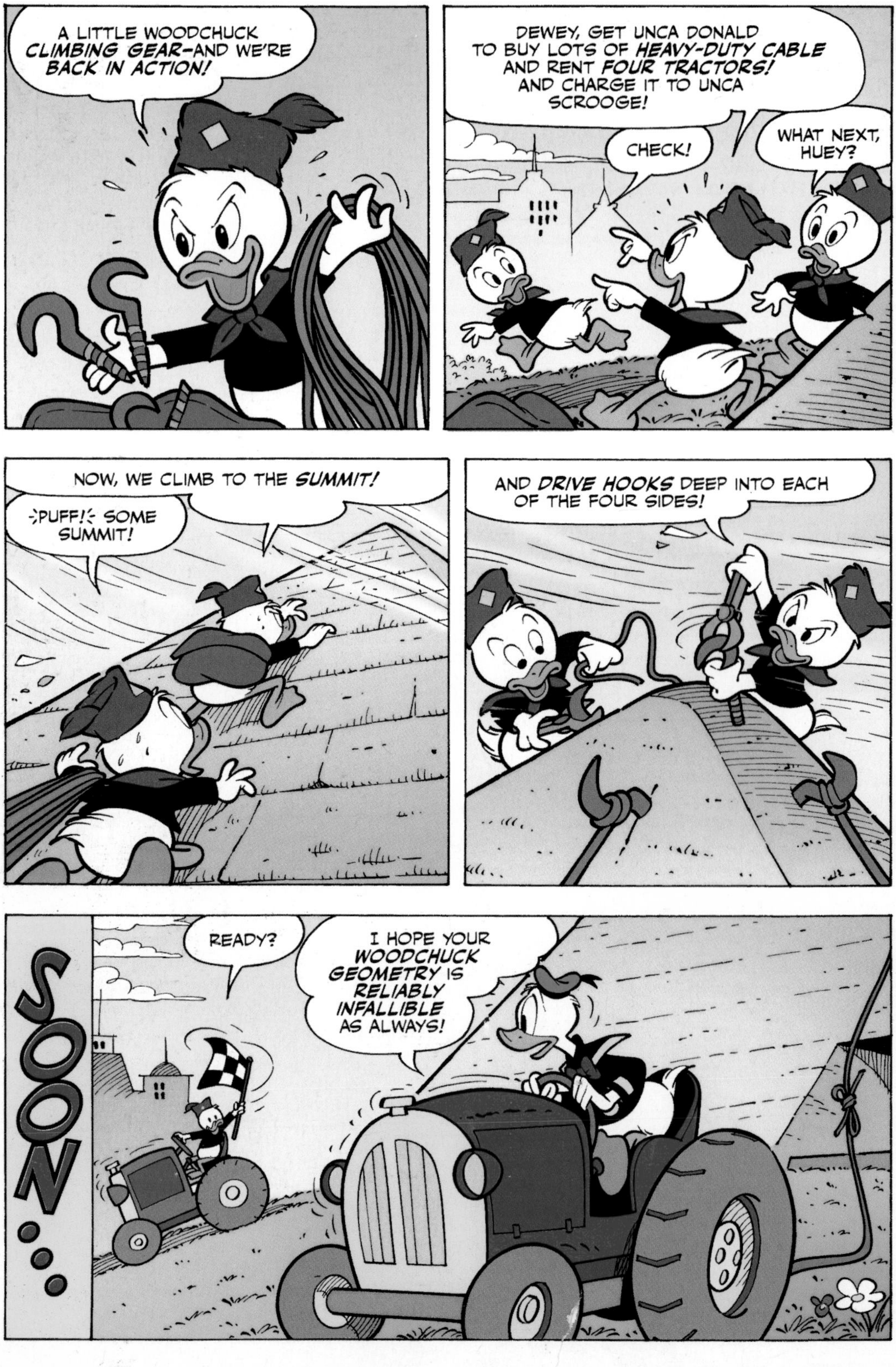
A LITTLE WOODCHUCK *CLIMBING GEAR*–AND WE'RE *BACK IN ACTION!*
DEWEY, GET UNCA DONALD TO BUY LOTS OF *HEAVY-DUTY CABLE* AND RENT *FOUR TRACTORS!* AND CHARGE IT TO UNCA SCROOGE!
CHECK!
WHAT NEXT, HUEY?
NOW, WE CLIMB TO THE *SUMMIT!*
PUFF! SOME SUMMIT!
AND *DRIVE HOOKS* DEEP INTO EACH OF THE FOUR SIDES!
SOON...
READY?
I HOPE YOUR *WOODCHUCK GEOMETRY* IS *RELIABLY INFALLIBLE* AS ALWAYS!

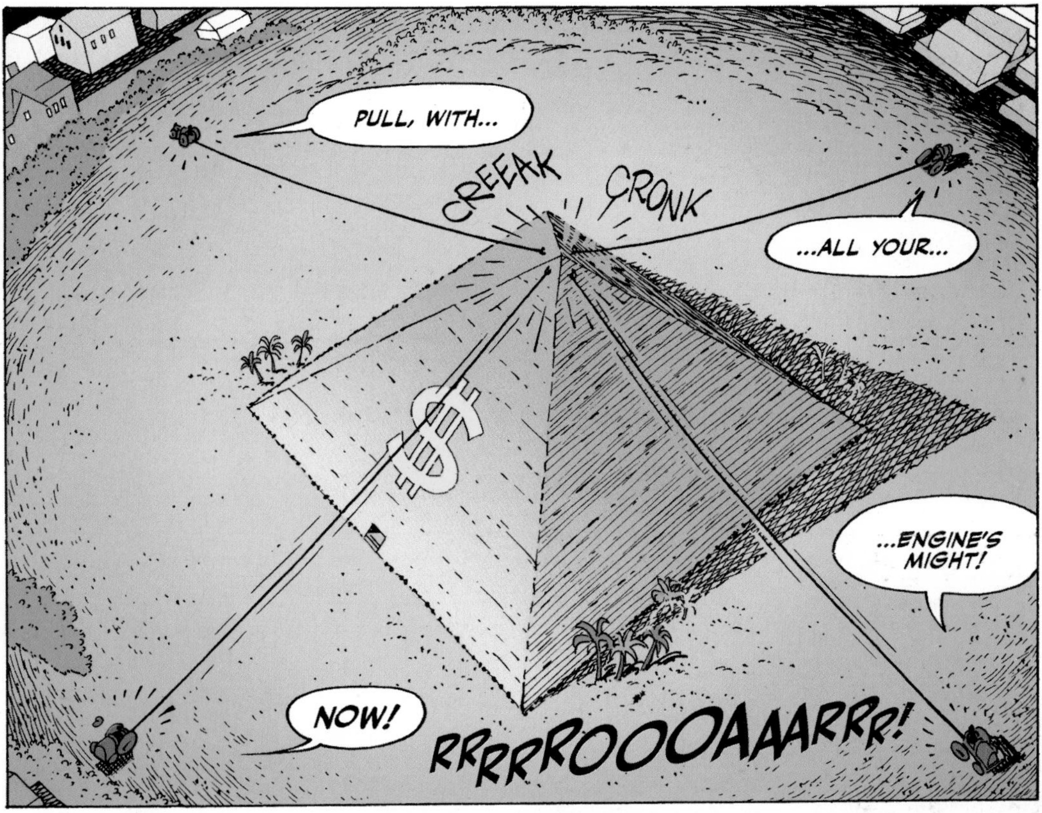
PULL, WITH...
CREEAK
CRONK
...ALL YOUR...
...ENGINE'S MIGHT!
NOW!
RRRRROOOAAARRR!

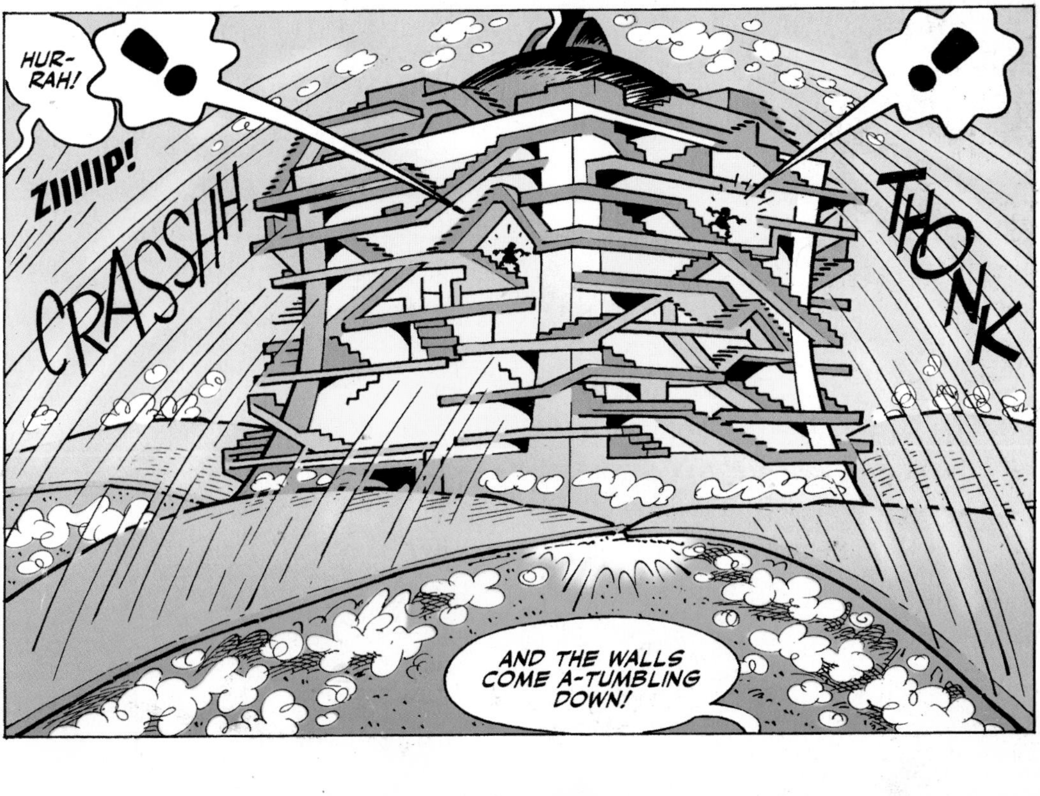
HUR-RAH!
!
!
ZIIIIP!
CRASSHH
THONK
AND THE WALLS COME A-TUMBLING DOWN!

ONE 9-1-1 CALL LATER!

WE'RE NOT THE HEROES TODAY! THE CREDIT ALL GOES TO THOSE *RESOURCEFUL KIDS!*

REALLY?

NUTS! WITH ALL THIS *RUBBLE,* NOW THE *VIEW IS WORSE THAN EVER!*

NOT AS BAD AS LOOKING AT *YOUR FACE!*

I'LL JUST VIEW MY CONDOS *CLOSE-UP* BY *WALKING* TO THE DOCKS.

I HOPE YOU GET *BLISTERS!*

SUB-WOODCHUCKS WE MAY BE...

JUST A MOMENT, LADS...

...BUT *WE STILL GOT IT!* YEAH!

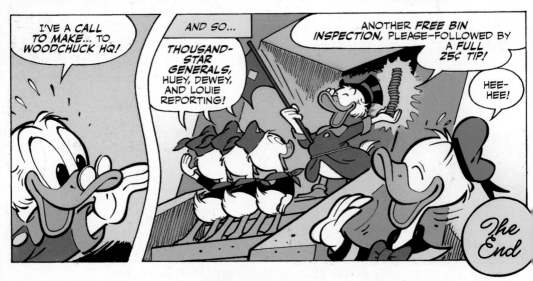

I'VE A *CALL TO MAKE...* TO WOODCHUCK HQ!

AND SO...

THOUSAND-STAR GENERALS, HUEY, DEWEY, AND LOUIE REPORTING!

ANOTHER *FREE BIN INSPECTION,* PLEASE—FOLLOWED BY A *FULL 25¢ TIP!*

HEE-HEE!

The End

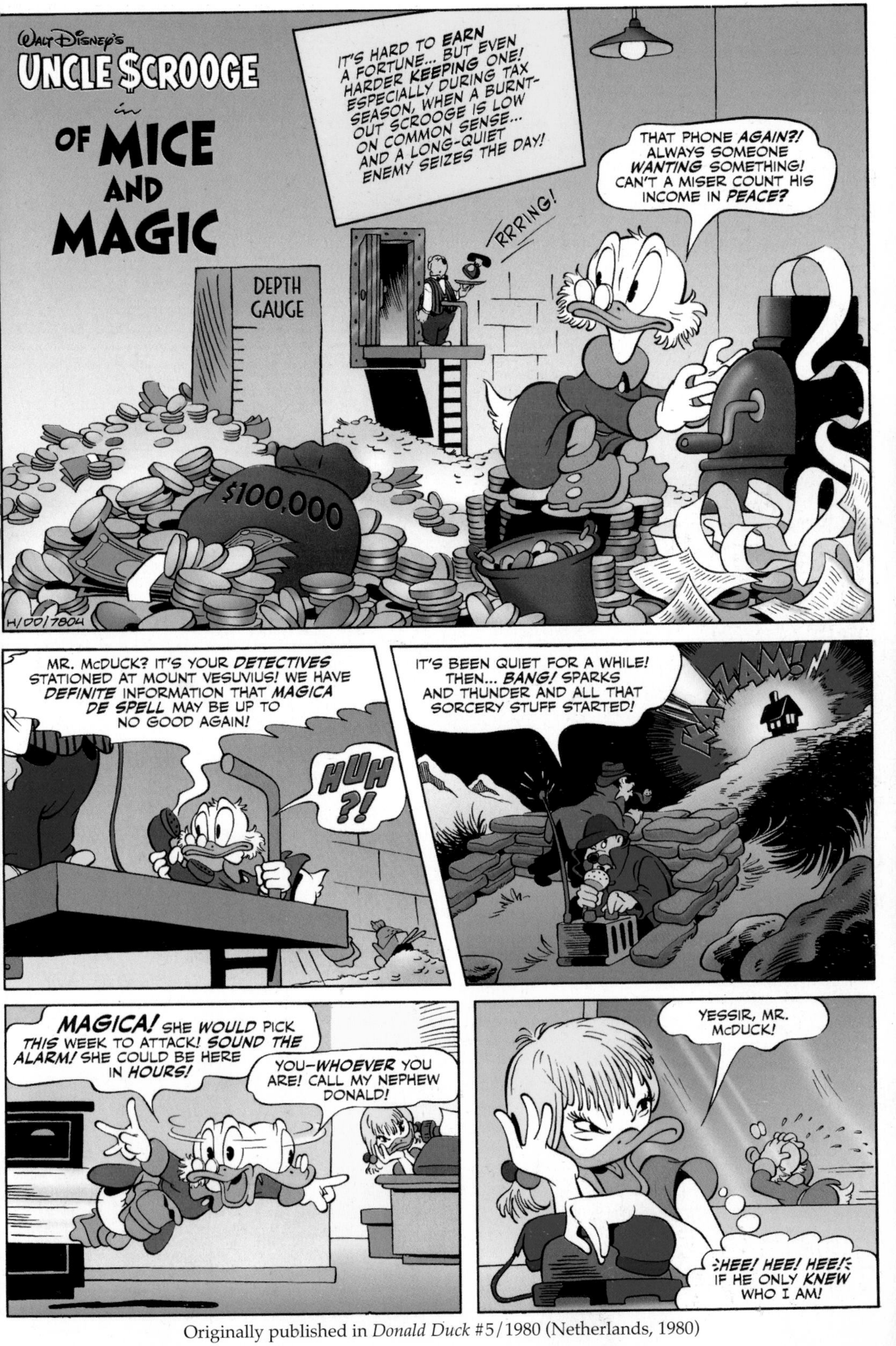

WALT DISNEY'S
UNCLE $CROOGE
in
OF MICE AND MAGIC
IT'S HARD TO EARN A FORTUNE... BUT EVEN HARDER KEEPING ONE! ESPECIALLY DURING TAX SEASON, WHEN A BURNT-OUT SCROOGE IS LOW ON COMMON SENSE... AND A LONG-QUIET ENEMY SEIZES THE DAY!
THAT PHONE AGAIN?! ALWAYS SOMEONE WANTING SOMETHING! CAN'T A MISER COUNT HIS INCOME IN PEACE?
RRRING!
DEPTH GAUGE
$100,000
H/00/7804
MR. McDUCK? IT'S YOUR DETECTIVES STATIONED AT MOUNT VESUVIUS! WE HAVE DEFINITE INFORMATION THAT MAGICA DE SPELL MAY BE UP TO NO GOOD AGAIN!
HUH?!
IT'S BEEN QUIET FOR A WHILE! THEN... BANG! SPARKS AND THUNDER AND ALL THAT SORCERY STUFF STARTED!
KA-ZAM!
MAGICA! SHE WOULD PICK THIS WEEK TO ATTACK! SOUND THE ALARM! SHE COULD BE HERE IN HOURS!
YOU—WHOEVER YOU ARE! CALL MY NEPHEW DONALD!
YESSIR, MR. McDUCK!
HEE! HEE! HEE! IF HE ONLY KNEW WHO I AM!

Originally published in *Donald Duck* #5/1980 (Netherlands, 1980)

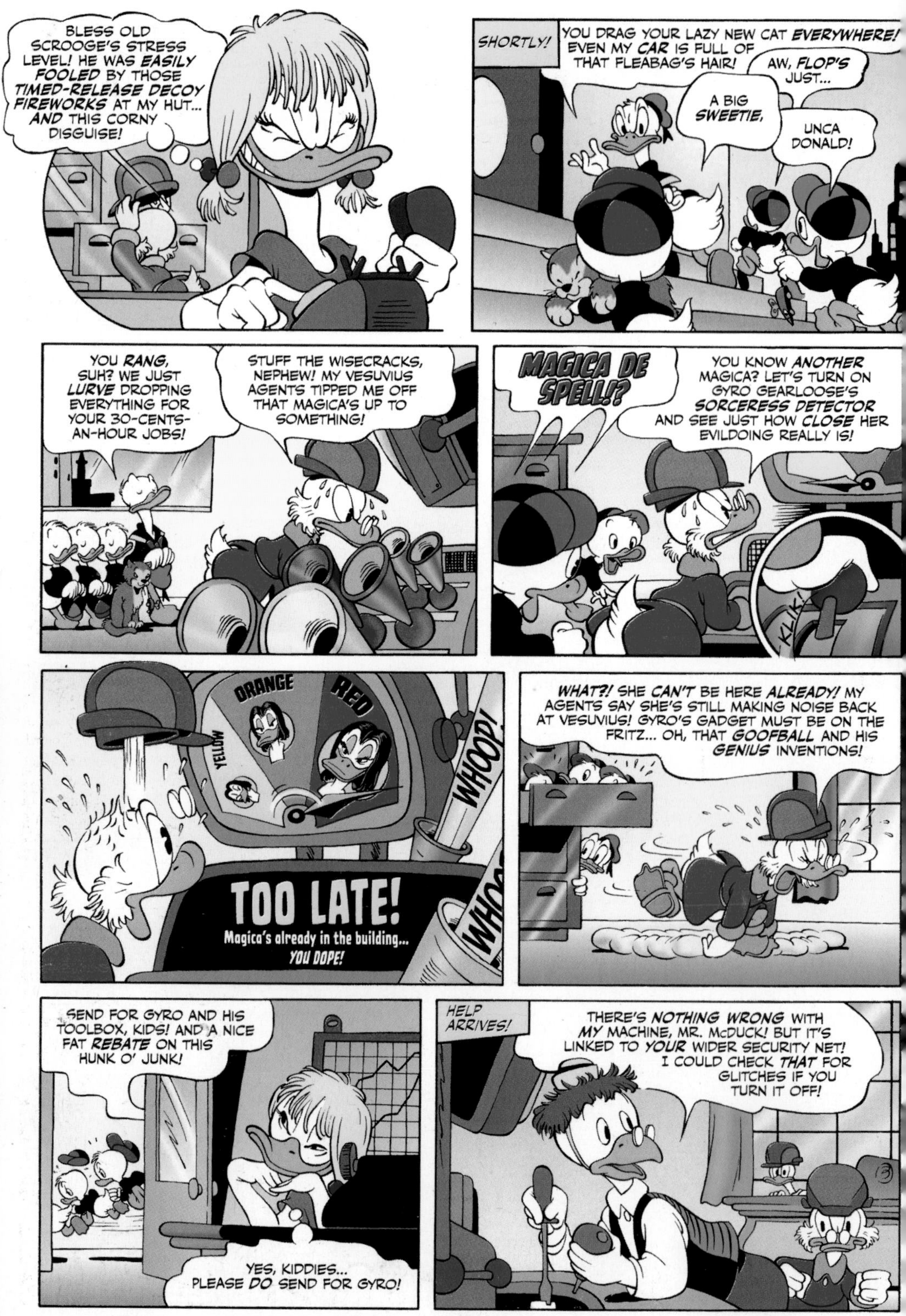
BLESS OLD SCROOGE'S STRESS LEVEL! HE WAS EASILY FOOLED BY THOSE TIMED-RELEASE DECOY FIREWORKS AT MY HUT... AND THIS CORNY DISGUISE!
SHORTLY!
YOU DRAG YOUR LAZY NEW CAT EVERYWHERE! EVEN MY CAR IS FULL OF THAT FLEABAG'S HAIR!
AW, FLOP'S JUST...
A BIG SWEETIE,
UNCA DONALD!
YOU RANG, SUH? WE JUST LURVE DROPPING EVERYTHING FOR YOUR 30-CENTS-AN-HOUR JOBS!
STUFF THE WISECRACKS, NEPHEW! MY VESUVIUS AGENTS TIPPED ME OFF THAT MAGICA'S UP TO SOMETHING!
MAGICA DE SPELL!?
YOU KNOW ANOTHER MAGICA? LET'S TURN ON GYRO GEARLOOSE'S SORCERESS DETECTOR AND SEE JUST HOW CLOSE HER EVILDOING REALLY IS!
KLIK!
ORANGE
RED
YELLOW
WHOOP!
TOO LATE!
Magica's already in the building... YOU DOPE!
WHOOP
WHAT?! SHE CAN'T BE HERE ALREADY! MY AGENTS SAY SHE'S STILL MAKING NOISE BACK AT VESUVIUS! GYRO'S GADGET MUST BE ON THE FRITZ... OH, THAT GOOFBALL AND HIS GENIUS INVENTIONS!
SEND FOR GYRO AND HIS TOOLBOX, KIDS! AND A NICE FAT REBATE ON THIS HUNK O' JUNK!
YES, KIDDIES... PLEASE DO SEND FOR GYRO!
HELP ARRIVES!
THERE'S NOTHING WRONG WITH MY MACHINE, MR. McDUCK! BUT IT'S LINKED TO YOUR WIDER SECURITY NET! I COULD CHECK THAT FOR GLITCHES IF YOU TURN IT OFF!

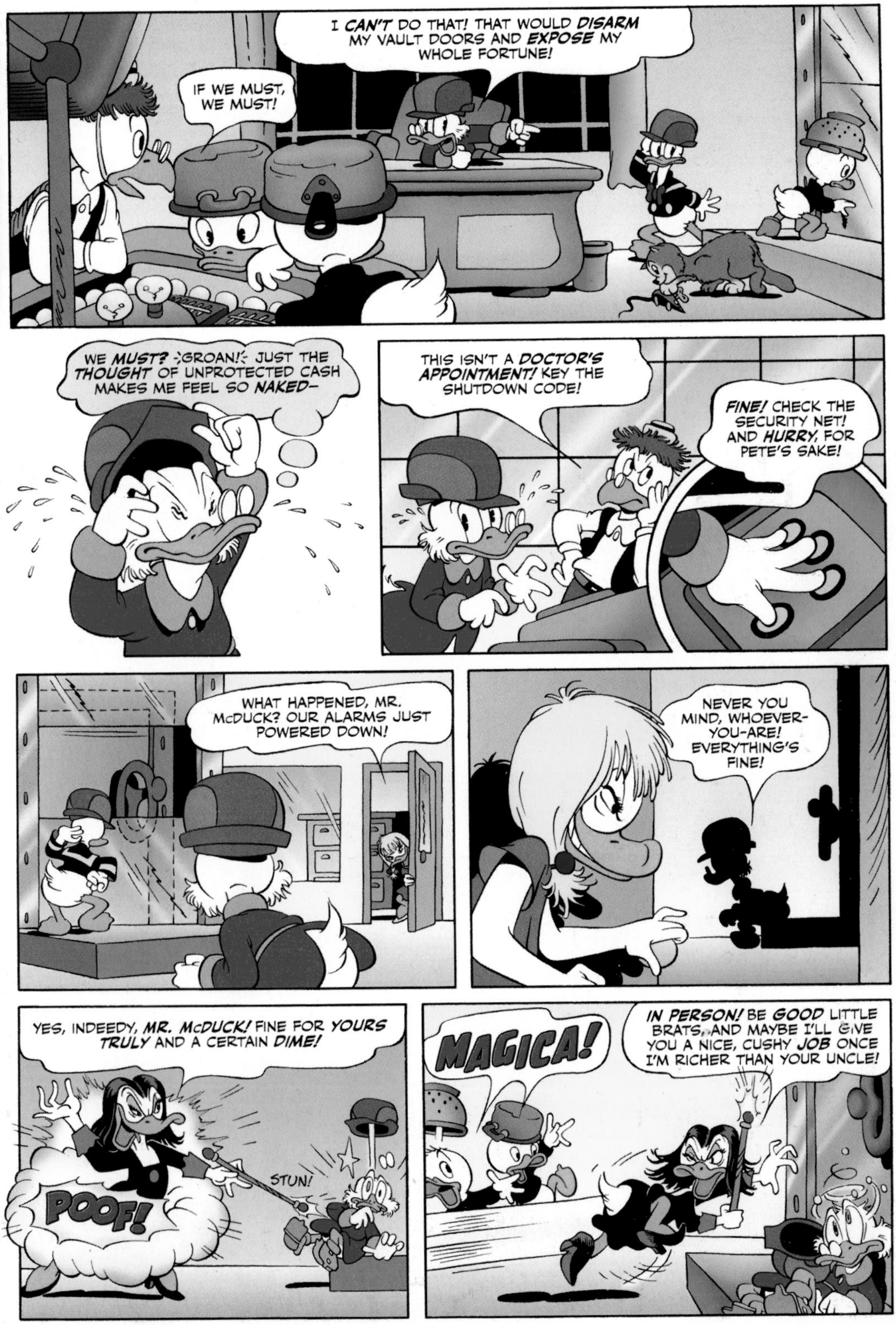
I CAN'T DO THAT! THAT WOULD DISARM MY VAULT DOORS AND EXPOSE MY WHOLE FORTUNE!
IF WE MUST, WE MUST!
WE MUST? -GROAN!- JUST THE THOUGHT OF UNPROTECTED CASH MAKES ME FEEL SO NAKED—
THIS ISN'T A DOCTOR'S APPOINTMENT! KEY THE SHUTDOWN CODE!
FINE! CHECK THE SECURITY NET! AND HURRY, FOR PETE'S SAKE!
WHAT HAPPENED, MR. McDUCK? OUR ALARMS JUST POWERED DOWN!
NEVER YOU MIND, WHOEVER-YOU-ARE! EVERYTHING'S FINE!
YES, INDEEDY, MR. McDUCK! FINE FOR YOURS TRULY AND A CERTAIN DIME!
POOF!
STUN!
MAGICA!
IN PERSON! BE GOOD LITTLE BRATS, AND MAYBE I'LL GIVE YOU A NICE, CUSHY JOB ONCE I'M RICHER THAN YOUR UNCLE!

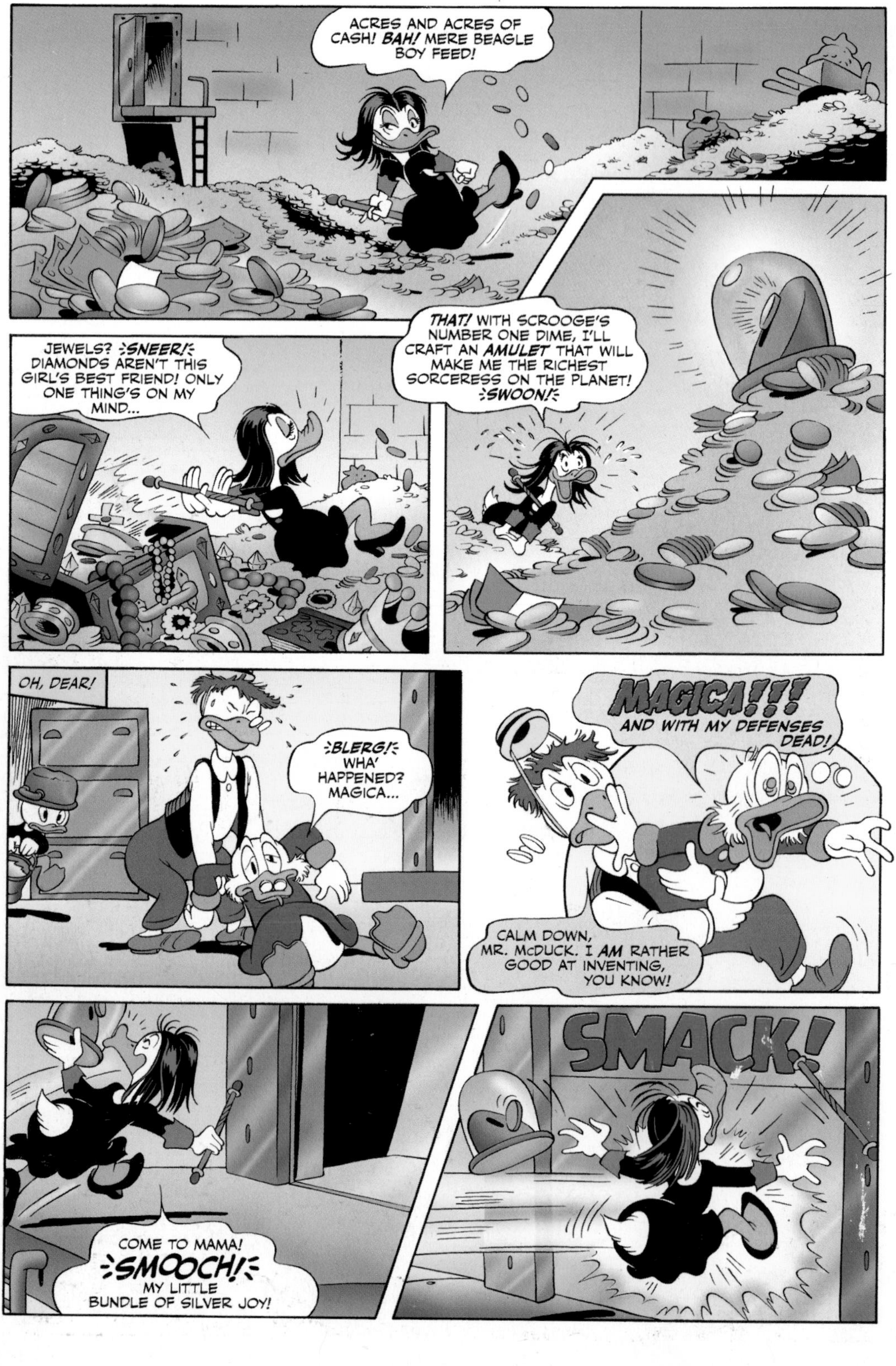
ACRES AND ACRES OF CASH! BAH! MERE BEAGLE BOY FEED!
JEWELS? SNEER! DIAMONDS AREN'T THIS GIRL'S BEST FRIEND! ONLY ONE THING'S ON MY MIND...
THAT! WITH SCROOGE'S NUMBER ONE DIME, I'LL CRAFT AN AMULET THAT WILL MAKE ME THE RICHEST SORCERESS ON THE PLANET! SWOON!
OH, DEAR!
BLERG! WHA' HAPPENED? MAGICA...
MAGICA!!!
AND WITH MY DEFENSES DEAD!
CALM DOWN, MR. McDUCK. I AM RATHER GOOD AT INVENTING, YOU KNOW!
COME TO MAMA! SMOOCH! MY LITTLE BUNDLE OF SILVER JOY!
SMACK!

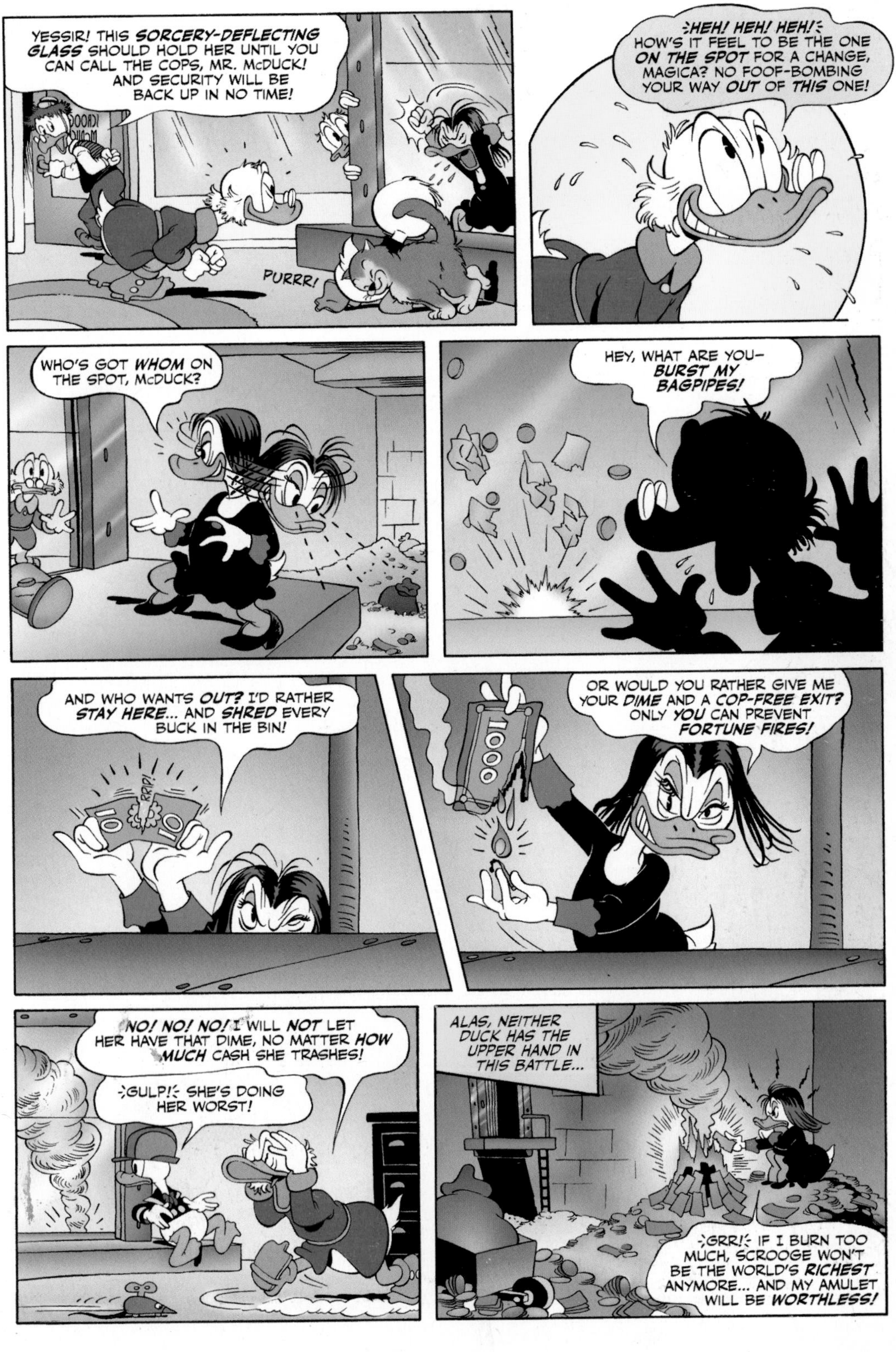
YESSIR! THIS SORCERY-DEFLECTING GLASS SHOULD HOLD HER UNTIL YOU CAN CALL THE COPS, MR. McDUCK! AND SECURITY WILL BE BACK UP IN NO TIME!
PURRR!
HEH! HEH! HEH! HOW'S IT FEEL TO BE THE ONE ON THE SPOT FOR A CHANGE, MAGICA? NO FOOF-BOMBING YOUR WAY OUT OF THIS ONE!
WHO'S GOT WHOM ON THE SPOT, McDUCK?
HEY, WHAT ARE YOU— BURST MY BAGPIPES!
AND WHO WANTS OUT? I'D RATHER STAY HERE... AND SHRED EVERY BUCK IN THE BIN!
RRIP!
OR WOULD YOU RATHER GIVE ME YOUR DIME AND A COP-FREE EXIT? ONLY YOU CAN PREVENT FORTUNE FIRES!
NO! NO! NO! I WILL NOT LET HER HAVE THAT DIME, NO MATTER HOW MUCH CASH SHE TRASHES!
GULP! SHE'S DOING HER WORST!
ALAS, NEITHER DUCK HAS THE UPPER HAND IN THIS BATTLE...
GRR! IF I BURN TOO MUCH, SCROOGE WON'T BE THE WORLD'S RICHEST ANYMORE... AND MY AMULET WILL BE WORTHLESS!

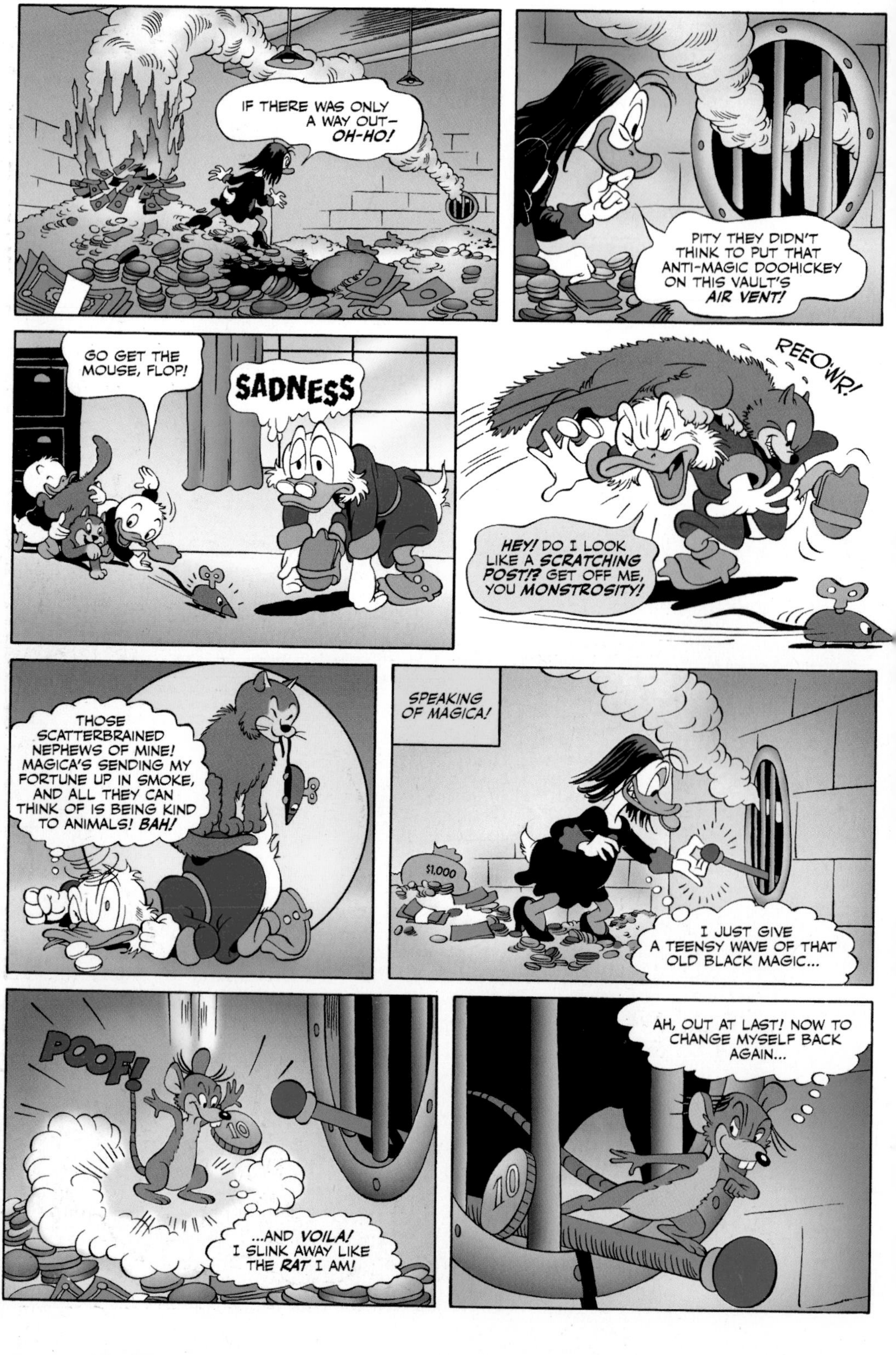
IF THERE WAS ONLY A WAY OUT— OH-HO!
PITY THEY DIDN'T THINK TO PUT THAT ANTI-MAGIC DOOHICKEY ON THIS VAULT'S AIR VENT!
GO GET THE MOUSE, FLOP!
SADNESS
REEOWR!
HEY! DO I LOOK LIKE A SCRATCHING POST!? GET OFF ME, YOU MONSTROSITY!
THOSE SCATTERBRAINED NEPHEWS OF MINE! MAGICA'S SENDING MY FORTUNE UP IN SMOKE, AND ALL THEY CAN THINK OF IS BEING KIND TO ANIMALS! BAH!
SPEAKING OF MAGICA!
$1,000
I JUST GIVE A TEENSY WAVE OF THAT OLD BLACK MAGIC...
POOF!
10
...AND VOILA! I SLINK AWAY LIKE THE RAT I AM!
AH, OUT AT LAST! NOW TO CHANGE MYSELF BACK AGAIN...
10

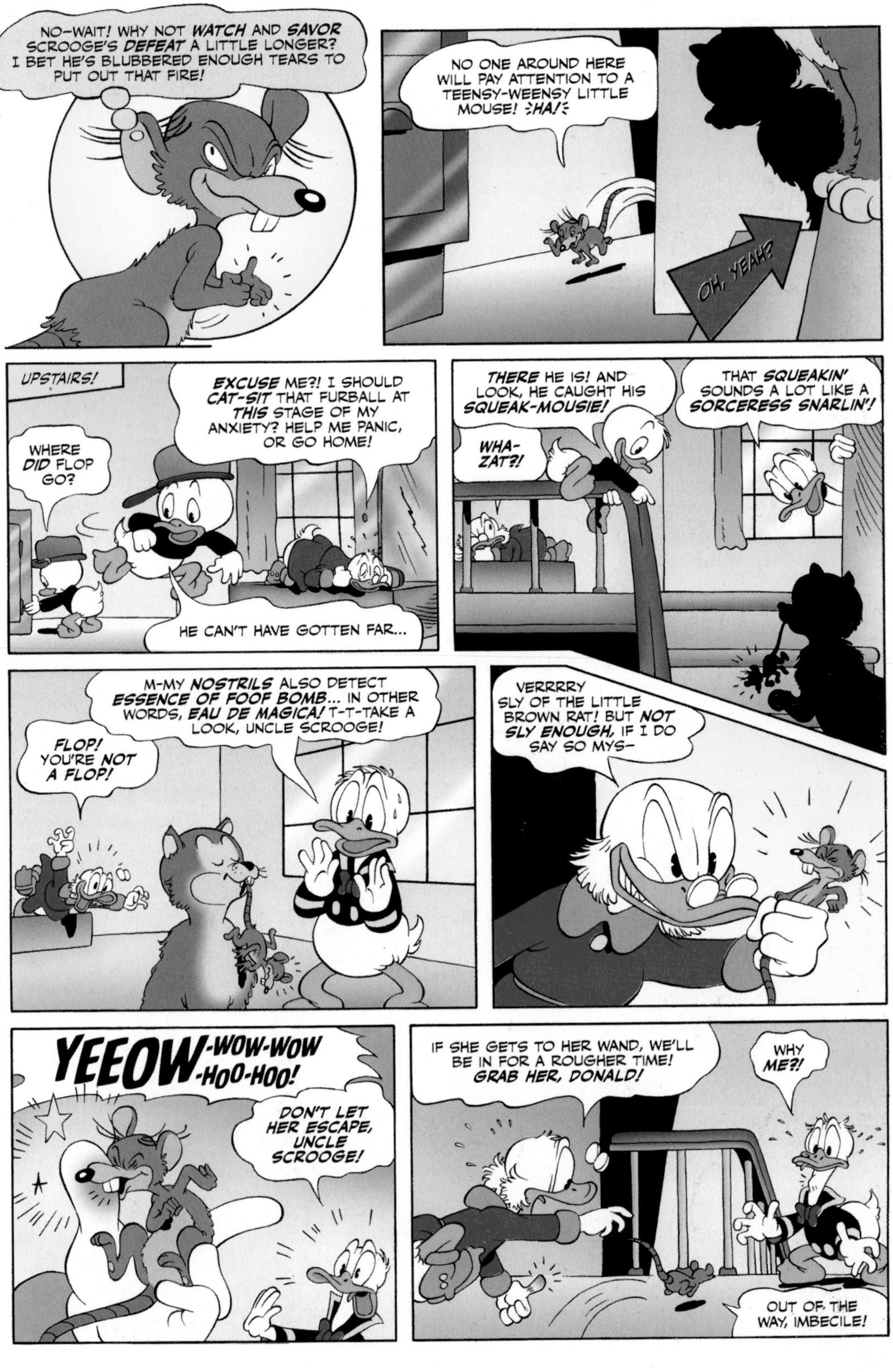
NO—WAIT! WHY NOT WATCH AND SAVOR SCROOGE'S DEFEAT A LITTLE LONGER? I BET HE'S BLUBBERED ENOUGH TEARS TO PUT OUT THAT FIRE!
NO ONE AROUND HERE WILL PAY ATTENTION TO A TEENSY-WEENSY LITTLE MOUSE! HA!
OH, YEAH?
UPSTAIRS!
WHERE DID FLOP GO?
EXCUSE ME?! I SHOULD CAT-SIT THAT FURBALL AT THIS STAGE OF MY ANXIETY? HELP ME PANIC, OR GO HOME!
HE CAN'T HAVE GOTTEN FAR...
THERE HE IS! AND LOOK, HE CAUGHT HIS SQUEAK-MOUSIE!
WHA-ZAT?!
THAT SQUEAKIN' SOUNDS A LOT LIKE A SORCERESS SNARLIN'!
FLOP! YOU'RE NOT A FLOP!
M-MY NOSTRILS ALSO DETECT ESSENCE OF FOOF BOMB... IN OTHER WORDS, EAU DE MAGICA! T-T-TAKE A LOOK, UNCLE SCROOGE!
VERRRRY SLY OF THE LITTLE BROWN RAT! BUT NOT SLY ENOUGH, IF I DO SAY SO MYS—
YEEOW-WOW-WOW-HOO-HOO!
DON'T LET HER ESCAPE, UNCLE SCROOGE!
IF SHE GETS TO HER WAND, WE'LL BE IN FOR A ROUGHER TIME! GRAB HER, DONALD!
WHY ME?!
OUT OF THE WAY, IMBECILE!

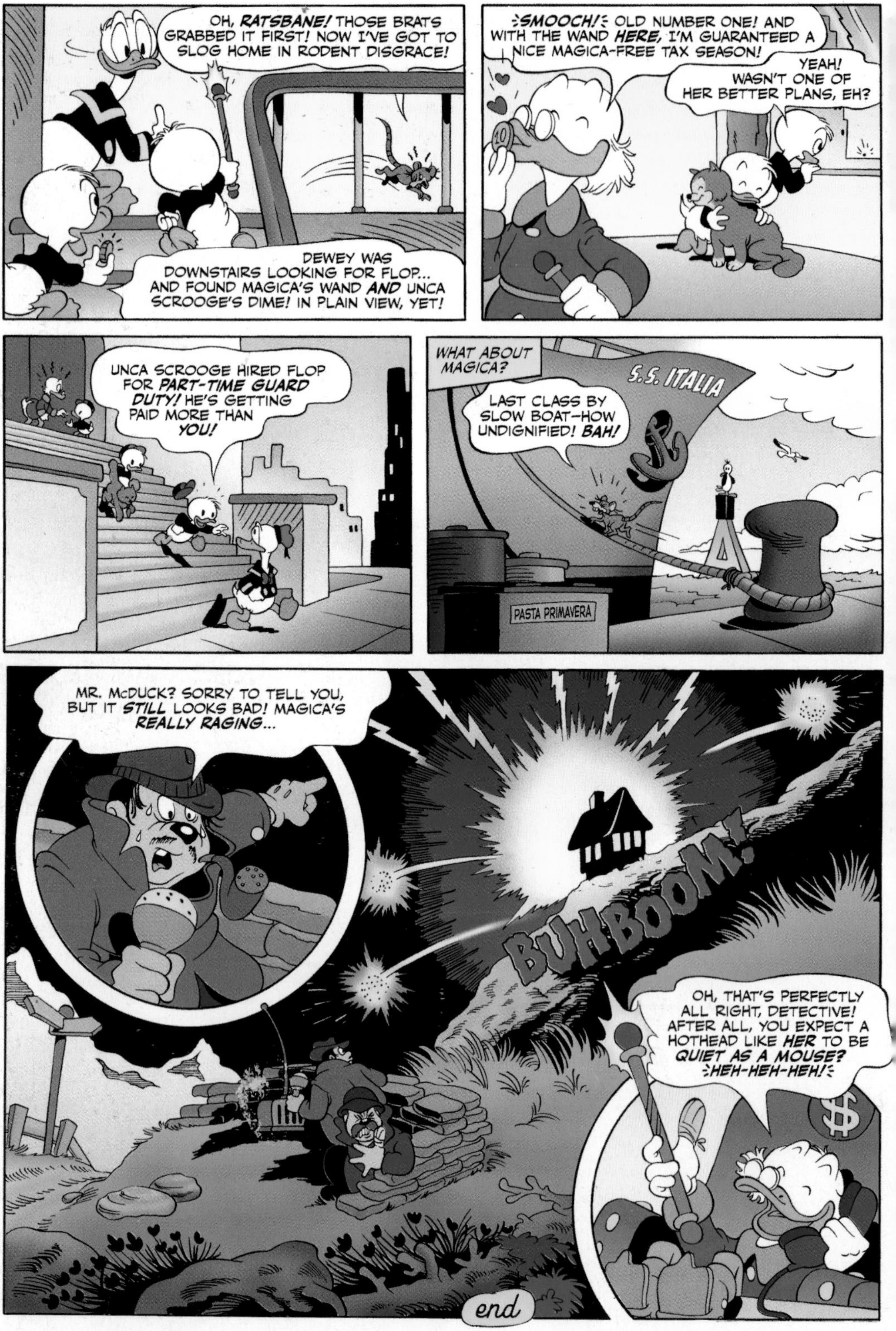
OH, RATSBANE! THOSE BRATS GRABBED IT FIRST! NOW I'VE GOT TO SLOG HOME IN RODENT DISGRACE!
DEWEY WAS DOWNSTAIRS LOOKING FOR FLOP... AND FOUND MAGICA'S WAND AND UNCA SCROOGE'S DIME! IN PLAIN VIEW, YET!
SMOOCH! OLD NUMBER ONE! AND WITH THE WAND HERE, I'M GUARANTEED A NICE MAGICA-FREE TAX SEASON!
YEAH! WASN'T ONE OF HER BETTER PLANS, EH?
UNCA SCROOGE HIRED FLOP FOR PART-TIME GUARD DUTY! HE'S GETTING PAID MORE THAN YOU!
WHAT ABOUT MAGICA?
S.S. ITALIA
LAST CLASS BY SLOW BOAT—HOW UNDIGNIFIED! BAH!
PASTA PRIMAVERA
MR. McDUCK? SORRY TO TELL YOU, BUT IT STILL LOOKS BAD! MAGICA'S REALLY RAGING...
BUHBOOM!
OH, THAT'S PERFECTLY ALL RIGHT, DETECTIVE! AFTER ALL, YOU EXPECT A HOTHEAD LIKE HER TO BE QUIET AS A MOUSE? HEH-HEH-HEH!
end

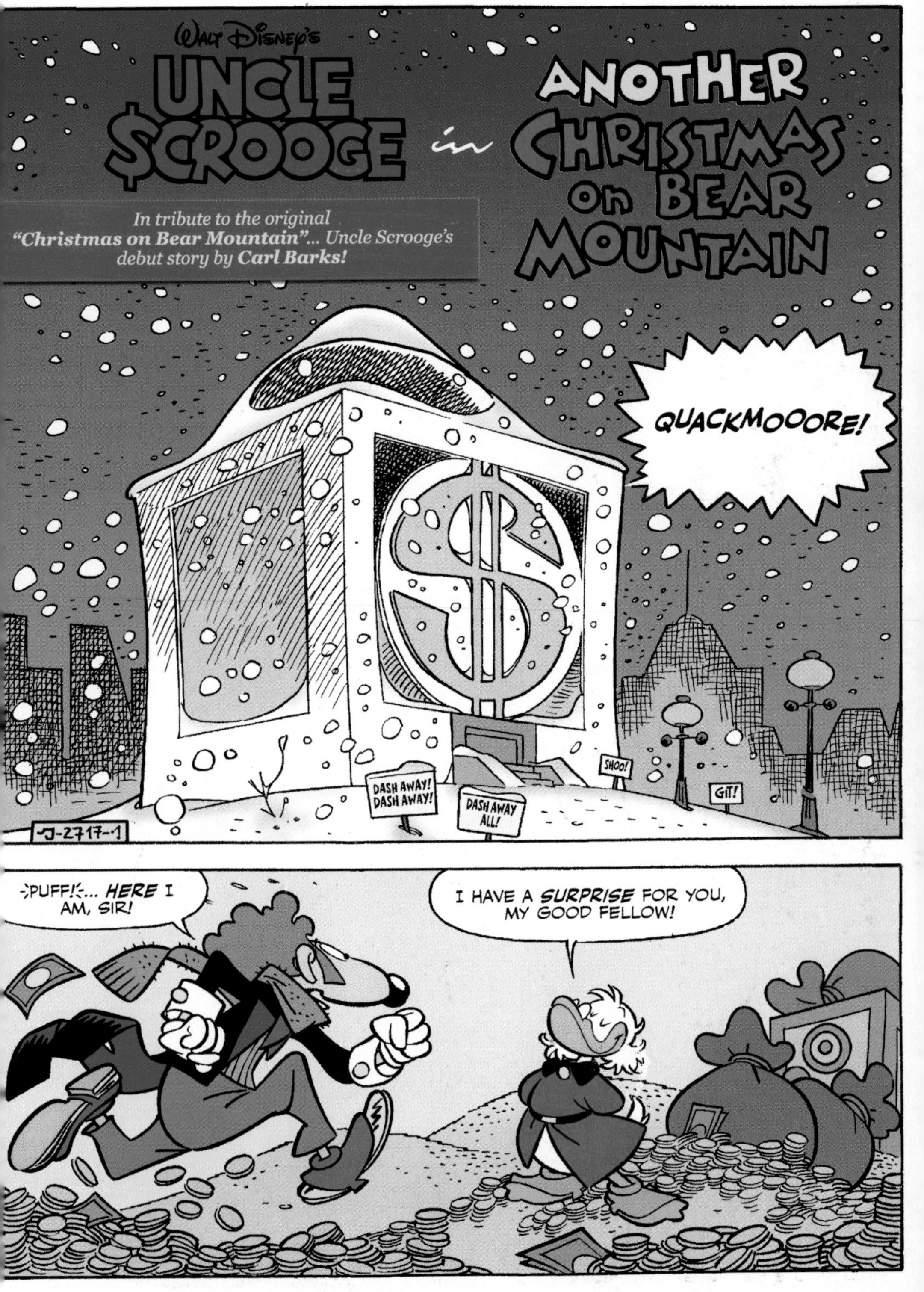
WALT DISNEY'S
UNCLE $CROOGE
in
ANOTHER CHRISTMAS on BEAR MOUNTAIN
In tribute to the original "Christmas on Bear Mountain"... Uncle Scrooge's debut story by Carl Barks!
QUACKMOOORE!
SHOO!
DASH AWAY! DASH AWAY!
DASH AWAY ALL!
GIT!
-J-2717-1
-PUFF!-... HERE I AM, SIR!
I HAVE A SURPRISE FOR YOU, MY GOOD FELLOW!

Originally published in *Topolino* #2717 (Italy, 2007)

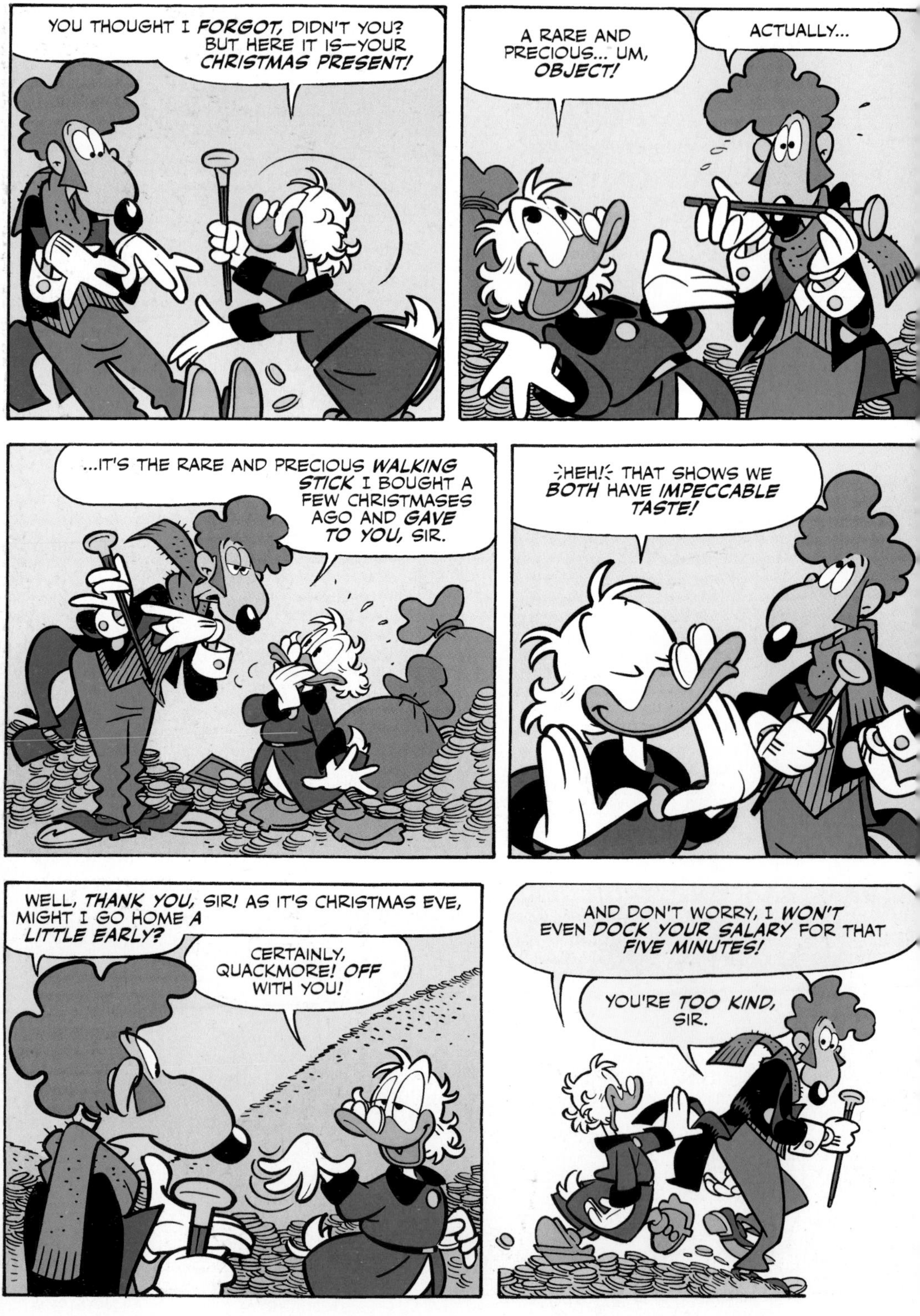
YOU THOUGHT I FORGOT, DIDN'T YOU? BUT HERE IT IS—YOUR CHRISTMAS PRESENT!
A RARE AND PRECIOUS... UM, OBJECT!
ACTUALLY...
...IT'S THE RARE AND PRECIOUS WALKING STICK I BOUGHT A FEW CHRISTMASES AGO AND GAVE TO YOU, SIR.
HEH! THAT SHOWS WE BOTH HAVE IMPECCABLE TASTE!
WELL, THANK YOU, SIR! AS IT'S CHRISTMAS EVE, MIGHT I GO HOME A LITTLE EARLY?
CERTAINLY, QUACKMORE! OFF WITH YOU!
AND DON'T WORRY, I WON'T EVEN DOCK YOUR SALARY FOR THAT FIVE MINUTES!
YOU'RE TOO KIND, SIR.

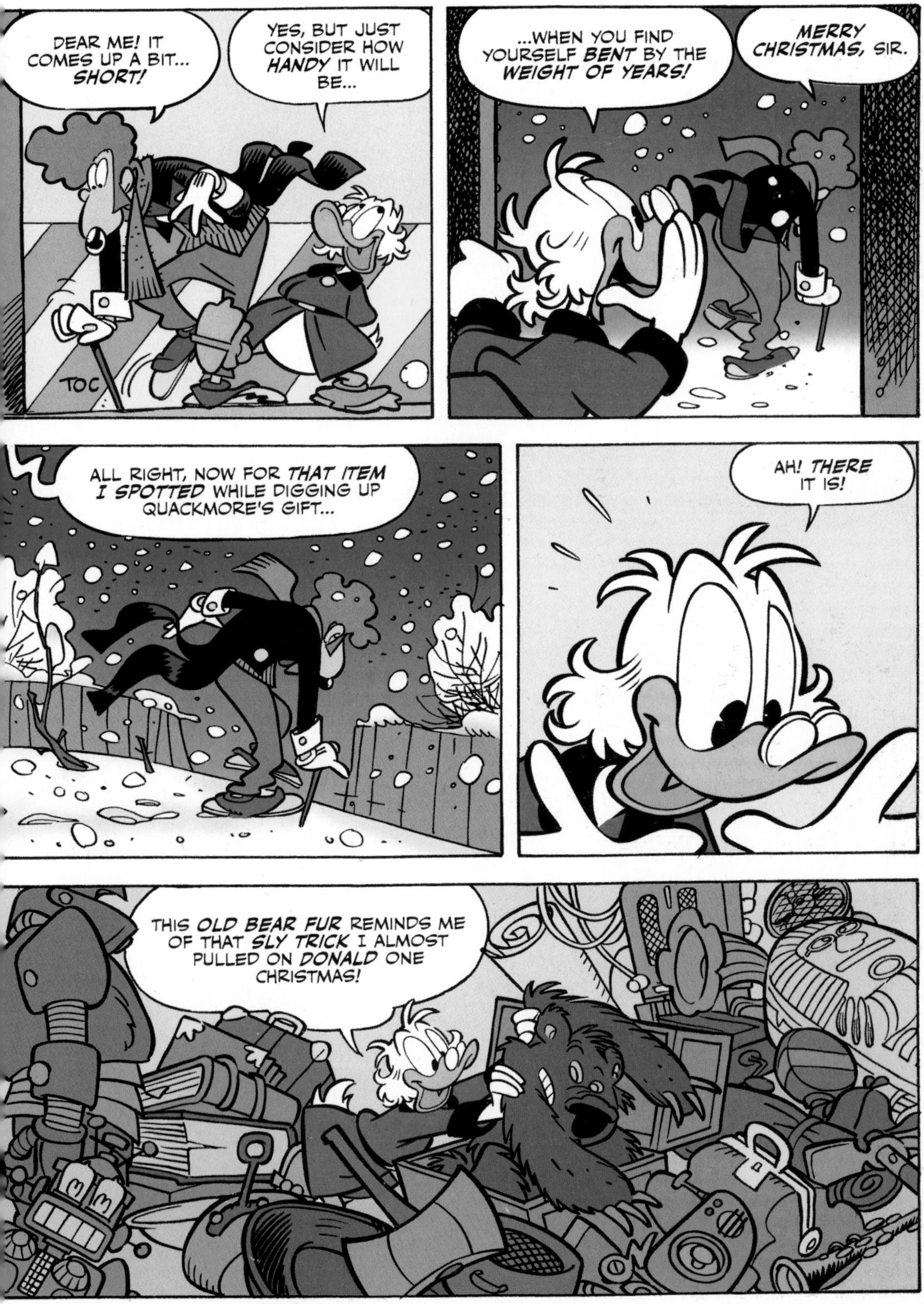
DEAR ME! IT COMES UP A BIT... SHORT!
YES, BUT JUST CONSIDER HOW HANDY IT WILL BE...
TOC
...WHEN YOU FIND YOURSELF BENT BY THE WEIGHT OF YEARS!
MERRY CHRISTMAS, SIR.
ALL RIGHT, NOW FOR THAT ITEM I SPOTTED WHILE DIGGING UP QUACKMORE'S GIFT...
AH! THERE IT IS!
THIS OLD BEAR FUR REMINDS ME OF THAT SLY TRICK I ALMOST PULLED ON DONALD ONE CHRISTMAS!

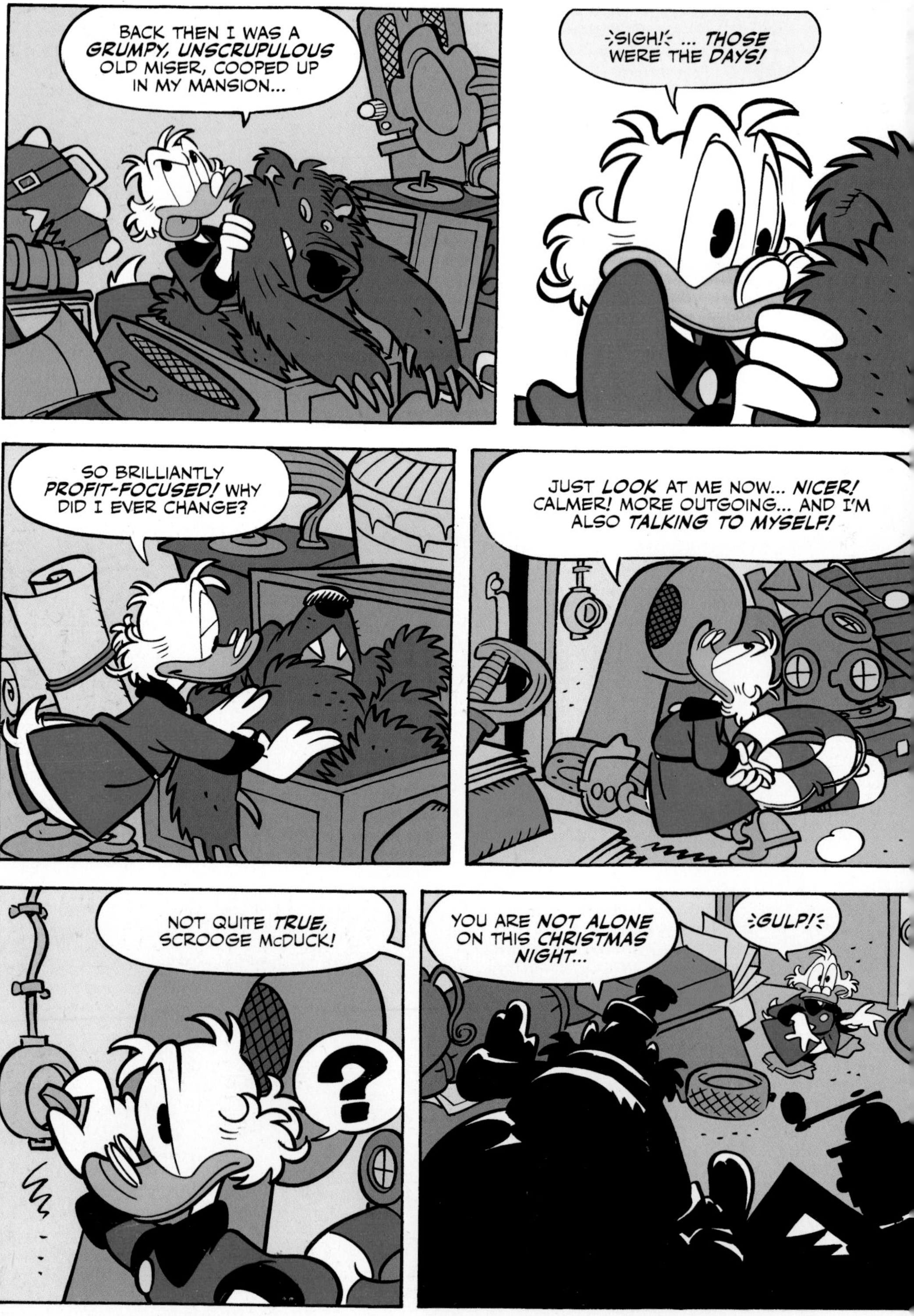
BACK THEN I WAS A GRUMPY, UNSCRUPULOUS OLD MISER, COOPED UP IN MY MANSION...
-SIGH!- ... THOSE WERE THE DAYS!
SO BRILLIANTLY PROFIT-FOCUSED! WHY DID I EVER CHANGE?
JUST LOOK AT ME NOW... NICER! CALMER! MORE OUTGOING... AND I'M ALSO TALKING TO MYSELF!
NOT QUITE TRUE, SCROOGE McDUCK!
?
YOU ARE NOT ALONE ON THIS CHRISTMAS NIGHT...
-GULP!-

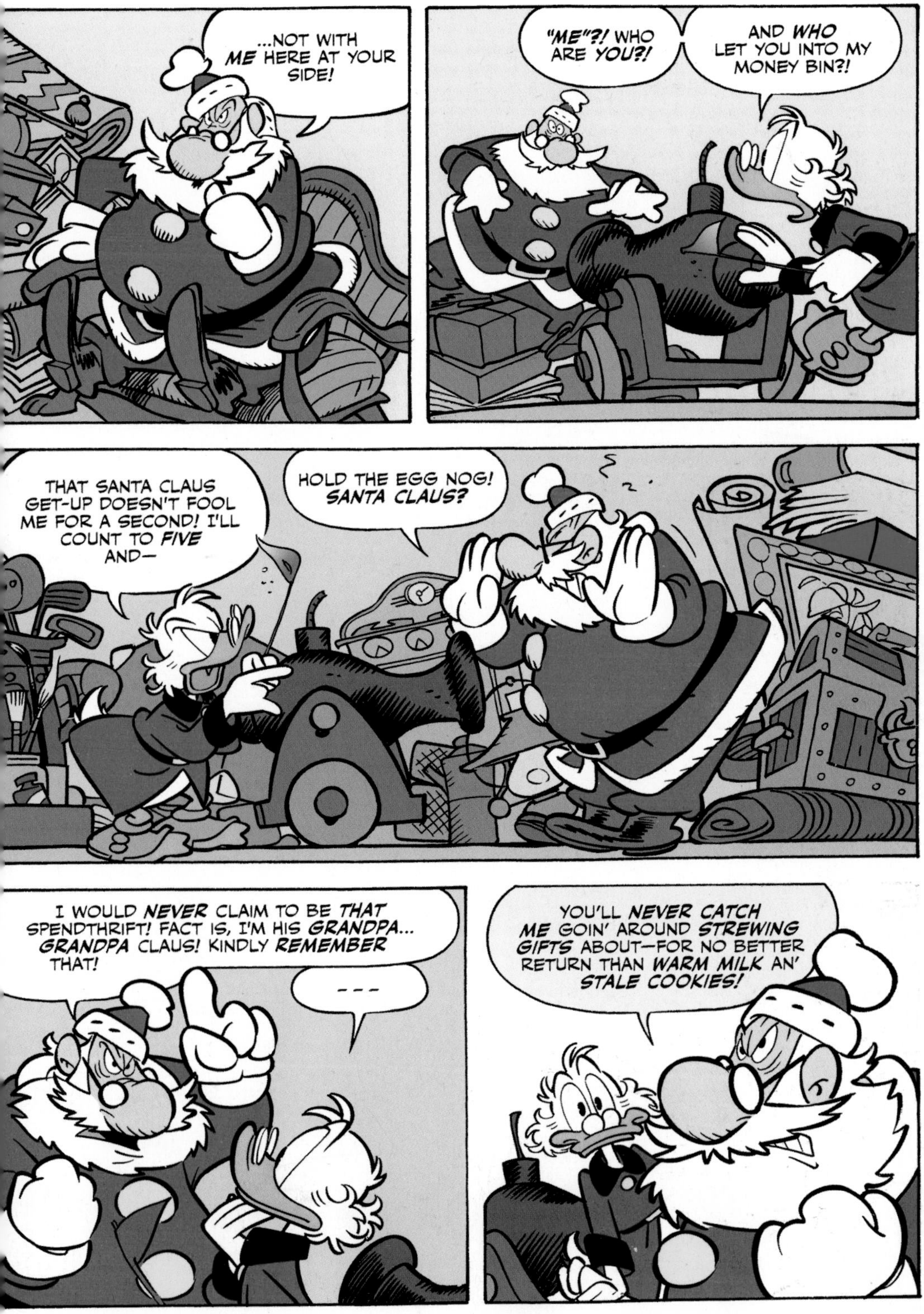
...NOT WITH ME HERE AT YOUR SIDE!
"ME"?! WHO ARE YOU?!
AND WHO LET YOU INTO MY MONEY BIN?!
THAT SANTA CLAUS GET-UP DOESN'T FOOL ME FOR A SECOND! I'LL COUNT TO FIVE AND—
HOLD THE EGG NOG! SANTA CLAUS?
I WOULD NEVER CLAIM TO BE THAT SPENDTHRIFT! FACT IS, I'M HIS GRANDPA... GRANDPA CLAUS! KINDLY REMEMBER THAT!
- - -
YOU'LL NEVER CATCH ME GOIN' AROUND STREWING GIFTS ABOUT—FOR NO BETTER RETURN THAN WARM MILK AN' STALE COOKIES!

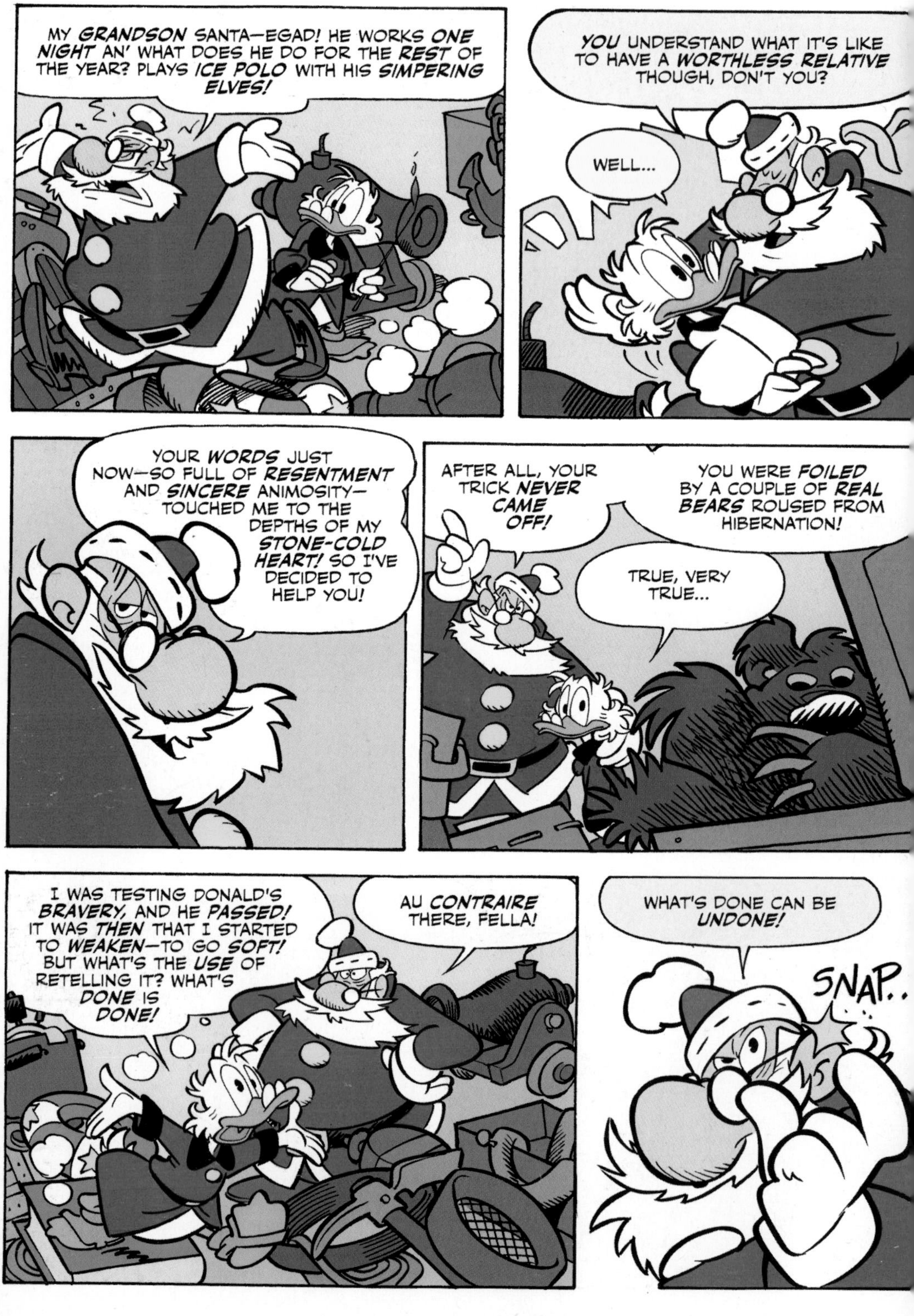

MY GRANDSON SANTA—EGAD! HE WORKS ONE NIGHT AN' WHAT DOES HE DO FOR THE REST OF THE YEAR? PLAYS ICE POLO WITH HIS SIMPERING ELVES!
YOU UNDERSTAND WHAT IT'S LIKE TO HAVE A WORTHLESS RELATIVE THOUGH, DON'T YOU?
WELL...
YOUR WORDS JUST NOW—SO FULL OF RESENTMENT AND SINCERE ANIMOSITY—TOUCHED ME TO THE DEPTHS OF MY STONE-COLD HEART! SO I'VE DECIDED TO HELP YOU!
AFTER ALL, YOUR TRICK NEVER CAME OFF!
YOU WERE FOILED BY A COUPLE OF REAL BEARS ROUSED FROM HIBERNATION!
TRUE, VERY TRUE...
I WAS TESTING DONALD'S BRAVERY, AND HE PASSED! IT WAS THEN THAT I STARTED TO WEAKEN—TO GO SOFT! BUT WHAT'S THE USE OF RETELLING IT? WHAT'S DONE IS DONE!
AU CONTRAIRE THERE, FELLA!
WHAT'S DONE CAN BE UNDONE!
SNAP..

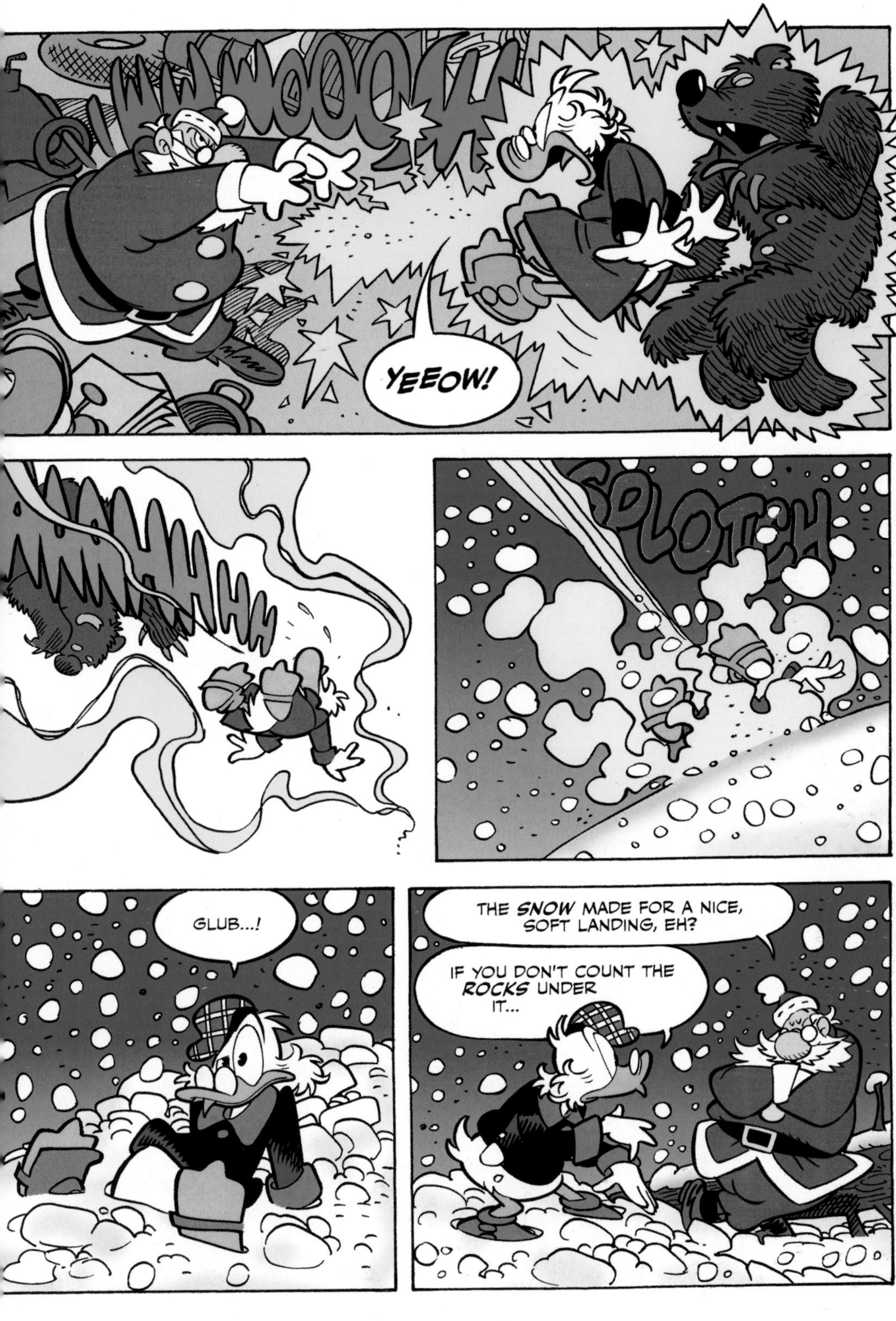
WHOOOOH!
YEEOW!
SPLOTCH
GLUB...!
THE SNOW MADE FOR A NICE, SOFT LANDING, EH?
IF YOU DON'T COUNT THE ROCKS UNDER IT...

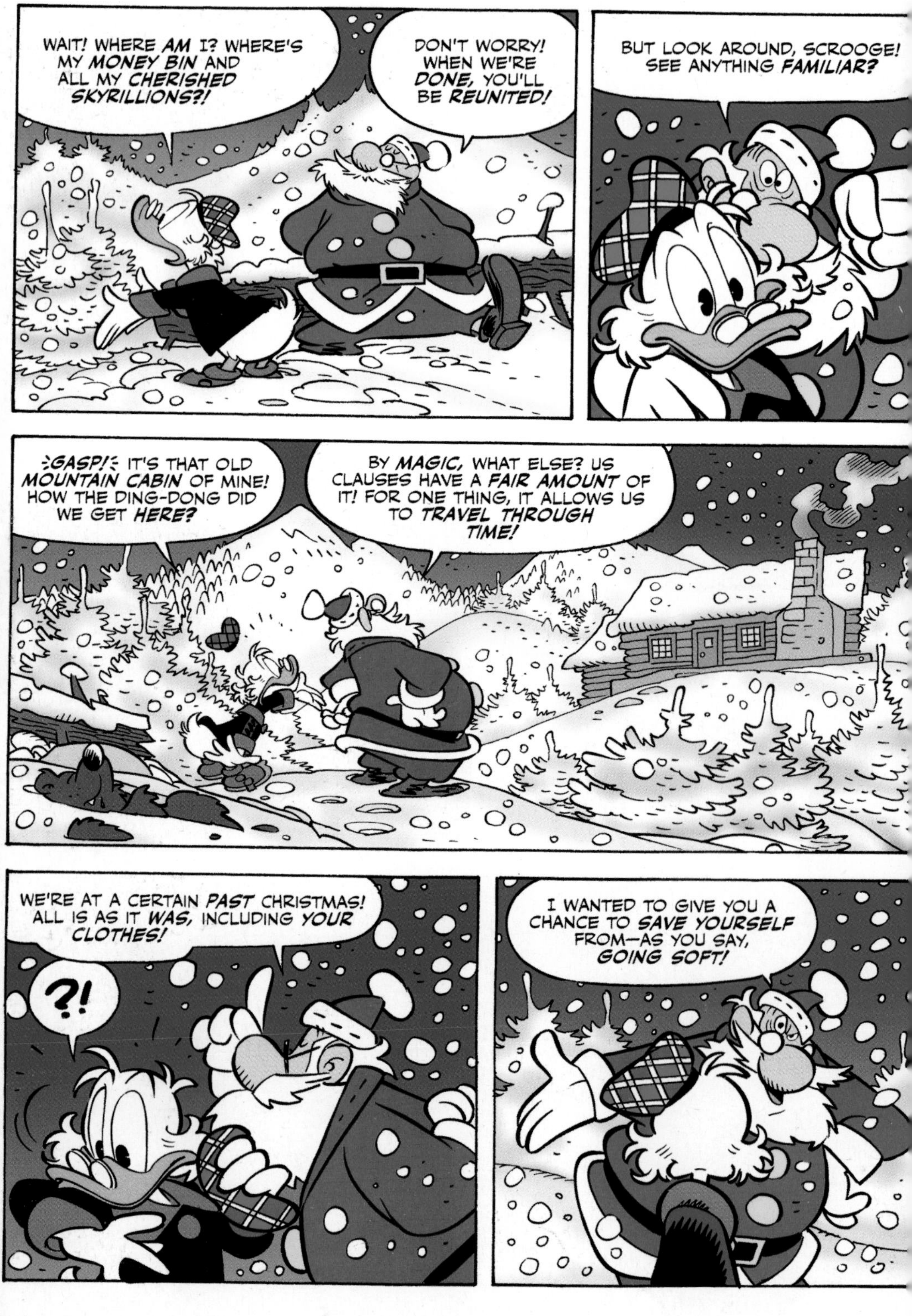
WAIT! WHERE AM I? WHERE'S MY MONEY BIN AND ALL MY CHERISHED SKYRILLIONS?!
DON'T WORRY! WHEN WE'RE DONE, YOU'LL BE REUNITED!
BUT LOOK AROUND, SCROOGE! SEE ANYTHING FAMILIAR?
GASP! IT'S THAT OLD MOUNTAIN CABIN OF MINE! HOW THE DING-DONG DID WE GET HERE?
BY MAGIC, WHAT ELSE? US CLAUSES HAVE A FAIR AMOUNT OF IT! FOR ONE THING, IT ALLOWS US TO TRAVEL THROUGH TIME!
WE'RE AT A CERTAIN PAST CHRISTMAS! ALL IS AS IT WAS, INCLUDING YOUR CLOTHES!
?!
I WANTED TO GIVE YOU A CHANCE TO SAVE YOURSELF FROM—AS YOU SAY, GOING SOFT!

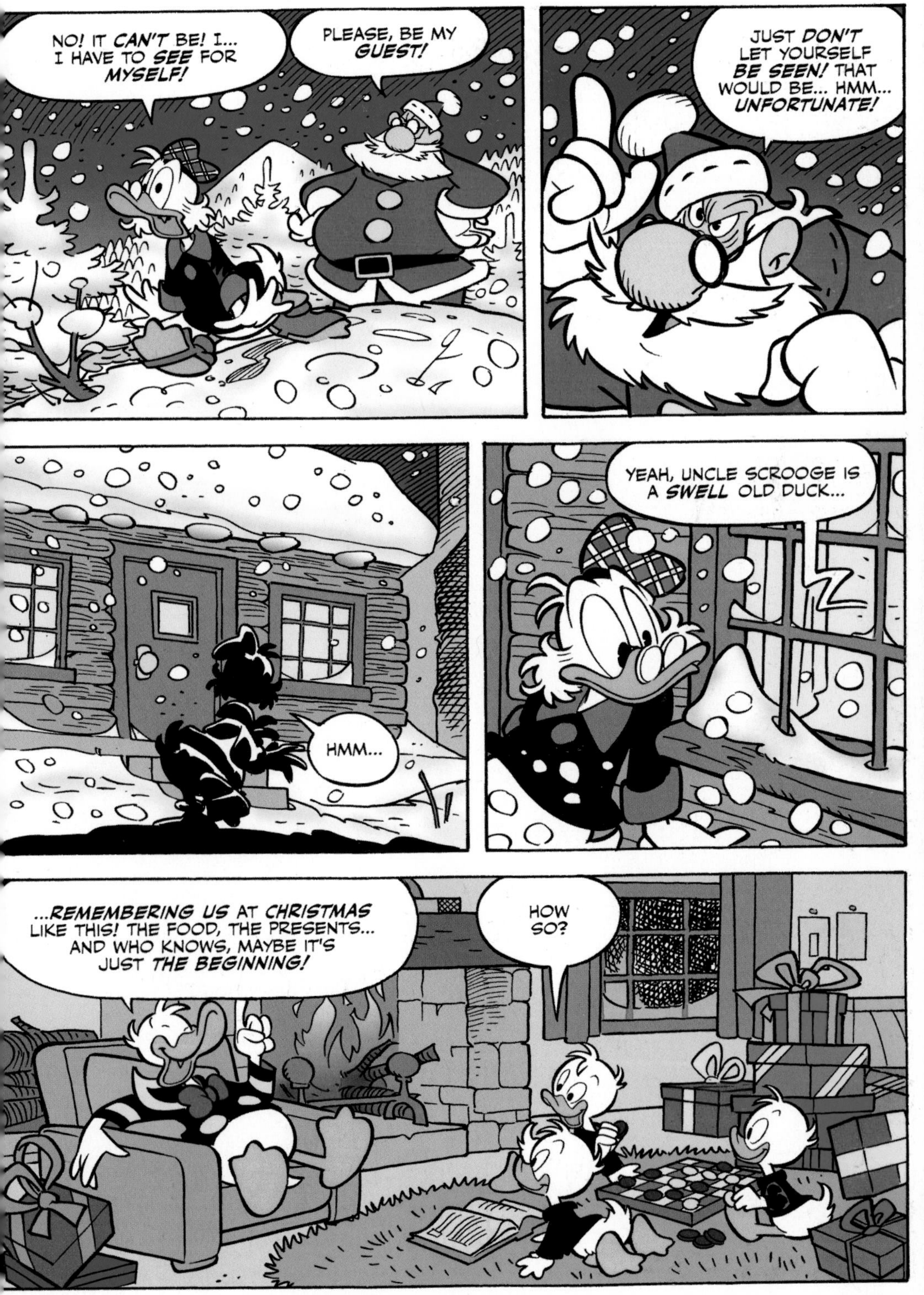
NO! IT CAN'T BE! I... I HAVE TO SEE FOR MYSELF!
PLEASE, BE MY GUEST!
JUST DON'T LET YOURSELF BE SEEN! THAT WOULD BE... HMM... UNFORTUNATE!
HMM...
YEAH, UNCLE SCROOGE IS A SWELL OLD DUCK...
...REMEMBERING US AT CHRISTMAS LIKE THIS! THE FOOD, THE PRESENTS... AND WHO KNOWS, MAYBE IT'S JUST THE BEGINNING!
HOW SO?

THE RICH OLD COOT MUST WANT TO SHOW US HE'S A *MORE GENEROUS SOUL* THAN WE THOUGHT!

NOT THAT IT *TOOK* MUCH...

AND MAYBE HE'LL *TAKE US* WITH HIM ON HIS TRAVELS *AROUND THE WORLD!*

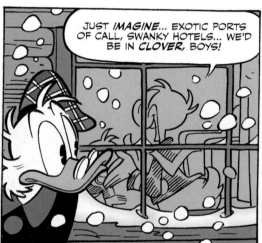

JUST *IMAGINE*... EXOTIC PORTS OF CALL, SWANKY HOTELS... WE'D BE IN *CLOVER*, BOYS!

AND MAYBE HE'D BUY SOME *FANTASTIC VEHICLE* FROM GYRO GEARLOOSE TO GET US AROUND IN *COMPLETE COMFORT!*

?

HEY, I'M *SERIOUS!* WHY ARE YOU *GIGGLING?!*

I'M NOT...

...ME NEITHER...

...NOR *ME!*

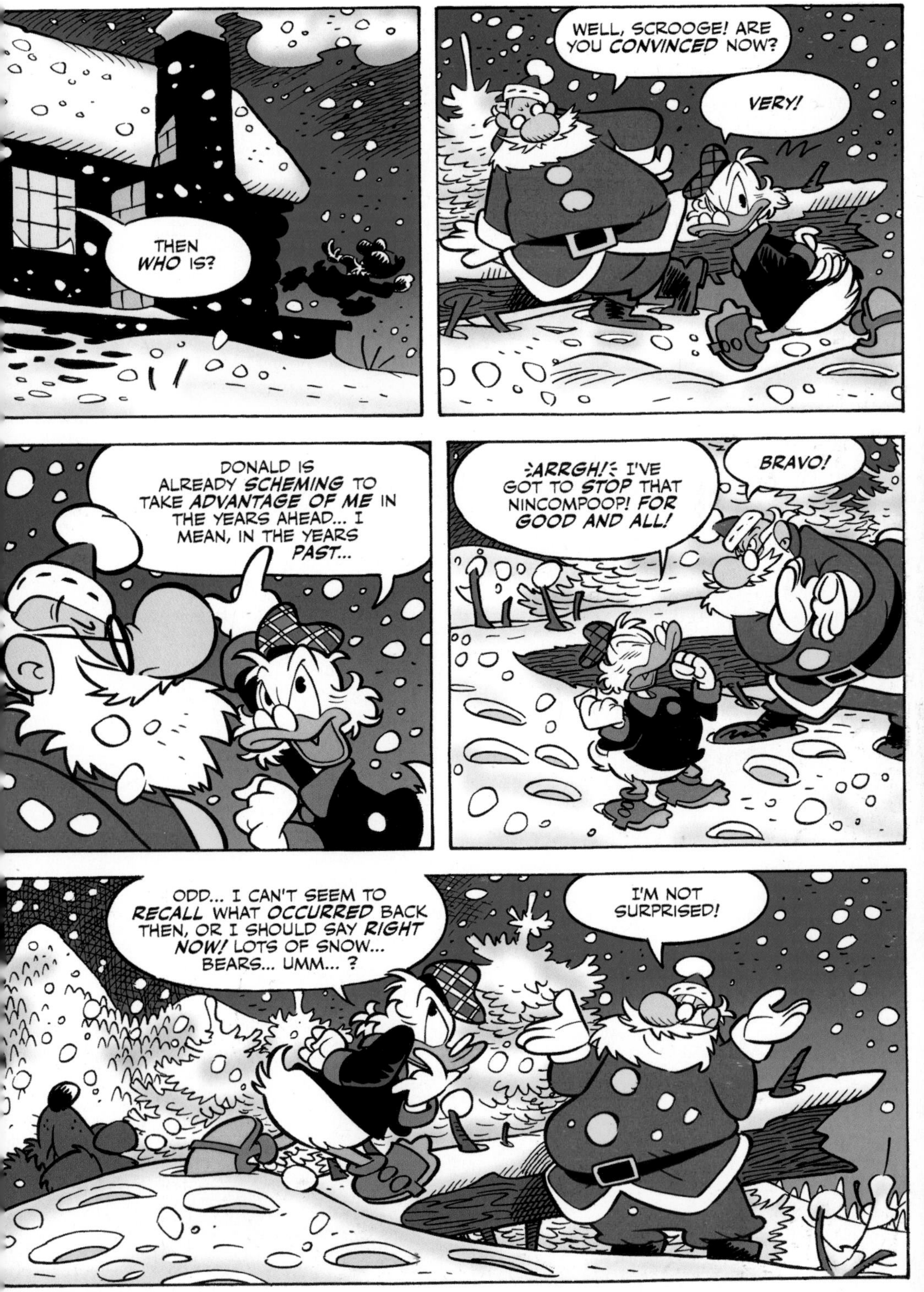
THEN WHO IS?
WELL, SCROOGE! ARE YOU CONVINCED NOW?
VERY!
DONALD IS ALREADY SCHEMING TO TAKE ADVANTAGE OF ME IN THE YEARS AHEAD... I MEAN, IN THE YEARS PAST...
ARRGH! I'VE GOT TO STOP THAT NINCOMPOOP! FOR GOOD AND ALL!
BRAVO!
ODD... I CAN'T SEEM TO RECALL WHAT OCCURRED BACK THEN, OR I SHOULD SAY RIGHT NOW! LOTS OF SNOW... BEARS... UMM... ?
I'M NOT SURPRISED!

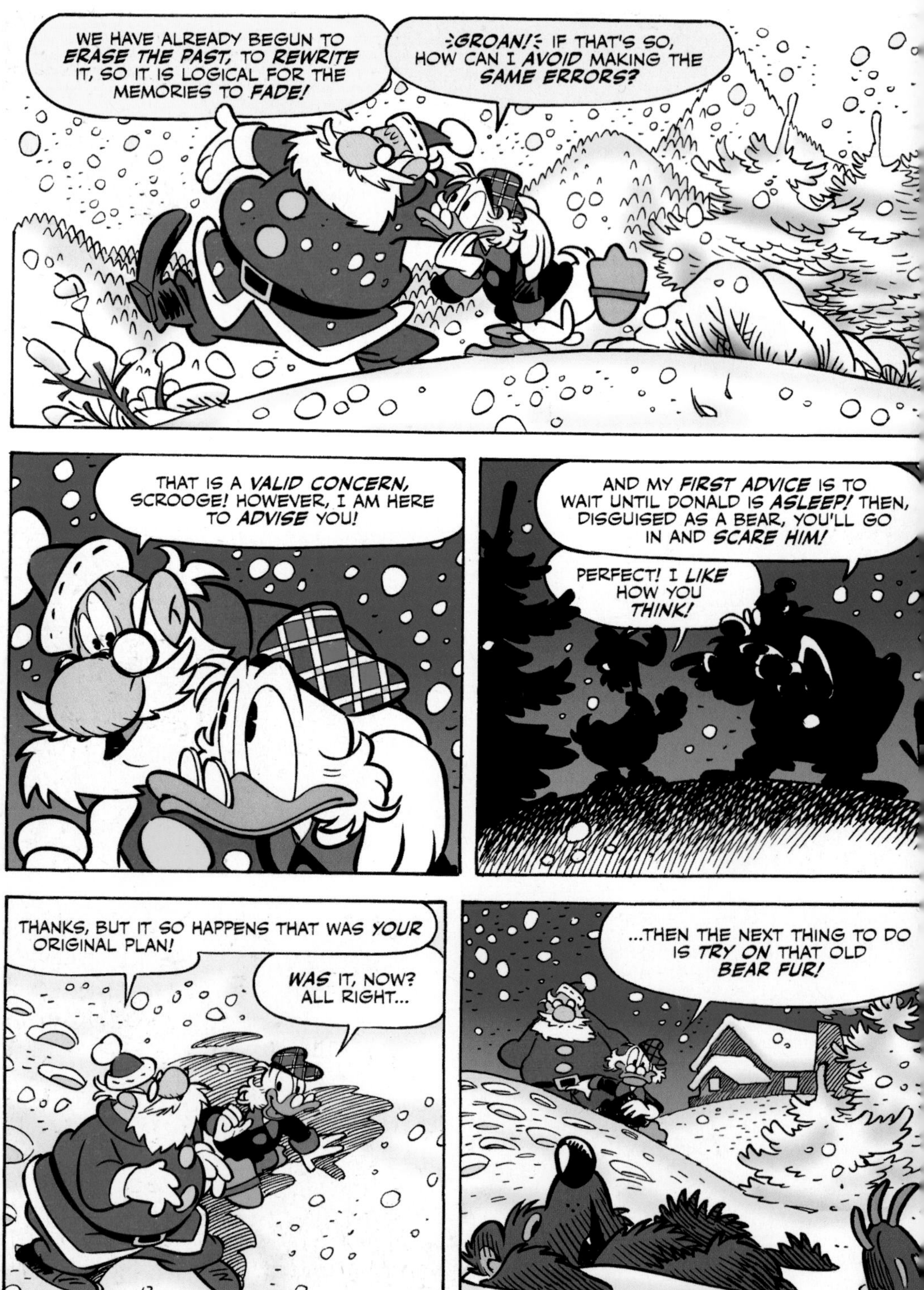
WE HAVE ALREADY BEGUN TO ERASE THE PAST, TO REWRITE IT, SO IT IS LOGICAL FOR THE MEMORIES TO FADE!
GROAN! IF THAT'S SO, HOW CAN I AVOID MAKING THE SAME ERRORS?
THAT IS A VALID CONCERN, SCROOGE! HOWEVER, I AM HERE TO ADVISE YOU!
AND MY FIRST ADVICE IS TO WAIT UNTIL DONALD IS ASLEEP! THEN, DISGUISED AS A BEAR, YOU'LL GO IN AND SCARE HIM!
PERFECT! I LIKE HOW YOU THINK!
THANKS, BUT IT SO HAPPENS THAT WAS YOUR ORIGINAL PLAN!
WAS IT, NOW? ALL RIGHT...
...THEN THE NEXT THING TO DO IS TRY ON THAT OLD BEAR FUR!

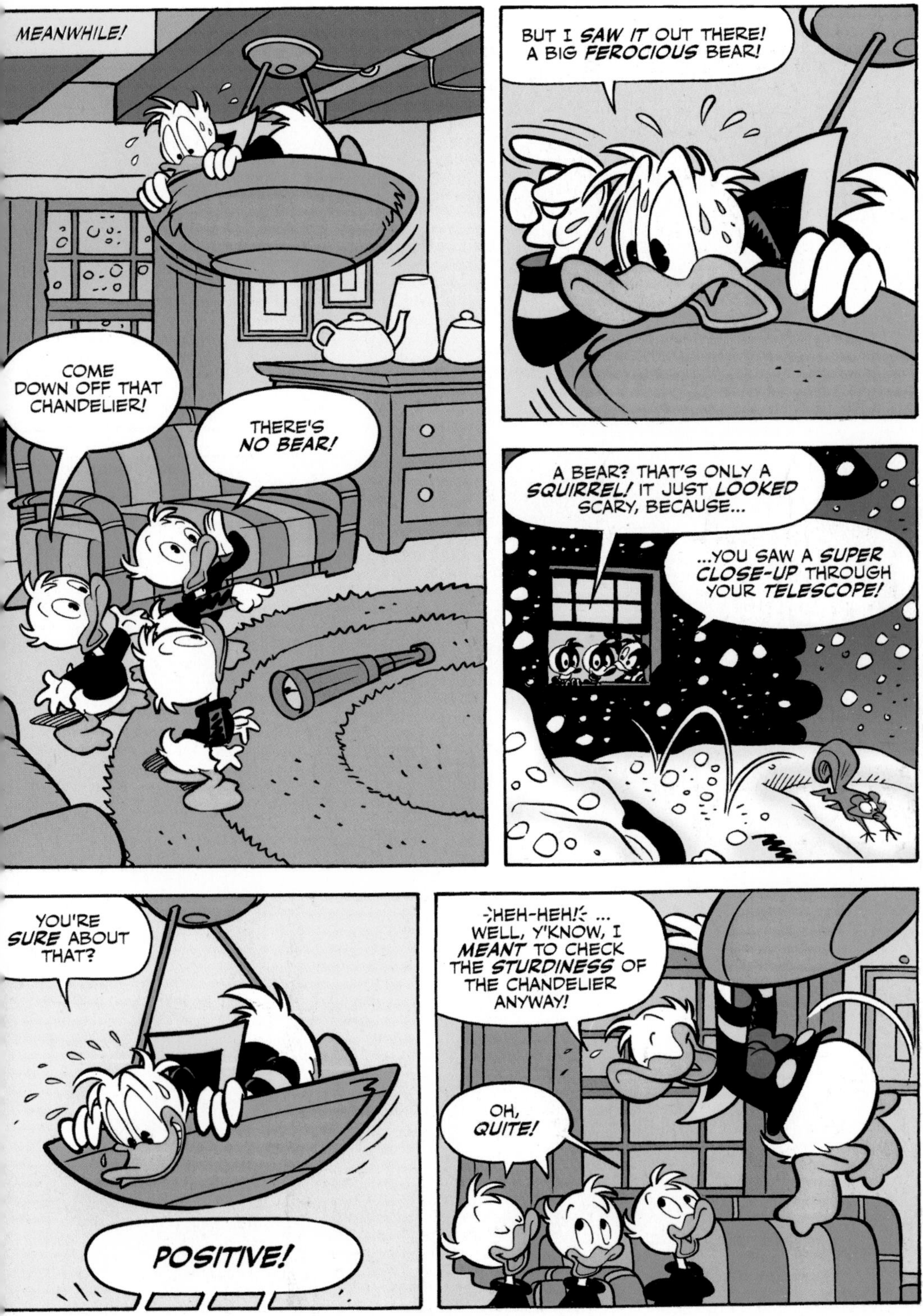
MEANWHILE!
COME DOWN OFF THAT CHANDELIER!
THERE'S NO BEAR!
BUT I SAW IT OUT THERE! A BIG FEROCIOUS BEAR!
A BEAR? THAT'S ONLY A SQUIRREL! IT JUST LOOKED SCARY, BECAUSE...
...YOU SAW A SUPER CLOSE-UP THROUGH YOUR TELESCOPE!
YOU'RE SURE ABOUT THAT?
POSITIVE!
HEH-HEH! ... WELL, Y'KNOW, I MEANT TO CHECK THE STURDINESS OF THE CHANDELIER ANYWAY!
OH, QUITE!

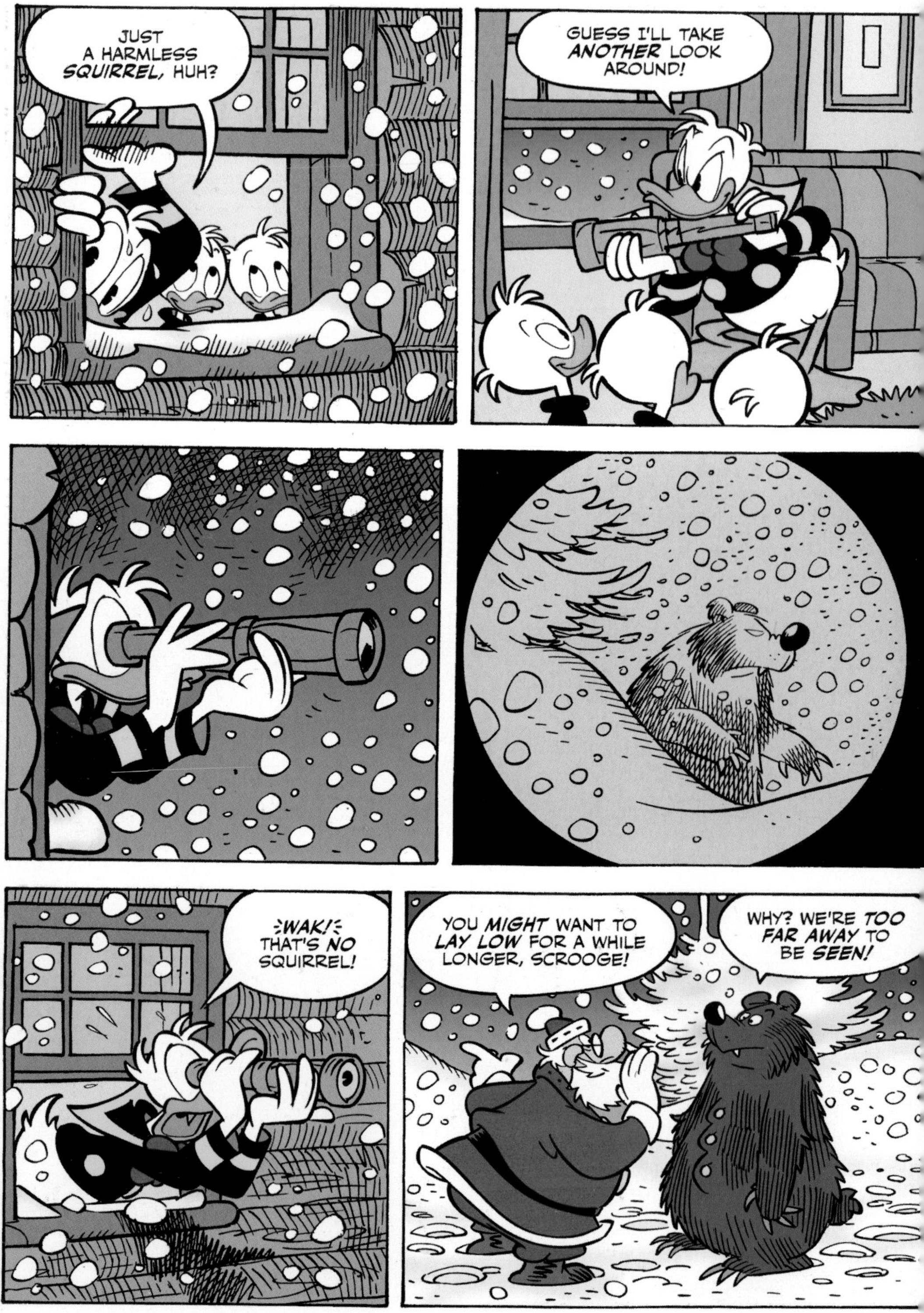
JUST A HARMLESS SQUIRREL, HUH?
GUESS I'LL TAKE ANOTHER LOOK AROUND!
WAK! THAT'S NO SQUIRREL!
YOU MIGHT WANT TO LAY LOW FOR A WHILE LONGER, SCROOGE!
WHY? WE'RE TOO FAR AWAY TO BE SEEN!

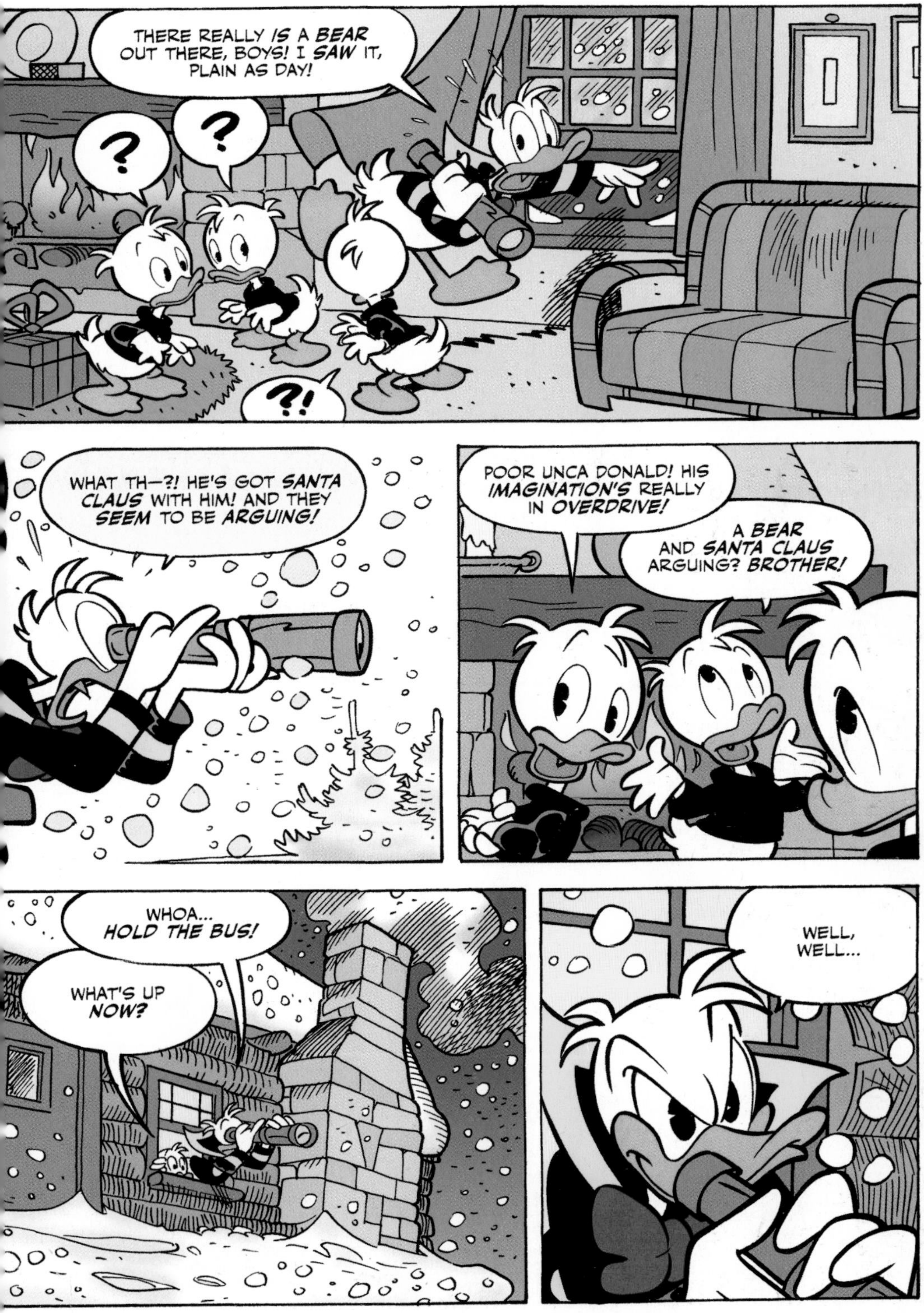
THERE REALLY IS A BEAR OUT THERE, BOYS! I SAW IT, PLAIN AS DAY!
?
?
?!
WHAT TH—?! HE'S GOT SANTA CLAUS WITH HIM! AND THEY SEEM TO BE ARGUING!
POOR UNCA DONALD! HIS IMAGINATION'S REALLY IN OVERDRIVE!
A BEAR AND SANTA CLAUS ARGUING? BROTHER!
WHOA... HOLD THE BUS!
WHAT'S UP NOW?
WELL, WELL...

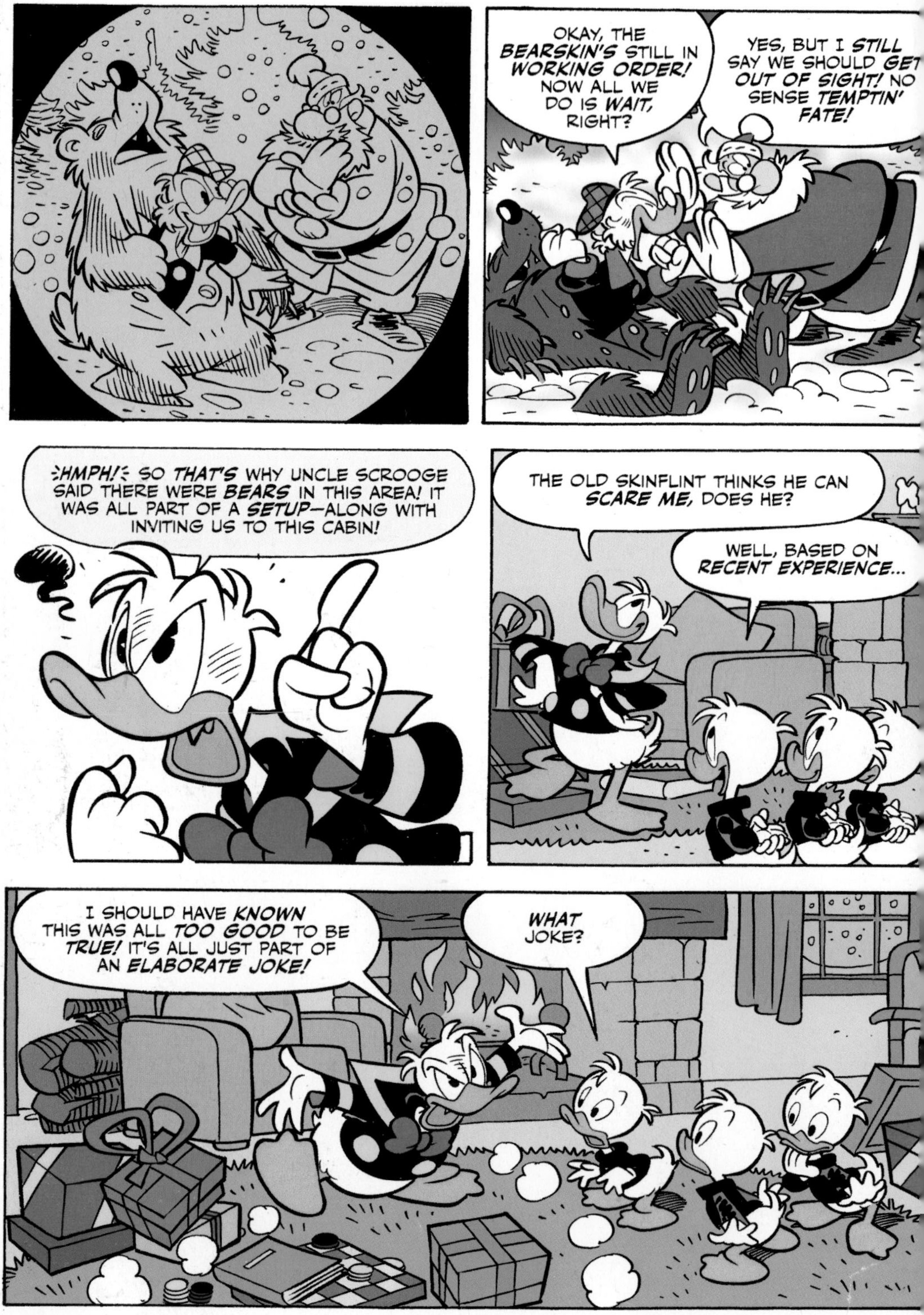
OKAY, THE BEARSKIN'S STILL IN WORKING ORDER! NOW ALL WE DO IS WAIT, RIGHT?
YES, BUT I STILL SAY WE SHOULD GET OUT OF SIGHT! NO SENSE TEMPTIN' FATE!
HMPH! SO THAT'S WHY UNCLE SCROOGE SAID THERE WERE BEARS IN THIS AREA! IT WAS ALL PART OF A SETUP—ALONG WITH INVITING US TO THIS CABIN!
THE OLD SKINFLINT THINKS HE CAN SCARE ME, DOES HE?
WELL, BASED ON RECENT EXPERIENCE...
I SHOULD HAVE KNOWN THIS WAS ALL TOO GOOD TO BE TRUE! IT'S ALL JUST PART OF AN ELABORATE JOKE!
WHAT JOKE?

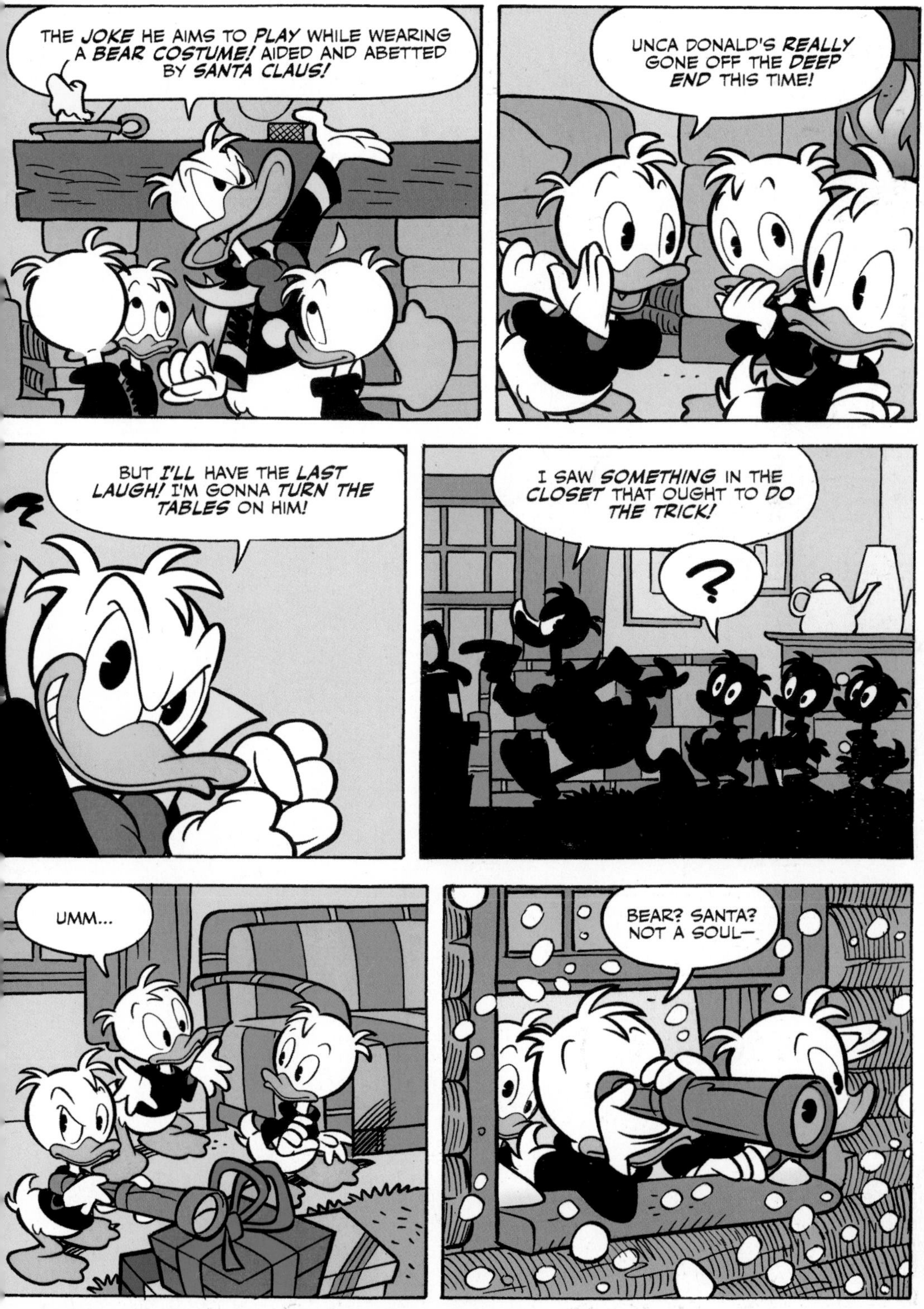
THE JOKE HE AIMS TO PLAY WHILE WEARING A BEAR COSTUME! AIDED AND ABETTED BY SANTA CLAUS!
UNCA DONALD'S REALLY GONE OFF THE DEEP END THIS TIME!
BUT I'LL HAVE THE LAST LAUGH! I'M GONNA TURN THE TABLES ON HIM!
I SAW SOMETHING IN THE CLOSET THAT OUGHT TO DO THE TRICK!
?
UMM...
BEAR? SANTA? NOT A SOUL—

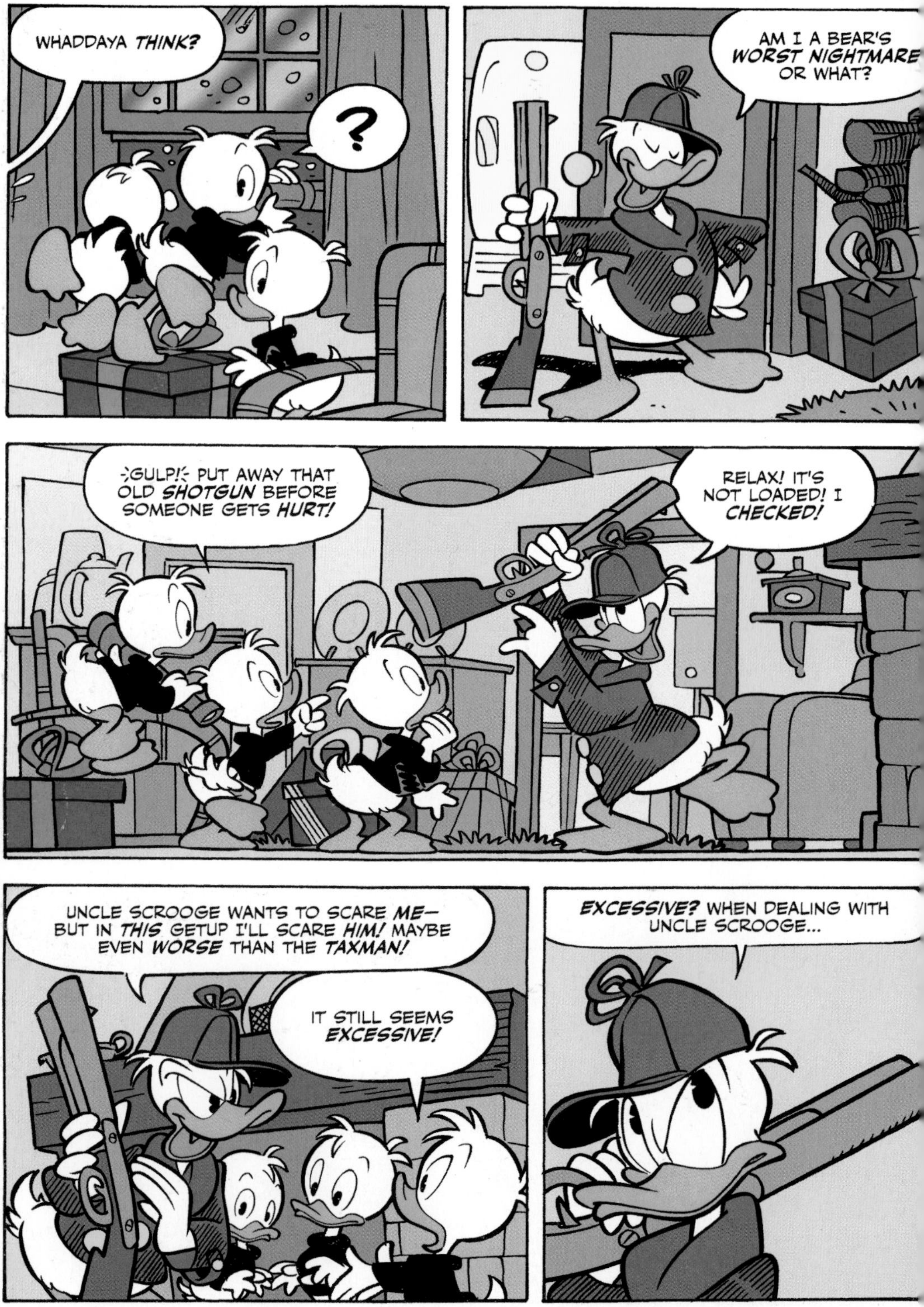
WHADDAYA THINK?
?
AM I A BEAR'S WORST NIGHTMARE OR WHAT?
:GULP!: PUT AWAY THAT OLD SHOTGUN BEFORE SOMEONE GETS HURT!
RELAX! IT'S NOT LOADED! I CHECKED!
UNCLE SCROOGE WANTS TO SCARE ME— BUT IN THIS GETUP I'LL SCARE HIM! MAYBE EVEN WORSE THAN THE TAXMAN!
IT STILL SEEMS EXCESSIVE!
EXCESSIVE? WHEN DEALING WITH UNCLE SCROOGE...

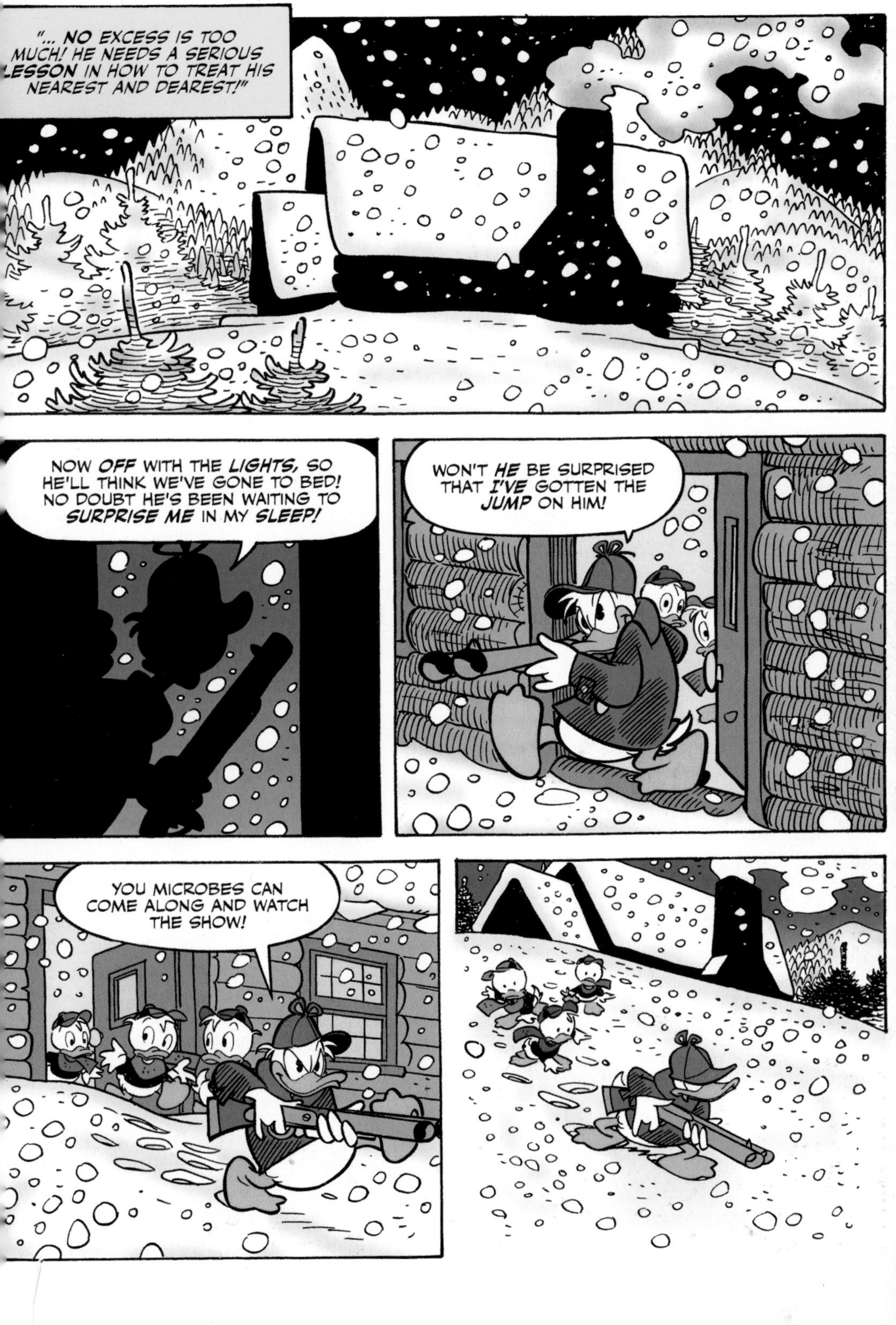
"... NO EXCESS IS TOO MUCH! HE NEEDS A SERIOUS LESSON IN HOW TO TREAT HIS NEAREST AND DEAREST!"
NOW OFF WITH THE LIGHTS, SO HE'LL THINK WE'VE GONE TO BED! NO DOUBT HE'S BEEN WAITING TO SURPRISE ME IN MY SLEEP!
WON'T HE BE SURPRISED THAT I'VE GOTTEN THE JUMP ON HIM!
YOU MICROBES CAN COME ALONG AND WATCH THE SHOW!

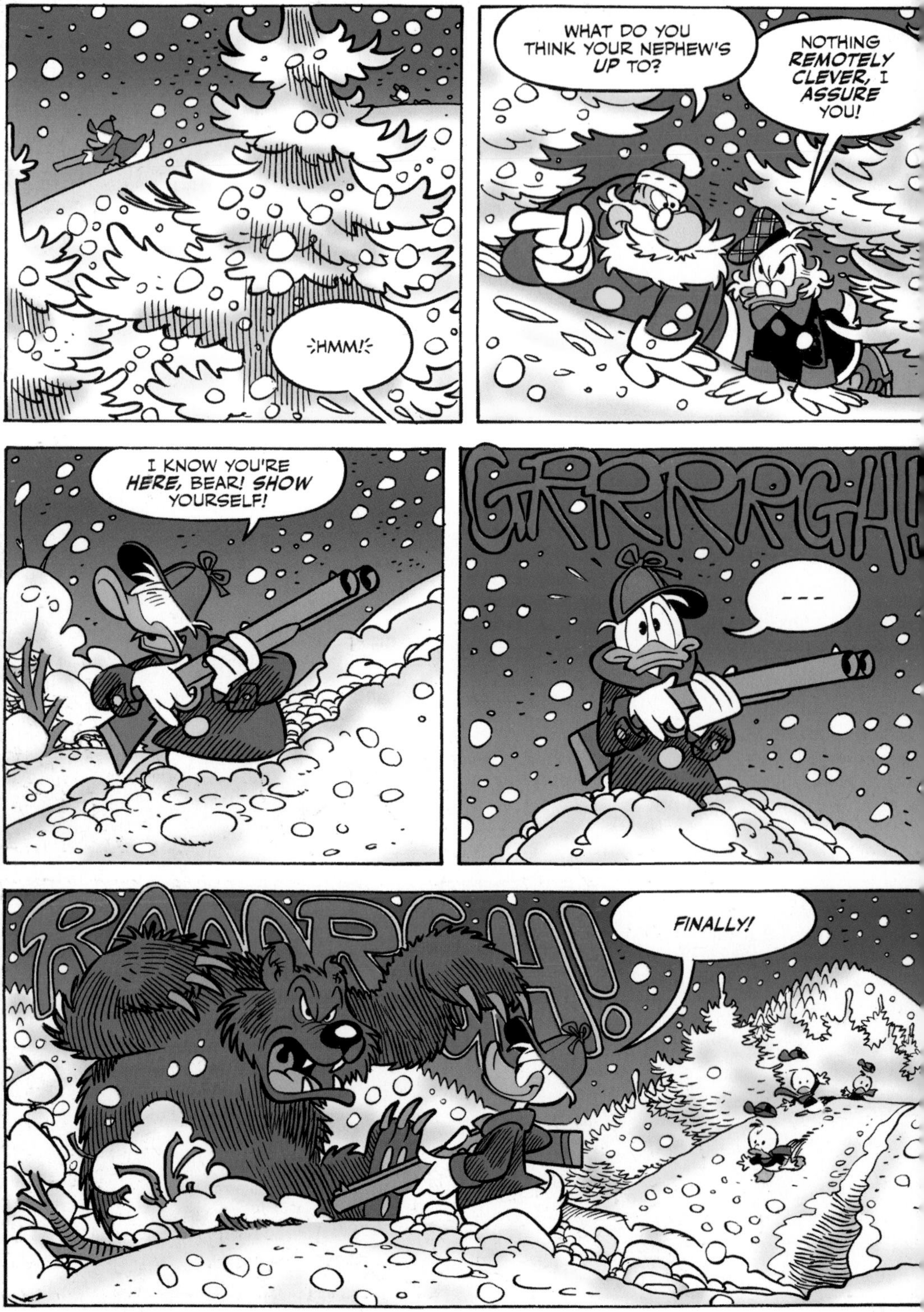

HMM!
WHAT DO YOU THINK YOUR NEPHEW'S UP TO?
NOTHING REMOTELY CLEVER, I ASSURE YOU!
I KNOW YOU'RE HERE, BEAR! SHOW YOURSELF!
GRRRRGH!
- - -
RAAARGH!
FINALLY!

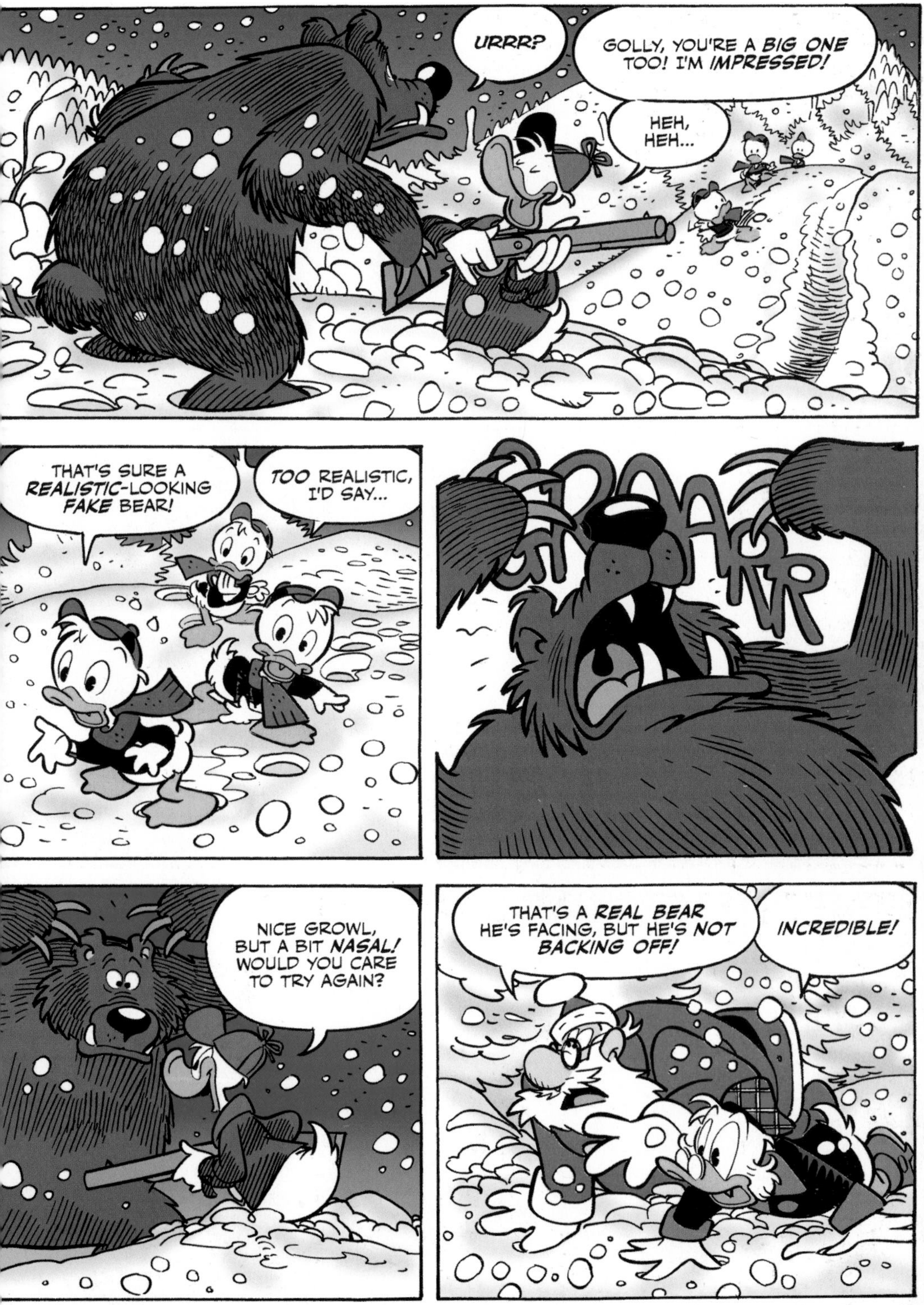
URRR?
GOLLY, YOU'RE A *BIG ONE* TOO! I'M *IMPRESSED!*
HEH, HEH...
THAT'S SURE A *REALISTIC*-LOOKING *FAKE* BEAR!
TOO REALISTIC, I'D SAY...
GRAAARR
NICE GROWL, BUT A BIT *NASAL!* WOULD YOU CARE TO TRY AGAIN?
THAT'S A *REAL BEAR* HE'S FACING, BUT HE'S *NOT BACKING OFF!*
INCREDIBLE!

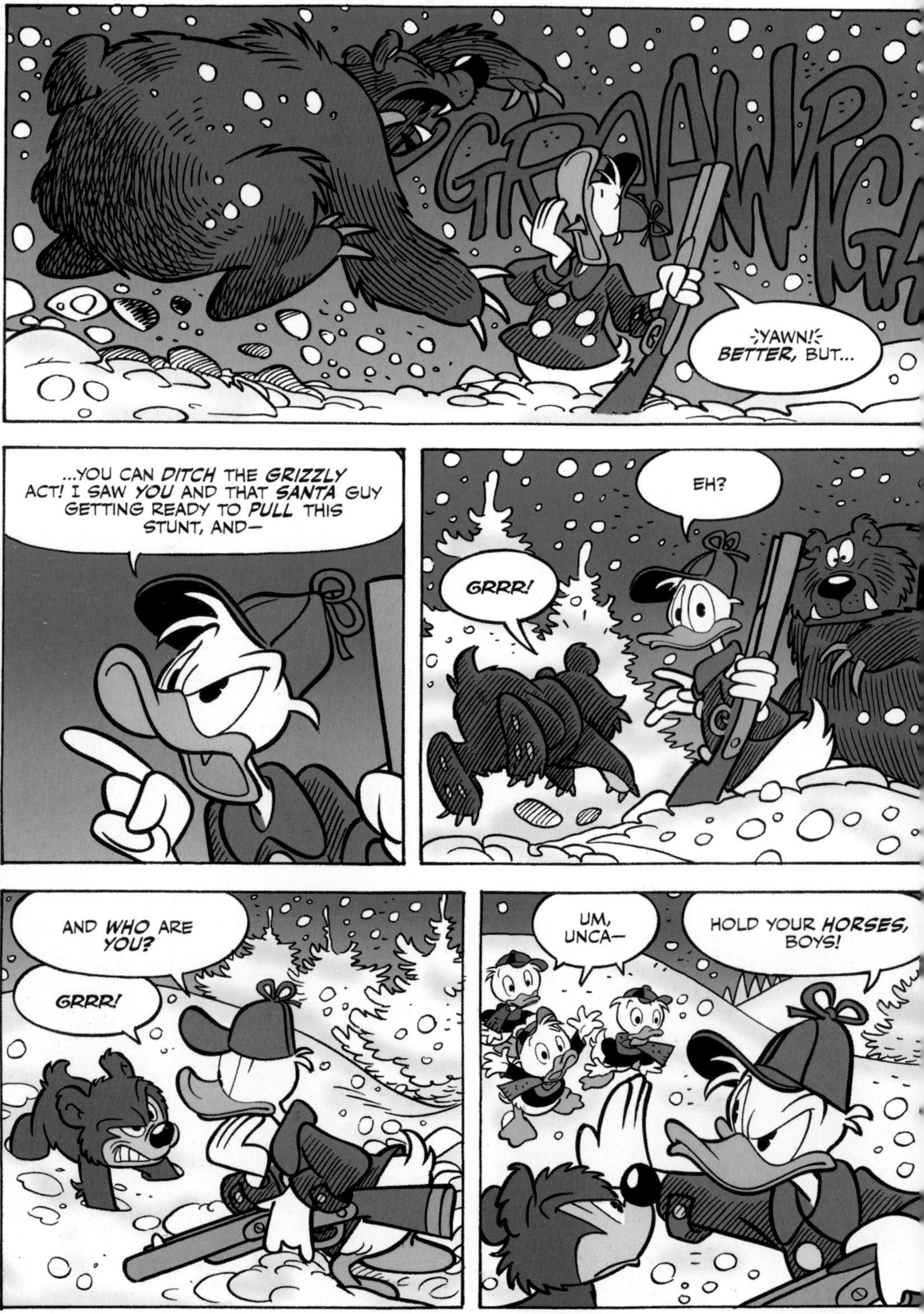
GRAAWRGA
¡YAWN!¡ BETTER, BUT...
...YOU CAN DITCH THE GRIZZLY ACT! I SAW YOU AND THAT SANTA GUY GETTING READY TO PULL THIS STUNT, AND—
EH?
GRRR!
AND WHO ARE YOU?
GRRR!
UM, UNCA—
HOLD YOUR HORSES, BOYS!

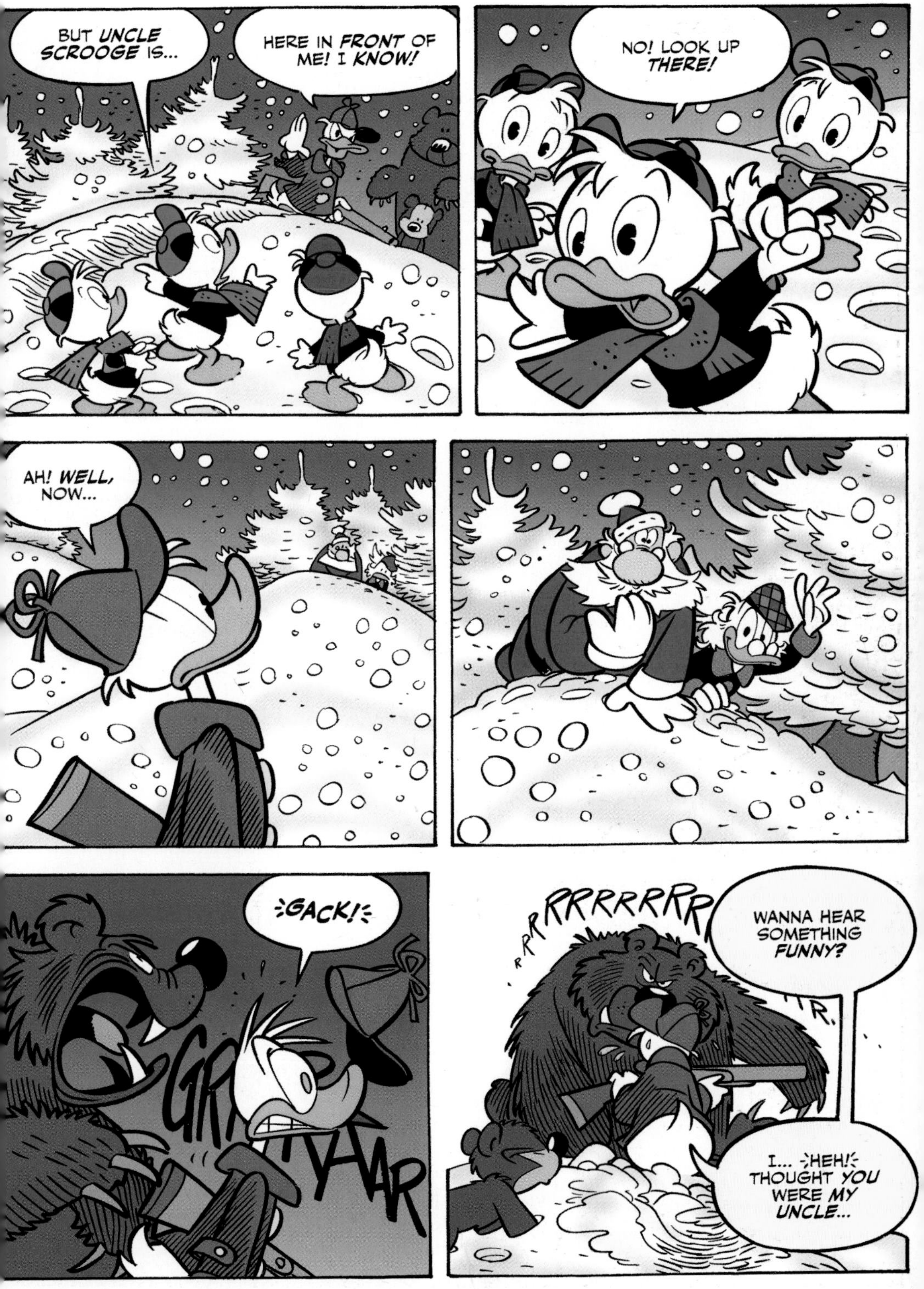
BUT UNCLE SCROOGE IS...
HERE IN FRONT OF ME! I KNOW!
NO! LOOK UP THERE!
AH! WELL, NOW...
GACK!
GRRYAAR
RRRRRRRR
WANNA HEAR SOMETHING FUNNY?
R.
I... HEH! THOUGHT YOU WERE MY UNCLE...

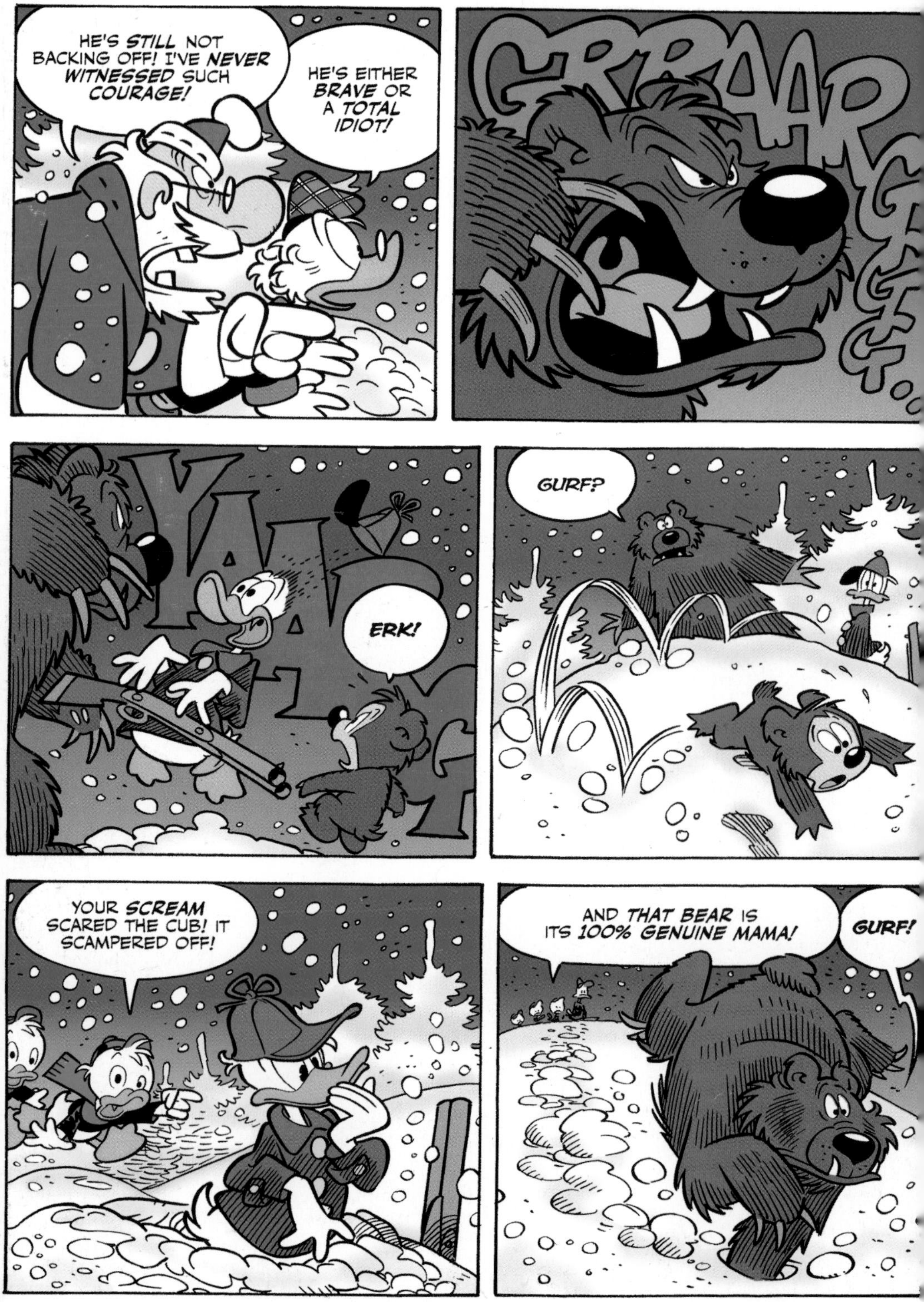
HE'S STILL NOT BACKING OFF! I'VE NEVER WITNESSED SUCH COURAGE!
HE'S EITHER BRAVE OR A TOTAL IDIOT!
GRRAARRGGGG...
YAAAH
ERK!
GURF?
YOUR SCREAM SCARED THE CUB! IT SCAMPERED OFF!
AND THAT BEAR IS ITS 100% GENUINE MAMA!
GURF!

AMAZING! YOUR *NEPHEW* MADE THE *BEAR* BACK OFF! *RUN* OFF, IN FACT! WHAT A *BACKBONE* HE'S GOT!

YES, BUT I *WONDER*...

COME ON! I WANT A CLOSER LOOK!

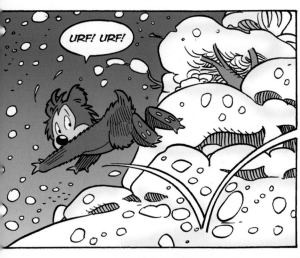

URF! URF!

?

EEERK!

SLIP!

GUUURF!

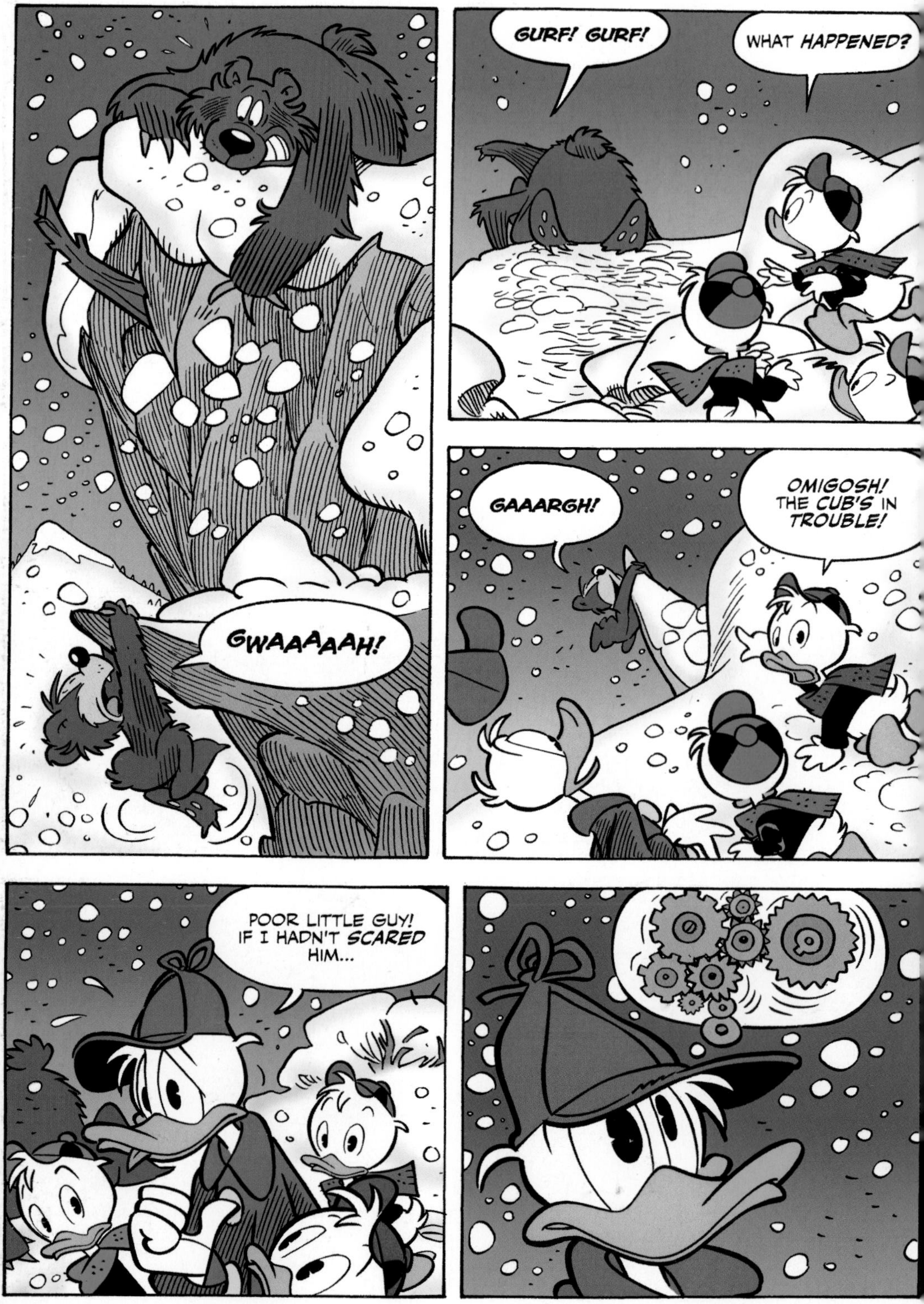
GWAAAAAH!
GURF! GURF!
WHAT HAPPENED?
GAAARGH!
OMIGOSH! THE CUB'S IN TROUBLE!
POOR LITTLE GUY! IF I HADN'T SCARED HIM...

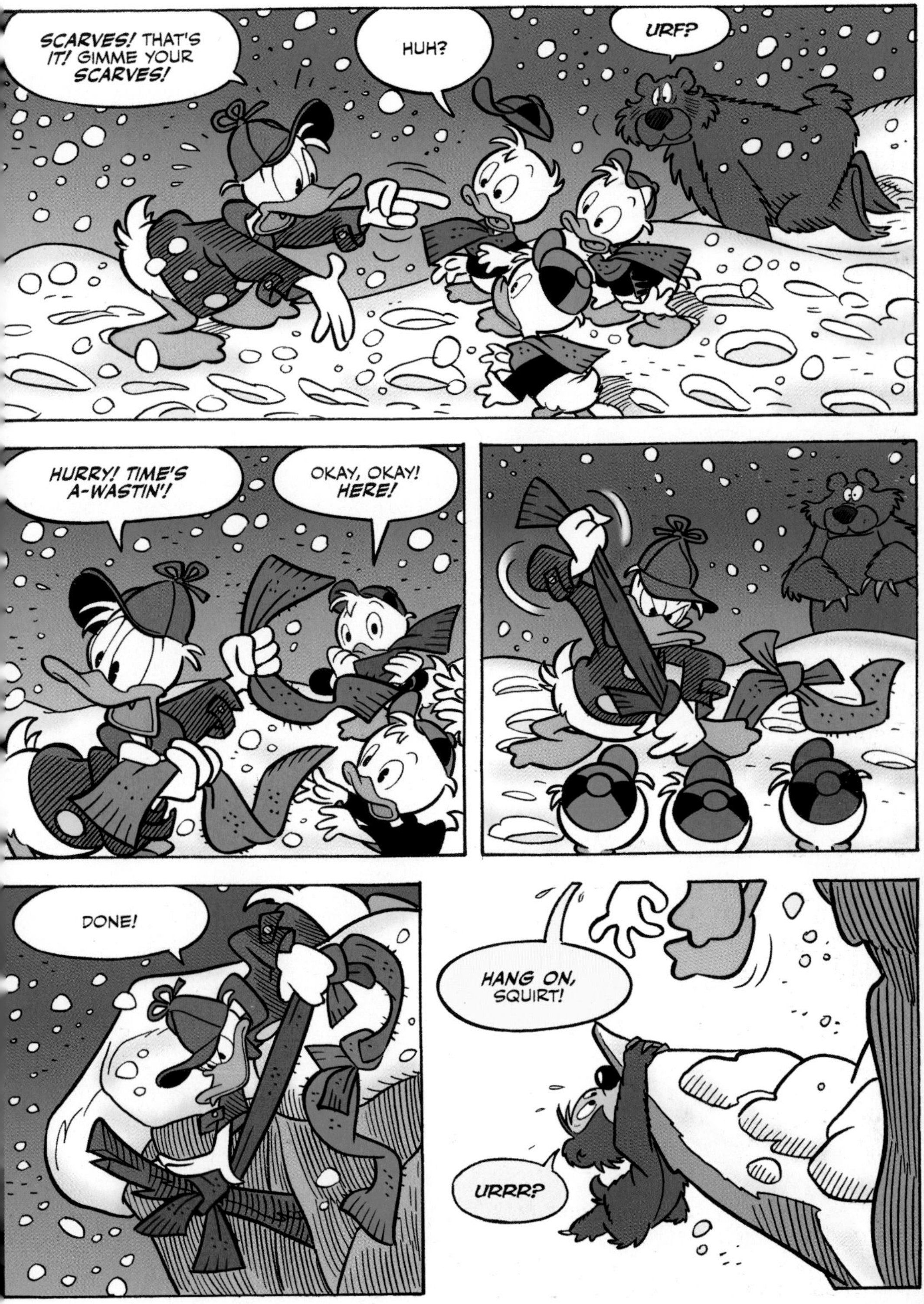
SCARVES! THAT'S IT! GIMME YOUR SCARVES!
HUH?
URF?
HURRY! TIME'S A-WASTIN'!
OKAY, OKAY! HERE!
DONE!
HANG ON, SQUIRT!
URRR?

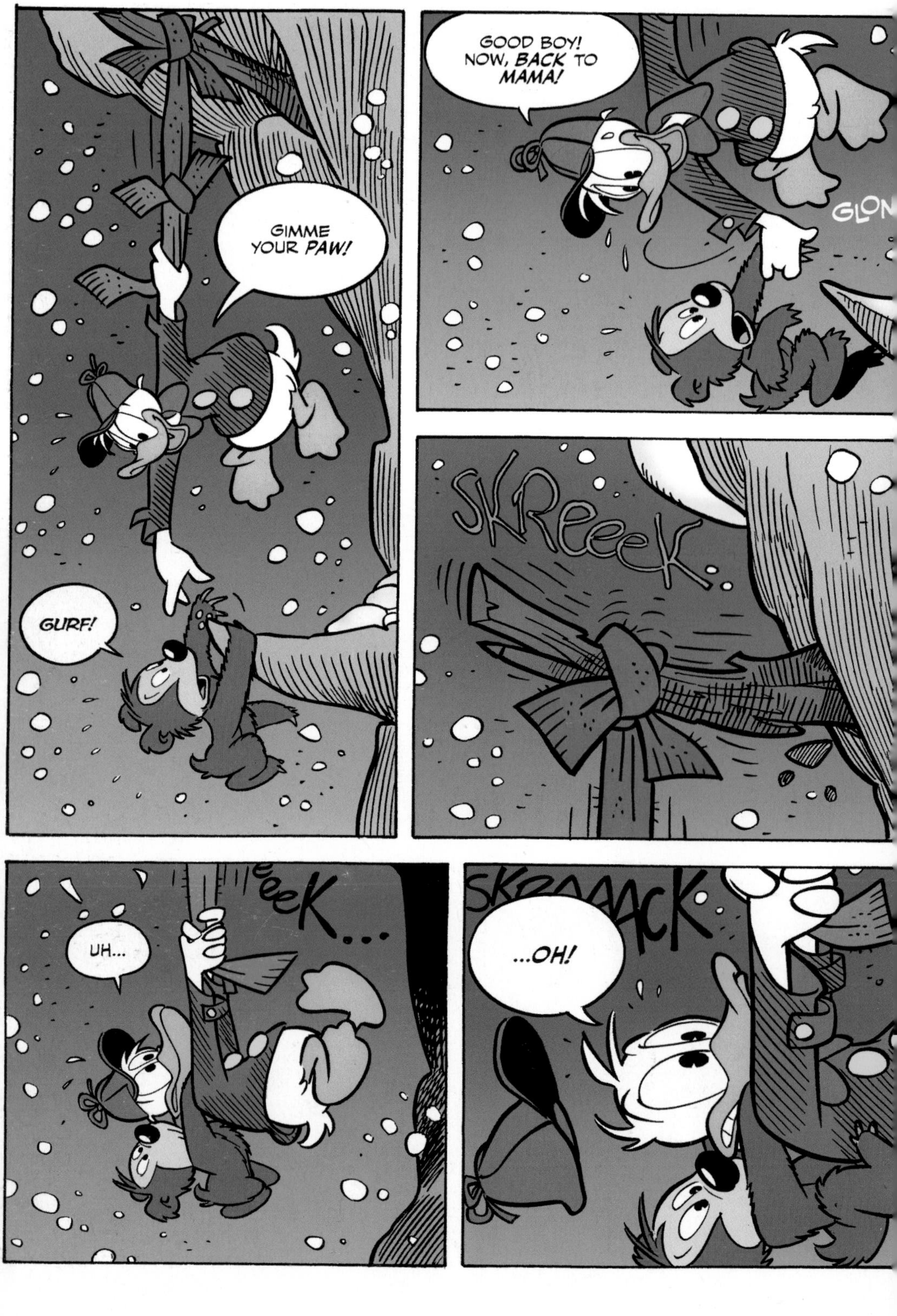
GIMME YOUR PAW!
GURF!
GOOD BOY! NOW, BACK TO MAMA!
GLON
SKREEEK
...eeeK...
UH...
SKRAAACK
...OH!

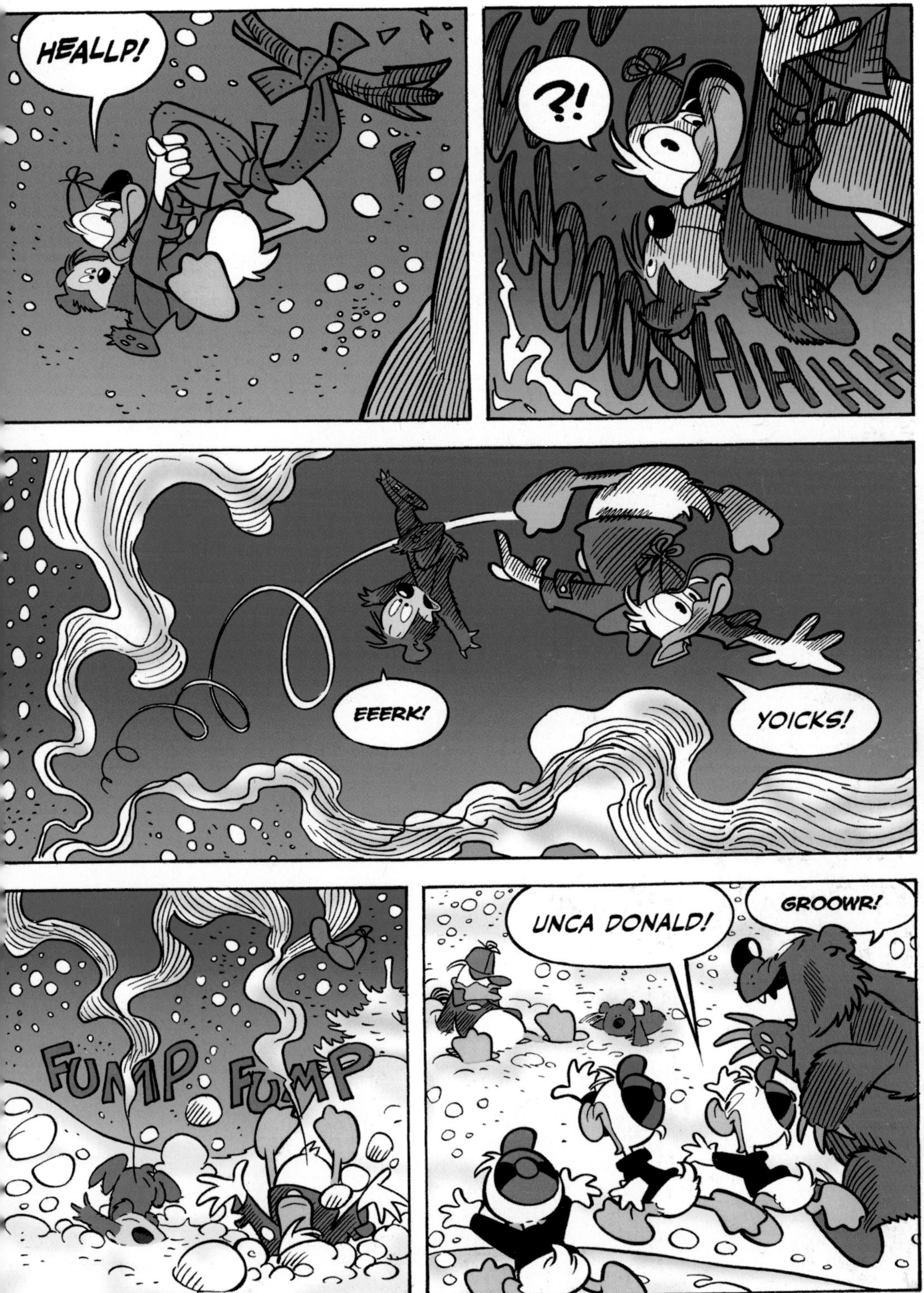
HEALLP!
?!
WHOOOSHHHH
EEERK!
YOICKS!
FUMP FUMP
UNCA DONALD!
GROOWR!

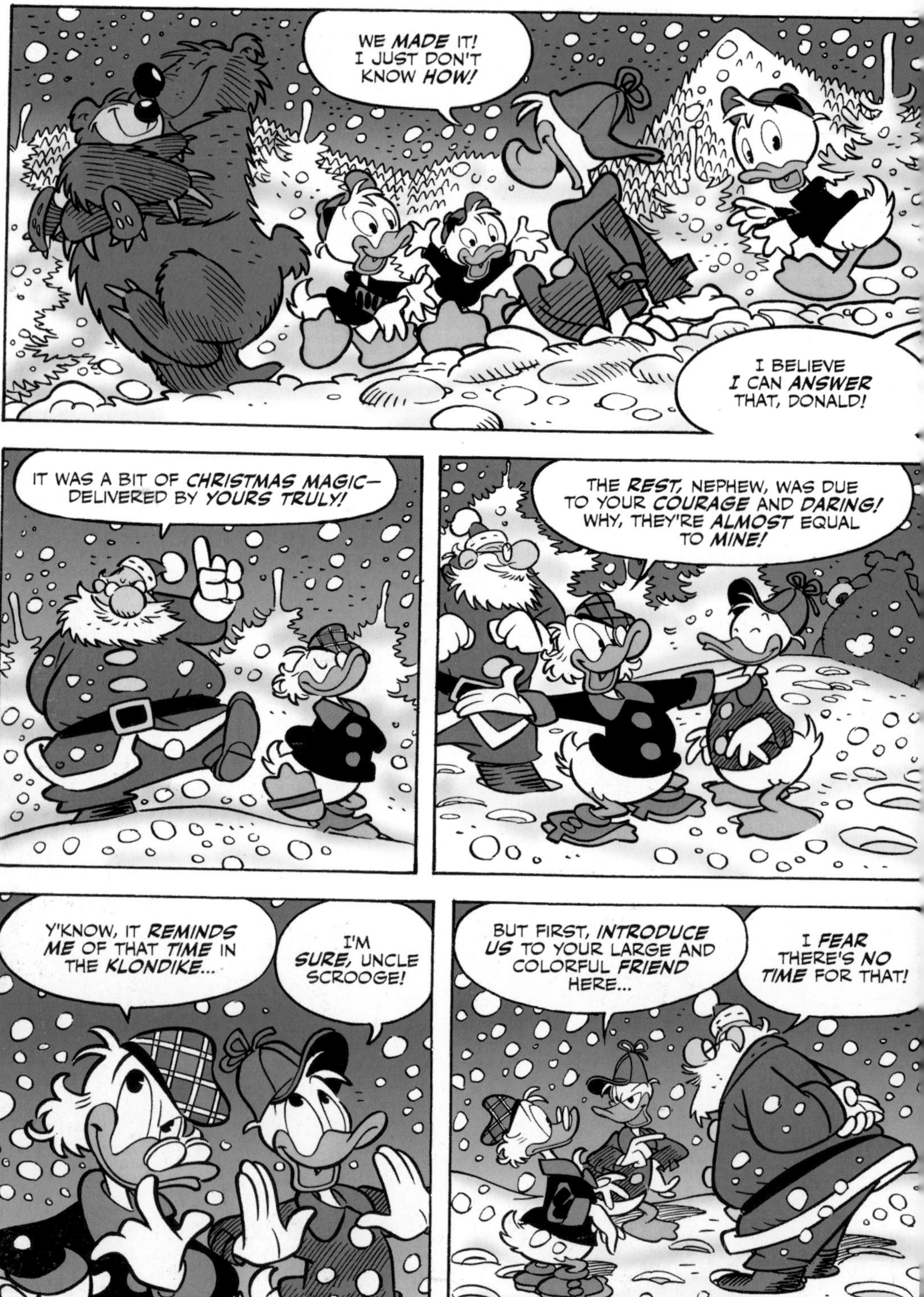

WE MADE IT! I JUST DON'T KNOW HOW!
I BELIEVE I CAN ANSWER THAT, DONALD!
IT WAS A BIT OF CHRISTMAS MAGIC— DELIVERED BY YOURS TRULY!
THE REST, NEPHEW, WAS DUE TO YOUR COURAGE AND DARING! WHY, THEY'RE ALMOST EQUAL TO MINE!
Y'KNOW, IT REMINDS ME OF THAT TIME IN THE KLONDIKE...
I'M SURE, UNCLE SCROOGE!
BUT FIRST, INTRODUCE US TO YOUR LARGE AND COLORFUL FRIEND HERE...
I FEAR THERE'S NO TIME FOR THAT!

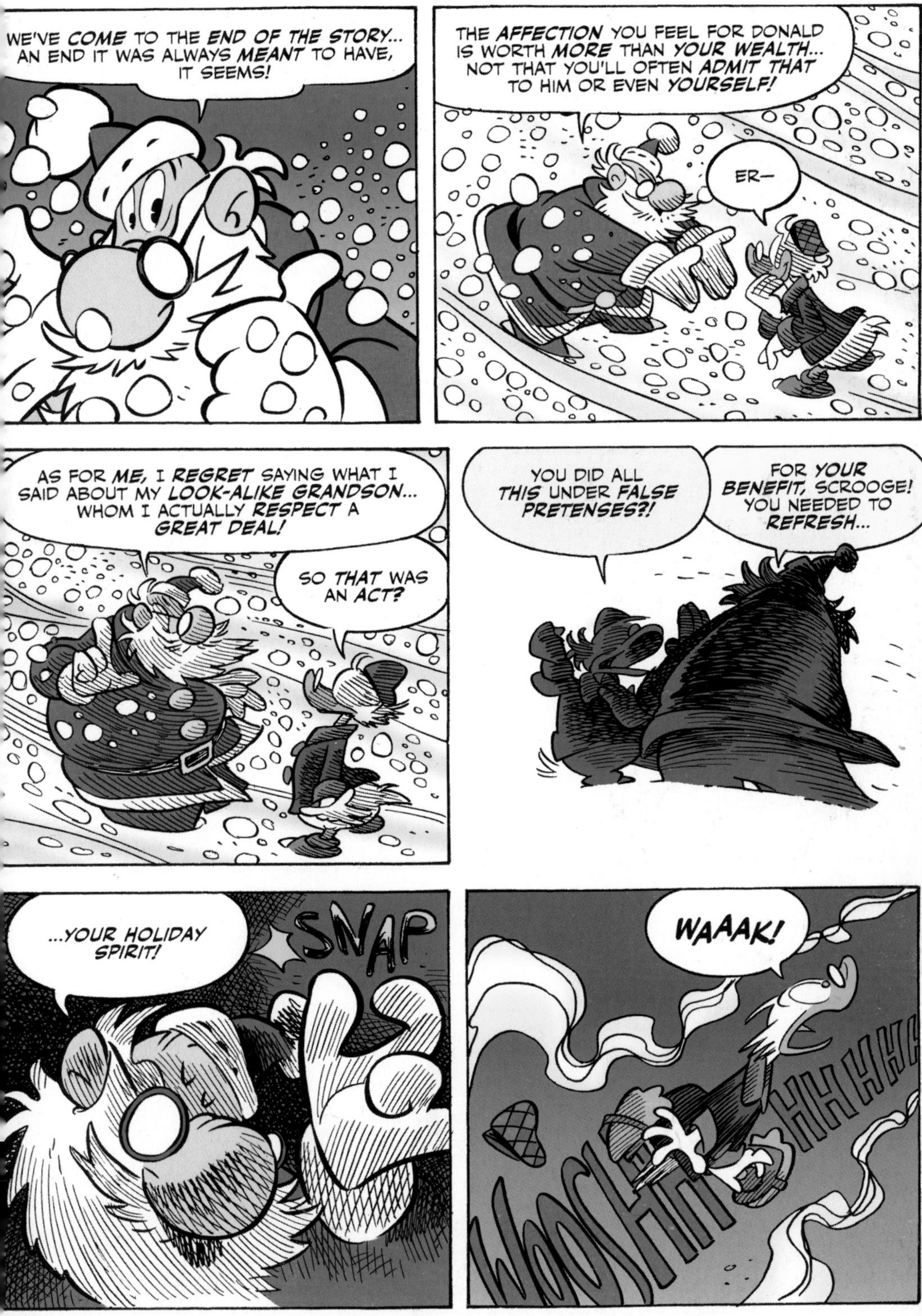
WE'VE COME TO THE END OF THE STORY... AN END IT WAS ALWAYS MEANT TO HAVE, IT SEEMS!
THE AFFECTION YOU FEEL FOR DONALD IS WORTH MORE THAN YOUR WEALTH... NOT THAT YOU'LL OFTEN ADMIT THAT TO HIM OR EVEN YOURSELF!
ER—
AS FOR ME, I REGRET SAYING WHAT I SAID ABOUT MY LOOK-ALIKE GRANDSON... WHOM I ACTUALLY RESPECT A GREAT DEAL!
SO THAT WAS AN ACT?
YOU DID ALL THIS UNDER FALSE PRETENSES?!
FOR YOUR BENEFIT, SCROOGE! YOU NEEDED TO REFRESH...
...YOUR HOLIDAY SPIRIT!
SNAP
WAAAK!

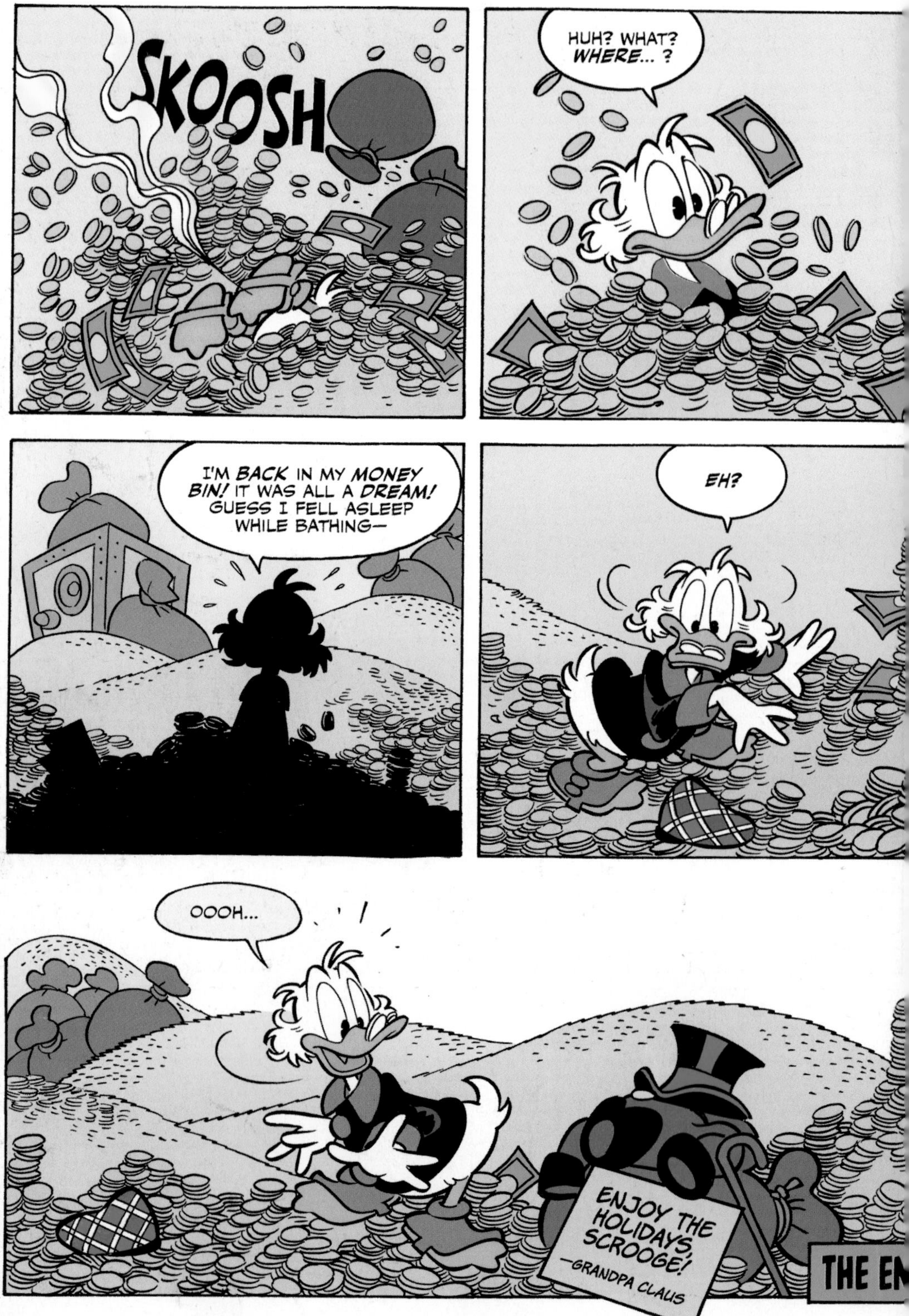
SKOOSH
HUH? WHAT? WHERE... ?
I'M BACK IN MY MONEY BIN! IT WAS ALL A DREAM! GUESS I FELL ASLEEP WHILE BATHING—
EH?
OOOH...
ENJOY THE HOLIDAYS, SCROOGE! —GRANDPA CLAUS

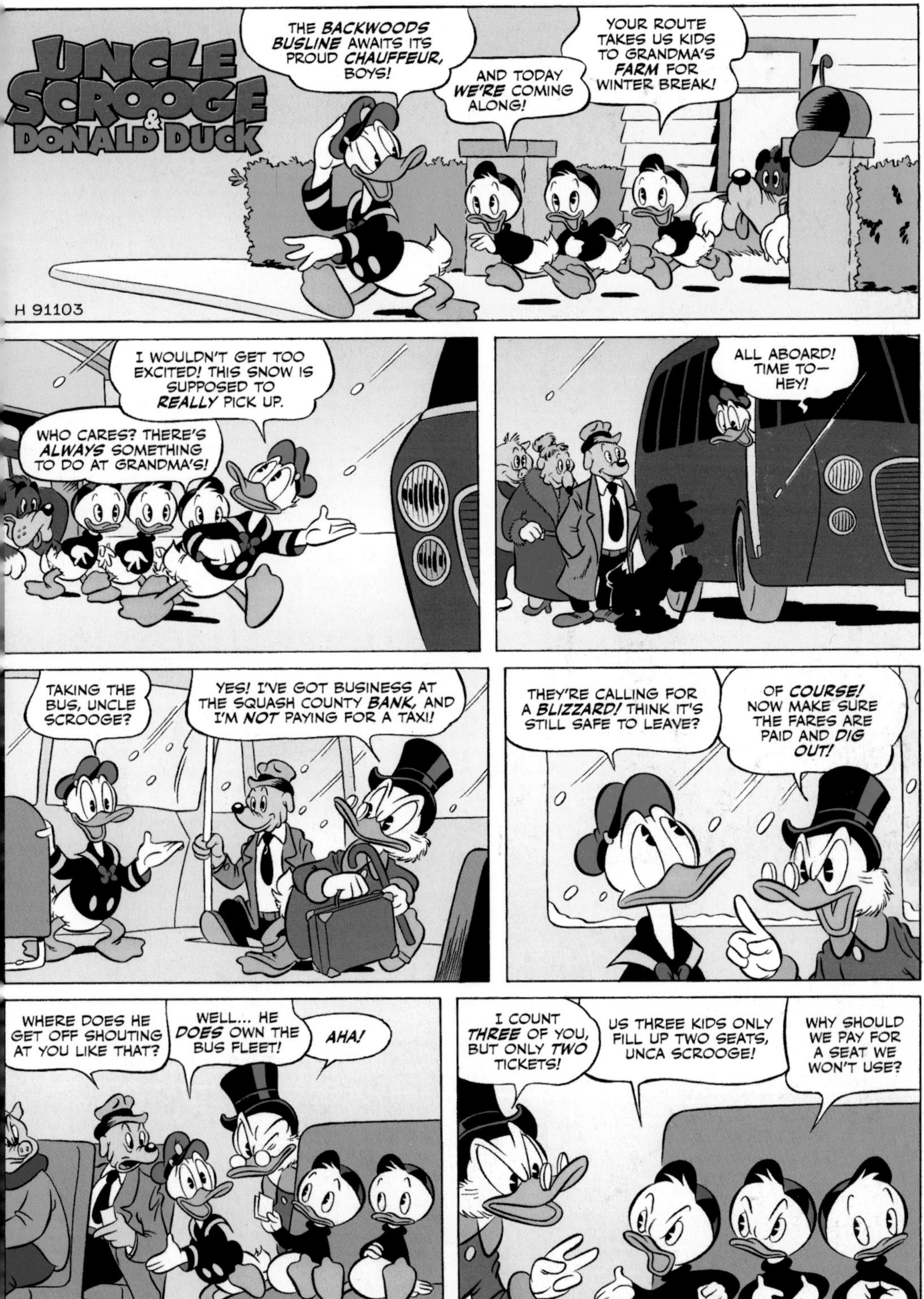
UNCLE SCROOGE & DONALD DUCK
THE BACKWOODS BUSLINE AWAITS ITS PROUD CHAUFFEUR, BOYS!
AND TODAY WE'RE COMING ALONG!
YOUR ROUTE TAKES US KIDS TO GRANDMA'S FARM FOR WINTER BREAK!
H 91103
I WOULDN'T GET TOO EXCITED! THIS SNOW IS SUPPOSED TO REALLY PICK UP.
WHO CARES? THERE'S ALWAYS SOMETHING TO DO AT GRANDMA'S!
ALL ABOARD! TIME TO— HEY!
TAKING THE BUS, UNCLE SCROOGE?
YES! I'VE GOT BUSINESS AT THE SQUASH COUNTY BANK, AND I'M NOT PAYING FOR A TAXI!
THEY'RE CALLING FOR A BLIZZARD! THINK IT'S STILL SAFE TO LEAVE?
OF COURSE! NOW MAKE SURE THE FARES ARE PAID AND DIG OUT!
WHERE DOES HE GET OFF SHOUTING AT YOU LIKE THAT?
WELL... HE DOES OWN THE BUS FLEET!
AHA!
I COUNT THREE OF YOU, BUT ONLY TWO TICKETS!
US THREE KIDS ONLY FILL UP TWO SEATS, UNCA SCROOGE!
WHY SHOULD WE PAY FOR A SEAT WE WON'T USE?

Originally published in *Donald Duck* #50/1995 (Netherlands, 1995)

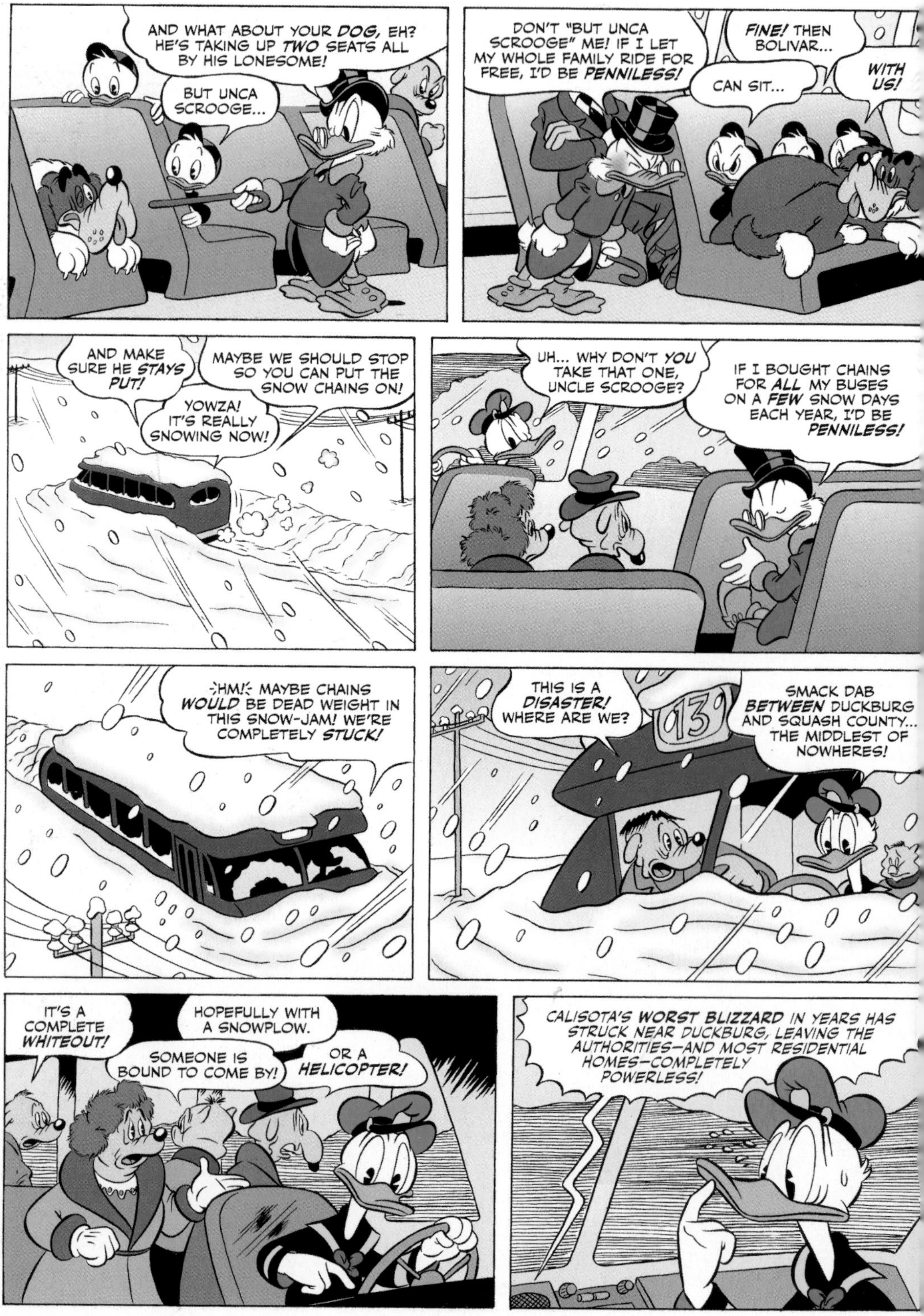
AND WHAT ABOUT YOUR DOG, EH? HE'S TAKING UP TWO SEATS ALL BY HIS LONESOME!
BUT UNCA SCROOGE...
DON'T "BUT UNCA SCROOGE" ME! IF I LET MY WHOLE FAMILY RIDE FOR FREE, I'D BE PENNILESS!
CAN SIT...
FINE! THEN BOLIVAR...
WITH US!
AND MAKE SURE HE STAYS PUT!
YOWZA! IT'S REALLY SNOWING NOW!
MAYBE WE SHOULD STOP SO YOU CAN PUT THE SNOW CHAINS ON!
UH... WHY DON'T YOU TAKE THAT ONE, UNCLE SCROOGE?
IF I BOUGHT CHAINS FOR ALL MY BUSES ON A FEW SNOW DAYS EACH YEAR, I'D BE PENNILESS!
HM! MAYBE CHAINS WOULD BE DEAD WEIGHT IN THIS SNOW-JAM! WE'RE COMPLETELY STUCK!
THIS IS A DISASTER! WHERE ARE WE?
13
SMACK DAB BETWEEN DUCKBURG AND SQUASH COUNTY... THE MIDDLEST OF NOWHERES!
IT'S A COMPLETE WHITEOUT!
SOMEONE IS BOUND TO COME BY!
HOPEFULLY WITH A SNOWPLOW.
OR A HELICOPTER!
CALISOTA'S WORST BLIZZARD IN YEARS HAS STRUCK NEAR DUCKBURG, LEAVING THE AUTHORITIES—AND MOST RESIDENTIAL HOMES—COMPLETELY POWERLESS!

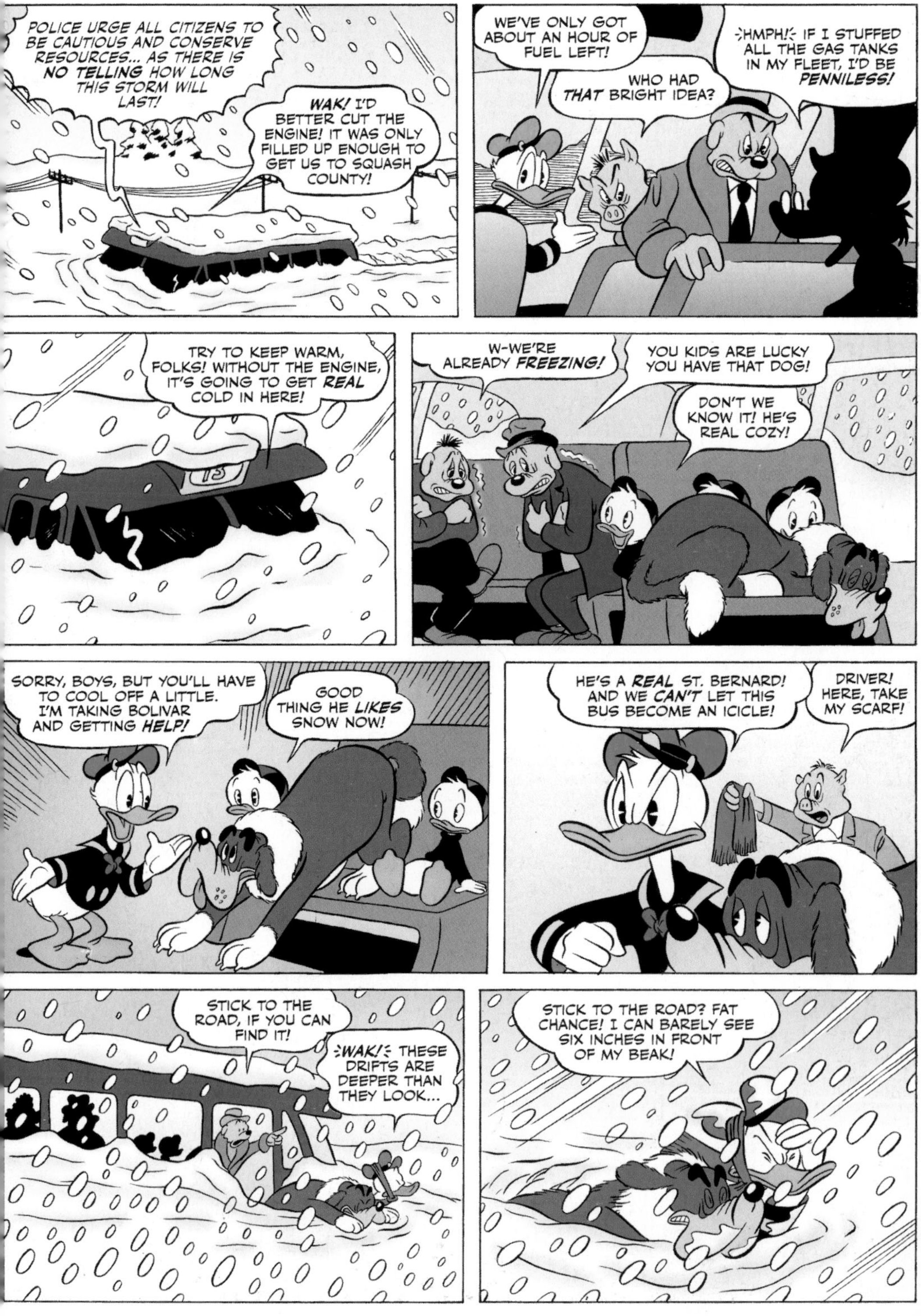
POLICE URGE ALL CITIZENS TO BE CAUTIOUS AND CONSERVE RESOURCES... AS THERE IS NO TELLING HOW LONG THIS STORM WILL LAST!
WAK! I'D BETTER CUT THE ENGINE! IT WAS ONLY FILLED UP ENOUGH TO GET US TO SQUASH COUNTY!
WE'VE ONLY GOT ABOUT AN HOUR OF FUEL LEFT!
WHO HAD THAT BRIGHT IDEA?
HMPH! IF I STUFFED ALL THE GAS TANKS IN MY FLEET, I'D BE PENNILESS!
TRY TO KEEP WARM, FOLKS! WITHOUT THE ENGINE, IT'S GOING TO GET REAL COLD IN HERE!
13
W-WE'RE ALREADY FREEZING!
YOU KIDS ARE LUCKY YOU HAVE THAT DOG!
DON'T WE KNOW IT! HE'S REAL COZY!
SORRY, BOYS, BUT YOU'LL HAVE TO COOL OFF A LITTLE. I'M TAKING BOLIVAR AND GETTING HELP!
GOOD THING HE LIKES SNOW NOW!
HE'S A REAL ST. BERNARD! AND WE CAN'T LET THIS BUS BECOME AN ICICLE!
DRIVER! HERE, TAKE MY SCARF!
STICK TO THE ROAD, IF YOU CAN FIND IT!
WAK! THESE DRIFTS ARE DEEPER THAN THEY LOOK...
STICK TO THE ROAD? FAT CHANCE! I CAN BARELY SEE SIX INCHES IN FRONT OF MY BEAK!

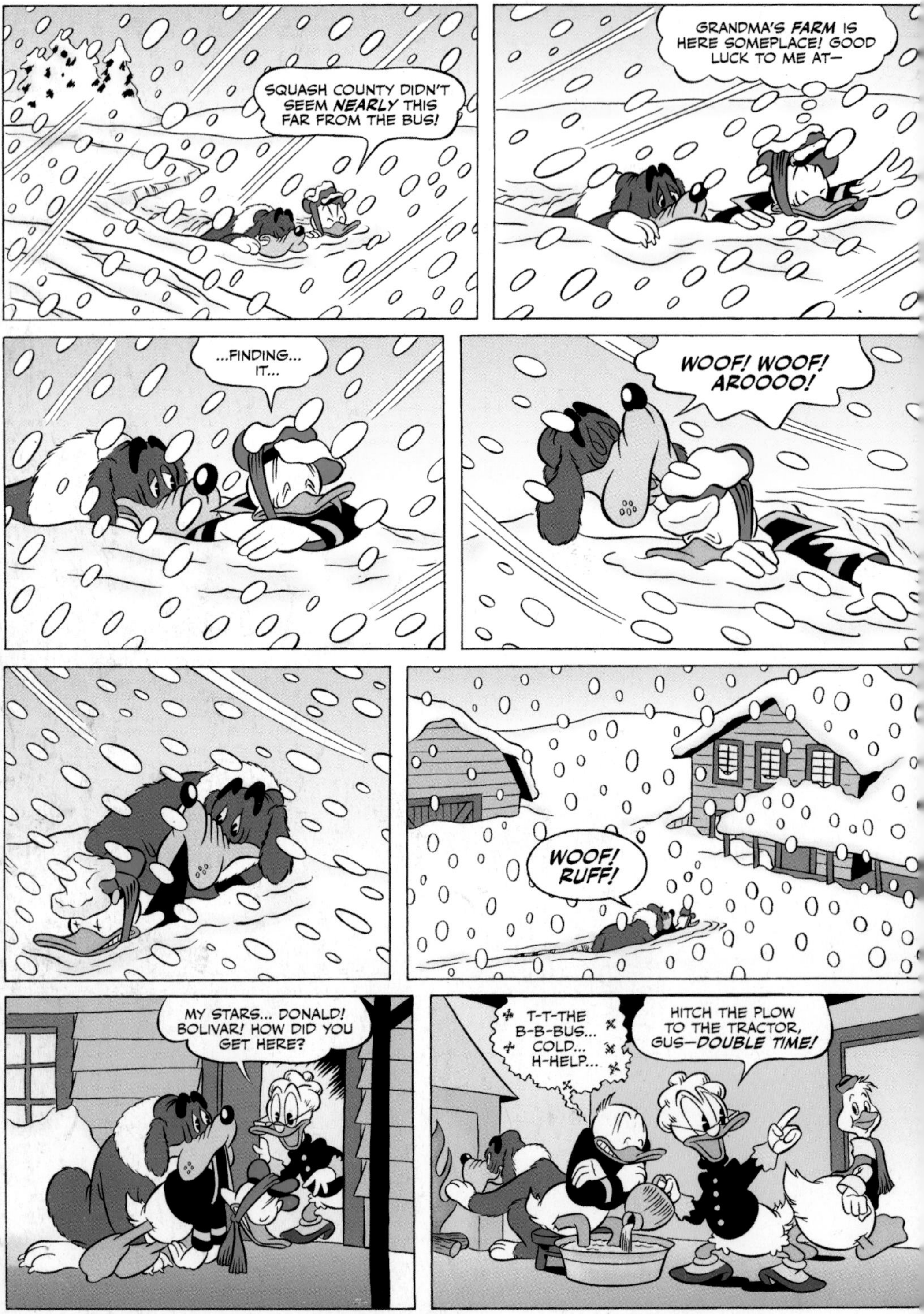
SQUASH COUNTY DIDN'T SEEM NEARLY THIS FAR FROM THE BUS!
GRANDMA'S FARM IS HERE SOMEPLACE! GOOD LUCK TO ME AT—
...FINDING... IT...
WOOF! WOOF! AROOOO!
WOOF! RUFF!
MY STARS... DONALD! BOLIVAR! HOW DID YOU GET HERE?
T-T-THE B-B-BUS... COLD... H-HELP...
HITCH THE PLOW TO THE TRACTOR, GUS—DOUBLE TIME!

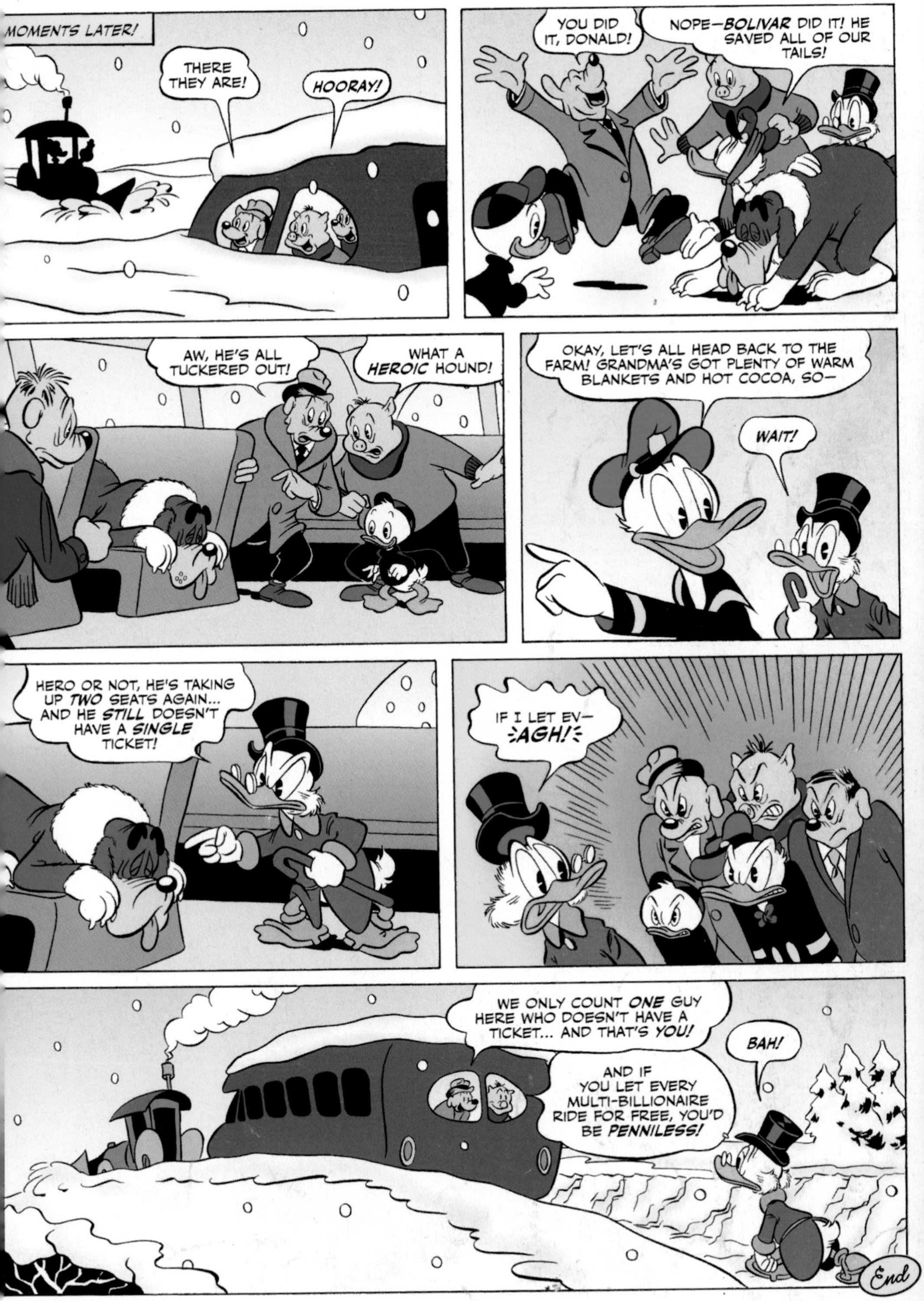
MOMENTS LATER!
THERE THEY ARE!
HOORAY!
YOU DID IT, DONALD!
NOPE—BOLIVAR DID IT! HE SAVED ALL OF OUR TAILS!
AW, HE'S ALL TUCKERED OUT!
WHAT A HEROIC HOUND!
OKAY, LET'S ALL HEAD BACK TO THE FARM! GRANDMA'S GOT PLENTY OF WARM BLANKETS AND HOT COCOA, SO—
WAIT!
HERO OR NOT, HE'S TAKING UP TWO SEATS AGAIN... AND HE STILL DOESN'T HAVE A SINGLE TICKET!
IF I LET EV— AGH!
WE ONLY COUNT ONE GUY HERE WHO DOESN'T HAVE A TICKET... AND THAT'S YOU!
AND IF YOU LET EVERY MULTI-BILLIONAIRE RIDE FOR FREE, YOU'D BE PENNILESS!
BAH!
End

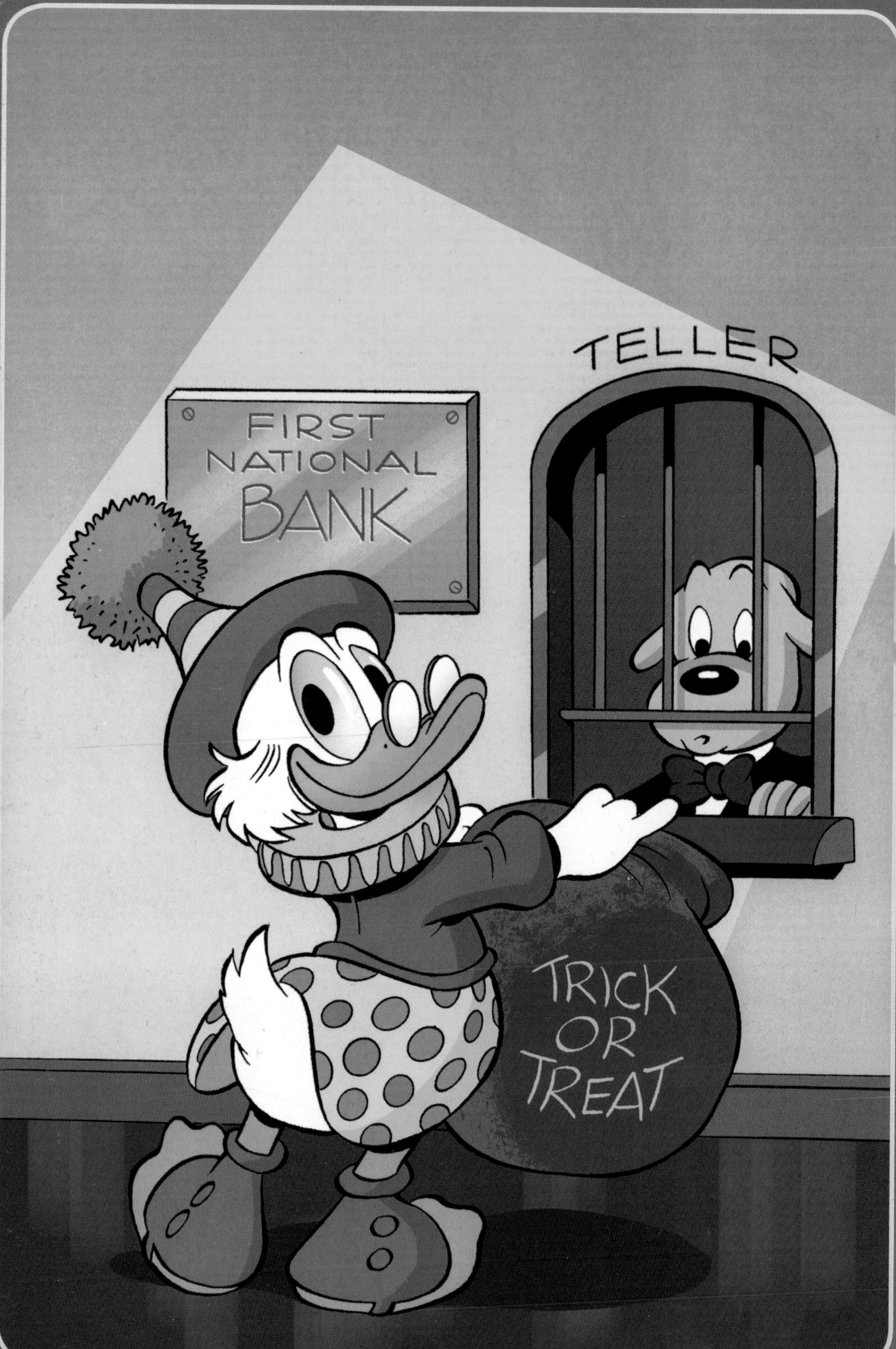
TELLER
FIRST NATIONAL BANK
TRICK OR TREAT

Art by William Van Horn, Colors by Derek Charm

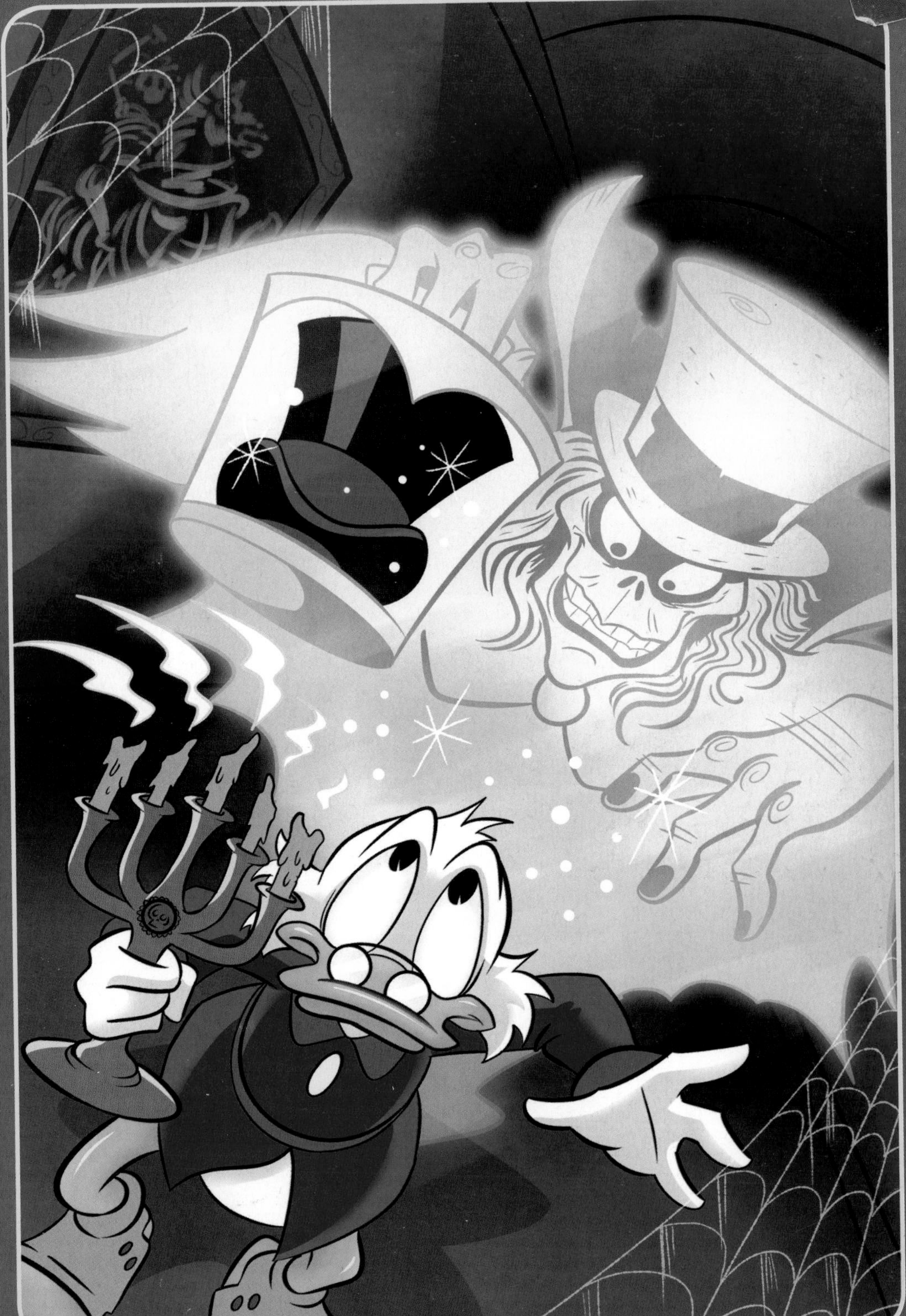

Art by Derek Charm

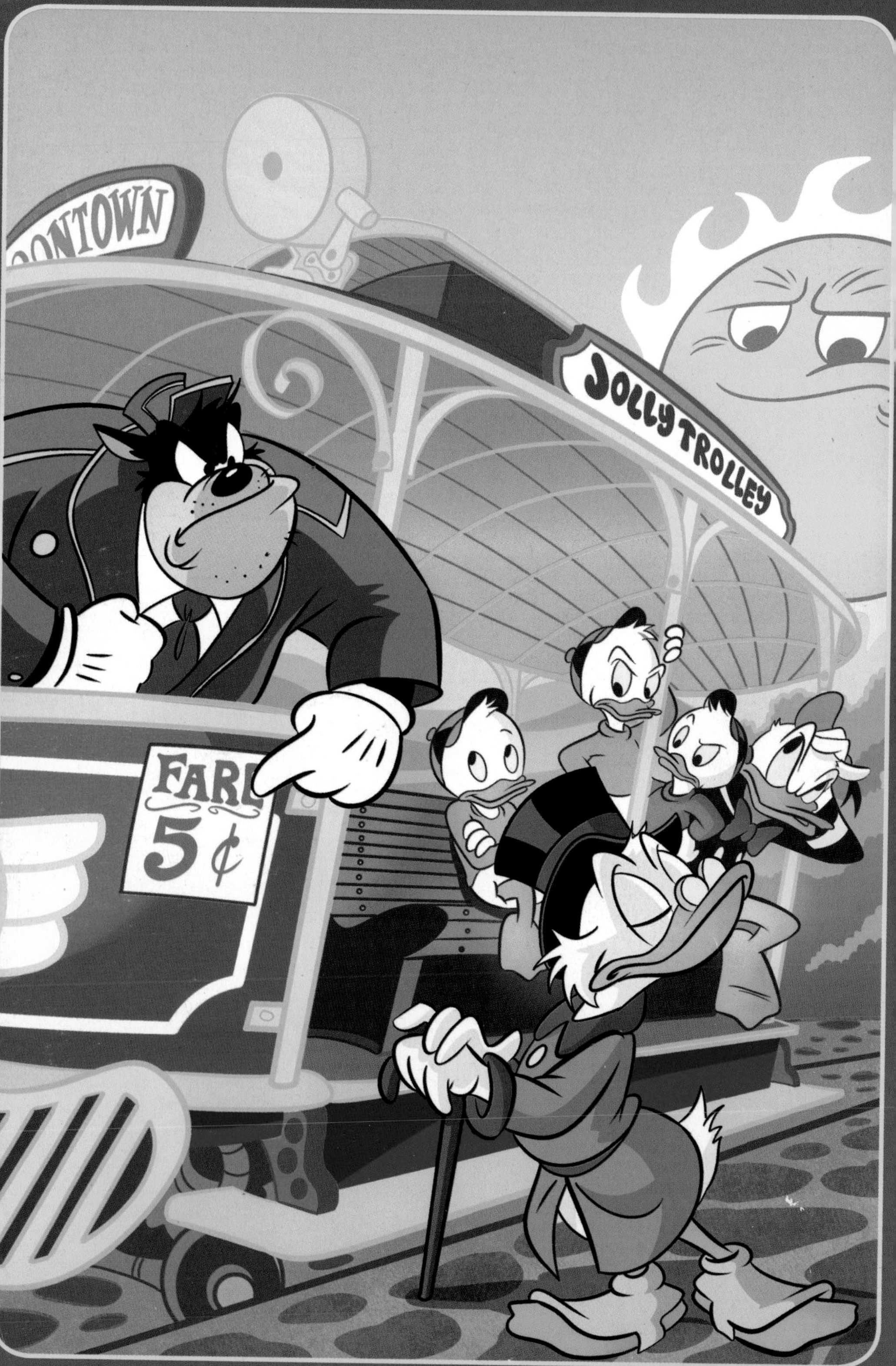
ONTOWN
JOLLY TROLLEY
FARE
5¢
Art by Derek Charm

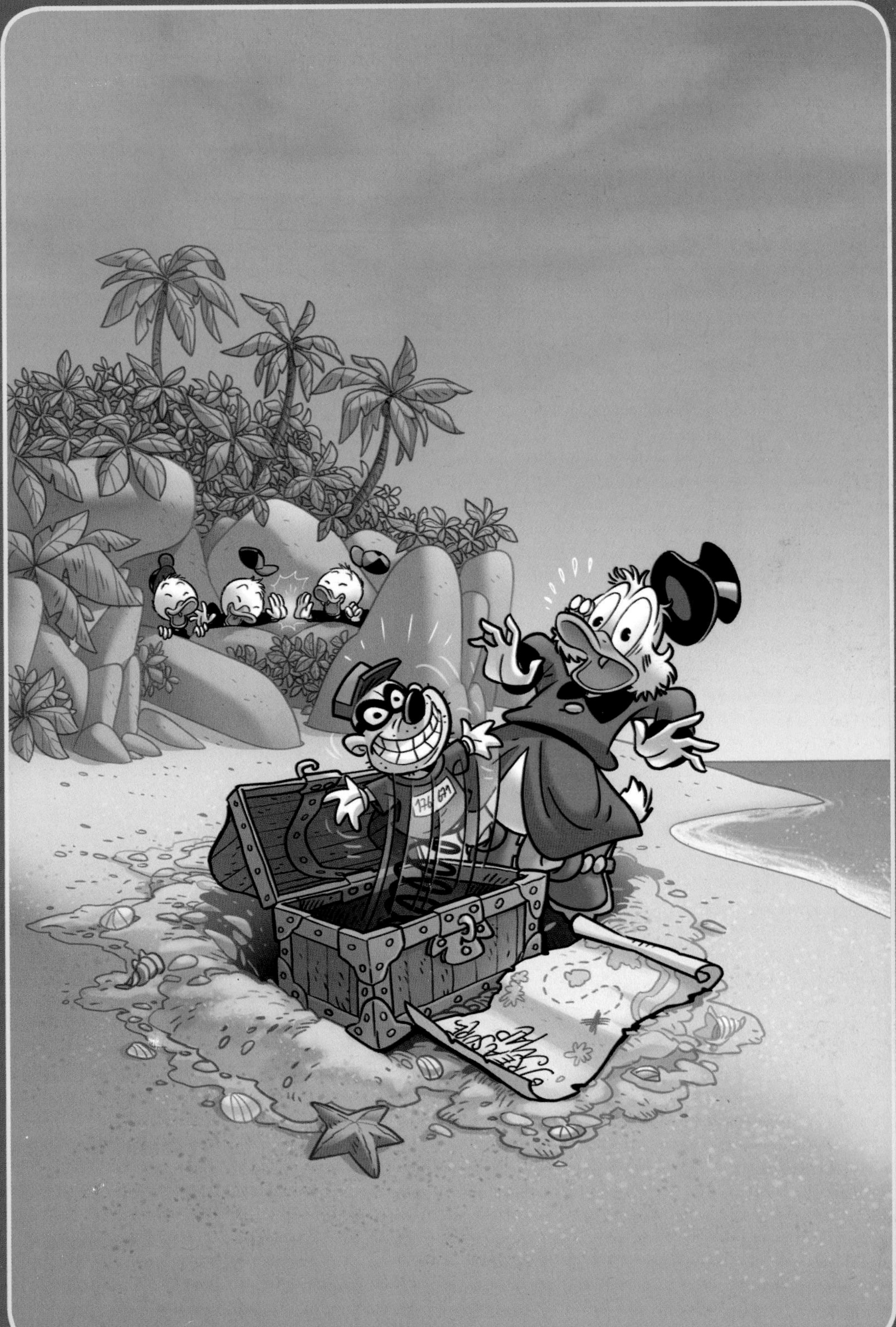

Art by Silvio Camboni, Colors by Mario Perrotta

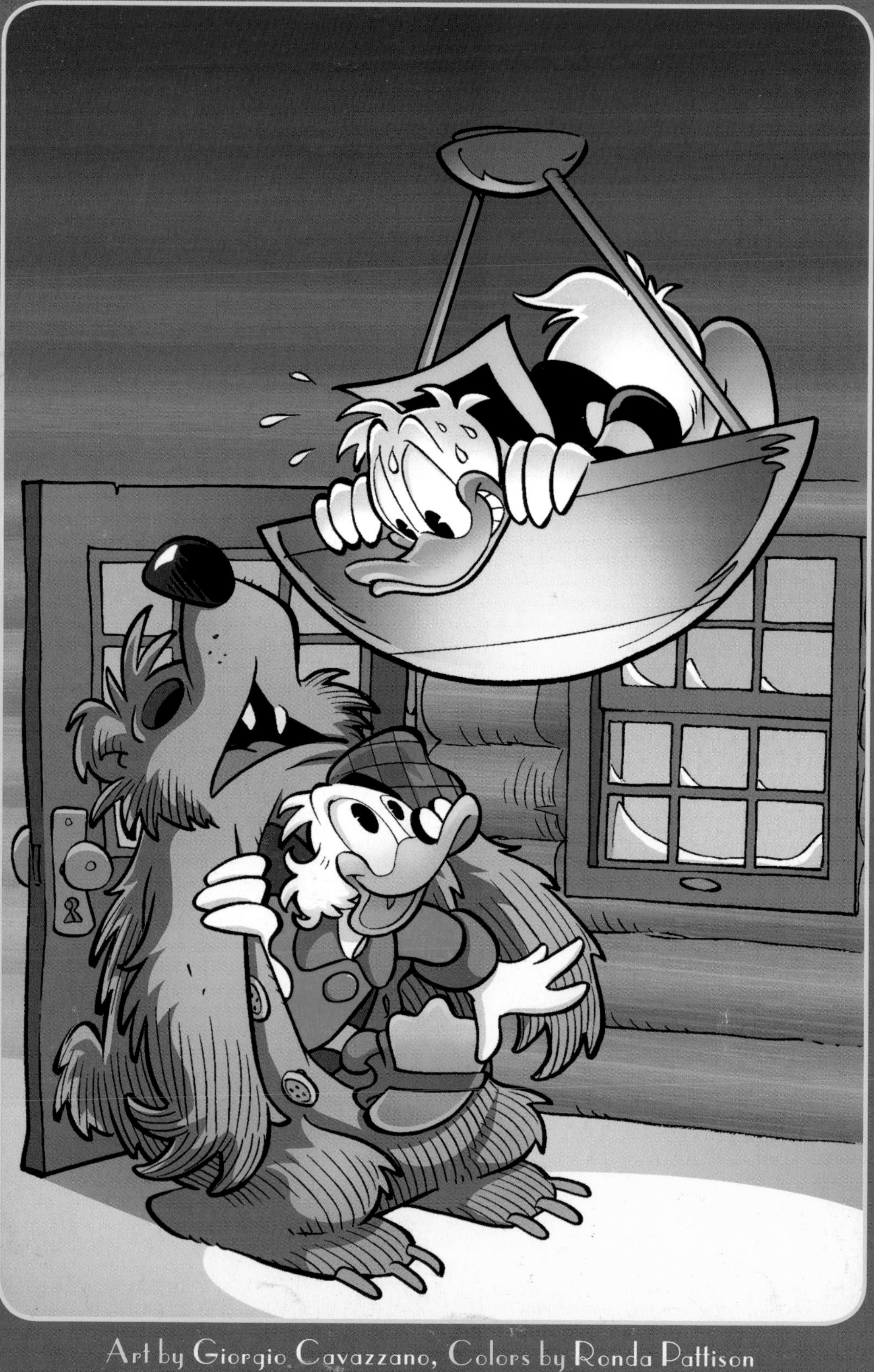

Art by Giorgio Cavazzano, Colors by Ronda Pattison

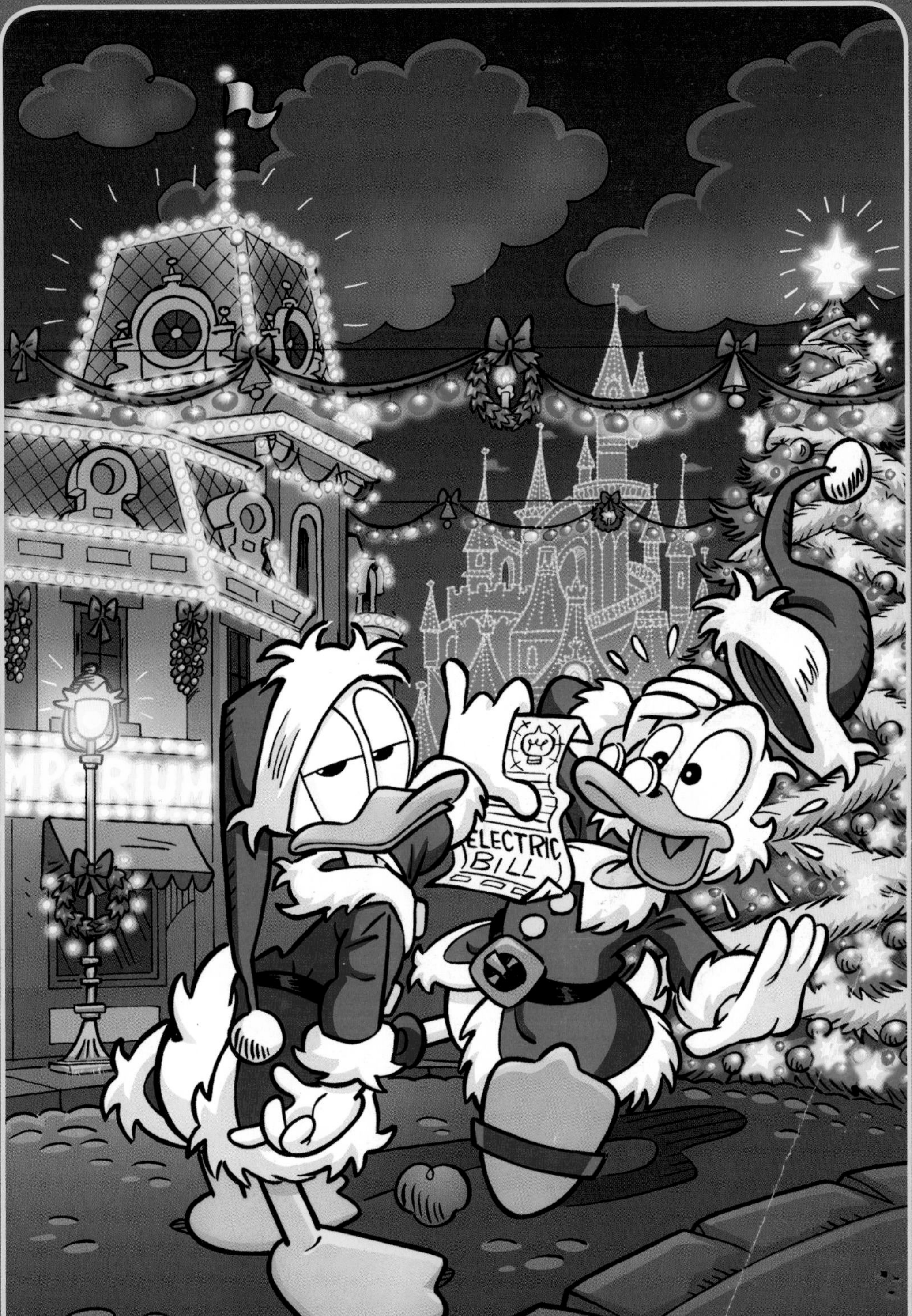
MPORIUM
ELECTRIC BILL
Art by Marco Gervasio, Colors by Ronda Pattison

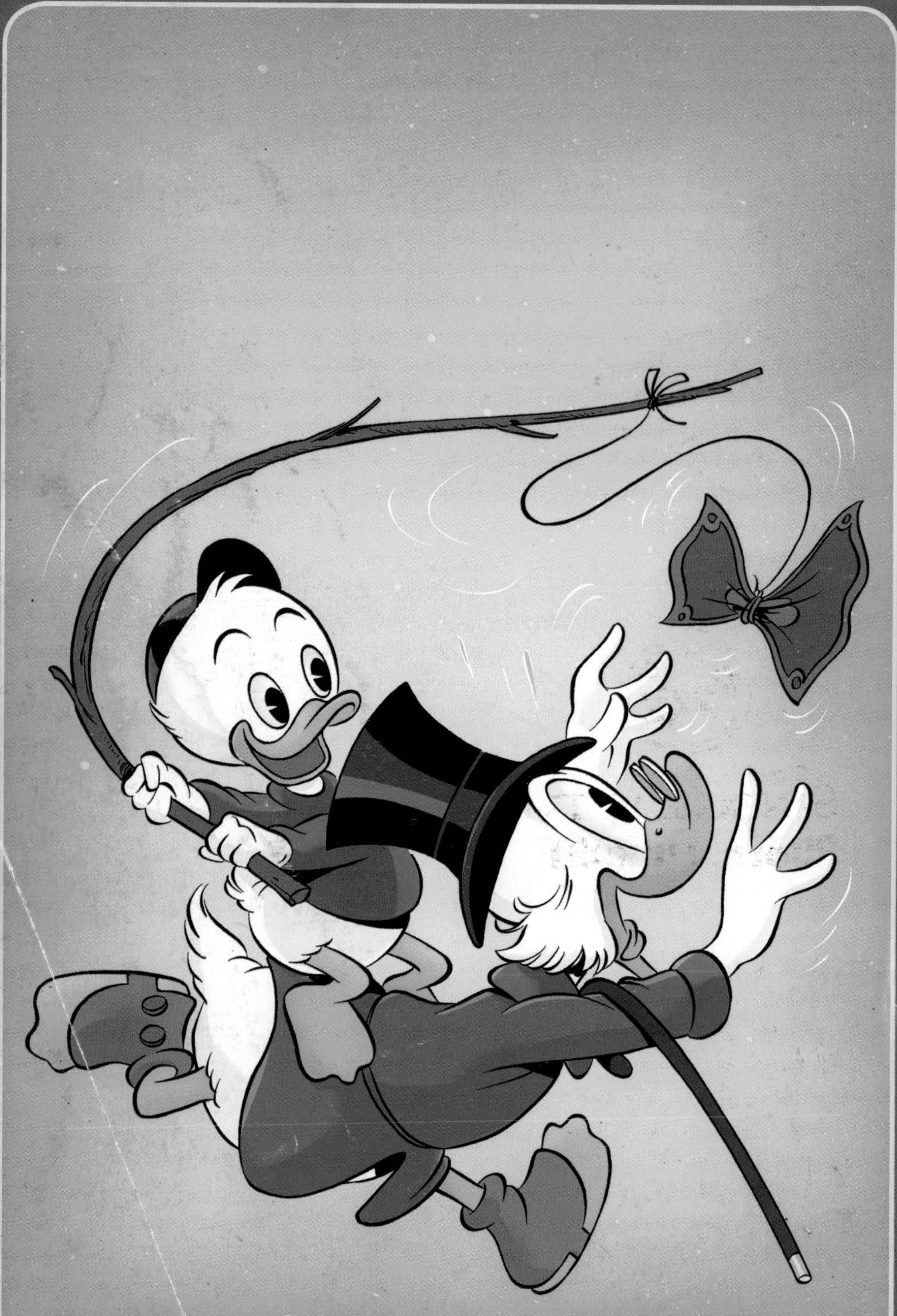

Art by Daniel Branca, Colors by Derek Charm